SELFIE

AMY LANE

RIPTIDE
PUBLISHING

Riptide Publishing
PO Box 1537
Burnsville, NC 28714
www.riptidepublishing.com

Selfie
Copyright © 2016 by Amy Lane

Cover art: L.C. Chase, lcchase.com/design.htm
Editors: Sarah Lyons, May Peterson
Layout: L.C. Chase, lcchase.com/design.htm

ISBN: 978-1-62649-385-8

Second edition
April, 2016

Also available in ebook:
ISBN: 978-1-62649-384-1

SELFIE

AMY LANE

To Mate, of course, because if we had worlds enough and time we would watch every sci-fi show on every channel, and all the movies. *Because that's who we are, and we've believed in sci-fi since we were little kids watching* Star Trek *and new lovers watching* Star Trek: The Next Generation, *and we will continue to believe it's the best of storytelling and the best of literature until our kids are watching their own shows and we're too old to get it and too deaf to hear.*

To Mary, of course, because she looked at a news article and said, "YOU must write this," and I said, "Why can't you?" And she said, "Because this is an Amy story—I'll bet you've already got half of it in your head." And I did.

And to Sarah, who makes me feel like I've won the lottery whenever I give her a manuscript, and to Amelia, who is right there next to her with the confetti, balloons, and noisemaker, making me feel like I did good.

I hate watching celebrities self-destruct via public media. It feels like the worst of voyeurism and the worst of ourselves. And the most awful part is all of the things we'll never see, and the knowledge that just the presence, the multi-thousand attention weight of the world is going to make every moment, every regret, every sordid article just ever so much worse.

So, for everyone who has ever felt the pressure of too many eyes, whether it's in front of the world and the national press or in front of a classroom with social anxiety, here's to finding out who you are and holding fast to what is true. We never look at a selfie and think, "Oh, that's *the best picture in the world!" Here's to finding the beautiful person in every snapshot we take.*

TABLE OF CONTENTS

CHAPTER ONE

CAN I COME IN
FROM THE OUT NOW?

Tere was a terrible sound—a shrill cacophonic assault—and I closed my eyes against the crippling brightness in our—my—beach house and whimpered.

Oh God.

What had I done?

The cacophony erupted again, and I rolled to my side, pulling the covers over my head, groaning. I'd left the patio door open, and the ocean roared carelessly on outside. It should have been a soothing sound, but my brain felt like a land-mine detonation facility. The phone rang again, and another bank of explosives went off, including a few in my stomach that would have sent me running to the bathroom if I could move.

I couldn't move.

"Vinnie," I moaned. "Vince . . . baby . . . get the phone . . . Oh fuck."

My voice pitched on the "fuck," because I remembered why Vince wasn't there. Suddenly my hangover was nothing, a torn cuticle, a pimple, a plucked hair, compared to that terrible, terrible voiding pain of the severed half of my heart.

Vince wasn't there. He'd been gone for 366 days, and he wasn't coming back.

Nope, Con, I'm not there. You need to get the phone, you lazy bastard.

The phone rang one more time, and I fumbled at the end table and answered it because that beat the alternative.

"'llo?"

"Do we need a Bloody Mary?" Jillian Lombard's voice was like a spring-powered launch of ice picks, all of them driven through my left eyeball to the back of the brain.

"I can't do bitchy," I whined. "Why are we bitchy? Make the bitchy stop."

"I'm sorry, sweetums, am I bitchy?" she asked pleasantly. In the background I heard the sound of a lighter flicking, and a heavily indrawn breath.

"You started smoking again?" I was concerned. Jillian was in her early fifties and built like a fireplug. "That's not healthy, Jillian—I thought you'd quit."

"I *did*," she snapped bitterly. "I *did* quit, because you and Vince were happy, and you were making scads of money, and suddenly, my shoestring operation was in the black and I could afford to worry about my health. Things have changed, buttercup, oh how things have changed."

I wanted to bitch and moan, but I couldn't. Instead I swung my bare legs off the white-sheeted bed, leaned forward on my knees, and massaged the back of my neck, trying to remember grown-up skills. I'd had grown-up skills once—I was famous for them. In a land where people were prone to excess, where you had to talk your boyfriend into rehab once every three years or so, the guy who didn't drink too much, didn't do too much blow, didn't party too much—*he* was considered a grown-up. I was that guy. I didn't get into fights, I didn't slip up our little cover, I didn't make scenes on set. I did my job, I did it professionally, and I enjoyed the hell out of it—my God, I worked hard on my reputation as a good guy in Hollywood, I really fucking did.

Or I had.

"I told you yesterday," I said, after a heavy silence between us. "I'm throwing my hat back in the ring. Go ahead—sell me. I'm product. Auction me to the highest bidder. I'll do it—I'm raring to go."

My voice held all of the excitement of a boiled eel. I was *not*, as I said, "raring to go." I was, in fact, *not* raring. And not roaring. And not going.

I was pretty sure that yesterday's conversation with Jillian, in which I pronounced myself so "raring," had been the beginning of last night's bender. I remembered, I was standing on the balcony, looking off into the poetic ocean distance, talking to Jillian and taking healthy swallows from a bottle of Pinot Grigio. In my head I could hear Vinnie chiding me for drinking what he called "flat 7 Up," because I never *had* developed a palate, and in my ear, I could hear Jillian telling me that I'd been grieving for a year, and it was time to jump back into the shark pond again.

"You wouldn't say that to me if we'd been out and married," I'd snapped, aching. Because you got more time to grieve a lover than a "bro," didn't you? With a bro, you were expected to carry on, but if we'd been married . . . if we'd even been *dating* . . . no.

For ten years Vince Walker had been my shadow, my lover, my best friend, the one person on the planet I could tell my secrets to. I'd chivvied him into rehab and supported him when he came out, and together we'd been the nonparty boys, the most clean-cut actors in Hollywood, hosting clean and sober parties in my place or his. We'd been photographed for three years in a row, having Christmas in his place, with his family, and pretending I only spent the night in his room on Christmas Eve so there could be space for his brother and two sisters and spouses and kids and such to take over his place for the holidays.

We'd bought houses right next to each other in Malibu, but so what? So had Leonardo DiCaprio and Tobey Maguire, right? We were like Alex O' and Scott Caan, or . . . or . . . oh Jesus, who cared.

Because we weren't like those guys at all.

We were in love, and we'd started working in this business when you just didn't fucking come out, not if you wanted to be leading men in big-budget movies, and so we hadn't. We'd just bought our big fucking houses and took turns sleeping over and quietly building a life together, only it wasn't together, it was separated by two walls, a hedge, and a big fucking swimming pool.

So, yeah. I may have been bitter when I told Jillian that I was willing to be thrown back into the shark tank.

I *must* have been bitter when I told her that. Because I remember taking a healthy swallow of flat 7 Up, and then another one.

And then another one.

And then sitting on the balcony, staring into the orange sunset, and thinking about Vinnie.

And *then* waking up to the phone.

"You're right." Jillian's voice came from an entire continent of pain away. "You're right. I wouldn't throw you back into the pit if you'd been married. But do you think you could have said that yesterday?"

"I thought I did," I mumbled.

"Yeah, and then you said okay."

"Then why are we having this conversation?" Oh God. When Vinnie was alive I wouldn't have gotten this drunk. When Vinnie was alive, I'd very, *very* carefully only had a social drink of wine in company, because Vinnie wasn't drinking *at all* and I knew how hard that was on him.

"Because it was most obviously not okay!" Jillian burst out, an exhalation of smoke hitting her receiver as hard as her voice.

"I don't remember saying that," I said plaintively. *Don't make waves. Treat your agent with respect. Remember, most people in Hollywood would sell their souls to be you and sell you out in a hot second if they even suspected you and Vinnie were an item.* I remember *thinking* all of that, but I don't remember *saying* anything at all resembling the truth.

"That's because you didn't!" she snapped, setting off a trash-can chorus in my head.

"Then how do you know it wasn't okay?" I demanded, because God, it was like "Carol of the Bells" was being played in broken glass between my ears.

"Uh, Connor?" For the first time something akin to sensitivity tinged Jilly's voice.

"What?" I asked suspiciously. "What's wrong? Why do you sound like that?"

"Connor," she said slowly, and I remembered the last time she tried speaking slowly to me.

My stomach wasn't feeling great, and when my bowels contracted in an icy heave I contemplated running for the bathroom. Oh, dear Lord—no. How bad could this be? I'd already survived the worst, right?

"What? What's wrong? Who's dead?" I asked, aware that after the last year this wasn't hyperbole and not the least bit funny. I needed to know how my world was going to be turned upside down as soon as possible, so I could hide all the hurt and pretend it didn't happen.

"Who's dead?" she repeated. "Your career, honey. You killed it last night on YouTube."

I closed my eyes and tried to think. What had been the last thing I'd done as the wine had weakened that brick wall between myself and my grief? I remember seeing the camera Vinnie had kept on the mantel. He'd been so good at social media—had taken short videos almost constantly.

And then edited them.

On *my* computer, I had the video of us kissing on a private beach, the camera held selfie-distance away from our faces, my blond hair riotous in the wind and Vinnie's shorter, darker hair barely ruffling. We'd both closed our eyes at the end, and the camera had dropped as we'd gotten lost in the kiss and the smell of the ocean and the wind and the sand under our feet. The end of the shot had been a ragged series of frames as Vince had struggled to turn the thing off one-handed so that kiss could be the focus of our lives.

The world had the first part of that picture—"Hey, here's the sunset in Hawaii! And here's my buddy, Connor, ready to do some surfing!" I'd waved and winked, and lights out.

Last night, I'd looked at that camera, thought of my computer memory, crammed full of what our life had really been, and thought of what the world knew. Who cared, right? Who cared if the world knew we'd been together since our first audition, both of us nervous and cocky at the same time, neither of us getting the part.

It hadn't mattered—we'd been in Vince's shitty one-room apartment about thirty minutes after leaving the studio, Vince filling the condom inside me, both of us screaming loud enough to wake the neighbors.

I'd been sleeping in a burned-out car then, two months into Hollywood after leaving my home in Northern California with the scornful injunction not to come back until I'd stopped being a fag. (Well, you know, get caught deep-throating the starter of your school's basketball team when you were a drama queer, getting kicked out of the house was bound to happen.)

I'd been desperate—desperate enough to blow a photographer to get my headshots. Desperate enough to have blown businessmen for food.

Vinnie had let me move in that day—a little banter, some hot eyeball action, and one quick fuck, and there we were, sleeping on his twin bed and throwing in for rent together. It might not have been love at first—in fact, at first I think it was mostly necessity—but after a year, and a few successful auditions, and a little bit of fucking around on both our parts, we had enough money to each rent our own apartments.

And we'd . . . decided not to.

Because what had started out as lust and convenience had turned into something more. Something bigger. Something that had us both getting tested and giving up condoms (most of the time)—but keeping the lube.

Then I'd landed a supporting role in a small television show on the CW. And then I'd been courted to be the leading man in another one when the first one folded. That gig had lasted three years, and when I'd left it because . . . reasons . . . I'd landed my first movie role. B-level action flick, yeah—but it paid decent, and I got another one, an A-level after that. Vince's career had taken off too—he was usually the broody guy who got offed, or sometimes the villain—but he worked consistently and got paid well.

Eventually, Jilly (who had signed us by that time—she'd gotten me the gig at the CW) said we *had* to get houses. If we didn't, the press would talk, the fan fiction would get out of hand, our careers would be in jeopardy.

I remembered asking, "Can't we just come out?" Neil Patrick Harris had come out. George Takei had come out. Six years ago there had been enough out celebrities that it shouldn't have made a difference, right?

Jillian had looked at me, pity in her cobalt-blue-tinted contacts. "Honey, you're just not that good." She shook her head. "Those other guys can do it because they've got balls-out talent—you and Vinnie, I love you guys, you're my first big hits and my bread and butter, but you're . . . you know. Beefcake. You're decent enough actors to not embarrass yourselves, but mostly, sugar, you're just a pretty face."

I'd done a shitty job of concealing my hurt—I'd *loved* drama in school. I hadn't wanted to be beefcake, I'd wanted to be an actor, damn it! But Vinnie had let it roll off his back.

"Whatever you say, gorgeous," he'd purred. "As long as we've got backdoor access to each other's pads, I'm good with that." But he'd looked at me searchingly over her head, with a little bit of pity and fear. *His* family still loved him, and I knew because he'd told me that he dreaded, more than anything, losing that support.

Jilly hadn't seen that look, though. She'd touched his nose like wasn't he just the cutest thing? Vinnie got that a lot. "You gay guys— you flirt like gangbusters, but do you ever put out? Done, then—I'll tell the real estate lady to look for properties next to each other, relatively private. No one will ever know."

And no one *had* ever known. Ten years of a relationship forged in the crucible of Hollywood, and my only proof was a laptop full of memories that only two people had shared.

And now it was down to one.

I pulled myself back into the present with a sick *thump*. "Jillian ... did I post a *video* last night?"

Her laugh was weak and stringy and hysterical. "Oh, honey." I heard a shaky draw on the cigarette. "That's like asking if the Washington Monument is a little bit of an erection."

I didn't look. I *couldn't* look at my Washington Monument of YouTube selfies. Just getting out of bed and into the shower took everything I had. After that, it was a fight against vomiting, and I needed all my strength for that.

Forty-five minutes after Jilly hung up, she was at my house—had arrived, in fact, while I was still in the shower. When I emerged, a towel wrapped around my waist, I was surprised and touched to see she'd pulled up my comforter and cleaned up the bottles for me.

Jillian was a four-time combat veteran of the marital wars, and the mother of two. She hardly twitched a sculpted eyebrow as I started rustling around in my drawers for some yoga pants and a T-shirt. She'd once walked into the tiny bathroom of a guest-star trailer to have me sign my next contract. I'd been taking a stellar dump at the time, but she hadn't even wrinkled her rhinoplasty. I loved her like a mother, but there was no doubting the fact that she had iron-clad tits in a stainless-steel bra.

Or so I thought.

She was sitting at my personal desk, sifting through my laptop browser when she cast a look over her shoulder and recoiled.

"Jesus, kid, you're scrawny as hell."

"I work out," I mumbled, taking a hungover look at my wardrobe. I had a maid service that came in and did laundry, which was awesome—but all of my clean, pressed yoga pants and T-shirts had holes in them, and I let out a sigh. Yeah, it had been a while since I'd gone shopping.

"Who gives a shit if you work out? Do you *eat*?"

I tried to remember the last meal I'd had, and drew a blank. "I must eat," I muttered. "Otherwise, I couldn't work out."

"Right." She shook her head and continued to browse. After a moment, she sighed. "You let your porn subscription lapse."

I made a hurt sound, and she looked back at my computer like it held the secrets of the universe.

"And you've been looking at this file with Vinnie every fucking day."

I stopped searching for clothes without holes and grabbed some boxer briefs, yoga pants, and a T-shirt and threw them on haphazardly. The T-shirt was a basic cotton tourist T—we'd gotten it on a trip to the Grand Canyon two years ago. For a while, we'd fought over it, playfully, because we never let ourselves get photographed in the personal shit, and if one of us woke up and put on that shirt, it meant he was staying inside all day and hopefully not alone.

"What do you want me to say?" I was working so hard on leeching the tears out of my voice that it came out flat, no affect, dead.

"I want you to say you want to live!" she half laughed. But she was looking at me soberly, and real concern showed, even through the trowel-thick mascara and the psychotropic contacts.

"Jillian . . ." I didn't know what to say.

She shook her head and waved her hands in uncharacteristic agitation. I hadn't seen her do that since the day we got back from Vinnie's funeral. I'd asked her if she wanted to come inside—basic courtesy, really, I hadn't expected her to take me up on it. The place had been . . . Well, I'd needed to find a different maid service after that week.

She'd helped me clean up the broken glass and the ripped-down curtains, all without a word. I'd apologized, humbly, feeling like a spoiled child, as she'd sat me down with some delivered pizza and a glass of soda, and she'd done . . .

That. Held her hands up, palms toward me, waving them back and forth as she'd tried not to see . . . me. My pain. The thing she couldn't fix.

She did that to me now, and then glared, her eyes watering. "This here is an intervention," she said briskly, and we both ignored the way her voice got thick. "Connor, you need to work again. You need to see people again. You need a fucking goal, even if it's just to know your line and hit your mark and look into the goddamned camera. You want to see how bad it is? You showed the *world* how bad it is."

And with that she shifted aside so I could see the computer. Then she hit Play on the Washington Monument of selfies.

I watched dumbly for a moment as the camera came on, the lens showing a fish-eye view from the mantel in the living room. The furniture was there, fabric couches, matching throw pillows, complementing love seat and recliner, as well as the little conversation pit, and, against the far wall, the 116" flat-screen TV.

Some bozo in board shorts and a tank top was blocking the view, but he backed up like he'd been trained with cameras, and knew about how far he needed to go to be seen in the whole frame.

I stared at my image for a moment. *Jillian was right. I look like hell.* My hair was usually sort of a sandy blond, but I highlighted it because it was Hollywood. You could see about three months of growth between my part and the blond, and there was some silver in that, even visible in the grainy, badly colored shot.

You could see my ribs. Yeah, sure, there were lumps of muscle, but you could *see my ribs.*

I had a sort of long face, with a bold nose and a full mouth—when I was full blond I was an Aryan wet dream, really—and really nice cheekbones, sharp and distinctive. It had been the cheekbones that had convinced me I could make it in Hollywood when my parents insisted that if I wasn't following my father into farming I would pretty much only succeed as a computer technician or an auto mechanic and nothing else.

I'd seen myself in the mirror, stared longingly at my heroes on the screen, and thought, *Look at that. We have the same faces. We can be the same.*

In the video I appeared . . . rodent-like, almost, and feral. My prized cheekbones threw the thinness of my face into stark relief.

I stared at my own image for a few wordless seconds before it hit me.

"What am I doing? And why isn't there any sound?"

"There's no sound through the entire thing," Jillian said irritably. "Did Vinnie not show you how to work the damned camera?"

I gaped at her, and then I gaped at the computer, because no. No, he had not.

I was actually grateful as I watched what followed.

If you asked me on any given day what the worst part of this video was, I'd give you a different answer on each and every different day. I could point out the fact that my eyes were half-mast and my mouth kept opening while I stared at the ceiling in between sentences. I could say it was the beginning sequence when I seemed to be just yelling incoherently at the camera, one hand on my cocked hip, one hand waggling my index finger like a teacher drunk on his or her own power.

But it was obvious that I wasn't drunk on power.

My tirade, whatever it had been, ended, and apparently it was time to fly. Yes, fly—flap my arms and run around the kitchen and pretend to be an airplane or a condor or a butterfly or what the fuck ever—I was gonna fucking achieve liftoff and zoom overhead, I just knew I was . . .

Right until I face-planted, arms outstretched, on the couch.

"Wow," Jillian said, like she was impressed.

"Wow, that's the end?" I prayed.

"No, wow, I can't believe your luck that you missed the floor. And you only *wish* that was the end."

I looked at the counter below the frame.

"*Seven minutes*?" Of which we were apparently only two minutes in. It went on. There was the Batusi and the bunny hop. At one point I was singing—obviously singing—head back, belting it out. I tried to read my own lips for a moment, before I gave up.

"'Sloop John B,'" Jillian said without glancing at me.

"What?" I could not seem to look away from the . . . the train wreck of my life, on display for YouTube viewers everywhere. Oh Jesus. I had over five hundred thousand hits, and it was less than twelve hours old.

"It's what you're singing. See? Right here, you can see that last part." Oh yeah. It was clear I wanted to go home.

"Oh!" And then, as a capper to the madness, we both sang along with my silent movie self as the timer counted off twenty more seconds of my career-dissipation light.

Holy fuck.

And then . . . Oh God. On the screen I was sitting on the couch, one ankle crossed philosophically over one knee, leaning on my elbow and talking earnestly to the camera.

And then . . .

"Turn it off," I said thickly.

"No."

I'd pulled up a picture on my phone and was showing it to the camera. It was nothing incriminating, just me and Vinnie, standing on my balcony, leaning back against the railing, sunglasses on, our faces toward the sun.

We looked so happy.

The other me, the skinny, drunk, pathetic me, just broke down and cried.

Then that same guy stood up and drew really close, so close you could see my rib cage through my tank top, so close the frame went black.

Jillian and I slumped in the desk chairs, while I thought of something to say.

"I'm sorry, Jilly," I managed after a moment.

"It's my fault," she said quietly. "I thought you were okay. You said you needed time to grieve, I said sure—that's what I did. Gave you time to grieve. I didn't realize you were here, all alone. You weren't getting better. You were just . . ."

"Just being sad," I said, closing my eyes. Behind them I could see that icky, rainy May morning we'd gotten back from the funeral, when Jillian had come inside and helped me eat, and I'd told her I just needed time.

There might not be enough time in the world.

"Well, you had a right." She clasped my hand. "I was sad—I don't know if that helps, but I was sad as fuck. You remember when I called Christmas Eve?"

I nodded. I'd been alone, in my house, while Vinnie's family had held a quiet celebration next door. They hadn't asked me over. They hadn't known about us, of course, but you'd think they might have asked Vinnie's *friend* over, right?

I wasn't sure if that meant they were insensitive, or grieving, or just . . . just users, hanging on Vinnie's fame like my family had offered to do with mine a couple of times since I'd hit it big.

I didn't want to think of Vinnie's family that way. For a few years, I'd been able to pretend I had family for the holidays. It had been nice. I didn't have much to pretend right now—I could probably just pretend they were grieving and had forgotten me.

That was easier.

"I remember," I said, to try to pull myself away from my post-Vinnie Christmas featuring me, a bottle of wine, a steak, and a laptop full of memories. "You were the only voice I'd heard in a week."

She rubbed the back of her neck. "Yeah."

"Is my career over?" I had money in the bank. I'd probably have to sell the beach house if I never worked again, but I could live pretty comfortably on what was left.

"No." Jillian rolled her eyes. "I thought it was when I called you—man, my heart almost stopped. But I'm telling you, on my way over here, I fielded about six different calls from people who want your story."

"No."

"Do you think I don't know that?" She simultaneously looked around for an ashtray and fished in her purse for cigarettes. Vinnie hadn't let people smoke in the house, but you know what? Vinnie wasn't fucking here.

Nice, asshole.

I'm not even sorry.

I opened the sliding glass door and grabbed an ashtray from outside—we kept a few for guests. The wind caught me square in the face, and I leaned into it, closing my eyes.

"God, I love the ocean," I said, thinking wistfully of when I'd have to sell the house.

"Do you?" she asked. I turned back inside and set the ashtray down for her, and she lit her cigarette with a shaky hand and a gold lighter.

I moved away from her and crossed my arms, leaning against the doorframe and letting the breeze cleanse away some of my despair.

"I really do. I wish I could live somewhere like . . . like Oregon, or Washington, or even Crescent City. Somewhere it's cold." Where it was cold, and the sky was blue, and the water fought an endless, frothy battle for dominion over cliffs and outcroppings of stone.

"You know," she said tentatively, "you've gotten a couple of offers from television in the past months. A lot of shows are still shooting up north. Are you game?"

I nodded, exhausted, even though I'd only been awake for a few hours.

"Yeah," I sighed, closing my eyes against the sun. "I'd love to go do something like that. Something not . . . here."

"Well, I think I've got just the thing," she said, checking her tablet. "It's late—they might have asked someone else, because shooting starts, like, *immediately.* Let me make a few calls—it might be temporary, you know. Just two months of relocation, and then back here. But it'll be enough to get your feet wet. And the show films just outside of Seattle—"

"Sounds great."

"Do you even want to hear what it is?"

With my eyes closed, I could hear the two pulses in the wind. The first one was the ocean, and it pulsed with everything I loved.

The second one was emptiness. And it pulsed with *He's not here. He's not here. He's not here. Vinnie's not here, he's not here, he's not here.*

It was that second one that made me crave another bottle of wine before I'd even eaten breakfast.

"It doesn't matter," I said honestly. "It's perfect."

"What makes it perfect?" she asked, exhaling smoke.

"It's somewhere not here."

If I could have teleported directly from my balcony in Malibu to a beach house outside of Seattle, I would have, but that would have been too easy.

Jillian, apparently chock-full of remorse after I almost torpedoed my career, set about making me "presentable" before sending me away.

I spent a day at a stylist's getting highlighted, vacuumed, manicured, massaged, and waxed, and then another day with her personal shopper. I fought bitterly for the right to my and Vinnie's old T-shirts, and in the end I won custody of three of them while she had the rest boxed and put into storage.

I got an entire drawer full of new yoga pants and underwear, as well as jeans, flannel shirts, and sturdy boots that really *were* made for the outdoors and not the movie set.

There wasn't a hole in sight.

Jilly also fed me constantly—by the time I got on the plane for Seattle two weeks later, I'd gained five pounds, but she still wasn't happy.

Oh well—agents. Jillian was the best of them, but it was the nature of the species.

And she really *was* the best of the lot, because I wouldn't be getting on that plane alone.

"I'm getting you set up in the house before I leave," she said sternly. "And you have a driver—"

"I can drive!" I protested, but she waved me off.

"Yeah, you say that, but you know what? We both know you still get lost in Hollywood, and you've lived there for ten years."

"Everybody gets lost in Hollywood," I grumbled. "This is Seattle—it's not nearly as big."

"Honey, you get lost in *Nordstrom's.*"

"Everybody gets lost in Nordstrom's." Yeah, right. I'd once wandered the women's department so long I'd bought lingerie for my supposed girlfriend and sent it to Jillian as a joke. But it rankled—my sense of direction was *horrible*. In fact, my horrid sense of direction was the reason Vinnie had been driving alone that night—that and exhaustion. He'd been going to a party out at the canyon, and I'd been fresh off the shoot for *Jupiter Seven*—I'd be no help finding the house and no fun at the party. I'd elected to stay in.

"I'm just going to drive out, make an appearance, drive back—it'll be a few hours, I know, but don't worry. We've got some making up to do!"

It was part of the job, right? We both knew that. You put in an appearance, air-kissed a few people, jumped back in the car, rolled down the top, and enjoyed the trip from the mountains to the beach.

Or got T-boned at an intersection by a guy with three times the legal blood alcohol and all the coke you never snorted pulsing through his bloodstream.

Jillian must have heard what was in my silence because she stopped buying tickets on my laptop and turned around to grab my hand. "Yeah," she said quietly. "I think about what if you'd gone with him too. You know what I think?"

"That I should have been there?" Who *didn't* think it?

"I think that he would have been driving anyway, Con. He had no alcohol in his bloodstream—you would have had no reason to drive. And then you'd both be dead."

My heart constricted, and I fought off the temptation to point out that I hadn't done much living in the last year. "We would have been legend," I said, trying to be blasé about it. "All our movies would have become instant classics, and you would have been rich beyond the dreams of avarice."

She slapped me.

It was weird; her expression didn't change. She just pulled back for some awesome momentum and *slapped* me.

"Don't be an asshole," she said shortly, and then she turned to the computer like it held the secrets to all of Christendom.

I rubbed my cheek and watched a hot tear plop down on the touch pad, and she swore. I'd done that before—the cursor started going batshit almost instantly.

I handed her a tissue, and she blotted the touch pad, and I handed her another one and she blotted her face.

"I'm sorry," I said, feeling empty. "I . . . I don't know how to be about that." When in doubt, state the obvious. "I miss him so bad."

"Of course you do." She patted my hand but didn't look away from the computer. "You guys lived here. These two houses, they were your heart. But there's more houses out there. Once you get away, you'll see."

"You want me to forget him?" I asked, my voice pitching querulously. *No!*

"No." This time she *did* glance at me. "I want you to remember you can live without him. Here we go." She returned her attention to the screen. "Two tickets, first class, no connecting flight. You get out the luggage and pack, I'll call the house and pool service, and we can leave in three days."

"You're sure you want to come?" I asked, confused but grateful.

She hit the appropriate keys on the computer to make her purchase go through and then looked me dead in the eyes. "I miss the motherfucking rain. You'd better bring all the new clothes we bought—it's going to be colder than you're used to, and I don't want you throwing some shitty sweatshirt you wore in high school over PacSun's finest. My boys . . . my *boy* doesn't go anywhere looking low-class."

I nodded, and pretended not to hear the slipup. She'd known we were lovers from day one, and she'd been great at helping us fool the world. She once rerouted me through four different countries to trick the paparazzi into thinking I was having a meetup with a girlfriend, when Vinnie and I had been fucking each other's brains out in a villa off the coast of Spain for two weeks. *"Anything to keep my boys sexed up and sexy,"* she'd said.

At the time, I remembered thinking that we were the best meal ticket she'd ever had. I felt ungrateful for that thought now, and unkind. Apparently she'd been doing what Vinnie and I had been doing—not the fucking part, just doing her best.

It was plenty right now. I found a smile—a real one—in the pit of my stomach and graced her with it like a gift.

"Thanks, Jillian. We can be in the rain together."

She lifted her hand, and for a moment I wondered what I'd said, but she only patted my throbbing cheek.

"So," she muttered, turning back to the screen, "designer umbrellas . . . who can I find that will deliver overnight . . ."

The flight was uneventful—and fun, even, in one of those new prop planes that they apparently use for north-south flights on the West Coast these days. Quiet, without that perpetual ear-roar of the jets—I was a fan.

So was the stewardess. I must have signed half the cocktail napkins in her stock by the time we landed—her sons, her daughters, her best friend, her mother. I'd say one for her husband too, but I got a napkin back with her cell phone number on it and figured *that* ship had sailed. Jillian ignored the woman and stayed pleasantly toasted during the journey. She was *not* a fan of air travel, really.

Still, she was pretty steady on her stilettos when we got off the plane. I had both our carry-ons—one wheeled behind me and one held by the handle on the side—as well as my briefcase (okay, man-purse with a computer pocket) over my shoulder. Against Jillian's strenuous objections, I was wearing jeans and a hoodie when we got off. I consoled her with the fact that the hoodie was high-end and the jeans were designer, but honestly, I just wanted comfort clothes.

That didn't keep me from feeling just a tad self-conscious when a driver—an honest-to-God driver wearing a suit and a hat and everything—greeted us in front of baggage claim with a tablet marquee-scrolling my name.

"Connor Montgomery," I read out loud, feeling stupid. "Uh, yeah. That's me. I mean us. I mean . . ."

The kid holding the tablet grinned. At least I think he was a kid—he had a long, square jaw, the thin neck of early adulthood, and a rather prominent Adam's apple. He also had deep brown eyes and skin to match, and brown hair in soft, glossy ringlets around his head, making me flail for his ancestry. African American? Native American? He had a straight, almost Roman nose, strong chin, and full lips. I flailed some more. Greek? Scottish and African American?

Oh hell.

Not white, and not fucking bad.

The smile he leveled at Jillian and me was blinding. "Mr. Montgomery? Really? So awesome to meet you. Anna Maxwell sent me to greet you. I'm supposed to be your driver for the next few months, so I'll set you up with my contact info and stuff when I drop you off."

I looked at Jillian, feeling a little embarrassed. "Jilly . . ."

She shrugged. "They were sort of hot for you, Con—and you need a driver. I can only stay here a week, and . . . you know . . ."

Lost at Nordstrom's. Awesome. I smiled at the kid, rather embarrassed and still trying to juggle our luggage. "Lead on, brave soldier. You have no idea what you're in for."

The kid flashed another supernova at us, and I almost covered my eyes and groaned. Jeez, kid, it was only one in the afternoon!

"Noah," he said, extending his hand. "Noah Dakers. Nice to meet you."

I took his hand and squeezed, liking what he gave back in return. *Nice kid*, I thought as we gathered baggage and hauled it out to the waiting town car. Maybe he'd be company in this unfamiliar place.

I could always use a friendly face, and as Vinnie used to say, a pretty face could make *everything* feel friendly. Not that I wanted to hit on him, no—but it was sure nice to remember I could look.

"So," he asked, after we'd stashed our luggage and slid into the town car (leather seats—I loved that in a car, I really did), "we're going to your cabin—it's out by the new development for the TV people. Nice place, you'll like it. But are you hungry? In need of coffee? Is there anyplace I can take you first?"

"Coffee," I said, my voice shaking with need, but I said it right at the same time Jillian said, "*Food!*" and she was louder and meaner.

Noah laughed. "Okay, food—do you want quaint and local, or fast produced and comforting? It's up to you."

I said, "Local!" because Vinnie and I had always liked trying to find the perfect hole-in-the-wall that only the locals knew about.

Jillian said, "*Anything!*" so guess what? I won!

Actually I won twice. Noah told us that he had the exact spot right outside of Bluewater Bay, but it meant we had to wait a bit—and since I was obviously jonesing for coffee, he took us through a drive-thru Starbucks on the way out of town.

"When we get to Bluewater, I'll take you to the Stomping Grounds—that's our local coffeehouse. Best stuff on earth. But let's get you coffee and a snack to hold you over until we get there, 'kay?"

"I like this kid," Jillian said with meaning, and I ignored her. But I let Noah order a spinach feta wrap to go with my Caffé Americano venti, so she got to win too.

I'd assumed Jilly and I would just sort of hunker down in the back of the town car and have muted conversations. The closest thing to conversation I'd ever gotten from a driver was the time one of them had been trying to get me to JFK at record speed. As my face had been plastered against the back window by the centrifugal force of taking a curve at ninety, the guy had muttered, "Time adjustment," in apology.

This guy was *not* the car driver in New York.

"You ever been out here before?" he asked after we'd cleared the Starbucks. He headed for 101, and the city—indistinguishable in the back of the car—faded to concrete, and rolling suburbs beyond.

"Yes," I said, enjoying the memory. "My first big break—*Warlock Tea*—that was filmed in Vancouver."

Noah let out an unabashedly fanboi sigh. "God, I loved that show. I'd forgotten that, you know? I was in high school, and Vancouver felt like a continent away. But *you* I remember."

I put myself in "TV star" mode. It was hard—people would gush over the stuff I was least proud of, but you don't want to crap on people's dreams. I mean, someone cared enough to tell you that your work meant something to them, right? So you said thank you, and I was *always* grateful. But I was also embarrassed.

It felt like I could have done more to deserve all that gushing.

"That was an awesome shoot," I told him—because being on the show had been great. The rest of the truth was I'd missed the shit out of Vinnie during those years. Of course I went back down to LA on breaks and holidays and over hiatus, and Vinnie visited me on *his* breaks, but still . . . we'd struggled so hard to get an agent and an audition and a break, oh holy God, just a motherfuckin' break, but once I had one . . . God, we'd learned how much we had together when we were forced to live apart.

"Yeah—it was a fun show," Noah said. I watched those remarkable brown eyes take me in through the rearview mirror. "Not your best work, really, but I get the feeling you haven't done that yet."

I gaped at him, a thousand critical reviews spooling behind my eyes. *"Montgomery did what he did best—amiable beefcake seems to be his calling." "Connor Montgomery is infinitely watchable, but he'll never be Oscar material." "Pretty and charming are Montgomery's calling cards, and he pulls them both out here with a flourish."*

Nice things—people said nice things about me. But they never, ever said I had more in me than what I'd put out there on the screen. Not even my directors—but then, Jilly told me straight out she picked the softball scripts for me. I could run from a fake explosion on a green screen like it was an Olympic sport. Just, oh God! Don't give him dialog, we're afraid the guy can't read!

In the course of the last week, Jilly and I had shotgunned the first season of *Wolf's Landing*, and sitting here, making eyes at the pretty kid driving my car, I had a flash of panic. That show was written *really well*—in fact, that was part of my planned press release to put a good spin on the fact that I wanted to ease back into the land of the living by doing TV instead of movies. "It's an honor to be asked to do a guest spot in a show written as well as this one. I hope I do the show's writers justice."

Oh God. What if I *couldn't* do the show's writers justice? What if Jillian was right? I wasn't good enough for more than amiable beefcake?

The flash of panic through my chest and the adrenaline dumping into my brain were pretty much the granddaddies of all surprises. If you'd asked me a week ago, I would have said it was *impossible* for me to care about my career.

I realized Noah was waiting for an answer—and whether she was looking at me or not, so was Jillian.

"Hopefully I can do my best work here." The words were clichéd, and probably sounded rehearsed—but the delivery was thoughtful and engaged. Wouldn't that be great, to find I wasn't done with my life at twenty-nine.

"We surely would love to see that, Mr. Montgomery," Noah said earnestly. "I've been waiting to see your best work since high school!"

My brain shot off a warning flare that a long-defunct operation was about to boot up, and I had another hit of panic.

"So, what was that? Two years ago?" I asked, hoping I didn't sound like a heel. Jillian smacked my knee, so I must have, and Noah stopped looking in the mirror, so I probably embarrassed him too.

"Closer to six." His voice kept that edge of good humor, and I blessed him. "I'm more a runner than a bodybuilder, you know?"

"Yeah," I said, regretfully. "I know all about that." My first year doing *Warlock Tea* had been spent getting phone calls from the studio execs every day, asking me to bulk up, while Jillian and Vinnie had been sending me vanilla whey protein to put into *everything* from my oatmeal to my fruit smoothies. "I miss the days when I could go running on the beach and call it good."

"Maybe if you'd just fucking eat, we could go back to those days again." Jillian inspected her manicure.

"Sure, Jilly," I soothed. I had a cookie leftover from our Starbucks run, and I took it out of my bag and offered her half. She took it and ate irritably, but she settled down when she was done. I offered her the other half, and she shoved it gently back to me.

"You eat it, pardnuh. You'll be fine."

I shrugged and put it back in the bag. I was hungry, yeah, but I needed protein.

I looked up to see what Noah thought of all of this, but the road took a few quick turns, and those sucked up his attention.

I turned my attention to the scenery—which was really quite spectacular. On the driver's side we had Mount Olympus in the background, and her northern slope seemed filled with wild flowers. To the passenger's side there were flatlands, heading out toward the sound. I remembered those days in Vancouver, when waking up and looking out over the sound seemed to be some sort of reward for living without Vinnie so long. Those days when I'd had Vinnie too, wrapping his arms around my waist and sharing the view—those had been the best.

I quick checked in my head, and I realized that it was early May—I'd start shooting in a week so the cast would have the rushes to tour with during convention season. I understood there was a small con here in March, but Comic-Con and Dragon Con happened later on in the summer. I used to love doing cons—being on panels, taking in the excitement from the fans.

I wasn't sure I was up to them right now—I'd have to ask Jillian if they were in my contract or not. The thought of all those people, some of them lying in wait to ask me what the press had been trying to ask me for a year, nauseated me.

How are you taking the death of your friend, Vinnie Walker?

How did they think I was taking it? It was like my world had ended. Because it had.

Maybe going out and doing something new would make that better, right? I mean, Hollywood had the attention span of a coked-up ferret. I was a special guest star—maybe everyone would pay attention to the show and forget about me. Pay no attention to the man behind the curtain! He died a year ago anyway!

Lost in my own thoughts, I didn't realize the road had leveled out again until Noah started talking.

"So, what do you like most about the Pacific Northwest?" he asked, and it was such a con question I found myself slipping into con mode to answer.

"The natural beauty," I replied promptly. "The genuine people. Being so near the ocean *and* the mountains."

He laughed, but the eyes in the rearview were skeptical. "Sounds like you've been asked that before," Noah said, putting his eyes firmly back on the road where they belonged.

I was going to laugh too, keep the moment light, but just that suddenly, I couldn't.

"I like the fog," I said after a thoughtful pause.

"The *fog*?" The distance was gone, replaced by surprise.

"Yeah—you know, the mist. I like that . . . that sometimes, when you're walking on the beach, it feels like you're the only person alive on an alien planet." That sounded pathetic enough, but I just couldn't seem to stop. "When I was a kid, I used to ditch out on my chores so I could walk on the beach. We lived by Monterey, so you know, six out of ten days, there'd be fog. I loved that. Those were the best days."

We hadn't lived so much *by* Monterey, but *below* Monterey, in one of the tiny seaside towns that were populated by the immigrant work force and the farmers who hired them. I was the son of one of each—the oldest son, and my father's blond, blue-eyed genetics had apparently latched on to some old Spanish ancestor of my mother's, because I had come out looking like a pretty white boy who tanned really well.

That hadn't stopped me from chasing brown-boy tail, though—apparently the hair and the eyes weren't the only thing I'd gotten from dear old Dad. Vinnie had been the poster boy for my favorite brand of pretty, which might explain the insta-lust on that first surprising day.

Which was, I told myself, why Noah the driver's opinion of my answer seemed to matter so damned much to me right now. He was my type—and here I was, still desperately trying to impress the boys who'd wanted nothing to do with me until I'd gotten on my knees.

I was almost thirty—how sad could I get?

The brown eyes in the rearview flickered to the road, then flickered back again.

"I like the fog too," he said, like it mattered.

I swallowed. "Yeah, not everybody does." Vinnie had hated it— he'd wanted to be in the sunlight as much as possible. It was why he hadn't moved to Vancouver when I'd lived here—he'd tried, during one of his breaks, but that had been his first lapse into depression, to drug dependency, to rehab. I'd had to leave the show after three years just to pull him out of it. The plot arc had fallen apart without me—I'd felt like shit, but the producers obviously held no grudges.

They were, in fact, some of the same people who were about to pay my salary.

"Hmm . . ." Noah nonanswered, and then he turned his attention to the road in front of him.

And I sank back into my thoughts.

Vinnie, leaden-eyed after too many pills to get to sleep. Vinnie, pale and self-deprecating in rehab. Jillian, using my freedom from the show as an excuse to launch me into movies. Vinnie had liked that—if I was gone, it was for maybe six weeks at a stretch, and usually some place with lots of sunlight and some parties.

And he'd made contacts at the parties, and I'd gotten to watch him rise like a meteor.

Was it wrong that I'd been as proud of his career as I was of my own?

But I'd missed the quietude of the cold ocean—I couldn't deny that either.

After about forty-five minutes, Noah slowed the car, and I looked up. We were close to the sound—I could tell by the foliage, by the dampness in the air, and the smell of the grasses that lived near the cold salt water—but I couldn't see the town.

What I could see was a small steak house set back into the overgrown foliage on the side of the road—dark paneled from the outside, and surprisingly large.

Rockin' Surf and Dockn' Turf.

I grimaced. "Food better than the name?"

We all sort of gasped—they were the first words spoken in a while.

But they got Noah to smile. "Yeah—the Captain isn't so great with words, but he's great with potatoes and *fantastic* with steak!"

"How is he with salads?" Jillian asked, properly horrified as someone who yearned to be a size two should be.

Noah grimaced, and I consoled her as we got out. "I'm sure he can do steamed veggies and some grilled fish."

Jilly brightened, and in spite of the heels and the skinny skirt, she strode up the moss-crusted flagstones like she was cruising Rodeo Drive in search of a bargain.

Noah was grinning and tilting back his seat, looking like he was getting ready to snooze, and I felt the remorse of the privileged class smacking me in the teeth.

I tapped on the window, and he rolled it down. "Want to come eat with us?"

He grimaced, obviously waffling. "I was going to call Cappy and have him bring me takeout while I waited, but . . ."

Hey—I was a movie star, and shameless about using it. I gave him the Connor Montgomery special smile, the one with the hint of shyness and a bulldozer's load of sex. I wasn't sure if the sex would work—contrary to all the tropes of fanfic, not all fanbois were gay—but I was pretty sure the shyness might. He followed my career, right? Everybody wanted to know if movie stars were approachable. We played someone's favorite buddy (or, in Vinnie's case, someone's favorite dickhead, thank you, typecasting) and don't you want to see if this person is nice in real life?

Hey—it explained most of my stalker mail, right?

And Noah bit.

"Sure," he said after a moment, shrugging. "I don't usually see the place in the day. At night it's sort of an after-hours dance club—and *then* the place is hopping, you know?"

A part of me wanted to fist pump, but a part of me was asking what I was doing. I didn't have an answer to myself. I talked to Noah instead.

The inside of the steak house was as modest as the outside—stained boards on the walls and floor, and basic, solid wooden tables.

But it *smelled* good inside, and not just of alcohol from the brass-fitted bar that took up the back wall. Noah led the way—his turf—and he smiled and winked at the waitress serving a family in the corner when he grabbed some menus from the hostess stand and found us a set table.

The napkins were cloth, I noticed in surprise, but every space had a small stack of those ultra-thick paper napkins as well.

"If you order something messy, they bring out a steam bath for you," Noah explained. Like me, he stood to let Jillian sit first, and I approved. It had taken me a while to learn that manners lesson after I'd moved to Hollywood—someone had schooled this kid well.

"It's pretty swank for the middle of nowhere." I wasn't sure if I was being complimentary or an asshole. I *wanted* to be complimentary—I liked the place. Along the back wall there were plaques of what *should* have been fishing trophies, but instead were ridiculous items of measurement. A length of pipe, a liter bottle, a plunger—along with a caption: *Caught a trout this big in 2010. Caught a rockfish this big in 2013.* (That one was under a mounted microwave oven.) Under a modest-sized bicycle were the words *The One That Got Away.* I mean, tacky fishing trophies that *didn't* look tacky—how could I resist?

My problem was that my dad and his family had money while my mom's family had not. A lot of times I mentioned stuff—class stuff like, oh gee, what a nice place you have here in what used to be a little fishing town—that made me sound like a snob. Vinnie used to say that I had social problems that teleported in like a cow into a nail salon. *You'll be sailing along, tap dancing the small-talk boogie, and BOOM, that cow will show up, thrash around, and destroy everything in its path, and then leave the charming Connor to clean up the mess.* Jillian claimed that was an apt description too—I'd once ranted about women with skull-cap perms in front of Vinnie's mom who'd worn her hair like that for twenty years.

But Noah seemed destined not to take exception.

"Yeah—it *is* pretty nice. Cappy did a twenty-year stint in the armed forces. *His* dad had been a fry cook, so when Cappy realized there was more to dining than a burger in a paper basket, he started to dream about a place that was comfy to eat at but classy too." Noah laughed a little. "He must have been a hell-raiser overseas, because he *also* added the dance floor. After ten there's only bar food—and usually live bands."

Jillian and I laughed appreciatively. I could see how a place like this would be a staple in a small town—especially once the small town did a tourist boom. This would be a locals-only sort of place—a secret.

"It was nice of you to bring us," I said sincerely.

A charming, self-deprecating grin made an appearance. "Well, you know. Not every day you get to meet one of your favorite actors in the course of your job. Had to make a good impression."

I felt an unexpected heat on my face and hoped that stupid cow would stay out of my conversation this time. "You mean Carter Samuels and Levi Pritchard didn't get the surf-and-turf treatment?"

Noah grinned wider, his cheekbones staining a darker red. "No, sir—but then, I haven't had a chance to drive for them."

"You're new to the company?" I looked over the menu and for the first time ever got excited about the choices. A small sirloin steak with mushrooms—that actually sounded *really* good right now.

"Well, yeah, but they usually drive themselves," Noah admitted. "I was hired for special occasions and gofering."

I cringed. "Oh God. I'm the only idiot who can't find my way around Washington, aren't I?"

He winked, which made me feel better. "Hey, you're keeping me employed, so as far as I'm concerned, you're brilliant. Besides, this job is sort of the answer to the age-old question, you know?"

I looked up from my mortification and took the bait. "What age-old question?"

"What kind of job can you get with a master's degree in philosophy?"

I laughed politely, but inside I quailed. I knew myself—the odds of the psycho cow popping up in conversation were inversely proportional to how embarrassed I was at being "amiable beefcake" in front of someone. Vinnie's parents were a cop and a nurse—psycho cow showed up *occasionally*. Jillian had three MAs. It had taken me five years as her top-grossing client to stop insulting her, her family, and her family's family at every turn.

"What are you having?" Jillian asked me, sotto voce, like she didn't want to interrupt my conversation.

"Baked potato, plain," I muttered, because the steak didn't sound as good anymore.

"Bullshit," she replied. The waitress showed up right then, and Jillian summoned her attention with an imperious click of her nails on the vinyl cover of the menu. "Yeah, we'll have the fried pickles as an appetizer, I'll have the low-cal chicken Caesar, and my friend here will have the twenty-two–ounce porter with mushrooms and bleu cheese on top, the loaded baked potato, the vegetable selection, and the small baby green salad after the app."

I stared at her. "Jesus, Jillian, that meal would feed half of Hollywood."

She ignored me and smiled warmly at Noah. "And what would you like, young man? Our treat since you took us to your favorite watering hole."

Noah blinked in surprise. "Uh, Char, I guess I'll have my regular—"

"How about your *favorite*," Char hinted, looking at Jillian meaningfully.

"His favorite," I said, winking at the waitress. She blushed and grinned and made the notation in her book.

"And to drink?"

Noah ordered lemonade, so I ordered that too—apparently fresh squeezed by the pitcher—and Jillian ordered a lemon *drop*. Well, that was usually *all* she had for lunch, so it was a banner day in the health department for both of us, wasn't it?

"So what did we just order you?" I asked curiously. "And how's it different from what we were *going* to order you?"

This kid's teeth should come with a warning label: Warning, will make grown men and women stupid as fucking hell. Should be flashed in small doses.

"Steak and lobster," he said, sounding greedy. "Usually I just get the chicken sandwich—but, you know, the boss insists . . ."

I laughed a little. "I ordered a plain baked potato and a mineral water for years before Jillian told me she expensed all our meals."

She shook her head. "Most actors can't wait to eat on someone else's dime—but not you and Vinnie. Gallant little assholes, both of you."

My breath caught, and for a moment I wondered if Vinnie's name was going to shut down all conversation. For the last week, whenever we'd gone out, I'd heard the name whispered as we'd walked into a place and heard it again when we walked out. But when we were actually *there*, I hadn't heard anything. Everybody—hairstylist, personal shopper at Nordstrom's, the sweet, flamingly gay kid who did my nails—walked around in a terror of dropping the one name that used to be my best and most favorite topic of conversation.

I guess I wasn't the only one with magic teleporting psycho cows on the brain.

In this case, Noah cleaned up the social carnage.

"You guys were close?" he asked without hesitation. "Good friends?"

"The best," I lied, grateful *for* the lie. At least I could talk about him.

"You must miss him."

Like that, the new locale, this kid's killer grin, the quaint restaurant with the weird fishing trophies, all of it, fell into the giant black hole that was my grief.

"Yeah," I said, looking at my clasped hands in front of me. "Every goddamned day."

Every goddamned minute of every goddamned day.

"Is that the reason you took the job up here?" Noah's perceptiveness was almost my undoing.

"Yeah." I glanced around. "Bathroom? My lease agreement on the coffee is up."

CHAPTER TWO

WHO DIED AND MADE YOU FUCKING KING OF THE ZOMBIES?

I had a long talk with myself in the bathroom: things like, "You're going to have to deal with it eventually!" and "Stop flirting with the chauffeur!" figured prominently, but so did, "Jesus, it's nice to talk to someone who's not afraid to mention Vinnie!" and "Jesus, it's nice to talk to anybody at all!"

Yeah—it was true I'd pretty much withdrawn from Hollywood after Vinnie died, but it was also true that had been because nobody would understand how much his life had meant to me.

Talking to a complete stranger—one who was easy on the eyes and charming and just starstruck enough to make it so I didn't have to work too hard—was like a refresher course in how to be a human being again.

I'd never really liked school until now.

That thought cheered me, and when I got back to the table they'd just served the fried pickles.

They were delicious—and that cheered me more.

There's a thing that actors and writers do—sometimes it's unconscious, but sometimes I think we do it in self-defense. It all comes from only having one life.

We want to live *all* the lives. We want to *be* all the people and *write* all the people—so much so that I know the weakest of us forget how to be ourselves. That's why Vinnie and the drugs, he told me once. He had to learn how to be Vinnie, and when Connor wasn't there to give him guideposts, he forgot. But with that weakness aside, the willingness to be other people makes us want to *talk* to other people, a lot.

Every person we've never met is a role we want to research or a character waiting to inspire.

The best part of this selfish, driving compulsion to be somebody new is that it makes us look like *spectacular* listeners—at least at first meeting—because we will flirt, cajole, and downright interrogate you like you are the most fascinating, fabulous person on the planet.

I used to feel guilty about this—the time I would spend at parties talking to the waitresses or the car valets or the maids. I would walk away never to see them again, but with somebody's life experience tucked close against my heart, like a treasure stolen from a secret box, and I'd wonder what they'd gotten out of it. How exciting could it have been to talk to me for an hour? All of my best stories were usually in print or pixels already. I didn't talk about my childhood, and as far as the public was concerned, I was a one-night-stand bachelor.

What did they get from me?

One night, lying on the bed next to Vinnie, I'd voiced the question, feeling silly and embarrassed, like I was overtaxing my amiable-beefcake brain with too much deep thought.

Vinnie didn't think so, though.

I remember that moment clearly, because it was at my house and we usually spent the night at Vinnie's. But every door and window in the house sat open, the white curtains blowing in with the breeze, the sound of the ocean sweetly singing in my ears.

And the sound of Vinnie's voice as he told me, *"Yeah, but think about it, Con. When we were just starting out, how many dicks would you have sucked to get one person—just one—to listen to the story of your life and tell you that you were special?"*

I grunted, thinking about it, and pulled the pillow I was lying on closer to my chin. Oh yeah—that gut-sick yearning for attention, for someone, anyone, to just look up and see *me*, Connor Mazynsky, and tell that kid he didn't need his big break to be a star.

That kind of neediness was depressing, and I kissed a sly glance up at Vinnie to lighten the mood.

"Turns out I only needed to suck one."

He'd laughed, low and dirty, and two dicks *did* get sucked, but after we swallowed, that moment stuck with me.

It wasn't a parasitic exchange after all—for just ten minutes, an hour, maybe two, I got to give something to someone. I got to make them a star.

I spent the next hour in the restaurant and forty-five minutes outside of it on the way to the cabin making Noah Dakers the star of my very own Oscar Award–Winning Movie.

By the time he pulled down a rather long gravel road toward an ocean-side block of two-story houses, each about a quarter mile apart, I knew the following about Noah:

I knew he had three younger sisters, all of whom were cared for by his father and paternal grandmother.

I knew their mother had taken off and their father was a handyman in Bluewater Bay. He was a member of the handyman's guild and everything, and if you needed anything from a weatherized house to a new driveway, Samuel Dakers was the guy you went to. The advent of the television show—now starting its third year—had been a blessing for Noah's family, because their father didn't have to look far for work.

I knew that even though Noah had worked his way through school—and the traditional mountain of debt still loomed—he'd jumped at a chance to come back to his family and work with the same film company that gave his father so much business. His father had gotten him the job, of course, but Noah had held it down for the past three months and he seemed to have impressed his bosses.

I knew that Noah's grandmother and sisters occasionally did local work for the movie people too—his biggest coup was when his oldest sister, Viv, got a job as a set dresser. She would wait until a scene was over, then run around and put all the stuff that had been disturbed in the course of the scene back in its original spot. Apparently she was great at making beds and repositioning fake guns, and Noah said she was looking forward to college with a little less debt than he'd built up.

I knew that in spite of the complaints about the debt, he thought the degree in philosophy was enough, even if he never used it to work.

I knew that he was twenty-five and his youngest sister was fourteen years old, and he and his other sisters had been working really hard to show her a bigger world than northern Washington.

But that was a hard sell, because they all loved where they'd grown up, and they all wanted to stay there too.

I knew that Noah had been twelve when his mom left, and he and Viv were the only ones truly pissed at her for going. But he tried not to be too vocal about that, because the girls needed to think their mother was a better person than she really was.

I knew that Noah was gay, and his family knew he was gay, and not even his grandmother thought that was a bad thing.

And I knew his oldest sister kept trying to set him up with boys she knew, and that he had a date tonight, back at the ol' Rockin' Surf and Dockn' Turf, and that it was his second time out with the boy.

That last one . . . Well, that last one left me stranded on the beach of my own intentions. *Just "researching" him, right?*

Yes. Absolutely.

"So don't forget your three-date etiquette," I chided lamely as Noah turned into the driveway with an earth-brown house with yellow trim. I was abruptly distracted. "This is it? This is my house? Wait—the backyard overlooks the water, doesn't it?"

We'd come down a rise as we'd driven in, and I'd been able to see that the "yards" had all been built out and built up, sod included, and they were all framed by wooden slats to keep the earth from tumbling into the water. The slats continued up, serving as a four-foot fence keeping the unwary from tumbling over the side.

"Yes, sir." Amusement tinged Noah's tone.

I didn't care. I mean, I *abandoned* my game of "research" so I could hop out of the car while it was still braking and take a good look at what would be my digs for the next two to three months.

"It's awesome," I breathed. "Look, Jillian, isn't it awesome? I think it's awesome. Can you see? The top gable or turret or window thing— that goes all the way through? Is that the main bedroom? You can look out the one side to Mount Olympus and out the back to the islands on the water? Oh, *look*, Jilly—it's got yellow trim! I mean, it looks just like a gingerbread house. Have you ever seen anything so fucking *dear*?"

I turned to her, heart thrumming from the sudden influx of enthusiasm. "It's great, Jilly. I love it. Can we keep it?"

She raised her sunglasses and glared at me. "What, are you twelve?"

"Yes," I told her sincerely. "I'm twelve, and I just got cast as Hansel in a place with fog. I fucking *love* this house!"

Noah pulled out of the car and laughed at me, and I glanced at him guiltily. I'd stopped, right in the middle of telling him to go out and get laid—how was I supposed to be a good listener if I didn't tell him what every American youngster desperately needed to hear?

And . . . damned teleporting cows anyway! Starting up on *that* conversation again was *not* particularly social.

Well, hell. The best I could do was to dork out so thoroughly about the house that he felt like he could leave this aging geek in the dust and forget about the most boring part of his job.

"You love the house," he said, laughing. "I get it. Here—let's get the luggage out, and I've got the keys. I can show you around, and we can talk about your schedule for the next few days. You start filming Monday."

"Oh." I was suddenly brought short by the idea of reality intruding. "Oh. Oh yeah." I smiled shakily. "I'd forgotten about that."

"Well, don't," Jillian snapped. "But do help us get this shit inside. I picked the decorations out for you, and you need to be sufficiently grateful, okay?"

"You ordered furniture in a week?" I asked, baffled. How did someone *do* that?

"Yeah, genius—and I'm pretty sure Noah's grandmother made the beds and stocked the refrigerator, am I right, Noah?"

That supernova smile made its appearance. "Yes, ma'am, she did. And my dad put together the furniture yesterday. Boy, that sure did arrive quickly."

Jillian raised an insouciant shoulder. "Shopping. It's a skill."

"I had no idea," I said, uncomfortably grateful. "I just sort of assumed we were getting a rental and rental furniture." I looked at the house with longing. "Would be the best rental ever."

Noah winked and hefted Jilly's "shoe bag," which must have weighed a ton. "I'm glad you like it—I picked the yellow trim."

I smiled, like a child with a clean past and only Christmas in his future. "That's the best part," I said earnestly, and then paused to look at it one more time.

A beach house at Malibu, with a balcony with steps that led right down into the sand? No.

This was a different ocean. The sound was calm—I knew that from my time in Vancouver, but it was still the child of a meaner ocean, the deep, cold breath before the icy currents that swept down from Alaska and the still-frozen north blew chaos on the shore.

As we loaded stuff into the house I was only more charmed. The inside was paneled in waxed pine, floor and walls, and the kitchen and bathrooms were tiled in basic white. It *was* a rental after all, but a high-end one, so the décor was basic. Jilly had ordered a plain wood kitchen table and chairs, complete with a pretty blue tablecloth and floor mats. The front door opened into a living room with comfortable furniture—rich-blue corduroy—all arranged on a dark-brown throw rug with a sturdy coffee table in the center and a television set—of course—on the wall.

Upstairs were three bedrooms and two baths, one attached to the master suite which was already made up. Carpeting up here, basic cream berber, and the furniture she'd ordered was sturdy and plain.

The whole house was comfortable, masculine and . . .

My heart fell.

Way too big for one person.

My enthusiasm plummeted to the bottom of the sound.

I trudged down the stairs and hefted Jillian's suitcase from the foyer without making eye contact with either her or with Noah, who was busy opening the windows and letting some air in.

"What's wrong, Peaches?" Jilly asked, naturally caustic voice sending a fresh arrow in. "You don't like the color scheme?"

Blue was my favorite. Okay—I had a lot of favorite colors, but blue and brown and yellow—that was my favorite combo. The whole house had been done on a minute's notice, with me in mind. Jillian's apology, I guess, for leaving me alone so long—not that it was needed.

Apparently she'd been sad too.

"It's amazing, Jilly," I said, infusing my voice with sincerity. I was an actor, right? I knew how to take real emotions and displace them to something that was needed. "Thank you."

Jilly buys nothing without biting the coin first. "Bullshit 'Thank you'—what's wrong?"

I cut eyes at Noah, whom I hoped was out of earshot. "This house, Jilly—it's awesome. But it's too much. Too big for just me, and too . . . too *nice* for temporary. This is supposed to be a short-time gig—"

Jilly looked away.

"It *is* a temporary gig, right?"

She shrugged. "You know how these things go," she said vaguely. "If your character is a hit, you get hired on for a while. I didn't want you to be in some temporary cabin with polyester sheets, is that so bad?"

"But who's going to be here after you go?" I asked, trying not to let my voice throb. That had been half the problem with Malibu. Four guest bedrooms, a gym, and a master suite that had room for a computer desk, a giant television, and two walk-in closets. And when Vinnie was gone I'd been the sole survivor of the zombie apocalypse, the head zombie himself.

Jilly stared at me as though I were deranged. "How about the cute gay guy who's been *throwing himself* at you for the last hour and a half."

I stared back at her. "He was being polite, Jilly. And I'm *straight*, remember?"

Jilly cringed—I guess I'd thrown a lot of venom into the word "straight."

"Yeah," she started, "uhm, about that—"

"I opened everything up so it's not all stuffy," Noah said, walking in from the kitchen. "You may want to close it when evening falls. There's food in the fridge for a week—you gave a list to my grandma, right?"

Jilly nodded, and I felt . . . useless, suddenly. I'd expected to show up to a crappy cabin and had ended up in a palace, and apparently Jilly had spent a very busy week getting the hookup on and making sure we were taken care of.

I remembered the week when Vinnie and I had survived on twenty bucks between us, with a little help from leftovers from the restaurant where I'd worked at the time. I'd had life skills once—but I don't know if I had life skills like Jilly.

"Thank you," she said sincerely. "I can see why the *Wolf's Landing* people rec'd your family so heartily—you guys ever want to start an actual business—you know, catering to rental companies and shit, I'll hook you up with the permits and publicity—you name it. You guys totally came through."

Noah grinned. "Well, Gran said you tipped in advance. Motivation—I'm telling you, it totally works." He flashed that destroyer of brain cells on me. "So, Miss Lombard, we've got a press conference scheduled for tomorrow at ten, a brief tour of the soundstage, and lunch with the producers in the specialty restaurant at the Global."

"A hotel?" I asked, surprised.

"Second best around here for dinner." Noah winked.

Next to the Rockin' Surf and Dockn' Turf, that was pretty high praise.

"You're not going to fill them in on your little secret?"

Noah shook his head. "No, sir, I am not. The TV people are nice and all, and really respectful of Bluewater, but I do *not* like to share. Besides—Cappy gets irritated if he gets too busy and the cooking gets bad. I like it as is."

We had not met the mysterious Cappy while we'd been eating—I guess Jilly and I didn't rank.

"Fair enough—I'll be sure to keep your secret," I said, teasing.

Noah stuck out a hand, like a grade-schooler swearing a blood oath. "And I, in turn, will endeavor to keep yours, good sir."

I blinked, puzzled, but took his hand. "And what secret would that be?"

Suddenly, Noah's confidence, his banter deserted him, and his hand grew sweaty in mine. "Nothing," he said. "Uh, I mean, you know, whatever secrets you might have. You know, secret pact between driver and driven or, uh, something like that."

He'd been thinking something completely different—I knew it. But I wasn't going to ask. If I didn't say it, he couldn't know it. If he didn't know it, this entire fantasy I'd been indulging in—the flirting, the "research," the pleasant stirrings of attraction—was just that. *Fantasy*. It was like playing a role where I got to flirt with the hot younger guy. We could banter and smile, and I could appreciate his body and his clean cheekbones and obsidian eyes, but I didn't have to open up—not emotionally. Because I knew that the minute somebody started to play "research" with *me*, all they'd find was the great yawning void of grief where Vinnie used to be.

"Well, I'll be sure to trust you with my secrets, then," I promised soberly.

He worried his lip, like I'd hurt him somehow. "No, you won't," he said, half to himself. "But it was nice to imagine." He straightened and looked at Jilly. "So, I'll come get you at nine; sometimes they run me around on errands between one gig and the other, but either way, I'll be back at the soundstage at twelve to take you both to lunch. They told me that it's going to be a long working lunch—they want the entire cast, and everybody's running lines for two scripts' worth, that's why the hotel. There's not a good place for the whole cast on the soundstage site—usually they do business in the little portable trailer office, but this is just too big."

"Oh," I said, a little surprised. "I thought we weren't shooting until next week."

"You're not," Noah supplied, then looked abashed, like he was embarrassed to know so much. "I mean, my dad's building some outside sets—he doesn't have to be done until your shooting date. But I think the writers want to see how the new additions to the cast go—you included—so they know what to do next."

"That's different."

Noah shrugged. "Yeah, well—the writers here are different. This show—you know, it's a labor of love, and it really took off last year. They want to keep up the momentum."

Wow. A labor of love. *Warlock Tea* had been that way. Again, I felt that sinking sadness for having to abandon that show when I'd loved the work. I didn't regret leaving so much as I regretted hurting the show—it had been really good.

"I can't wait to work on it." Some of the awkwardness dissipated, burned away by the sincerity in my voice.

"Well, good. I'm mostly just a pair of ears and sentient transportation, but I think everybody's really happy to have you on board."

Yeah, he'd like to board you, Connor, don't doubt it.

Shut up, Vinnie, you're supposed to be dead.

Noah left shortly after that, and Jilly and I both went up to our rooms to unpack. We met downstairs about an hour later, and to my surprise Jilly was a good six inches shorter.

"Holy hell! What just happened?"

"Don't be an asshole," she snapped, looking at the obviously new and pricey cross-trainers on her feet like they were alien babies eating her toes. "I thought we'd go for a walk before dinner."

"What's for dinner?" Don't ask me—I'd been eating whatever the maids had pitied me with over the last year.

"I know you can cook, moron. Go throw something together for us. We can walk while it's cooking."

I had to think for a minute. Oh, yeah—I *had* been the one cooking for Vinnie and me. I remembered our first dinner party in the apartment *before* the beach houses. Jilly and a few friends from our restaurant days. I'd made enchiladas, because cooking with my mother was still one of the few good memories I'd brought from home.

I rooted through the fridge, as ordered, and found no tortillas, cheddar, or salsa, but there *was* some broccoli, feta cheese, and lasagna noodles, as well as some high-end canned sauces.

Broccoli lasagna—natch. If you added extra water to the sauce, you didn't have to boil the noodles. Just dump, wrap in foil, and bake—there were even black olives, a small bag of mozzarella, fresh garlic, and some sourdough. Prep took twenty minutes and the lasagna was in the oven.

I worked quietly, the basics of cooking coming back to me like I'd never lived on takeout and maid service, and I left the garlic bread for when we got back. The whole time, I was wondering what was on Jilly's mind. The old Jilly would have brought down her laptop and watched trashy television while she worked through the afternoon. The walk sounded like me, actually, but before . . . before, she would have snorted, stayed on the couch, and told me she'd call me when the fire alarm went off.

I remembered, like from a long distance, time at the bottom of a well, that when Vinnie had been alive, Jilly had come to my house sometimes—a couple of times a month, really—to do nothing but work and sip wine and throw casual barbs at Vinnie and me that we would return happily, because she was our friend.

Clients, yeah—she had a shitload. Family too. But she'd come to our house because there'd been something there, something she'd treasured.

I'd thought Vinnie's death had taken that from her, the way his death had taken everything from me. I guessed maybe Jilly wanted it back. But still . . .

"Why the tennis shoes?" I asked as we padded companionably down the road together. It was six o'clock and sunset wasn't for another three hours here, but high clouds softened the sun. An island was visible across the sound—close enough to swim to if you were *really* fit and the water hadn't been bone-breakingly cold. The side facing us was pretty sheer—difficult to build on, more difficult to get to. I wondered if there was a ferry port on the other side, a small boat dock and a cabin, or if it was just a growth, a protrusion of forest and wildlife that nobody ever visited. Thousands of people could have seen this island, and thought it was beautiful, but only a few might have touched it, because it wasn't meant for them.

I loved that idea—but given the premium land went for here, I was guessing there was a cabin or something.

"'Cause," she muttered. "No goddamned cigarettes, half an hour of—" she shuddered "—exercise every day."

I tried to remember what we'd been talking about— Oh yeah! Tennis shoes! Then it hit me. "Why the life changes?"

We'd managed to convince her to stop smoking two years ago. After Vinnie's second stint in rehab, we said if he had to quit the booze, she had to quit the smokes. She'd agreed—but only if Vinnie did a full sixty days. I remember her face when she'd told me she was tired of seeing kids end up in the headlines, dead of addiction and stupidity.

It had been taut and oddly middle-aged and vulnerable without the makeup and the hand gestures and the cigarette wielded like a fencing foil.

She looked like that now. She'd even washed some of her makeup off when we'd been unpacking.

"Because I'm fifty-five." She shrugged.

"You don't look it," I said sincerely, and she turned and patted my cheek wordlessly before continuing on.

I followed, thinking we were probably heading for the little beach I'd seen driving in. Oddly, I thought it would be a good place for a dog, which was funny because I'd never wanted a dog before in my life.

"McKenna's in rehab," she said abruptly. "Jerome *should* be, and in Weight Watchers to boot."

Her kids—I was aghast. "McKenna . . .?" Last I'd seen McKenna, she'd been sixteen years old, and still a little girl who wanted to be just like her mom. I knew that she'd become involved in LA's party scene since high school—Jillian had been worried, but not overly so. I remember *that* pat on the cheek, when I'd asked if McKenna was okay. *"Don't worry, doll. You and Vinnie made it through your party years, and you're fine!"*

Well, yeah, sort of. Vinnie did rehab. Twice. Once for pills, once for booze—he'd been fragile.

But Jilly had seemed to think her daughter could take it, tough as nails, just like mama.

Apparently not.

"Sorry, hon." I was at a loss. "Is there anything—"

"I was not a great mother," she said ruminatively.

"They're not *dead*," I told her, my voice sharp. If my mom showed up on my doorstep and offered to help me cook again, I'd break down and cry. But she wouldn't because I was gay, and because the last time I'd had any contact with them was signing the payoff papers that Jillian had given them: for a fixed payment every year they agreed to never say anything to the press but the brief that Jilly had provided.

No mom for me.

But that didn't mean *Jilly* didn't have time to fix *her* relationship with her children.

"I know that!" she snapped, voice hurt. "I do. And what I meant was that I wasn't a great mother *then*, when they were growing up. But the thing is, they're *still* growing up. They still need me. So I gotta be around."

I sighed happily and looped my arm over her shoulders. *That* was the direction I liked to hear. But the tension in her spine didn't relax, and I wondered what else was wrong.

"You're still growing up," she said abruptly.

I looked at her in surprise. "I'll be thirty in September."

"Bully for you. You're still a kid. You're still *my* kid. Do you remember when I called to say I'd rep you?"

I thought about it. "Yeah—Vinnie and I were still in that first apartment. I'd finished filming that commercial—the one for lip balm—you remember—"

"I remember that you and Vinnie were in bed."

I gasped, shocked. "How in the hell did you know that?" She was right. Vinnie was still *inside me*, jerking in climax, but *I'd* tried to keep my voice steady. My cell phone had been on the bed next to me, and I'd been waiting back then—waiting for call backs, waiting for an agent, waiting for my sources to tell me about another audition. Vinnie's cell phone had been next to mine—we'd laughed about it.

But we'd still answered every call at two rings, whether we were fucking each other's brains out or not.

"I know that because I know that, idiot," Jillian confirmed. "You were out of breath, Vinnie was panting like he'd run a mile—"

"We could have been running," I said, wounded.

"No. No, you couldn't have. Because when I said I'd rep you, you asked if I'd rep Vinnie too, and I heard his voice practically in the mouthpiece. I found his file on my desk, and he kept pounding away."

I'd pulled my arm off her shoulder, and put my cold hands to my heated face. "*Jilly!*"

"Yes, I knew that too. But the thing was, you asked for him. Which was classy—unlike, say, answering the phone when you're getting ass-fucked at three in the afternoon."

"How do you know I—"

Jilly just gave me a look—the kind of look that says, *Shut up, bottom boy, that's the least of your secrets.*

Whatever.

"And I would have taken you on as a client if you'd answered from a meth lab," she continued, after the look was done. "But you didn't—you were having celebration sex from the commercial, and your first thought wasn't, 'Yay! Let me dump this guy!' it was 'Yay! Let me take him with me!' and you did. I mean, I wasn't happy when you gave up *Warlock Tea*—"

"I thought you said it was an opportunity!"

"Yeah, that's what I said to you and the press. What I said to my plant was that you were a dumb-shit kid who wouldn't know an opportunity if it bit you on the peter. But you *turned* it into an opportunity, and I was proud."

I swallowed, not sure if I was up to any more introspection today. I mean, I'd flown up the coast and had lunch with someone I didn't know. Didn't that mean I got a cookie?

The beach was nice—round rocks lapped by clear water. The air had cooled to the low sixties, and I raised my face, feeling the beginnings of mist.

"Do you want to keep walking?" I asked. We'd only been gone ten minutes.

"I want a fucking cigarette," Jilly snapped, looking around. Someone had built a fire pit a little ways down, and Jilly made for that, me tagging reluctantly along. A few logs lay, framing the pit, obviously impromptu seats, and she eased gingerly onto one of them, even though most any part that would splinter had been sanded off many bottoms ago. She cast a sour glance at me and patted the seat next to her.

I sat, suddenly tired. Too much talking. Too much talking that felt important. I longed for a party and small talk—but only a very, very short party.

"See," Jilly said, just plowing ahead, "the thing is, I don't always do that."

"Do what?" I looked out over at that island and wondered how long I could live there. Like at the beach house, I could have a little cabin, and I could pay someone to ferry in supplies—not so much wine, this time—and I could just eat and vegetate and stare into space and feel nothing. Forever. If snows crept down in the winter, I'd just close my eyes and sleep and sleep and sleep.

"I don't always say the thing that will make you feel better."

"Who says?"

"McKenna," she told me, voice somber. "I came into her room while she was going through DTs—"

I cringed. Vinnie had said some heinously bitchy things to me when he was going through rehab. I tried to forget them—our good times had been so *very* good.

"You can't believe anyone during that part of the process," I said gently. "Jilly, they're shaking apart—they need so fucking bad, and they're—"

"Yeah, no—I get it. I visited Vinnie too, remember? I also got his flowers the week after he called me an interfering old twat. And I remember visiting him again, and watching him tear up because he hadn't meant it. So I get it—I *get* when someone says something they don't mean. But this . . . I said, 'Jesus, kid—I didn't know you had it in you to fuck up this bad.' And she usually laughs when I say shit like that, but . . ." Jilly's voice got thick. "She just rolled over to her side and started to cry. She said, 'Mom, couldn't you just once blow sunshine up my ass? I don't need to know I fucked up, I need to know you think I don't have to!'"

I was stunned by the simplicity of that. "She's really smart," I said, because that was true. That was what you needed in a mother, right? A cheering section? My mom used to do that for grades, for cooking, for soccer—for the times I'd let down my old man. You expected straight talk from your agent—but a mom, that was a different thing.

"Yeah." Jilly pulled a tissue out of her pocket and blew her nose. "She really is. And I came home and remembered the look on your face after the funeral, and how I hadn't heard from you in a few, and thought, 'He needs to hear me say he can get back on the horse!' so I called you."

"She takes after her mother," I said gruffly.

"She's way the fuck smarter than I am, Sparky," Jillian muttered. "But here's the thing."

I waited, not sure what to expect. Her eyes were red-rimmed, and she looked blotchy, but there wasn't a photographer in sight.

"You think I don't remember, don't you?"

I thought of her revelation about the first time she'd called me. "I think we've covered the fact that you pretty much remember everything."

She laughed and patted my cheek. Then she stroked it, like a mom would.

"You asked me if you should come out. I said no. You said all sorts of other people had come out. I said—"

"It was true," I muttered, not necessarily wanting to hear her say it again.

"No. I needed to have faith in you. I *should* have had faith in you. Both of you. Not coming out—it's what drove Vinnie to rehab.

And . . . God, Connor, I probably should have dropped your ass in there before we caught the plane."

I shook my head. I didn't crave alcohol—no trembling hands. No need. I'd seen Vinnie, face contorted with rage the morning we'd had the fight about the pills. There was none of that for me and my glass of wine. I just . . . *appreciated* what it could do for me when the world was all edges.

I'd been cutting myself bloody for a year.

"I don't need alcohol," I said, not defensively, even. "I just need—"

"To live your life," Jilly said, matter-of-factly. "So, that's what I'm saying to do here. I don't mean come out right now—but if you got that excited about *anything*, I'd be all for it—"

"I got excited about the *house*," I defended.

"Shut up, Connor," she snapped. "I'm trying to be nice here. All I'm saying is that, all those years ago, when I told you that you weren't good enough to come out, that it would fuck up your career—that was bullshit. I should have had faith in you. You've done every goddamned thing I've asked of you, and you've done it well. If you get a chance to be happy—here, or on the next job, or in a fucking opium den in the Orient, I need you to jump on that soapbox, grab life by the balls, and tell the world exactly who you are."

A part of me . . . Wow. A part of me, the kid who'd hit my new agent up to back my boyfriend while he was still inside of me, *that* kid wanted to take her up on it. Like, *now*. Like to just drop that bomb in the middle of the press conference tomorrow and fucking crack that bitch wide open.

But most of me was still . . . tired. Tired and sad and afraid that this thing she'd asked of me, this whole "moving on and living" thing, was going to be hard enough as it was.

I stood and stretched, turning my face to the glowing dime of a sun that kept trying to shine through the high clouds. "I think the lasagna's getting close to done. It would be a shame to burn down the house. I really like it."

"Connor . . ."

I looked at her and smiled weakly. "Later," I said simply. "Today I got on a plane and I talked to a stranger and I got excited about something I didn't expect. Let's—"

"*Connor*!"

She was starting to cry again, and for the first time in a while I felt that pressure—that love pressure—the insistence that you put someone else's feelings in front of your own.

I offered my hand. "It was a real good speech," I told her gently. "It was brave. And generous. And all the things a good mom is supposed to be. I think you and your kids have a real chance."

"But—"

"You don't need a second chance with me, Jilly. Whether it was good advice or shitty advice, it came from a really good place. I'm just . . . I need to wake up tomorrow and see if I feel as good as I did today. And maybe the next day I'll feel better than that. But I'm not there yet. I can't balls-out do the big brave thing. That was Vinnie's shtick anyway—"

"The hell it was," she snapped, taking my hand and hauling her chunky butt up. "You saw him through rehab twice. You rearranged your world for him. You're the good guy, Connor. It's why you don't play assholes."

I shrugged. "You know us actors. We just want people to like us."

"I like you." Her hug surprised me, but I returned it.

"I like you too. Your kids will too. When are you going back to them?"

"Five days," she said, her voice thick. She pulled away then, and we started walking toward the house at a decidedly faster clip. "I'll be desperate for a little fucking civilization by then. Jesus, do you think people have to mail order their clothes out here?"

"Seattle's two hours away, Jilly—I'm pretty sure there's some posh places to shop there."

She sniffed. "You can't find Manolo Blahniks at the fish market, Sparky."

"I don't know—aren't they sort of passé? I mean, maybe a fish ate them."

She laughed then, even though I'd probably insulted her god or something, and we made our way back to the house in time to get the lasagna out.

I tossed a salad too, and we ate dinner with a glass of wine apiece before watching TV and going to bed.

As I fell asleep, I pictured Noah Dakers's gut-punch of a grin. *If I did something to make him happy, would that thing just glow and glow and glow until we* all *passed through toward the light?*

I dreamed of holding Noah's hand and walking through bright sunshine, waving across the sound to the deserted island.

For some reason I thought Vinnie was there.

CHAPTER THREE

WHAT IF WE WAKE UP AND THE PRESS IS INSERTING A PROBE INTO OUR ANUS?

I thought I was prepared for the press conference.

Not so much, no.

It was held in front of what was apparently the office for the soundstage, a little portable cabin, painted a cheery red, and high enough off the ground to need its own stairs. They'd taken advantage of that and had a platform built, so press conferences had a natural venue.

The conference itself looked almost friendly as far as those things went—the reporters were standing around in jeans and boots, sturdy sweaters and flannel shirts. None of the women were wearing heels—I wondered if the press for a show like this was made up of true believers. That was helpful if it was so—it meant you didn't get those annoying "sci-fi is for babies" questions, because that shit pissed me off.

Noah walked us up to the platform, which surprised me—I hadn't expected him to get out of the car. I took Jilly's elbow, like she'd schooled me years ago to do in the presence of a lady, and he took our backs, with his hat on, looking official and actually a little bit imposing.

It was because he didn't smile.

But he *was* reassuring behind Jilly and me as Simon Conklin, one of the show's producers and occasional directors, addressed the press in jeans and a fleece jacket, with a familiar smile on his face. He talked about the direction the show was going to take, citing some new characters, and adding that if the fans reacted as well to the new characters this season as they'd reacted to the addition of Levi Pritchard last season, then they might consider a spin-off. He was in his early forties, with thick black hair and only a few grays—very attractive, in a happy professor way—and the press ate out of his hand. When he introduced me, it was like he'd led plump fuzzy bunnies to come nibble at my palm, which was sort of a superpower considering the Hollywood press was more like a sleek, muscular shark.

We took questions for a moment, and the first ones were the ones I'd practiced in my head—why this show, would I miss big-screen acting, how did I like the area—and that was great.

And then, right when I was expecting questions about Vinnie—and had my answers and my smooth mask of grief all ready—they hit me.

"Connor—your selfie hit the internet big two weeks ago. What the hell was that about?"

I stared at the reporter, caught flat-footed for a moment, before eleven years of hard-earned professionalism kicked in.

And surprised me even as I was the one with my mouth open.

"I knew Vinnie Walker for ten years," I said baldly. And why not? Who *wouldn't* figure out that some of that was grieving, sound off or sound on. "We were roommates, best friends, neighbors"—*lovers!*—"brothers." The lie shriveled my throat for a moment, and I almost couldn't go on. Jilly shifted next to me, and I remembered our conversation the night before.

And I wasn't ready for that. Not yet.

"Grief isn't predictable," I said after a lonely moment in front of people holding their phones up to record me. "I had a drink too many—or a bottle of drinks too many. I thought about my friend who'd been gone a year, and I grieved. I've lived in the public for a long time. I guess the only thing I'm embarrassed about is that I thought that was a good thing to share with the world."

There's this moment after you've given a really good performance. It's like the world holds its breath. And even though this wasn't a play, or a bit on screen, for that moment nobody breathed.

Then the voice—a girl with half her hair scalp-trimmed and a long braid pulled to the side—spoke up again. "That was really sincere, Mr. Montgomery. Thank you."

A sudden bout of applause broke the silence, and that was the end of the press conference.

I wasn't aware that my hands were shaking, or that my heart was thundering in my chest, until I felt Noah's hand on the small of my back, turning me, steering me inside the cabin for my meeting, making sure I made it up the last step on the stoop without tripping and falling on my face.

"Thank you," I mumbled.

"You look really fucking pale," Noah insisted. "You go sit down, and I'll get you some coffee. I know how to work the machine. Steamed milk?"

"And two sugars," I told him. "But I can go—"

"Sit down and pretend to be a movie star," he ordered, and you'd think that, you know, as a movie star, I'd have a problem with that.

I sat docilely at the table—probably the one where everybody read lines when they weren't doing a full cast—and Jilly shed her puffy white coat before excusing herself to go get her own coffee. It was around fifty degrees outside, which was pretty cold compared to Hollywood, and I didn't blame her for losing the coat, but I wasn't ready to lose my sturdy bomber jacket and scarf yet.

I was shaking like it was five degrees outside.

"How you doing?" Simon asked, looming over me now that Noah had left. I looked up at him and smiled, smooth and professional, because he was the boss. Yeah, I'd given my share of casting couch blowjobs in the early days—shocker! But being on your knees for some douche bag who wielded his power over you like a fucking mace taught you lessons, the first and foremost was to always let Daddy think he was in charge. While Simon didn't seem like a douche bag, he was definitely "Daddy" today, and showing deference was the order of business.

Besides—he seemed like a nice guy. Interns were running around with organized efficiency, not panic, and he greeted pretty much everyone with a sincere, if sometimes absentminded, smile. No, this guy was probably not getting blowjobs from new actors—which was an even better reason to be decent to him.

"I'm doing great," I lied. "Thanks so much for the nice intro—it makes a difference."

Simon shrugged unhappily. "I'm not excited about that last question," he said frankly. "That was supposed to be a hands-off topic—we picked our people, Mr. Montgomery—I promise, we won't let her on the lot again."

I remembered the girl's honest gratitude for some frankness in this business.

"Please don't," I said impulsively. "I mean, I don't necessarily want to talk about that again, but maybe just give her a warning or something. I mean, I *had* to talk about that eventually—I know Jilly's been saying 'no comment' for the last two weeks. Maybe this way people can stop speculating, you know?"

Simon was regarding me with a little bit of shock just as Jillian came back over, nursing her coffee and a serious grudge.

"Jesus, Conklin, you were supposed to pick your fuckin' people! Wasn't that one of my caveats? Wasn't it? That question did *not* come up—"

"Easy, Jilly," I said, a reluctant smile on my face. "We all survived."

You would have thought I dropped a bomb.

Or a psycho teleporting cow.

Their dismay was a hair away from comic, and I pushed it over the edge with a laugh I didn't feel. "People, he's going to get mentioned—around me even. Trying to pretend he never existed is only going to make more moments like this."

Simon smiled, revealing laugh grooves. "Fair enough. We won't treat his name like a box full of plague." He sobered. "I worked with Vinnie, you know?"

I hadn't. "No," I said, keeping my smile if it killed me. "Which gig?"

"*Comet's Tail*—you remember, the space opera one for SyFy?"

"Oh yeah!" I remembered—Vinnie had worked that gig for five years as a guest spot—maybe two or three episodes a year. He'd fit it in between film jobs because he enjoyed the cast so much. "He *loved* your show!" Another memory—Vinnie gushing about Simon this and Simon that—and how Simon was quietly out, but he wasn't a big enough name for it to attract attention. "He couldn't stop talking about you!"

I'd been horribly jealous. *Hellishly* jealous. Vinnie had been fresh out of rehab when he first worked that job, and the things he'd said during detox had hurt me so bad. I'd gotten over it—but yeah. Not a good time.

But meeting Simon now, a small part of my faith was restored.

"Yeah," he said, nodding. "He was the greatest guy. When I first met him I was going through a breakup. He listened one afternoon—you know, just let me dump on him because he was there. Gave the best advice. Told me that a good relationship isn't built on the flash-in-the-pan sex, but on the hand-holding that comes after it—I actually Googled it to see if it was one of his lines, but nope. He really meant that."

I couldn't decide whether to laugh or to cry. He'd been talking about me then—*me*—and he'd thought we were good. Even then, when I wasn't so sure myself, he'd believed in us.

Cry. I really wanted to cry.

"Yeah," I said, "Vinnie was usually sincere. I'm glad you've got good memories of him."

"I don't know how you hang out with those people, Vinnie. They're horrible and shrill, and they make my head hurt."

"They give two million dollars a year to animal charities. Seriously, Connor—there has got to be a heart of gold somewhere in all that pony shit, you know?"

"Well, most of them were about how much fun you guys had. He was your brother, man—don't think I don't know you're hurting."

For the love of hell. Could this nice man stop talking to me? I was going to wave my hand and say something about shows and going on when Noah came up behind him, tripped, and spilled just a few drops of coffee on his sleeve.

"Oh my God! I'm sorry, sir! I'm so sorry, Mr. Conklin— I didn't mean to— Are you okay?"

Conklin checked his arm and grimaced. "Yeah, but geez, Noah—you usually move like you're on ice—when'd you get so clumsy?"

"Sorry, sir—the carpet caught my shoe just right. Here's your coffee, Mr. Montgomery." He held a napkin and was wiping the top off as he handed me the large, lidded paper coffee cup. "Would you like a pastry?" He also gave me a chocolate croissant, and I took them both from him gratefully, even though I wasn't particularly hungry.

He'd gotten Conklin away from that conversation—I'd eat sawdust if he gave that to me in a cup.

"Thanks, Noah." I took a sip from the coffee, and it was ... perfect. "Oh wow—did you have to get the degree to learn how to make this, or are you just a natural?"

Noah's grin popped out—the lethal one that made the angels sing and my stomach do backflips. "I waited tables at a deli while I was getting through school," he said proudly. "They had a cappuccino machine, and I got damned good."

I took another sip and shuddered, feeling some of the heat of the room seep into my bones finally. "You're hired," I told him lightly, and his courtesy laugh warmed me more.

At that moment Simon stood up at the head of the table and called order, and I looked around at the room that had grown a little more occupied while we were talking.

"Okay, folks—we've consolidated some of the sets to Soundstage One and added Soundstage Two. We also have three new locations to shoot at, and only one of them is accessible via golf cart from here. So returning people, you get to take the short tour, new people, you get the slightly longer tour. When the new people are done, we're all motoring to the Global, the European Suite, and we'll be served lunch and get a chance to mingle before we have our first reading. Hunter Easton and Kevin Hussain will be there, and they're going to brief us on the basic story arc—you've all signed your NDAs, right?"

"Yes, Simon," came an amused voice. "None of us are going to the Pentagon with our secrets." I looked and saw, oh my God! Blond, blue-eyed, the darling of the small screen and everybody's favorite boy-wonder actor, Carter Samuels! The star of *Wolf's Landing* had actually come in unannounced, which was pretty impressive given that he and his husband Levi Pritchard were together and their bodyguard was right on their heels.

My eyes widened as I took in the three of them, the bodyguard looming large in the background. Carter's career had *taken off* as a result of this show—and Levi's had revitalized in the extreme. It was a good idea to remember that. I may have been coming from the big screen, but as of yet I hadn't been beating the paparazzi off my lawn with a stick the way they had.

"Thinking of trading up?" Noah murmured in my ear, and I grinned at him.

"I already got the premium model," I joked, and he gave me a "damned straight" nod in return. But Simon wasn't done talking yet, and I didn't want to be a shitty student on the first day of class.

"You laugh!" Simon complained good-naturedly, because as I looked around most of the cast and crew *were* laughing. "But Finn Larson is going to meet us at the Global, and he's going to be jumping up and down and screaming to make sure we understand—no spoilers, no dropping hints, not even to our special sources, you all understand?"

"I understand Larson's a douche bag," Levi Pritchard muttered not so quietly.

A mid-sized woman with Jilly-style maquillage *and* impressive heels spoke up. She was the only woman in the trailer not casually dressed in jeans or stretch pants, and her no-bullshit black business suit and bun told me that this was someone with clout.

"You need to keep that to yourself," she said sternly. "*Selves,*" she corrected with a look around at the rest of us. "We are a small cast and crew working in an isolated location—we need to be the proverbial big happy family or we *will* end up at each other's throats, do we get that?"

Conklin grimaced. "Thanks, Anna—we were going to try to keep the scary teacher lectures in reserve for the mid-season, when we get the fuck on each other's nerves, but it's good you broke that out now. We know what's coming. Ladies and gentleman, if you haven't met Anna Maxwell, she's usually a little less uptight than this." Ah—Anna. She was one of the show's producers, so, yes, she did get to be the scary mean teacher, didn't she?

Anna rolled her eyes and visibly relaxed. "Yes, well," she said, sending a comic glare at Levi and Carter, "if you had to work with these two overgrown fifth graders, you'd pull out your ruler and your dunce caps too!"

General laughter, and Simon went on talking while Anna started pulling packets and folders from the desk at his back to hand out to us. Noah got a copy too, and as I glanced around I saw that bodyguards, PAs, and gofers were all getting the same set of papers. I took a look—shooting schedules, what was needed when, availability of everything from food to gum to soda to cigarettes, including feminine protection and extra clothes.

Impressive—and considerate.

I leafed through my own packet and realized everything pertaining to me personally had been highlighted. "Anna, I think I love you," I said facetiously, and she turned from her duties with surprise.

"Why? What'd I do?"

I didn't want to tell her that I'd worked on shoots so disorganized the *director* didn't know where he was shooting next or from what part of the script.

"This right here is a work of art—even an idiot like me can find his way around with this. Thank you!"

She smiled at me like I was her favorite son. "Honey, praise like that will get you asked back at the very least. You're welcome."

"Nice job kissing up," Jilly murmured in my ear. "Now stop being so earnest, you're going to make everyone else fuckin' puke."

The meeting was moving on, so I didn't have time to retort. What I wanted to say was that she'd been right about this move. Looking at my shooting schedule, at the envelope with my script pages in it, at the maps and the facilities and the whole shooting match, had actually started my heart beating again.

I was going to walk onto a soundstage and become another person again. I wasn't going to have to hide a thing—it was going to be my *job* to make that person on the pages as transparent, as perfectly obvious as possible.

I remembered that feeling, saying words that weren't mine, having reactions, emotions, *presence* that had nothing to do with me. It was like getting struck by lightning and filled with someone else's soul.

Oh, holy God, blessed were the actors—I was going to be somebody *new*.

The rest of the morning was sort of a blur. Soundstages were the same—Vancouver, Hollywood, the Midwest, New York—they were big buildings full of pretend places and real light racks, where the center of the action was always surrounded by what felt to be a hundred people. We got shown around and told which sets were used for which locations on our schedule, where our trailers were, how to check out a golf cart, where the catering was—basic things. It was like learning the word for "bathroom" when you were visiting a new country: there were some things everybody needed to know.

As we were getting walked around by Simon, I realized that about three quarters of the people who had filled the small room had vamoosed, leaving me with two actresses and another actor, and *their* assorted entourages.

Simon was going on about how to get to the bathroom while sets four through eight were engaged, when I heard one of the actresses whisper, "Oh my God, I know—he's even hotter in person!"

I looked over my shoulder, surprised, and they both saw me and squeaked. They were completely unfamiliar, both the tall brunette and the elfin blonde—they must be *brand*-new blood.

Suddenly I remembered *my* first gig, and how every name on the cast list was someone I recognized from another show, and how *exciting* that had been.

I smiled and edged away from Jilly and Noah's protective looming and into their little gossip circle.

"Hiya," I said, turning on the charm. God, there was so much crap in this business—and they were so young. I wanted to be the person who was nice to them when they were just starting out, because I remembered a couple of people who had been that for *me*, Vinnie among them. "So, are you going to be the new pack members?"

They both nodded, and the tiny blonde stuck out her hand. "Lissa Harvey—I'm actually going to be *your* pack member, Mr. Montgomery."

"Connor." I took her hand automatically. Strong grip—good girl. Smart blondes survived in this business.

"Nice to meet you, *Connor*." Her eyes went to half-mast and she lingered on my name—and on her fingers as they fluttered by my wrist.

I quirked my mouth and quirked my eyebrows, making it clear I wasn't in the market, and she blushed.

"Brenda Tracey," said the taller woman, and we shook hands too—without the come-on chaser. "Obviously we're both fans."

"It's nice to have a fan," I said simply, aware I was quoting *Spider-Man* and unable to help myself. If I'd grown up watching plays, I'd be in New York.

They laughed like they were supposed to, and we chatted as our group moved on. I was just thinking about how to disengage from them when Noah appeared at my elbow again, swapping out one cup of coffee for another and doing that thing, that one with his shoulders and personal space, that pushed me back into his and Jilly's orbit without it looking like I was being rude and trying to leave the conversation before it got awkward.

"Try to stay with the group," he murmured primly, eyes narrowed and dancing over his own cup of coffee.

"Yes, sir," I responded, just to see him smile.

He nodded sternly instead, and I had to swallow, hard. I was suddenly caught in the mock seriousness of his eyes and the way his brows drew together.

And an intensely private moment between Vinnie and me.

"Not yet, boy!"

"No, sir!"

"Who's fucking you?"

"You are, sir!"

"Whose cock's inside you?"

"Yours, sir!"

Vinnie fucking me, stretching my asshole to the hilt of his outsized cock, one hand pushing between my shoulder blades, one hand issuing irregular, sharp cracks on my thighs and ass as his hips snapped forward at dizzying speed.

The smacks on my ass, the slaps of our bodies colliding, our harsh breaths rasping through the air, the squeaking of the bed, and the smell, sweat and sex and cum, because this was round two, and I was sore, tender, but jazzing on the pain.

We'd been together for four years, and this was the first time he'd ever gotten rough with me.

The "sir" had popped out of my mouth like it had been lying in wait. Every time he smacked my ass I had to pinch my cock to keep myself from coming.

"I'm gonna come, sir!"

"Not yet!"

"Please, sir!"

"Hold on!"

"Vinnnnnieee . . ." My eyes closed, and my voice broke. I couldn't hold it off anymore, and the game was almost not fun.

"Oh! Sorry! Come, baby. Go ahead! Come!"

"Yes, sir!"

My breathing quickened, and my face grew hot. Noah was regarding me intensely, mouth parted to reveal the pink of his lips. We were locked in that semiplayful look, but my body was responding, filling with blood and the pounding of my heart, as the pleasure nerve centers I'd thought had withered and died woke up, decided to boogie down my nipples, my abdomen, my cock, taint, and asshole.

It was like acknowledging the want acted as accelerant. Desire roared through me like an arson fire, and I gave a little whimper as my knees threatened to give way.

Oh God. Oh holy God. To have a man's touch on my skin, the flat of a rough palm on the inside of my thigh, a mouth, hot and relentless, sucking to the point of pain . . .

I was hardening in my jeans, and Noah's expression had changed, from desire to intensity bordering on anger.

That change let me yank my eyes away, and I took a few shaky steps forward. I stumbled, and only Noah's firm hand helped me forward.

"Easy, *boy*," he muttered for my ears only.

Oh. Oh hell. I couldn't . . . Nobody was supposed to know, to guess . . . I couldn't do this again.

"I'm nobody's boy," I said coolly, and tightened my proverbial sac, grabbed my figurative nuts in both hands, and strode away.

I tried to maintain my distance for the rest of the day. I even thought maybe we could resume the friendliness between us, which was something I'd really enjoyed.

I hadn't counted on the read-through, though, for lowering my emotional barriers. I guess I could blame it on the caterer, right?

Because lunch was . . . damn. In-season fish, a sauce to die for, and rice that actually had flavor. I mean, there was a name for it, but my Hollywood sophistication had never extended to memorizing food names. I just sort of looked at the menu and said, "Yes! Chicken! With some buttermilk fried stuff on the outside! And gravy! Good!" But this was catered, and the fish made me want to lick my whiskers and purr.

They offered a full bar, but I abstained, figuring Jilly and I had another couple of bottles to split before she went home. Instead, I nursed my flavored water and lingered over the miniature mousse cakes for dessert, and enjoyed talking to Levi and Carter, who were so hopelessly in love I couldn't even hold it against them.

"Yeah, it was funny," Carter was saying, that all-American face lighting up when he talked about craft. "Anna talked about bringing you on, and the first thing Levi said was, 'So, blond Carter and blond Connor—*I* might get them mixed up!'"

I laughed—and winced—because yeah, I'd noticed the similarities myself.

"But then Anna pointed out that it would work out *great*," Levi said, picking up the thread. "You'd be like this dark, shadowy *echo* of Gabriel, and so when you did like, morally questionable things, the audience could ask themselves, 'Hey, isn't Gabriel close to being that much of an asshole?' And I thought that was *genius*!"

I smiled—and pretended any of that had actually crossed my mind when Jilly flashed me the offer two weeks ago. I *did* remember something she'd said later that afternoon, though.

"I'm just glad you guys held on to the part," I said earnestly. "I can't believe you hadn't cast it yet."

"Yeah, well," Carter looked over his shoulders, "honestly, Anna didn't want to film these episodes if she couldn't have you. You know that nice, neat, highlighted stack of papers we just got? I think there's a whole other set for what we'd be filming if she hadn't gotten your name on the contract before this round of filming."

"Me?" I said blankly. I *was* a name on the big screen—but I was still a B-list name. I'd read my press: by all counts, "amiable beefcake" was infinitely replaceable.

Carter and Levi laughed like I was making a joke. "It's like he doesn't even know!" Carter crowed.

"Know what?" God, I was starting to feel dumb. I mean, yeah—I *played* dumb, but usually that was just what it sounded like. An act.

"You're like a big fucking deal around here!" Carter said, and while he wasn't that much younger than me, I heard the same tone of voice that *I'd* used when I'd gotten to work with Gary Oldman in *Pirating Stars*. It was, uhm, odd to hear it turned toward me. "And man, Hunter Easton was *pissed*, too. Because he's usually totally 'Keep your grubby mitts off my plotline!' and that goes for casting too."

I blinked, wanting to be surprised, but the fact was I'd heard that. When Jilly and I had shotgunned the series, I realized that Mr. Easton had become, like, *legendary* for being one of the few writers who actually had a say. "So, he *didn't* want me?"

"Oh no," Levi said. "At first, he was doing his usual diva, but Anna apparently saw the rushes on *Jupiter Seven*—she must know someone there. Anyway, I heard that fight from outside the trailer. And then today, you totally sucked up to her without knowing it. Genius!"

"No, no," I said, a teeny bit panicked. It never paid to have people expect too much from you. "I'm an action figure." I winked, trying to dial it down. I hadn't reckoned on this. I'd wanted to come play with my fellow actors—this sort of thing from . . . from *Carter Samuels* and *Levi Pritchard* was really uncomfortable.

"Whatever," Levi muttered, rolling his eyes and looking away.

"Oh, not you too!" I protested, about done. "You're a *legend*." And he could *act*. I'd been a fan of Pritchard's before he'd disappeared from Hollywood ten years before—now that he was back and gay and rising again? Well, the Levi Pritchards of this world gave the Connor Montgomerys faith.

"Yeah, yeah," Carter finished amiably. "You just keep playing it modest, Mr. Nice Guy—we'll pull that shit out at the next con, trust me. *Especially* because your role here is going to sort of dick with that whole image."

I blinked, and suddenly realized what a big leap I'd made without looking. I'd signed on to be Slade Lupin—one of three surviving members of what used to be a rival pack to the one in Wolf's Landing. I'd read the extract for the character, and words like "morally ambiguous" had been thrown around—but I really *had* been ready to throw my career in the crapper, because until right now I hadn't stopped to consider what that would mean.

"Well," I said, swallowing and remembering that talk I'd had with Jilly about being okay with selling the beach house, "a new character is always a risk."

"Right on!" Carter agreed, and he was so young and so happy and so *hopeful* I refused to fuck with that and tell him that I hadn't risked myself for a character *ever*. Jilly and I had *always* gone for "amiable beefcake" because we'd *always* known that until I made the A list, one bad role, one series flop, one tanked picture meant obscurity.

Carter and Levi wandered off to talk to their costar, and I was stuck, nursing my flavored water and thinking that two weeks ago, obscurity hadn't sounded that bad.

Which was maybe a good thing, if my blind leap was going to help me tank a good show!

"What'd they say?" Jilly asked at my elbow, and I turned and smiled weakly.

"They said I signed up to play a challenge," I said, trying not to make a big deal out of it.

Jilly frowned. "That's a problem?"

"Jilly . . ." I didn't want to whine. "You had to haul me out of bed this morning."

Literally. By the feet, covers over my head as I practically begged her not to make me go.

She shrugged and waved me away. "Forget about it. You'll be fine. You've been *dying* for a challenge. Did you think you were going to grow old running away from a green screen?"

"Would you like me to name all the actors who did?"

"I've banged some of the actors who did," she said, making me curious. She and Bruce Willis would be *dynamite* together. "But that's the thing—they're all better than people gave them credit for. Smarter. More able to craft. It might not be this role, kid—but it might be. You've got nothing to lose right now. Not a damned thing. Be reckless and brave—at least professionally. See what it can get you."

"Sexually it could get me HIV. Do you have a body condom for my *job*, Jilly?"

She gave me a toothy grin. "Sure I do, doll. That's what reality shows are for."

I looked around like she'd just dropped state secrets. "*Jilly*!" I hissed. "For God's sake—"

But she was relentless. "Yup. You're single. You're young. You're closeted. If you don't make this work—" she stopped to snag a leftover mousse cake off the discarded plate on the table next to me "—I could always boost your career by booking you on *The Bachelor*. It would be *phenomenal*—"

"I'd sooner eat toe cheese!" I snapped, and Jilly spit mousse crumbs all over both of us. And then burst into raucous, hysterical laughter.

"*Buahahahahahahaha—*"

"Jilly, calm down!" I patted her on the back and offered her a napkin.

"*Hahahahahahahahahaha!*"

"Here, hon, you're scaring me!" Together we blotted off her face and her brushed linen suit, but the laughter—loud enough to turn heads—continued. Finally I just pulled her to my chest and held her, laughter muffled against my shirt until the noise stopped.

When she was done, I looked down and saw to my horror that she was crying. Here. In public. "Jilly?" I asked, in the sudden quiet of the room.

She'd taught me from the very beginning to always have tissues and a lighter on hand, and I fished the tissues from the pocket of my jacket because the napkins were all used up. She took them, and looked at me, tears spiking her lashes, mascara running down her face, and all other makeup with it. A wistful smile graced her features.

"It's just," she said brokenly, "that I remembered Vinnie, and the psycho cow. And . . . you just did it. You just did the psycho-cow thing, and I thought, *I have to tell Vinnie about that.*" She dabbed her eyes with her tissue, and I kissed the top of her head.

"Yeah," I said, not sure what to do with this. Not here. Not in the crowded place. The words "I miss him too" hovered between us, but I couldn't say them. Not because anyone would suspect the truth, but because, bless her, Jilly had finally gotten me to the place she'd been trying for. The place where I had something that mattered besides the big black hole of trying not to think about him.

I wanted to act. I wanted to be on the set with Carter Samuels and Levi Pritchard. I wanted to be Anna Maxwell's favorite actor. I wanted Simon Conklin to give me stage directions and tell me what to do, and for Hunter Easton to write me beautiful boys with fractured souls. I wanted to be a part of this again, like I wanted my next breath.

Oh God, let me be somebody new.

She calmed down and then excused herself to the ladies room. I headed toward the gents to see what I could do about the T-shirt under my bomber jacket, and found Noah on my heels.

"It's toast," he said as I wiped futilely at it in the mirror. "What set her off?"

I shrugged, not wanting eye contact with him right now—not if it meant he was going to dip deep into my soul and see all my secrets.

"She had one of those, 'I have to tell Vinnie' thoughts, and then..."

"Remembered that she couldn't," Noah filled in soberly.

I gave up on the shirt. "Think the gift shop has something that doesn't look like...like..."

"Like a cum rag in a clown orgy?"

I gasped, and the effort not to laugh, hysterically and out of control just like Jilly, pressed against my chest until I could hardly breathe. I don't know what he thought, me hanging over the sink, hauling in breath and fighting for control over my own goddamned face, but he didn't say anything. Just stood there, his hand on my back between my shoulder blades, rubbing circles until I could breathe easily again. I closed my eyes and—

His hand on my back.

It felt so good. I remembered Jilly, wrapped up in my arms, seeking comfort, and wondered—would Noah comfort me if I asked for it?

Subtly, I hoped, I squared my shoulders and moved away.

"Yeah," I said, like I was responding to something when I wasn't. "Is there any way you could go get me one of those T-shirts? I'd be grateful—"

I started digging into my pants pocket, looking for my wallet, but Noah waved me off. "I'll expense it," he said, not looking at me.

He disappeared, and I took off my bomber jacket and my pricey long-sleeved microfiber thing that Jilly had picked out that morning.

God. Poor Jilly. I wish I'd warned her—I should have warned her. I'd been having *I have to tell Vinnie* moments for a *year*. In fact, since I'd woken up hungover and on YouTube, he was starting to answer back. I was beginning to see that hanging out in my house— my empty house—with nothing to do but watch his movies and nothing to report but grief, had been a way to *stop* having those moments. When his absence was slapping you in the balls with every breath, there was no way to forget, ever, that he was gone.

I leaned on the sink and closed my eyes, resting my forehead against the mirror, shivering a little in the chill.

Pull it together, Connor, Vinnie's voice said in my head. *You weren't this much of a pussy for your* Warlock Tea *audition, remember? You were like, "Forget about it—I'll blow this audition and we'll go out for burgers," remember?*

Yeah, Vinnie. I remember.

But we didn't go out for burgers, because you got a callback for that evening, and we were starving. I brought you sandwiches from home.

Yeah. We called it champagne and caviar on wheat.

Yeah. Go out and have yourself some of that, for me, okay?

Yeah, Vinnie. Okay.

"Connor?" Noah's voice yanked me out of my communion with the dead.

"Hi, yeah, oh, I was just—" I jerked away from the mirror and smiled at him, holding my hand out for the bag. I wondered if anyone had come and gone while I'd been zoned out over the bathroom sink.

"You look awful," Noah said, but his voice was all concerned.

"Bathroom lights don't make anybody look good," I temporized. "I don't know how—" *I don't know how I used to get blowjobs in bathrooms, because it probably makes your penis look like green cheese* "—to make that stop," I finished lamely, well aware that Noah was rolling his eyes and shaking his head and looking irritated as hell. "Let's see what the gift shop had to offer, shall we?"

Forest green with redwood-colored lettering, and a logo with a giant globe and trees growing out of perspective on the part where

Washington would be. *The Global, Bluewater Bay* was wrapped around the circle. So, not imaginative, but it could have been worse.

"Wouldn't you think they'd have a bay and not trees?" I asked inanely, unfolding the shirt and yanking the tag. I made the mistake of glancing at Noah for a reaction and saw that he was focused entirely on my face.

"Nope."

That was helpful. I grimaced at him and realized his glare was focused on my chest now, my abs, and I blushed.

"I hope you got the large and not the XL," I chirped, pulling the thing over my head. "I mean, even when I'm bulked up I *still* have a neck."

"I got the XL," he said without a note of apology in his voice. "Because you *should* be an XL, but you haven't eaten in a year."

I scowled at him and opened my mouth to tell him what I told Jilly—that I must have eaten because I could clearly remember working out—but he looked at his watch and started shoving my discarded shirt in the retail bag from the gift shop.

"Grab your jacket and hurry back into the ballroom," he ordered. "I'll be in there with a soda on ice, and make sure Ms. Lombard's okay."

I paused, not wanting this kid—this *kid*—to just order me around like this, but he leveled that "know thyself" glare at me and pointed an imperious finger. "Now *go!*" he snapped, and I found myself striding through the corridors of the hotel, wondering where it had all gone wrong.

Read-throughs aren't supposed to be your favorite thing. Everybody sitting around the table, reading through the first scripts, getting a feel for what the episode—hell, the *season* is going to be like.

But I've always liked them.

It's a terrible thing to confess for an actor, but I can't actually visualize a movie from the script. I can't visualize a character from the words on a flat page. Thank God for Jillian and Vinnie, or I would have spent my career performing shit.

But at the read-through, when I heard other actors doing *their* parts, suddenly I knew who I was. I'd look at the words, and they became me, and I didn't have any other words for the process than that.

And as I listened to Carter, Levi, and Marianna read their opening scene, that magic thing happened, where the words took shape and built whole new people. When I looked at my part, I wasn't Connor Montgomery, closet case in mourning, anymore.

I was Slade Lupin—and I was *magnificent*.

The story unfolded: the Wolf's Landing universe developed a portal to another dimension, and suddenly the two females left of my pack and I were spit from our time and place and into Northern Washington.

And we were brokenhearted and furious.

"Slade," said Wind (the little elfin blonde whose real name I couldn't pull out of a hat right now). "We're all alone here. I mean . . . the others . . . I saw . . . We saw—"

"We *all* saw!" I snarled, as the hotel room around me became an outdoor location shoot on one of the San Juan Islands. "We saw the bodies, Wind. They . . ." My voice broke, and the tiny part of me that *was* me had just walked into a viewing room in Cedars-Sinai, where the world turned gray. "They were bloody and lifeless and . . ." I shook my head, unable to go on—because the script told me so. And the script told me to start again. "And we can't think of that right now. We *can't* think of that right now!"

"But what are supposed to *do*, Slade!" Wind shrieked. I would shake her, on the set—but gently, because of the tiny part of Connor still in my body.

"We are supposed to *stay alive*," I ordered. "And if we have to murder every alpha, beta, and cub between here and our entrance portal, we are supposed to go. Back. Home."

End Scene.

And the world held its breath again, and I—Connor Mazynsky— swam slowly to the surface of my consciousness, and smiled at Wind, who was Lissa in real life, and Brenda, who was Swift in the show.

And the table erupted into applause, which was a first for this read-through, especially because we weren't at the end of the episode.

I smiled shyly around and noticed Simon, nodding at Anna as though they'd seen something that confirmed their earliest impressions. Hunter Easton—silver fox and writer genius, who had merely regarded me from the far corner of the room skeptically— looked eager, like a school kid who had just discovered a book was *way* more interesting than he'd first suspected. Jillian nodded at them, encouraging them to like me as much as they wanted.

I glanced across the table, to the little group of PAs and bodyguards, etc., who were sitting and waiting on the rest of us. Some of them had their phones out, a few had books. A few of them had knitting, which always impressed me.

Noah had a paperback in his hand—but he wasn't reading it.

He was staring at me, eyes liquid and deep, mouth set as though he knew something the whole world didn't, and it cut him to the bone.

I looked away.

I didn't want to know what he saw—and I couldn't keep feeding myself the line that he was research or that his opinion didn't matter.

It was very clear to both of us probably that his opinion *did* matter, and I didn't want to ask myself why.

CHAPTER FOUR

I AM A MEAT POPSICLE

By the time Noah got us home, Jillian and I were both exhausted and taciturn. I expected to maybe forget to make myself a sandwich for dinner, but Noah parked the car in the garage next to the house and then, to my surprise, let himself inside.

Jilly and I were wandering around numbly in the kitchen, and he ordered us both to sit while he pulled the leftover lasagna out of the refrigerator and started dishing it up. While he was waiting for the first plate to nuke, he pulled out some carrots and green beans and started to prep them. By the time he had three plates of lasagna melting on the counter, he also had some veggies with herbs and butter ready to serve with them.

Jilly and I couldn't think of a word to say while he did this. Every thought we had centered around the guy who wasn't here.

Noah didn't ask us for conversation—not at first. Instead, he served everybody a plate of food and a glass of milk—*milk*—and then sat down across from Jilly and kitty-corner to me, and gestured.

"Dig in."

"Thank you," I managed. "This was really kind."

"You guys would have been eating out of the casserole dish with a fork if I hadn't stepped in to make things civilized."

I shrugged. "Two forks." Because it was true.

He flashed a ghost of his grin, and turned to Jilly. "Ms. Lombard, I sure was glad to see you felt better today."

Her lips twisted, a smile's wraith, drifting on by. "Thank you, Noah. I . . . Vinnie meant a lot to me. I don't know if I realized . . . you know. How hard it would be to do the public thing—either of us—without him."

Noah nodded like that was fair. "Yeah, I get it. Have either one of you thought of . . . you know. Grief counseling?"

I let out a bark of pain. Sounded like laughter. Close enough. "Junior, this *is* grief counseling for us. Welcome to the unhealthily repressed."

I took a bite of lasagna because it was something to do.

Noah decided to take another tack. "How did you meet?" he asked, imposing. "The interviews all say it was at an audition."

I nodded. Good. Well-covered ground. "Yeah. We were both auditioning for a commercial. Neither of us got the part, but you know. I was crashing in my car back then, and Vinnie had actually sold his"—*ass*—"soul for an apartment. But we enjoyed"—*flirting*—"talking at the audition, and we ended up having"—*sex*—"lunch at his apartment. He let me crash on his"—*cock*—"couch forever after."

Noah heard the story with his head tilted, like a dog listening for the whistle.

"That's not . . ." He took a deep breath. "I have a feeling there's more to it than that," he said quietly. "But still—that's a long history. You can't just expect to wake up and think it's all going to be okay."

"Do you think I did that?" Anger began to congeal in my chest. "Do you think I woke up two weeks ago and said, 'Hey! Mourning's all over—I can say good-bye to my . . . my *friend* and I'm going to be all okay!'? I woke up *hungover*, and Jillian was on the phone saying, 'What did you *do*?' and I was like, 'Oh *fuck*, if I don't change something, anything, someone's going to find me here, dead for no other reason than I just didn't get myself the fuck up!'"

I pushed myself away from the table then, my lasagna half-eaten, but I couldn't take another bite.

"I'm sorry," I said into the silence. "I'm sorry. You've been nothing but kind, and I'm being an asshole. I . . . I just need to go walking, okay? I'll be back in ten."

I trotted out of the house and down the road toward the same little prayer circle Jilly and I had visited the night before. The sun was starting to set—that read-through had gone really long—and I tried to remember what I was supposed to do tomorrow. I *thought* it was nothing, but I should probably ask Noah about it. I was happy that there might be something—happy, because I wanted to not have to decide what to do for myself.

I half jogged down the road in the pink twilight until I found the inlet with the fire pit. My blood was rushing just a tad in my veins, and I thought that I should pull out my running shoes tomorrow and give that a go. I could use the gym on set when I was working, but who didn't love cardio? (I didn't. I loathed it. If I could have exercised in my sleep to stay healthy and fit, I would have.)

I flopped onto the log bench, not caring about obesity even if it hit me in the ass *right now*, and stared out across the water, my mind a fuzzy blank. The mist was coming in with the cool of the night, and it rose off the surface, which gave the view the same emotional impact as looking at TV snow.

Perfect.

No hard thoughts, no hard decisions, no tripping over my tongue in an effort not to out myself. God, it had been easier when Vinnie was alive. We used to compare stories when we got home from a party, fill in the blanks for ourselves, laugh about a play on words or a joke that only the two of us got.

We had told each other it made up for sitting on opposite ends of the room during weddings, and escorting young models we had no interest in at all to events we cared a great deal about. Who needed to hold hands at the movies? We could wait for it to hit Netflix and fuck on the couch if we lost interest. Dinner parties with friends? Real married couples didn't hang together during those things—wasn't that the whole strategy? Split up and compare notes later?

We were actors. We lied for a living.

We lied to live.

I closed my eyes, hoping for snow, and what flashed behind them was the last thing I'd expected.

It was my parents' wedding picture, Mom decked out in a traditional white wedding dress—meringue-y as hell—and Dad looking fierce and irritated in a tuxedo. But that wasn't the only picture they had. One of them—the one they kept in their bedroom—was a close-up of Mom. She was feeding her best friend's baby cake, laughing because the little brown face was smeared with icing, ear to ear. In the background, Dad was looking at her with this softness in his face.

Every now and then, we'd see that softness there again, and we could figure it out, why Jack Mazynsky, redneck farmer, would marry an immigrant farm girl when his parents were so obviously against the match.

He loved her. Against everything his parents tried to tell him was true.

Weird, wasn't it? How some people just couldn't *apply* the knowledge life so cruelly dished out for free?

So that image behind my eyes—Mom being warm and vibrant, Dad being quietly, painfully besotted—that's what I saw.

Except I couldn't picture my parents anymore—not without seeing their faces when they kicked me out of the house. Instead, I saw Vinnie, laughing with that child, because God, he'd been good with kids. And I saw myself in the background, looking at him with this half-ashamed, half-hungry look, like the thing I wanted the most was right beyond my reach, and it almost hurt to stretch my body out to grasp it by the hand.

I wiped at my eyes with my shoulder to stop the burning.

Think puppies. Think kitties. Think wombats or aye-ayes, but for fuck's sake don't think about—

Who are you kidding, Con? Vinnie's voice sounded in my head again. *Pets just weren't your thing. Neither were kids, remember?*

I want a dog, I thought stubbornly.

Yeah, fine, Con. Get a dog. I don't give a shit. Just stop running away from every memory of me like I've got zombie makeup on!

Augh! Because zombies really freaked me out—it was the one sci-fi trope I'd never done. *Jesus, leave me alone!*

"No."

My eyes flew open at the quiet voice in the evening.

"Noah?" I asked, squinting through the mostly fallen darkness. How long had I been out there?

That long-boned, lanky frame was easy to spot, even against the darkness. The too-large suit made identification a sure thing.

"Who else were you talking to?" he asked, crunching across the tiny pebbles of the beach and sitting down about three feet away.

"Sorry," I mumbled. "Just . . . you know. Having one of those imaginary arguments."

"Yeah? Who won?"

"Zombies," I muttered darkly. "Those fuckers *always* win."

"Seriously," Noah said. In the darkness I could see those loose, glossy curls bobbing as he nodded his head. "When I'm really stressed—deadlines or shit—I have zombie dreams."

That caught my attention. "You too?" I asked, feeling pathetic. "You can *never* get away. You're just running, constantly, and they keep popping up and trying to get you."

"Right? And I don't know what movies I've been watching, but the zombies in my head get scarier with every dream!"

"Oh, yeah, man, I know that. I won't do a zombie picture. *Walking Dead*? Forget about it. I'd have nightmares every time I got a script."

Noah's soft laughter healed something in me, replaced that zombie picture of Vinnie in my head with the real Vinnie, and I was so grateful my eyes burned again.

"Yeah," Noah said, when his laughter faded. "Zombies. Northern Washington has werewolves, but not a lot of zombies."

I tilted my chin up, wondering if it was dark enough to see stars. "Well, it's a selling point. I can't imagine zombies are good for the real estate market, you know?"

"My dad says they're hell on the carpet," Noah said, and I closed my eyes and let a chuckle flow through me.

I had to swallow that chuckle down, because it was about to get out of hand, like Jillian's laughter during lunch today.

An icy silence hardened around us, and I didn't have the strength to break free.

"You know," Noah said after two or three solar years had passed, "I had to sign a nondisclosure agreement to get this job."

It was such a non sequitur. "I did too," I said, because they didn't like it when actors dropped spoilers.

Noah was quiet, like he was waiting for me to keep talking. I didn't. Finally, he said, "So, like, if someone's doing hookers and blow in the back of the car as I drive, I can tell the producer, but I can't tell the press."

"Has that ever happened?" I asked, not particularly curious.

"Nope, but I'm waiting patiently."

I gave a courtesy laugh, afraid if I really engaged, things would get out of hand. "Well, if it ever happens, be sure to tell me," I told him. "I won't tell a soul, I promise. I just want to know so I can laugh at people behind their backs."

"That's sort of dealing dirty, isn't it?" he asked, but he knew I was bantering.

"Yeah, well, that's me. I have no moral compass. Ask anyone."

"Should I ask Mr. Conklin?" he asked pointedly.

I had to think about that for a minute. "He wouldn't know," I said, trying to remember what he looked like. "We only just met today."

Noah grunted. "Well, he's interested in knowing you better," he said, sounding disgusted.

I frowned. Was it possible Vinnie had told Conklin? Why wouldn't Vinnie have told *me*? I shook my head. Who cared? If Conklin hadn't told the press now, he wasn't interested in exposing us, and if it wasn't about keeping my gods-be-damned secret, I didn't give a crap.

"I assume I'm going to get to know *everybody* better," I said mildly. "Just, not, you know. Biblically." *Please laugh, Noah, please laugh.* That ease of the day before, the lack of stress in our conversation—I wanted that back.

There was a short bark of sound next to me, and I closed my eyes and gave thanks. A laugh. But before I could silently beg him to just let it drop, he spoke again, lowering his voice to an intimate rumble. He had a *really* deep voice for such a lanky guy.

"Point taken. Mr. Conklin, not on the menu."

"No," I said firmly. I wondered . . . if I *was* out to Simon, and he *was* interested . . . but I got nothing from that thought but a friendly smile. "Not on the menu."

I didn't add, "I'm straight!" because . . . well, there was no way to say it that wouldn't feel like a lie, even if it had been true.

"So, forgetting about Mr. Conklin and what's for dinner—"

"Lasagna?"

"Shut up, Connor. I want you to hear me. I've signed an NDA. Now that you know that, you know that you can tell me pretty much anything. If you asked me to score drugs, I couldn't tell the cops."

"Would you?" I asked. "Because you seem a little wholesome—"

"Of course not!" Noah snapped. I fell silent, because the kid had that thing—that *thing*—in his voice, the thing that made you listen, even if he wasn't wearing the director's hat. "But if you wanted to, say, tell me something, something that was weighing on you, so when Jilly leaves you could have, you know, one person you can talk to, someone you see every day, you know who to turn to. Do you understand what I'm saying?"

He's saying I can come out.
He's saying I can talk about Vinnie.
He's saying I don't have to switch pronouns or fake it or lie.
He's saying I can be free.

"Yeah," I said, throat suddenly swollen with all the things I hadn't said to anyone but Vince Walker and Jilly Lombard for the last ten years. "Yeah. I hear you. That's . . . that's . . ." Oh God. All the words I had in my head sounded stupid. "Kind," I finished at last, the word a lamed leg on a swaybacked nag. "Generous," I tried again, and that horse barely passed the first. "I'm grateful."

And yes—*yes*—I was so terribly grateful.

There was an expectant silence then, thick and hopeful, but . . . but the dark wrapped weighty about me, and Vinnie was so close. He hadn't gone away like I'd told him to. He was right there, over my shoulder, asking me if I really wanted to do this, really wanted to share this part of us, really wanted to expose him to even the frail starlight that was beginning to pierce the night.

I couldn't. And after three or four solar years had passed, Noah knew it too.

He sighed and got heavily to his feet. "I'll wait for you to get back to the house before I leave," he said, defeated.

Fuck.

"Noah?" My voice sounded thin and childish in the dark.

"Yes, Mr. Montgomery?"

"Mazynsky," I said, the Polish name crashing consonants into the air.

"God-bless-you?"

I laughed, feeling lighter already. "You signed an NDA. Mazynsky is my real name. I—" my voice fell "—spent a lot of food money changing that shit." Vinnie and I had spent an entire night talking about who I'd be when I finally got my SAG card, and we'd stuck with it.

"Mmm . . ." Noah said, the syllable conveying tremendous disappointment.

"Not good enough?" I was absurdly hurt.

Then, even in the weak light, I could see the dim sparkle of his supernova grin. "Naw—for right now, Mr. Mazynsky, it'll do just fine."

I winced. I'd always hated that name. "Maybe Connor," I said humbly.

He moved, coming to squat right in front of me, and taking my hands as they dangled limply between my knees. "Okay, Connor," he said, his voice so gentle I almost—*almost*—didn't realize he'd taken this conversation to a sudden intimacy.

"Okay what?" I rasped. His hands on mine were warm and strong, and my neediness rose up, almost choking me.

"We'll start with your name." His thumbs rubbed circles on the inside of my palms. "Maybe eventually we'll get to who you really are."

He stood then and turned to leave, and I watched him, hungering for something, anything, to hold on to in the still darkness of the fallen night.

"Noah?" I said, hating myself for the pitch in my voice.

He turned halfway. "What's up?"

"What are we doing tomorrow?" Like a little kid, I fuckin' swear to fuckin' God.

Noah turned all the way then. "You don't have anything at the studio, but how 'bout I come get you around ten, and show you and Jilly around our little town. There's a bike shop—I'll put the rack on the back of the car if you like. You can buy or rent a touring bike and maybe have some independence if you're not going to get your own car."

My voice squeaked with embarrassment. "That's a really good plan," I said. "I . . . The bike's a good idea, but, uh, Jilly and I weren't kidding when we saw you in the airport. I can't, uh, navigate out of a paper bag."

Noah laughed a little. "Don't worry, Connor. It takes two turns to get to Bluewater Bay. Even *you* can't screw that up. You'll like it, trust me. Besides, it's good exercise, and you won't risk turning an

SELFIE

ankle—the roads here are for shit because the ground's so soft. There's not a road shoulder for miles."

"Two turns?" I said, puzzled. I mean, we'd driven through the town on the way to the studio this morning, and it had seemed like we'd been running through a maze.

"The road's a little squirrely, but I swear, there's only two stop signs between here and town. I'll let you sit up front tomorrow, you'll have a better view."

I smiled suddenly—I had something to do, then. Something to look forward to.

"Okay," I said, happier than I had been. "That sounds like a plan." Creakily, like an old man, I stood and stretched. "I'll walk back to the house with you. I don't want you to feel obligated to wait."

"Sure. But it would have been no problem."

We started back, shoulder to shoulder. He loomed an intimidating height over me—and I was pretty tall for Hollywood.

"I don't like to put people out," I said apologetically.

He chuckled, and the air between us lightened. "Aren't you a movie star?"

I laughed too. "Jesus, don't start that shit. Just get me my coffee and give me my pedicure and I'll go be big and important somewhere else."

This time his laugh echoed off the water, and the island across from us, and the houses down the hill in our little block.

"Noah?"

"Yeah?"

"Do other people live on this block?" The houses were well spaced—if there were lights on, it was hard to see in the twilight.

"Yeah—a family in each house."

"How come I don't see them?"

"Timing."

"Huh. Hey, does anybody live on that island across from us?"

He made a surprised grunt. "I don't know. I can find out for you."

I thought about it for a few steps. "No, that's okay. I can make up better scenarios on my own."

"That's . . . narcissistic. Any other questions?"

How far away was Mount Olympus? How many stores were in town? What were the locals like? Was it possible to swim to the island? Could I plant flowers even though we were renting the house? How many miles was it to town? To the hotel? Were there helmet laws in Washington? Were they enforced? What exactly was a touring bike? Was it different from a mountain bike? Which one would be better?

We got back to the house, and he opened the garage with the press of a fob on his keychain, stopping me in midquestion.

"God, you're exhausting," he muttered, almost to himself. "I had no idea one little truth was going to set so much free!"

I smiled, a slow, sweet, sunshiny kind of smile. "Yeah, well, I'm surprised myself."

The light from the garage let me see his features, and I remembered all over again that he wasn't a bad-looking kid.

That thought, of all of them, killed my smile and shut me up.

"No," he snapped harshly.

"No what?" But my shoulders were hunching, and I could already feel my body hiding all my secrets.

"No—we were in a place. A good place—you're not shutting me out."

I held up my hands, forcing my shoulders back with an effort. "Absolutely, Mr.—"

Oh God, he moved fast.

He suddenly stood so close I could smell him—something dark and Old Spice-y—rum and sweat and wool. I could feel his body heat through his suit.

"Noah?" I said uncertainly—although I didn't feel threatened. Just really, really close.

So close that when he captured the back of my head with one long-fingered, bony-knuckled hand, I had no way to pull back.

And when he pressed a short, brutal kiss against my lips, I froze in surprise.

He paused, and I parted my lips slightly, prepared to tell him . . . what? He went in again, and this time his tongue swept in. For a moment, I relaxed, and in that breath—

I was safe. Cared for. Protected. Comforted in a way I hadn't felt since . . .

Ever.

Treacherous and ungrateful—that feeling forced me to step back and hold my hand to my mouth like an outraged Victorian heroine.

"But . . ." I stammered.

"Don't say it," Noah ordered. "Man, if you actually say that fucking lie out loud I am going to lose my shit."

I'm not gay.

Oh for fuck's sake, Connor—you blew half of Hollywood before I fucked you up the ass.

But Vinnie!

He's hot. Please don't fuck this up.

"Uhm . . ." I was still staggered, and when Noah's hand came out to cup my cheek I almost flinched.

But he wasn't mean or angry—he just rubbed my cheekbone with his thumb. "I'll see you tomorrow, Connor Mazynsky."

"Okay," I said, like this was normal.

"Good." And like that he turned around and hopped in the car. He backed out and gave me time to get into the garage before he closed the door and left me to wander into the house.

Jilly had cleaned up and apparently gone to bed, and I made it to my room before I stripped to my shorts and collapsed, wondering what in the hell had just happened.

CHAPTER FIVE

I Wish Like Hell You Were Elsewhere

J illy declined to come to "the village" as she put it, stating work reasons. I honestly thought she just needed to put her head in a different place, a place where she was forced to realize "I have to tell Vinnie" meant she had to do it like I did it—in her head, where Vinnie could reply and she didn't have to tell anybody about the conversation.

Noah picked me up, right on time. We were both wearing cargo shorts and hooded sweatshirts, which relieved me on some level. Actors play the part—and right now my part was to blend in and be casual.

"I think," I said, looking out the window to the greenery that surrounded the winding road, "that the last year was like . . . like we insulated ourselves. Like when you wrap a bandage tight around a cut so you don't have to feel it until you're ready."

I felt rather than saw Noah's startled glance. "You haven't spoken for three miles, do you know that?"

I looked at him. "This road is really long. I'm surprised I don't get carsick on the way out."

"Is that another of your quirks—like the getting lost?" he asked, not like he was irritated, just like he was taking note.

"Only sometimes," I confessed. "Usually if I've played it fast and loose with the diet."

"Which means . . ."

I sighed. "Okay, fine. Let's play 'Getting to know Connor Montgomery—'"

"Mazynsky."

"Connor *Mazynsky* better. I rarely get carsick, but when I do it's usually after too much sugar and fat. So, sausage and cheese with a milkshake chaser is a bad idea for me."

"It's a bad idea for my little sister," Noah muttered. "It's a bad idea for *anyone*."

"Yeah, Vinnie used to complain. I loved burgers and fries and milkshakes, and that shit's cheap, but I couldn't eat it, even when we were younger. Not more than once a week. So we'd have wheat bread and hummus with turkey, and we'd call it champagne and caviar on wheat."

"That's good." Noah laughed.

I smiled back. I'd made him happy—and the memory had slipped out so naturally it hadn't hurt at all.

"Vinnie could turn shit around like that," I told him. "Just . . . just stupid optimistic. I started to pick it up from him, way back—it's a better way to live."

"Like how?"

"Like, well, if you blow the audition for the chewing gum, you'll have time to make it to the one for the fabric detergent and that one has a hot director. You know, that sort of thing."

"What was his name?" Noah asked casually.

"Whose name?"

"The hot director's name?"

Oh, very tricky.

"It was a hypothetical," I returned mildly.

"Sure. So, what else did Vinnie give you?"

"Besides a place to live?"

"Was it a nice place?" It seemed like such an innocuous question.

"It was a dump," I said bluntly. "Mold in the bathroom, a hot plate and a minifridge, a couch that would break your back if you slept on it, and one window, from the bedroom, that looked out on a brick wall."

"But you guys lived there for a year?"

"Yeah." I smiled nostalgically. "Until Jilly signed us on and we started getting a better class of commercial." This was basic history— you could find it on any website, or clickbait site for "best bromance" really. I know it had found its way into fanfic, which was fine. As long as Vinnie and I didn't have to read about one of us having ass-babies or getting gangbanged by aliens with latex tentacles, we'd been sort of proud of popping up in the imaginations of schoolgirls everywhere.

It was like being a movie star in their dreams, right? Except some of the scripts were *way* better.

"And then you moved into a better apartment?"

I smiled. "Yeah—this one actually had a kitchen. It was awesome." It had been a studio.

"And a year later, you signed on for *Warlock Tea*."

I sent him a sideways look. "Yeah, why?"

Noah shook his head. "Just getting a timeline here. You know—how long you lived in each other's back pockets. Didn't that get wearing?"

"No." I realized that I'd managed to answer his questions honestly, and that made me feel good. "In fact, we missed each other when I moved out."

My voice dropped. That was a truth I had difficulty sharing. It led to so many truths I *couldn't* share.

"How'd you handle that?"

"Friends separate all the time," I said vaguely.

"Yeah. What'd you do?"

"Email, texting, Skype—it's not the dark ages. Is that the town? It's sweet!"

It was a tourist trap—but a nice one. Log cabin facades, boardwalks above streets that probably flooded when the rain melted the snow off the mountains. The stores themselves were eclectic—art galleries featuring local artists, coffee shops, candy by the barrel, locally designed and manufactured clothing. There was a store with yarn spun from everything from arctic bunny to yak, and a store with carved Native art. Noah cruised the small, maybe four-block area slowly, and I took in the shingles hanging above the boardwalk with a kind of delight.

They even had men's outdoor clothing, and it was apparently doing brisk business. Good—the clown cum rag had come out of the wash that morning, and it was never going to be the same.

"I like this place," I declared. "This is a very good place!"

I looked at Noah and could tell by his smirk that he'd just assessed my mental age to about five. I didn't care. One of the first things Vinnie and I had done when we started getting good commercials was learn to shop. Not for headshots or clothes we had to wear for auditions or hair products. Just for *us*. We'd furnished that second apartment with an eclectic assortment of things we'd seen and loved—and could finally afford.

A throw rug the color of a summer sky? Yes. Plates shaped like steak? You betcha. Quilts, pillows, throws, and afghans that matched the season, or the day, or the month, or the premiere we looked forward to the most?

I thought of my beach house, which had been all hardwood floors and white drapes and windows, and the joy leached from my day.

All of the fun stuff had ended up at Vinnie's house. It all belonged to his parents now. His family. From the Hairy Otter throw we'd gotten in Monterey to the 3-D poster board of *Shrek 2* we'd actually bid $100,000 on at a charity auction.

And the steak plates.

Ooh—I bet someone here has some moose-head plates, Vinnie's voice said, pressing its nose against the window like mine had been.

We're here for a bike.

Oh, come on, Connor—if I'm living through you, you're doing a piss-poor job of it.

Where do I start, Vinnie? Do I start with the plates? With that picture on the wall from the artist who retired? Do I buy a Dora the Explorer *blanket and hope the collection gets better? Everything. Everything we loved was in your house, and now it's just me, floating like a ghost—*

But you're not anymore! You're here, in this new place. Remember when we used to split the heel of the bread because it was the only thing in the house? You're not in that place! You will never *be in that place again! Now go get some fucking steak plates to prove it!*

"Where do I start?"

Noah and I jumped—both of us startled by my voice in the quiet car.

"I don't know—how about we start at the far end and walk down the boardwalk to the other side where we'll buy the bicycles? We can ride them around and then back to the car. How's that?"

God, he had the best ideas. "What if I want to get something?"

"Don't worry—the stores have a co-op and a delivery truck. Fifty-mile radius. You're more than within limits. And I can always fetch it on the way back. Or—" He wrinkled his nose with impatience. "Whatever. There's ways. Do you want to see the town or not?"

I smiled, feeling shy. "Yeah!" I was feeling it! "Let's go shopping!"

I did not find plates that looked like big cuts of beef—but I did find a complete set with pictures of small dogs instead.

"I love these," I said, looking at them in awe. A Shih Tzu stared back at me, limpid eyes peering out from a gray pouf of hair. "I . . . I mean . . . imagine finishing off your chicken tetrazzini and seeing this?" I held the plate up so Noah could see.

He blinked, very, very slowly.

"That's terrifying," he muttered, almost to himself.

"You wouldn't come over and make lasagna if you had to eat off a Chihuahua?" I held up that plate too.

"I would," Noah said. "But I'm *gay.*"

I blinked, and it occurred to me that I was not having the most "heteronormative" of conversations. "Not all gay people like small dogs," I said with dignity. "V—" *Vinnie hated them.* "Very many of my friends who are gay don't like small dogs at all."

Noah gazed at me with this baffled, irritated expression that I pretended I couldn't read.

"Seriously—we can't be friends if I get the small-dog plates?"

He had dark, brooding eyebrows, and they did something complicated as his eyes narrowed and widened by turns. "Sure," he said after a pause. "But only if you get the cat coffee mugs too."

My relief suffused my entire body and beamed out in my smile. *Thank you, Noah. Thank you for playing along and pretending you don't see what I don't want you to see.*

He did that for me for the next couple of hours. I bought— well, random crap, mostly, but almost all of it was for the house, *any* house since this setup was only supposed to be temporary. I bought a delicious seascape from the art gallery and a lawn sculpture from the woodworking place. I found a quilt that featured movie werewolves and a matching set of throw pillows that did the same thing for vampires.

Noah added a T-shirt to match. We had the other stuff set to ship, but I kept the T-shirt. I was just about to do a quick change in the back of the store with Noah blocking the sight lines, when it hit me.

Sorry, Vinnie.
What, we're the only ones who change our shirts in the store?
That's not what I'm sorry about.
You can't do T-shirts with the other guy?
He's a friend.
Connor—
No. No, I'll take it home.

I stopped then in the act of pulling my shirts off, and winked at Noah, trying hard to hide the fact that the laughter and the momentum that had carried us here had disappeared in one random Vinnie-and-I thought.

"I'll take it home," I said, keeping my best actor smile in place. I turned abruptly and walked out of the store, T-shirt shoved back in its little bag.

Noah caught up to me, and I felt him moving his arm restlessly, like he wanted to do something with it but couldn't.

I turned to look at him, affecting amusement. "What? Are you twitching?"

"Yes," he said, irritated. "I am definitely twitching. You know, if you and Vinnie did a thing with T-shirts, it's not going to destroy my world if you say so. 'Gee, Noah, I'm sorry, but Vinnie and I used to buy stupid T-shirts together and now I'm sad.'"

"'Gee Connor, you're always fucking sad. Get over it, people fucking die!'"

I swallowed in the suddenly shocked silence.

"That came out with a little extra bitterness," I apologized. "I, uh . . . you know. I'm not that callous, I swear."

"No." He took a big deep breath. "Grieving—you know, I get it."

Here was the place where in the movies, I'd say something self-serving, like, "Yeah, who'd you know who died?" But when you asked that question in the movies, the other person's story was way worse than your own, so I decided to skip the humiliating come-to-Jesus moment and be a human being.

"I'm sorry," I said softly. "Did you lose someone close to you?"

He nodded, like we both should have expected this conversation. "Yeah." He paused. "You know when you're too young to know about sex, and your best friend is the most important person in your world?"

I thought about that. "No," I said honestly. "I . . . My whole life, when I looked at . . . a friend, I looked at the potential to crush."

"Huh." It sounded innocuous enough, but the look on his face was akin to horror. He shook his head, like he was trying to shake it off, and continued. "Well, *I* had a friend who was like that. Her name was Sharra and we were . . ." He held up his crossed fingers.

"Peas and carrots?" I said gently.

"Yeah." Benches were situated periodically on the boardwalk, and as the morning mist burnt off, they beckoned invitingly from spots in the sun. He chose one of them and gestured for me to sit down. I did, and he sat next to me, not so close that we were touching, but close enough to feel the heat from his body, and to smell whatever it was he wore that just sort of turned my key. Rum and musk and spice—so, like a car freshener with some horse sweat thrown in.

Whatever—I had a sudden instinct to nuzzle his neck, to offer physical comfort, to throw my arm around his shoulder at the very least. Oh dear God—what was the math? 366 days plus fourteen plus two, that equaled 382 days without a ma . . . without Vinnie?

The silence between us stretched, and I reminded myself that I was trying to be there for Noah like he'd been there for me.

"What happened?" I asked, remembering his friend.

"Drowning." He looked away. "It was . . . Well, they lived in one of those houses that fronted the sound, sort of like yours. They think she went wading and slipped and—it's cold. She could swim in a pool, but . . ."

"But not in the sound."

Unforgiving. Just like the rest of life.

"That's horrible," I said, hating the thought of children and tragedy—and a child living through a tragedy. "I'm so sorry. How old were you?"

"We were twelve," he said. "But see—that's how I know. You lose that friend—that peas-and-carrots friend, and for months—even years—you'll be thinking to yourself, 'I've got to tell Sharra—'"

I swallowed and nodded. I couldn't even fit "Yeah" out through the tightness of my throat.

"You know, like, 'Hey, Sharra, the first day of high school sucked,' or 'Hey, Sharra, I think I'm gay.'"

Oh. Oh fuck. "Who'd you tell?" I wanted to know.

"My father," he said, surprising me.

"How'd that go?"

"'Dad, I think I'm gay.' 'Son, I'm pretty sure I still love you. You think all you want.'"

I choked and ran my thumbnail against the weathered wood of the bench. "Your dad sounds too good to be true."

"He yells," Noah said, but it sounded like he was fishing for reasons his dad wasn't perfect. "What are your folks like?"

I buried my face in my hands for a second. "Oh God. Noah—there is nothing we can talk about, do you understand? There is nothing we can talk about that isn't a tap dance through a minefield. If you haven't read it in a certified interview, I . . ."

And this time he really *did* make a growl of frustration.

And he draped his arm over my shoulders, which I needed so, so very badly.

"What's the worst that could happen?" he asked softly. "The absolute worst that could happen?"

I turned to look at him, wondering if there were paparazzi around the corner, or under the boardwalk, or stalking us through the stores.

"I could tape a seven-minute video with the sound off, so stinking drunk I don't know what the fuck I was singing."

He nodded, dark eyes unfathomable. Then: "'Sloop John B.' You wanted to go home."

I looked away. "I was in my own living room. You may recall the wine." He didn't say anything, so I stuck to a safe topic: him. "When did it . . . when did it get better?"

"What?" he asked.

"The . . . the 'I've got to tell Sharra' thing?"

"It never goes away, not completely," he said.

"Not *ever*?" I asked, suddenly near tears. "*Never*? Because—" *Vinnie, I can't do this all the time. I can't be this sad. It's pressing down on me so hard, I can hardly breathe.*

"Well, yeah," Noah said, his voice gentle and absurdly close, like he was talking into my neck. I couldn't have shaken him loose or made him move farther away in this public place—not if there were explosions and bullets across the street. Not if there were paparazzi or the top reporter from *Variety* walking down the boardwalk.

"But . . ." Oh hell. I had to say it. "But . . . it *hurts*. *Everything* is something he won't hear or see, and I want to tell it to him, and there's no space in my head for *me* because it's all about telling *Vinnie*—"

"Shh . . ." He just held me, face next to mine, arm around my shoulder like a comforting anchor. "It gets better. If you talk about him. You don't have to get personal, but . . . you know. My friends from school, my family—we all *talked* about her. And when we had an 'I've got to tell Sharra' moment, we *all* had it. And we shared it. And we all sort of filled in the comfort when we needed it. Man, the way you and Jilly *don't* talk about Vinnie, it's making it hard for *me* to breathe."

"He loved to watch me shop for kitsch," I said, wondering why *that* would be the first thing out of my mouth. "We taught each other how to shop. We *filled* his place with . . . memorabilia and stupid junk and color and pictures and . . . and Jilly made me stop wearing his T-shirts because they were falling off my body."

I felt him stiffen next to me and thought, *Oh. There's the line. Now I know.*

But he relaxed in a moment. "Well that was probably a good idea," he said. "So, the T-shirts?"

"That was a thing," I told him. God. It was a personal thing. It was a *living with another man* thing. But I couldn't help it. "We . . . we only got one T-shirt whenever we went somewhere together. And then we . . . we'd fight over who got to wear it. But then we got . . . you know. Paparazzi were everywhere when *Warlock Tea* got big, so we couldn't wear them in public—speculation was fun for the fanfic sites, but Jilly was like, 'Guys. No.' So if we just wanted to—" Oh God "—hang out and play video games or something, we'd . . . steal the shirts from . . ." We'd kept them all at my house, because his got all of the fun decorator stuff. "You know. Our kitschy travel T-shirts were like a 'let's have a friend day' signal."

If friends used the T-shirt for a cum rag after they were done doing inventive, consensual, sexual things to each other's bodies because that was their favorite way to spend time when they were alone.

"Friend day," Noah said without inflection.

I shook my head and turned my face to the emerging blue sky. "That's what I said."

"I think I've had 'friend days' like that."

An image of Noah—naked, head back, face contorted in climax, while someone younger, hotter, and with less baggage than me swallowed his cock down to the root—rocked me.

I stood up, no longer interested in T-shirts or sadness or even, God forgive me, *Vinnie*.

"There's a jewelry store," I said, because Captain Random does random shit. "Let's get something for Jilly. She's . . . stressed." Two kids with substance-abuse problems and I was her best client? Yeah. Jilly was fucking stressed. "I think we should do something for Jilly."

And I took off across the boardwalk like I was shot out of a cannon.

I hovered over the jewelry counter for a while, which was ludicrous, because the giant chest piece in turquoise and jade was the obvious choice, fuck the price tag. Noah lingered outside, pinching the bridge of his nose and squinting, like he was trying to comprehend a particularly irritating child.

Well, fucking sue me. I'm an actor—emotional maturity is *not* the hallmark of my people.

"Excuse me—you're Connor Montgomery, aren't you?"

I looked up, and the sales clerk was addressing me shyly. Pretty girl—strong, African American features with light-brown skin and a wide smile.

"Yeah." I smiled. "So pleased to meet you."

"We're not supposed to fawn all over the Hollywood people," she said, looking around like she was checking for the manager. "It's sort of a . . . I don't know. All the shop people got together, and we had sort of a meeting about it. But . . . you know, I just wanted to say that it's nice to have you here. I mean, I know the magazines and the tabloids totally lie, but . . . but you just have this reputation of being a good guy. And I was so sorry about your friend."

"Thank you," I said, genuinely touched. "That's really kind."

She smiled back, and after an awkward pause made the realization that she had something to do. "Oh, can I help you?"

"Yeah," I said, pointing to the necklace and the chunky earrings that matched. "Uh, that."

"Oooh—pretty." She lifted it out of the case. "Girlfriend?"

"Agent," I said succinctly. "But she's sort of amazing so—"

"Ah," the girl—her name badge said *Stevie*—nodded understandingly. "So she gets the best."

At that moment, Noah walked in, looking official even without his suit and hat. "How we doin'?" he asked, like he hadn't just been ready to throttle me.

"Got Jilly a present," I said, like I hadn't been seesawing between spilling my guts and spilling my tears all day.

He watched as Stevie boxed it up, looking surprised. "That's really pretty—you are one thoughtful bastard, Connor M . . ." He paused infinitesimally—but I still heard it. "Montgomery," he said, and his eyes hit mine in realization.

No. Not easy.

"I have my moments," I said, trying for cocky, and then he stepped forward to make arrangements for pickup and delivery. We left the store, shoulder to shoulder, and my stomach clenched.

God—I just wanted to hold hands with him. I'd had this feeling with Vinnie too, and big bleeding parts of me were suddenly furious that this one stupid simple thing was something I wasn't going to let myself do. We weren't even *sleeping* together. But we were friends, and I felt close to him and straight guys didn't do that.

Believe me, after all these years I had a really firm grasp on what the straight guys didn't do.

"So," I said after a moment of wants and needs and thoughts and angst colliding in my head like excited electrons, "how's the whole delivery thing going to work?"

"I'll pick everything up tomorrow," he said, "and bring it by."

I grimaced. "That doesn't sound like fun. I thought there was a delivery—"

"Wanted an excuse to stop by," he admitted simply, and God. Suddenly I didn't want to bring him in on my little pity party or my repression or my stupid career.

"Noah," I said gently, "I am so grateful for—"

"We're not breaking up," he said, voice mild. "We haven't gone out. There has not been dating, and you haven't even told me with your own mouth all the shit I already know. So no. I'm not listening to you when you say 'Don't get attached.' So don't bother."

"Fine," I muttered. "I'm a fucking mess, so why listen to *me*? What would *I* know about how hard it is to crawl down this rabbit hole—I've only *lived* here for the last ten to twelve years, right?"

He bumped my shoulder then and grabbed my hand.

I turned at him, mouth agape, but he stared straight ahead. "If anyone asks, you got lost," he said. "But you and I—not today, maybe not this week, but sometime in the next few months, we're going to have a talk, a scary-assed talk, where every fucking thing that comes out of your mouth is nothing but the truth, do you hear me?"

Oh God. Someone just told me what to do.

I wanted to cry. I felt like I'd been waiting for someone to tell me what to do for my entire life.

I'm gay—should I tell my parents? Someone tell me what to do!

My parents just kicked me out—should I lie to them and say I was sorry? Should I hang around town and hope they love me again? Should I talk to my sisters and see if they'll hate me?

Should I hitch a ride to LA so I can go be somebody new? Someone tell me what to do!

I just turned my first trick for food and I feel… I feel… I feel… Oh God, someone tell me what to do!

This guy just took me home and we fucked and it was awesome, but who falls in love after one fuck? Someone tell me what to do!

Jilly says we shouldn't come out, and Vinnie needs his career too, but I don't want to live a lie, oh, God, Vinnie, I don't want to live a lie, Jilly, do we have to live a lie, oh God, someone tell me what to do!

I clung to Noah's hand like it was a lifeline in a frozen ocean. "You are awfully goddamned old for twenty-five," I said with dignity. "How'd you get to be so old?"

"I fucked everything that moved in my freshman year." He nodded judiciously. "That meant I had it out of my system when it was time to grow up."

I laughed, like he meant me to, and kept hold of his hand. Yeah, I knew straight guys didn't hold hands with other guys.

Noah knew that too.

The touring bike was sort of a simple thing—upright frame, two gears, kickback brakes.

I loathed it.

I looked at Noah apologetically. "I mean, I know it sounds like a good thing for a tourist," I apologized, "but I sort of want something kickass."

Noah rolled his eyes and nodded to the proprietor, a short, scrawny white guy with a blond beard that went down to his waist and blond dreadlocks the same length. "Cheddar, he wants something kickass—maybe a mountain bike, okay?"

Cheddar nodded, because I don't think he talked, and disappeared for a second, into the back.

He came back with a mountain bike my size, in a lovely seafoam green.

"Ooh," I said. "I like the color." I smiled at Noah guilelessly, and he raised an eyebrow.

"Of course you do," he said, like I'd answered every question he'd ever had about the cosmos. "There is no reason why a perfectly straight guy wouldn't love a bike in weenie-ass green."

I rolled eyes at Cheddar. "Ignore him," I muttered, and then brightened. "Actually, better than that! *Get him one.*"

Cheddar practically hurt my eyes, looking at Noah with a shiny, glowy, positively *diabolical* expression on his face.

"No." Noah watched in horror as that little figure disappeared behind the counter again. The whole store was bicycles and tires and equipment, all of it neatly stacked and organized, but apparently they had Aladdin's cave in the back for special nutjobs like me.

"Yes," I said, excited about what he'd come back with.

Noah shook his head as Cheddar emerged. "No," he muttered, covering his eyes with his hands.

"Definitely," Cheddar said, sounding smug.

"*Yes!*" I crowed. I looked in triumph at the pink and white confection. It was actually the same bike I was getting with a different paintjob, and I couldn't be happier. Even the seat was pink.

"It's perfect," I told Cheddar, and he leveled a look of pure bathos at Noah.

"I'm so telling Viv."

"I hate you." Noah sounded like he meant it.

"No, you don't, bro," Cheddar refuted. "I'm the best boyfriend your sister ever had."

Noah looked bad-temperedly at the bicycle. "My dad has a gun," he warned, and Cheddar took that threat so seriously he burst into raucous, chortling laughter—which surprised me, considering I didn't think he could talk a minute ago.

"Dude!" he choked, as I pulled out my credit card. "Dude! No!" He ran the credit card, still laughing. "Oh my God. Dude! Your dad can't kill spiders!" He wiped his eyes as the receipt printed out, and nodded at me like I was in on the joke. "Oh my God, that was a good one. You know—Mr. D, he's like . . . like a *muppet*, he's so sweet. I'm going to tell him. He'll probably laugh until pee comes out!"

"Please don't knock my sister up," Noah said sourly, and Cheddar straightened and shook his head, completely sober.

"Dude, no. No—Viv, she's going places. Man, I want her to like me enough to come back, you know?"

Aw. I pleaded with Noah for forgiveness, using my puppy dog eyes alone.

Noah shook his head. "Dude. *Duude*."

Cheddar beamed at him. "See? Dude, you love me, right? You totally love me."

"Pink, Cheddar. You got me a pink bike."

Cheddar and I looked at each other and nodded. "Dude," I said, adopting Cheddar's smile.

"Totally," he said, so serious it hurt.

Noah glared, but his full lips quirked in a smile. "Fine." He barely managed not to roll his eyes. "Thanks for the bike, Connor. I can—"

"It's a gift," I said quickly, not wanting to hear about him expensing something or paying me back. "You've . . ." I turned my face away. He'd been irritable and cranky and pushy and demanding.

But he'd also really, really wanted me to not feel like shit.

"You've cared," I said truthfully. "And you didn't have to. So, you know. Maybe we can ride together."

Cheddar startled like he'd been shot. "Oh! Dudes! I totally forgot to sell you helmets!" He knocked the helmet *he* was wearing and grinned. "You want they should match the bikes?"

"*Yes!*" I cried out, beating Noah by a mile.

Noah sighed. "No. Please, God—"

Cheddar grinned at me and disappeared into the back again. If he didn't keep popping out with bicycle equipment, I'd expect he had porn in there or something.

He returned with two helmets and some elbow and kneepads, and we got down to the business of inflating the tires and adjusting the seats and the brakes.

Noah was right—when we left the store, we rode out in style.

We had to swing a wide arc around the commercial part of town because it was mostly paved with cobblestones, which made for shitty riding and a potential danger to the old peanuts and swings, if you know what I mean. The town itself skirted the edge of the sound, and Noah, after making sure I had my eyes on him, swung us down 101, where we kept to the unstable shoulder. It was bumpy, but after about a mile, the bulk of the Global hotel filled our view, and I realized that this was where we'd eaten the day before. I was actually hungry after our little test ride, but Noah shook his head when I asked.

"Let's go to the coffee shop," he said seriously. "They've got pastries, and you can see why I think Starbucks is bullshit."

So we swung around, and he took us in a big arch to get us to the car, which was parked in one of the few parking lots in the small commercial area.

The bike rack proved invaluable, and after securing the bikes, we walked back to the shops, and he took me into Stomping Grounds.

The store was separated from the entrance by a partial wall, and we could hear the conversation and banter overhead as we walked up a boarded ramp. On the other side was a corkboard with community happenings—everything from LGBTQ mixers to slam poetry to a singles BBQ to PTA meetings covered that board. There was even a schedule for "open shoots" for the show. I'd been warned with my contract that some of the outside shoots would give the public limited access, and I was expected to meet my people, as it were.

I was looking forward to it now—something about seeing that flier in the coffee shop, meeting Stevie with her careful respect, and meeting Cheddar who was just . . . just fun as hell, made me want to invite this town in.

Fun feeling. If I'd been forced to do the same thing in Hollywood, I would have held my breath and beat my feet against the floor until Jilly took it out of my contract.

The boarded ramp ended up on a landing, and voila! The world's cutest coffee shop with a view of both the town *and* the sound from the front window.

The place was filled with small tables and couches, most of them occupied. Noah shooed me to one of the tables and said, "I'll get your order, just sit."

"But pastries—" Because they were lining the case and they looked awesome.

"Trust me." He nodded, for the first time that morning looking impossibly young.

"Yeah," I said. "Fine."

A short, wiry woman with short blonde hair and serious ink on her arms was running from table to table, mostly just checking up on customers, and as I sat one of the men by the window called out, "Hey, Tori! Is Avery working today?"

Tori gave a pained wince. "Uh . . . no." She grimaced. "Not today. But, you know, that's no guarantee it's gonna happen a—"

I hadn't thought about it as we'd come in, but this building actually had two stories. I realized it now when a very suspicious thump and squeak echoed from the floor above us.

"Oh Lord," Tori said, slumping resignedly.

Around me, the rest of the coffee shop broke into applause.

I looked up at Noah, and he seemed to be pointedly avoiding my eyes. And smirking.

The thumping and squeaking continued.

The same guy from the window said, "I think they're finally getting quieter—"

And then we could all hear it. I knew that sound—or I remembered that sound. Or sometime in my life I'd *made* that sound.

Usually when Vinnie's cock was so far up my ass I thought my lungs would collapse.

I let out my dorkiest laugh, buried my face in my arms, and kept laughing.

Above us, the sex of the century was commencing apace.

My stomach muscles were aching by the time Noah got back with our coffee, fruit, and a couple ham and cheese croissants that I probably shouldn't allow anywhere near my hips.

He set the food down next to my head and poked my shoulder.

"Come out and eat."

"No," I said, my voice muffled by the table.

"We're not an orgy kind of place," he said soberly. "Nobody is going to force you to have sex just because Avery and Cal . . ." His voice softened. "Let's just say that Cal has all the good sex in the world coming, okay?"

I peered out of the shelter of my arms. "You know these people?" I couldn't decide if that made this more or less pornographic.

"Well, Avery Kennedy came to town a couple of months ago—"

"Wait," I muttered. "I know him—"

"He's a writer?"

"Oh yeah!" He'd come up during my and Jilly's research. "He did that piece on fan fiction, and then another one about the town and the show. I like his stuff!" He was succinct, and funny, and . . . and . . . uhm . . .

"*Cal, harder!*"

Apparently getting ass-fucked by someone named Cal that Noah used to know.

"Not that stuff," I said with big eyes.

Noah's smirk broke, and he chortled. I looked around, and the entire coffee shop was in various stages of hysterical giggles.

"God—it's a good thing there's no kids in here," I said, torn between horror and . . . oh hell. Arousal. There was no mistaking it. My groin was tingling, my nipples were puckered . . . three hundred and eighty-three days. My body had gone over a year with no stimulation—I'd been effectively dead.

And now I was not.

Noah laughed shortly. "You missed the woman hustling her preschooler out, but yeah—I don't think they know how loud it is down here. Tori doesn't want to kick them out yet—she's been trying to rent out that top room forever, and, you know, ninety-nine percent of the time, they wait until after dark."

"*Now . . . now . . . now . . . God, wait!*"

"Well," I muttered, finding refuge in politics. "You never know when the one percent is gonna sneak out and kick you in the nads."

Noah patted my hand. "You'll live," he said gently. "Now drink your coffee and eat your pastry. I actually have another movie star to run errands for this afternoon, so I'm afraid I'm going to have to drop you off."

"You have another movie star?" I said, stunned into letting my actual feelings show. "I'm not your only movie star?"

There was another burst of noise from above—a climactic burst as it were—and then a sudden, relieved silence.

When I looked back at Noah, he was smiling at me crookedly.

"You're my favorite movie star," he said with a courtly little incline of his head. "But yeah—I'm on the clock in two hours. I gotta go home and get my suit."

I blinked. "Hey—the suit thing. Uh . . . you don't *have* to wear that for me, do you?"

He shrugged. "Not if you don't want me to. I have to admit, though, I look more like a bodyguard in the suit."

I grimaced. "Noah, I hate to break this to you but—"

A self-deprecating smile crossed his features—a bit of vulnerability I didn't think he'd possessed. "Yeah," he admitted. "My dad was rail thin until he was about thirty—no amount of working out did it. Now he's got to fight to keep the weight off. I expect I'll be the same way."

Thirty. I sighed. "I need to start watching what I eat," I said, pointing to the pastry.

He broke off a bite for me. "Yeah. When you turn thirty—"

"In September."

"In September," he acknowledged with a head bob. "I'm sure you'll be all about the foodie stuff."

I shrugged. "Hollywood. You want the bod, you work out, you eat the chicken and veggies, you—"

"Supply the world with methane," Noah filled in dryly. "Yeah, I get it. But right now, you need a croissant."

"I do?" I looked at him dubiously.

He nodded. "Before I go pick up *Shalene Cross*, my assignment for today, you need a croissant."

I couldn't help it. I brightened. "She's a nice girl," I said, because she was, and we'd worked together before. "I didn't realize she was on the cast."

Noah rolled his eyes. "As far as I know, she's not—she's visiting someone. But," he held his hand up in a mock Boy Scout salute, "mine is not to reason why, mine is just to do or drive."

I laughed and reached for the pastry. "Then let's get it done so we can drive."

From the room above, we heard bed springs creaking, and a low, drawn-out moan. "God, Avery, are you trying to kill me?"

I looked at Noah weakly, and the boner that had wilted with the conversation and the food and the idea of not being the center of the known universe came back with a vengeance.

Noah pursed his lips and nodded judiciously. "Maybe we could get it done on the way out."

I grabbed my cup and the bag of pastries and we made a graceful exit, accompanied by the music of young (I assumed) love.

I couldn't help thinking it, though, as Noah and I walked slowly down the boardwalk under a crisp blue sky.

Vinnie, how many people do you think heard us having sex in that first apartment?

I dunno, Con—how many people actually lived in the building?

Yeah. That many. That many people knew when we were getting lucky.

I wasn't sure why, but in the days that followed, that thought gave me a lot of comfort.

CHAPTER SIX

OFFICE SPACE

Jillian was still working diligently when we got back, but she stood up from the table to say hi to Noah while he unloaded my bike into the garage, along with my helmet and pads.

"I'll bring mine from home tomorrow," he said brightly, and before I could object—for whatever reason—he'd hopped into the car and spun out of the garage, closing the door in his wake.

"So?" she asked meaningfully, as we walked back into the house.

"So what?" God, *so much*, but I was done talking—I'd bled my quota during the early part of the day.

She let out a little snort of disbelief—but the matter dropped.

That night though, after a dinner of chicken and wine sauce (that I managed to pull off very well, thank you), she sat and played with her wineglass thoughtfully.

"Connor?"

"Yeah?" I said, loading the last dish into the washer. "You want dessert?"

"Always, but that's not why I'm talking. I . . ." She grimaced.

And I knew.

"You need to go back sooner." I got it, but I hated how needy I felt.

"Just a few days," she conceded. "Day after tomorrow—I already traded in the tickets. But there's more."

I sat down and poured myself the last of the bottle. Well, I'd used part of it to sauté the chicken. "Hit me."

She glanced up from her fingertip on the edge of the glass. Today had been another no makeup day for her, and I suddenly realized this was a privilege. It was like Vinnie and me, spending the day in bed without showering. *We* were the only ones who got to see that. I was one of the few who got to see Jilly like this.

All those years of being her "kids" and this was an unexpected reward.

"I thought about Vinnie today," she said, and I let out a bitter breath.

"Join the fuckin' club."

She concentrated on her finger again. The manicure was starting to chip.

"But, see, that's what I thought about. The tiny club of people who really knew Vinnie. I had this long conversation with him—I told him about your new project, and how you were getting back into television and that you liked the script and you were hoping you could stay a little longer if the audience liked you."

"Talk about getting ahead of yourself—"

"Shut up. I told him about that kid who took you out today, and how he . . ." She looked up and this time locked my gaze and held it. "How he seems really good for you, even if it doesn't go anywhere. And I told him how lost you've been, and how work is going to be good for you too, and how maybe, since you won't be trying so hard to take care of *him*, you might be able to work a little on your own career—"

"You shouldn't have told him that," I said tautly. "Jilly, you had no right—"

"I told him *now*, Connor, because *now* I can't hurt his feelings the way you and I were afraid to before."

"That's not fair. We worked together, we had a relationship, that's what you *do* in a relationship—"

"I told him this time I wouldn't make you stay in the closet," she said, voice shaking. "That if you came out, I'd find you work if I had to kick some producer in the balls, and that me and Vinnie, we were wrong to say you couldn't, and that the silence is killing you—"

"*Goddamn it, Jilly!*" I shouted, standing up and trying to hold back the tears. But I'd been fighting them for weeks—ever since I'd left the house that first time, to get my nails and hair done, they'd been burning in my throat, behind my eyes, and here, in front of Jilly, with her makeup off, I realized I was just as defenseless.

"Connor, I—"

"It was a good day," I told her, my voice broken with tears and nothing else. "I was just going to tell him it was a good day—why do we have to tell him all that other—"

"Because you deserve more good days," she sobbed.

And that was when I turned and left the room.

I don't remember getting undressed, and I'm pretty sure I didn't brush my teeth. But crying myself to sleep—*that* I remember.

I'm sorry, Vinnie. I didn't mean any of that. Jilly's talking out her ass—

She's right—

No.

Just, be honest, Con—

Shut up—

I held you back—

I don't want to talk about it.

Let's talk about two trips to rehab, and how you put your life on hold for me.

I don't want to.

Let's talk about how I wouldn't let us—

SHUT UP.

Okay. I still love you.

"I still love you, Vinnie. For always."

But I didn't hear his voice in the dark. I hadn't for too long a time.

The next day, true to his word, Noah came by and dropped off all the packages. He hung out with Jilly and me as we ran around the little rental and put all the kitsch in its appropriate place, and then, after we'd *ooh*ed and *ahh*ed at it all (and it looked *craptastic* if I say so myself), he produced the necklace I'd gotten for Jilly.

She pulled it out and lit up, like a little kid.

"Seriously? Con? This is awesome. What's this for?"

I blushed. "We blew off Christmas this year," I said, shamefaced because it was true.

"Yeah," she conceded. "What'd I get you?"

"You got me here." I waved my arms around the rental, but we both knew it was bigger than that. "And I don't know what you threatened the paparazzi with, but I'm telling you, I feel remarkably unmolested." The unthinkable hit me. "Do you think I'm just passé?"

She laughed, and the sound had an edge of hysteria. "I think the producers of this show and the town made a deal with the devil, that's what I think. But yeah—I've been pulling some strings, baby."

I felt suddenly weak. "I'm . . . I'm not going to disintegrate when you go home, am I?"

Because she was another living, breathing person in the house.

"No," she said, completely serious. She patted my cheek and then looked in wonder at the necklace. "Your heart is just as whole as it's always been." Then she met Noah's eyes and nodded. "You'd think that in his profession he'd be Mr. Cynicism, but he's not."

"I figured that out," Noah said dryly.

She patted his cheek—it was his turn—and then she held my gift to her chest. "I'm going to go have a little heart-to-heart with Vinnie," she announced, and before I could gasp—shock, horror, bewilderment—she ran up the stairs.

"You didn't do that," I told Noah, meaning it. "She'd already decided she was going to be tight with Vinnie's ghost before I got home yesterday."

"How about you?" he asked.

"Vinnie and I reached détente." I looked around the rental again, happy with all the new stuff, but suddenly constrained. "Did you bring your bike?"

He winked and nodded. He'd come dressed in cargo shorts and a hoodie again, and, hello, it was a uniform.

"You want to get out of here?"

"I thought you'd never ask."

He drove us out to the Forks area, to the Bogachiel Rain Forest, and I'm sayin', if you've never biked through a state park, well, you're missing something.

Driving through is nice—on the way to the trail you get the light, you get the sights, and if you lower the windows, you get the air, delivered in your face at full power.

But if you're riding a bike along bumpy roads, looking at fields of wildflowers and breathing air regularly scrubbed by hundred-year-old trees . . .

It's like being reborn.

And then Noah took me off the gravel road and onto the trail.

For a moment, I hated it, hauling my scrawny ass up that hill, one pump at a time, thighs and glutes screaming, arms trembling on the handlebars as I grunted, growled, and screamed up the hillside.

"God, you're noisy," Noah panted. "If you're this noisy during sex, it's a good thing *you* don't live upstairs from anyone."

"You . . . should be . . . so lucky . . ." I wheezed, stopping gratefully at the top of the hill where he was perched.

"Yes," he said, with one of those slow blinks of his that indicated he'd just had a very different thought. "Yes, I should."

For a moment, in a quiet forest, we stared at each other, and all of the things I hadn't said lingered between us.

"Are you sure that's a trail?" I said, desperate for *something* and looking at the downhill slope with a sort of bare patch through the fallen logs and big fucking rocks and not seeing anything resembling a path.

"Yes." He nodded.

"That's not a trail."

"Watch me."

And he threw himself and his pretty pink bicycle down that hill like there were werewolves on his ass.

With a startled "*Yeehaw!*" I did the same thing.

Oh yeah. I'd forgotten what this shit was like. Parasailing, horseback riding, wakeboarding—these were some of the rewards of keeping fit. The bike thumped down the hill, and I gave up trying to ride it and stuck with trying not to kill myself, shrieking all the way.

Glorious—fucking *glorious*—right up until the tree root rose up like an evil goblin. If I'd had more control, I would have jumped it, but I didn't, so I went ass over teakettle, sticking my foot hard while I tried to control my spill.

I ended up on my back, staring at the peaceful filter of leaves and needles, watching the sun dapple the forest floor with shade as the quiet returned and the world stopped roaring in my ears.

"*Connor*!"

Noah was running up the hill toward me, bicycle over his shoulder, and I had a moment to think he looked really amazing, rugged and hot and . . . well, worried as hell, as he bent over me in concern.

"Noah? Is that you?" I was dicking with him, and he knew it.

"You asshole. Are you okay?" He scowled, and the ruggedness disappeared, leaving him unbearably cute.

"Honestly, I think my ankle is . . . amok."

"Amok?" He propped his bike against a tree and bent down to offer me a hand.

"Amok," I confirmed, taking his hand and pulling—while putting my weight on the ankle that did *not* feel amok.

He took me in and grimaced. "Oh, Jesus, you're fifty percent road rash—Simon and Anna are never going to forgive me."

"Why you? You're not the asshole who just wasted yourself on a beginners' bike trail."

Noah shook his head. "Yeah, but I'm supposed to be protecting you—can you put any weight on it?"

"My ankle?"

"What else?" he asked, his sarcasm fully in place.

"Well, I'm sort of worried about my face!" God, you should hear the makeup people bitch if you got so much as an ingrown beard hair.

He squinted at me. "Yeah, we're going to need to call Junior before you go in to makeup, but don't stress. He's good. Now try the ankle."

I tried—gingerly—but it wasn't going to happen. And the road rash wasn't a joke—my chin, my cheek, my back, my knees—everything fucking stung, but I'd never been afraid of physical pain.

"Fuck," he muttered, as I tried and winced again. It was starting to swell visibly, looking like a ripe peach under my sock. "How are we going to get back?"

I looked at my bike, and the thing must have been built of ogre spit and adamantium, because nothing was bent, broken, or incapacitated. Hell, the paint was barely scratched.

"Okay," I said, using my reason and not my poor-poor-pitiful-me skills. "Bike still works—I was mostly coasting anyway. The road reconnects at the bottom of the hill, right?"

He cocked an eyebrow at me, like he didn't like where this was going. "Yesss . . ."

"So, you ride down to the bottom and go get the car, and I . . . you know, sort of coast down the hill and wait for you."

"That's a horrible idea," he said, like I hadn't seen it coming. "'How'd you lose *Wolf's Landing's* hottest property, Mr. Dakers?' 'Oh, I deserted him in the middle of the forest and he got eaten by a bear.' 'That was a bad idea, Mr. Dakers, how did that happen?' 'Well first I took him mountain biking and broke him, and then he couldn't outrun the fuckin' *bear*!'"

"Bears don't eat people," I told him.

"Yes, they do." He nodded so I would take this seriously.

"Well not often!" I laughed. "Now come on! I'm not getting heli-lifted off a bike trail for a sprained ankle. Now go down the hill and get our ride, and I'll just sort of . . . you know . . . do what I always do and fuck along feeling sorry for myself."

He shot me a glare. "You do *not* feel sorry for yourself!"

I snorted. "Tell that to the twenty-three million people who've seen me on YouTube." Yeah. I'd checked the stats that morning. Wiping out on the mountain bike was a picnic with pie, it really was.

He grimaced. "Look, I'm not going to—"

He still had one hand around my waist from my abortive attempts to walk, and I put my near hand on his shoulder, hoping it looked like camaraderie. "C'mon, Noah—don't take it so seriously. I'll be fine."

He grunted and avoided my eyes. "I don't want to do this."

"Clearly."

"You . . . you should not be left alone."

"Yeah, but I already tried suicide by mountain bike and failed. You've got nothing to worry about."

He swung his head around again, eyes blazing, lower lip thrust out in fury, and my brain caught up with the obvious. He *had his arm around my waist*, and we were *standing really close*.

So close I could feel the whoosh of his breath as he gasped in anger.

"Wha—"

He kissed me.

Surprise didn't even begin to . . .

He *kissed me*. Mouth crushing mine, hand coming up to hold my head still, tongue sweeping in to taste me.

I gasped and let him go deeper, harder, until I closed my eyes and conceded to the inevitable fact that I *really wanted this kiss*.

I moaned and let him plunder my mouth for another second, another minute, another breath, until *I* wanted more, and I turned my body, putting weight on my stupid ankle.

I let out a high-pitched shriek and stumbled. He caught me, holding me tight against his side, shoring me up when my body let me down.

There was a moment of roaring silence.

"You need to start down now," I said into it, not meeting his eyes. "Help me get on the bike, I'll be fine."

"Connor—"

"I can't talk about that." Oh, boy. I'd rather ride down the hill, swollen ankle and all. I'd rather do it twice. I'd rather ride back to town.

"Connor, nobody can see us here—"

"This has nothing to do with the press," I snapped, and for once, I was being completely truthful. "Not a goddamned thing."

"Then what—"

"What do you think?" Jesus. He'd been the fucking elephant in the car since Noah had picked me up. "*Who* do you think?"

Noah let out a frustrated growl, and stared at the sky. "You know, you'd have an easier time getting over him if you could ever, just once, fucking admit what you were getting over."

Oh, a thousand things surged to the tip of my tongue—some of them true and some of them cruel—but he didn't give me time to say them.

"Here—get on the goddamned bike." His words were surly, but he was gentle as a nurse as he held the bike and helped me swing up. I'd injured my left foot, which was lucky because I tended to use my right to prop up on. We worked for a moment to see if I could put my foot on the pedal, but that hurt too much. Instead, he pulled a towel from his pack and slung a loop of fabric around the strut of the bike, then, gingerly, he helped me stick my toe into it.

That worked. I could coast down the hill, taking most of the drag and the steering with my right foot, and my left foot was extended slightly out, with enough flexibility to move it so I didn't hyperextend my knee.

"You good?" he asked, worry etched between his eyes. In spite of the thing—the thing I didn't want to think about—that had just happened, I smiled.

"You fret too much," I chided, winking. "Now get down the stupid hill and get my chariot."

He shook his head, and then, like he had a right to me, he grasped my chin and gave me a hard, quick kiss. He hopped on his bike and left before I could formulate a response to that. The trip down was going to be so much worse than I let him believe.

I had to stop to get sick about halfway down. I'm not proud. Pain, exertion, and the fact that I hadn't eaten yet all combined to make me puke stomach acid in the brush.

The going was slow, miserable, and awkward—and by the time I reached the road, I could feel the sweat stinging in every pore of my body, not just the parts missing skin.

And all I had room for in my head was his kisses, and the things he'd said before and after the kisses, and the way I still missed Vinnie.

All of it.

And hey—the sprained ankle too.

But still, as confused as I was about Noah, about Vinnie, about my entire freaking life, I have to say that when I saw the car coming around the corner on the winding paved road, I thought he was the most beautiful thing I'd ever seen.

He helped me into the car and gave me some more water to rinse my mouth with, as well as some cloths and antiseptic so I could work on the road rash while he put the bike on the back. I unhooked my helmet wearily just as he got into the front, and he reached behind him and ruffled my hair.

"To the doc's?" he asked, hopefully, but I shook my head.

"Sprain," I muttered. "RICE—rest, ice, compression, elevation. You know the drill."

"But you have to be on set in four days!" Bitch, bitch, bitch.

I shrugged. "I don't trust doctors." That was the simple of it. That Vinnie had gotten his prescription meds from a guy who'd treated his tennis elbow with oxy was the more complex. "Trust me—I'll be okay."

He grimaced. "I don't believe you. If you can't put some weight on it by tomorrow, we're going to the doc."

I smiled, closed my eyes, and nodded, thinking, *One more reason to see him tomorrow. After Jilly leaves, of course.*

Maybe it was that thought—that I'd be alone and hurt in the house and Jilly would be gone—that prompted what happened next.

It didn't happen immediately. Immediately, I closed my eyes and let the shadows pattern the throbbing red of my lids. Immediately I let Noah's music—lots of Motown and blues—slow the thundering of my blood.

But the problem with knowing how to relax your mind and body is that it works. And once you're relaxed, allowing your endorphins to conquer the pain, it's hard to keep the truth at bay—from other people, or from yourself.

"We were lovers," I said into the silent car.

"I know," he responded gently. I was a coward because I couldn't look at his face when we did this. I could only see his brown eyes, flickering to the rearview when it was safe.

"From that first meeting," I said, half smiling, closing my eyes so I could see Vinnie, young and flirty, and irrepressible. He'd done what Noah had done—just kissed me, taken me, because I'd been so obviously ripe and for the taking. It hadn't occurred to me that I could still be that way.

"You little slut," Noah said, but he said it with a smile, like he didn't care.

"You have no idea," I muttered, and then, because I wanted him to know that it was real. "We . . . we didn't start out exclusive. We were just fucking around and sharing an apartment." Unvarnished truth. "But . . ."

"But it stuck," Noah filled in.

"Yeah."

"Uh, Connor?"

"Yeah?"

"I don't want you to go."

"Oh, thank God."

"You're not just saying that so you don't have to look for an apartment, are you?"

"I love you, Vinnie. Jesus, you're stupid."

"You do?"

"Yeah."

"Oh, thank God. I love you too."

"Connor?" Noah said, pulling me back from that sweet, sweet moment past.

"Yeah?"

"It's going to be all right. You know that, don't you? You're going to be all right."

I half laughed, but then I thought about it. I'd just wandered through the wilderness and found a friend. *Literally*. And figuratively. And with a hot bath and some antibiotic cream and a wrap, I'd be just fine.

And my heart might survive too.

"Thanks, Noah."

"I took you to the woods and broke you, Mr. Mazynsky. It's the least I could do."

I don't know why I thought that was funny—but I giggled most of the way home.

After Jillian called the makeup artist and told him to get ready for road rash on Monday, she fussed over me and I let her. Yes, I have a mommy complex; I'm not proud—it felt good to have a mom bring me a milkshake and make sure my ankle wrap was cold and give me ibuprofen. It felt even better to have her come up to my room and watch TV after Noah had left. He'd been remorseful and full of promises to be there in the morning to collect Jilly and her luggage, as well as to check on me and my injured body.

She sat next to me on the bed and snuggled, which was *not* a thing she would have done before Vinnie died, or before the last three weeks. We'd grown closer since that stupid video, clinging harder, because grieving alone had left us lost, but grieving together was just easier to do.

"You sure it's okay?" she asked for the umpteenth time.

"That you go?" I kissed the top of her head. She needed to get her hair done—her grays were showing through her bleach job. "Yeah."

"I'm leaving you all alone," she complained, working on peeling her polish some more.

"Jillian, you have a life. You have four ex-husbands, and kids who need you, and a really thriving business."

"Yeah." She sounded so sad. "But . . . but right now, you're the one friend who knows the worst things about me, and you still love me. Why would I want to leave that?"

I thought about it. Thought about the way we'd left things the night before. My arm tightened around her shoulders.

"Because now that we've said the hard things, we're free," I told her. "You can go to your kids and say, 'I'm not a saint. I've fucked up. But I've faced the hard things and you can too.'"

She shuddered against me. "Will that help?"

I let out a bitter laugh. "Oh, Jilly. You have no idea. None. It's helped *me*. It'll help them."

Was that why Vinnie had ended up in rehab *twice*? Because we'd never said the hard things—not to the press, not to his family, not to each other?

God. That was one question it was too late to ask.

"Connor?"

"Yeah?"

"I want us to stay like this. I promise, you know."

I looked down at her, but she was pretending to watch *The Expendables 3*. I wondered which of those guys she'd boned, because most of them were pretty rockin'.

"Promise what?"

She returned my gaze, eyes red-rimmed. "If you get a chance to stay here, do it. I promise I'll come visit. Next time I'll actually use the clothes I bring. I swear."

I smiled, thinking of all that luggage, and she'd showed up on set once and hung out in her sweats for less than a week. I kissed her forehead and gave thanks for her.

"Jilly, you are welcome. In any home I live in, you're welcome."

She nodded and settled in just a little closer.

The next day Noah arrived bright and early to pick her up. She'd done her face up and was wearing a white pantsuit that was pure LA, along with some four-inch patent-leather platforms that made her look bigger. She insisted on me staying in the bedroom, with the lunch she'd just made me, and the television and Netflix and my Kindle, and she hugged me long and hard before she left.

Noah watched the proceedings with a half smile on his face.

"I promise, Ms. Lombard, I'll take good care of him."

And just that quick her cynical agent was in place. "Yeah, I'll just bet you will," she muttered, rolling her eyes. "You just make sure the press conference is his idea—I don't like my girls knocked up or my boys outed without their consent, do you hear me?"

Noah widened his eyes in surprise and backed up, letting her sweep imperiously out the door and down the steps.

"I'll be back," he said softly.

"I don't want to talk," I warned, because I wasn't up for that. Not today.

He lifted a shoulder. "Who said anything about talking?" Like he hadn't been the driving force of my emotional reckoning. "I'll bring chess."

"I suck at chess. Bring Scrabble."

His smile blinded me again. "I rock at Scrabble. Bring it on."

They left, and I settled in for a nap and a read and some relaxation. When he got back, we played Scrabble, and then he made me dinner, we watched some television, and he left.

I lay in the dark, alone at home since that first morning after Jilly woke me up with a phone call to say I'd almost ruined my life—almost three weeks ago.

I realized that I didn't want wine. I didn't need Jilly. And while the promise of seeing Noah again the next morning made me happy, it wasn't what kept me from the wine.

It was the promise of *everything* that kept me from the wine. Of Noah, of Jilly as a friend, of the show that started in three days. It was the hope of more mountain biking, and shopping, and maybe some trips out into the sound. It was the idea that I could have friends here, like Carter and Levi, or Cheddar, or Noah's sisters whom I hadn't met.

I was lying alone in a dark house, but my thoughts weren't bleak or lonely.

I had hope. I had promises.

The thought alone let me close my eyes to sleep.

CHAPTER SEVEN

RUN LOLA RUN

W ell, I'd been right and wrong about RICE.

On the one hand, it *had* helped me get my mobility back in a relatively short amount of time—but the ankle was just not as stable as it should have been.

The day before we started shooting, Noah snuck me in to see a doctor *not* affiliated with the show, and he gave me some steroid injections—and told me to stay off the ankle.

Noah helped me set up a gym in one of the spare bedrooms so I could continue to work my upper body and core—but on the condition that I stay off the damned ankle.

And for the first two weeks of shooting, I basically walked in, hit my mark, and dialoged with the girls so we could figure out what to do with our poor pack, displaced out of time and space, and stranded in this strange world.

It was great stuff—stranger in a strange land is one of my favorite bits, and this was made even better by my character's intensity. He was such an object of pathos that I refused to play him for pity. I wanted people to admire his grit, his need to defend his pack, even as tiny as it was, and his determination to survive.

Man, as long as I could support most of my weight on my right foot, I was loving life.

And the days were long—so long. Nothing like shooting a twelve-hour day to kill your urges for any more soul searching than was absolutely necessary.

Noah was my driver, my employee, and, steadily, he was becoming my friend. But we didn't even have time to *talk* about those two kisses on the hilltop, much less allow them to happen again, and I was grateful.

For twelve hours a day, six days a week, I got to concentrate on being somebody new—complete with makeup.

For me, the makeup was sort of like the read-through: it wasn't supposed to be fun, but when you had to do it, it was also my favorite part.

So, Friday morning, as we were shooting outside in the first location, I wasn't actually stressing about *anything*. I was mostly just getting my full werewolf kit on for the last scene of the week (we hoped!) and bouncing my lines off Noah, since he tended to follow me around the dressing room and the set anyway.

"Oh, Mr. Montgomery," Junior, the makeup and prosthetics whiz muttered, "your ankle— It's . . . Are you sure it's okay if we put a prosthetic on that?" He'd done a bang-up job covering my road rash—if he was worried, I should take him seriously.

I looked down and grimaced. Yeah—still swollen, today especially because I'd been on my feet almost continuously the day before.

"Toldya," Noah grunted sourly.

I stuck my tongue out at him. "Yeah, Junior—go ahead and wrap an ACE bandage around it and cover it up. I can still walk on it—no big deal."

"What's no big deal?" Simon Conklin hopped into the trailer looking revved and excited as only a zealot to his profession *could* look. In the last two weeks I'd seen why Anna Maxwell had gone out of her way to recruit Conklin. Young enough to be energetic and cutting edge but old enough to have the patience to walk his actors through what he needed, I thought he was going to take this next season of *Wolf's Landing* through the top of the charts. I knew he was directing four of my eight episodes—this pleased me to no end. Yeah, I'd gotten some of my first breaks by blowing the boss—but I'd made up for every blowjob with hours upon hours of craftwork. I'd studied the greats, I'd read their biographies, their books on craft, the critics' works—you name it. One year, I downloaded the reading list for the drama classes from the local state college and made it my life's mission to read that shit.

I read plays from Albee to Ibsen, and damn if I didn't appreciate someone else who thought making science fiction was just as important if not more so than making contemporary drama.

"Nothing's up." I smiled at Simon, wanting to *not* be a pain in the ass. A couple of the writers had sounded me out about staying for longer than my established gig. I'd said yes—you bet your sweet ass I did—but the first thing you learn (usually after your first blowjob gets dismissed and forgotten) is that promises aren't worth jack until you sign the contract.

I really wanted to sign that contract. Being a speshul snophlake who got hurt at the drop of a hat was not the way to have that happen.

"Is Junior almost done here? We're moving right on schedule to get out of here by nine—just as long as you pretty much come out of the makeup trailer and onto the blood puddle, okay?"

Today's location shoot was carefully scheduled. First Wind and Swift (Lissa and Brenda, who had been doing an awesome job as my costars in our little pack) had been forced to kill a predator of the male rape-y kind. They'd filmed *their* scene about twenty minutes ago, and Noah's sister and the other gaffers had been dressing the set to make sure all the details they needed—entrails strewn on trees, tennis shoes ripped in two, that sort of thing—were in place. When the set dressers were done, Carter and Levi would go be the detectives and try to figure out why Mr. Sleezebucket Octopus Hands (as Lissa and Brenda had called him when they were running lines) had to die.

When they left, it would be my turn to come running up in werewolf form and decide whether to kill the detectives or to run off and find my pack. I pick the good guy option, which will make it harder to hate me, and the story goes on.

It meant I got makeup as soon as Brenda and Lissa left the trailer, and it meant I had to run through the woods, looking fierce and predatory and pissed off.

I thought I could fake it, and any residual pain would make me look fierce—I could use that!

So I was fine—patient, like you have to be in the makeup chair— and relaxed, right up until Conklin came up behind me and started rubbing my shoulders. No, I hadn't asked him to do that and, well— proximity alert!

I must have stiffened up because he gave an apologetic mutter.

"Sorry, man, usually I ask. I'm just trying to do the coach thing, right?"

He nodded like a little kid, and I nodded back and winked.

"I hear you," I said mildly. "Just, you know . . . getting to know people."

He nodded and patted my shoulder and then moved back. "So, the 'How ya doin', champ?' speech doesn't have as much pull when I'm not doing the massage thing, but I'll ask you anyway. How ya doin', champ? You up for the fight?"

I grinned at him in the mirror. "Oh yeah—definitely. I'm totally looking forward to this!"

And I was. Because once you get the makeup on, being in the role was so much cooler.

"Really?" And Conklin sounded like that favorite best friend from grade school again. "You're like, the only actor I've heard say that!"

I grimaced. "Well, it's easier since they haven't started working on my face yet—but I'm looking forward to it—lots of 'loping' if I read the script right."

Conklin tilted back his head and laughed, and I thought again how handsome he was. Silver strands in his brown hair, piercing blue eyes, a long, angular face that normally I would have found quite attractive.

Maybe if Noah hadn't been glaring at the two of us in the mirror.

I caught Noah's eyes and crossed mine, making him roll his own eyes and smile. *Yeah, he's cute, and he's my boss, but he's not you so just deal.*

I should have questioned, right then and there, that we even had to have that sort of eyeball-rolling conversation, but that's when Junior pulled—hard—on my foot to get it into the prosthetic, and I had to concentrate one hundred percent on my acting.

I'm doing fine, nothing to see here.

Even the trailer smelled like redwoods and ocean. And *nothing* reminded me of Vinnie.

God, I wanted to stay in the Pacific Northwest.

"Mr. Conklin," said a young voice, "they're ready for you on the set."

"Sure thing, Viv!"

I looked toward the door and waved, because Noah's little sister always made me smile. Not nearly as tall as her brother—but not short either—Viv Dakers was a *stunningly* beautiful girl. Where Noah's hair did big, glossy, springy curls, Viv's were tight ringlets, unapologetically African American—and she wore them big and poofy, like springs sticking out all over her head.

Everything about Viv was unapologetic and stunning, from full lips that she painted bright red to big-hooped earrings that were probably impractical but I couldn't see her giving up unless they snagged on something. She wore a tight yellow T-shirt and mildly bell-bottomed jeans, and damn, she was good at her job.

I could see why Cheddar was solid gone in love with her—and why he'd be sure she'd move on and leave him in the dust.

But I'd chatted her up in the last week, and I didn't think Cheddar had anything to worry about.

Viv might go to college after she'd saved up enough money, but she was as obsessed with Cheddar as he was with her.

It sort of gave me heart to know they were young and in love, and there was something so vibrant and wholesome about Viv that pretty much everyone on the set responded to that romantic possibility in her.

If Viv thought something wasn't right, it didn't matter that she was low man in the company, people would by golly listen to her before they dismissed her intuition out of hand.

So Conklin didn't dismiss her when she told him it was time to go. Instead he gave me one more animated wave before rabbiting out of there, probably so he didn't have to try *not* to touch me.

Noah waited until we could hear Conklin shouting instructions to the cameraman before he spoke.

"He likes you," Noah said. There wasn't any recrimination in his voice—but he wasn't all hearts and flowers about Conklin either.

"He does that to all the actors," I muttered, blushing.

"No, he doesn't," Junior said, applying glue to my ankle. "I think Simon has had a crush on you since he and Anna talked about getting you for the part."

Oh God. "That's really flattering," I said, meaning it. "But I'm pretty sure he's crushing on the actor, not the guy."

Junior looked up at me and rolled his eyes. "I'm straight," he said, raising a triple-pierced eyebrow over a narrow, freckled nose. "I've got a girlfriend. She's cute—goth like me, likes helping me come up with concepts. Nice girl. I'm gonna marry her next year, and we're gonna dye our hair green together for the ceremony. You're invited if you're still here."

I stared at him, bemused, wondering where the hell this was coming from. "That's, uh, great, but, uh—"

"I would totally crush on you, Mr. Montgomery. You're so hot you're making me question my own sexuality, and the last person to do that was Carter Samuels. Now are you going to promise not to go mountain biking again? I mean, I covered the stuff on your face, and I can just use this as part of your werewolf persona and deal, but I'm saying, you are not making my job any easier."

"I was on the easy trail," I mumbled, completely mortified. In the mirror, Noah was laughing so hard he couldn't breathe. "A tree root reached out and grabbed me. Not my fault, I swear."

"See?" Junior shook his head, his floppy purple hair falling into his eyes. "Even your fuckups sound more spectacular than a regular person's. If you don't want Conklin to hit on you, you're going to have to give him the 'I'm sorry, you're a great guy, but I'm not interested' speech."

I don't know—maybe it was the pain in my ankle, or the way Noah had been looking at me for two weeks. Maybe it was that epiphany that Vinnie wasn't coming home and I was going to live through it.

But I had to ask.

"Why not the 'I'm sorry, I'm straight' speech?"

Junior was this tall, thin guy with a big nose and a big Adam's apple—one of those skinny people like Noah with the bigger-than-life voice.

He had a laugh that shook the trailer.

I stared at him, appalled.

"Am I missing something?" Oh, Jesus—I'd followed the press since my YouTube disaster. I had. And yeah—the fangirls had gone apeshit in the archives, and there'd been some tabloid speculation as well. But nothing for certain. Nobody had reported lip-reading "Vinnie I miss your cock!" from that damned video. *Everybody* has done the primal scream thing, and hey—who *didn't* burst into uncontrollable sobbing? It was all as it had always been—pure speculation—which was something everyone in the limelight had to live with, straight, bent, or very, very gay.

Junior's expression took "bewildered" to a whole new level. He looked at Noah for help. "Seriously?" he asked.

Noah looked back, equally puzzled. "What? I'm not seeing it either."

Junior shook his head and finished gluing a fur ruff above my knees. I'd shaved my legs in prep for this, and I had to congratulate myself on my forethought—one way or another, I was losing that hair.

"*You!*" Junior said, half laughing. "*You* are looking at him like . . . like I look at my girlfriend. It's written all over you, and he's . . . I don't know. Is it an artist thing?" And it sounded like he was asking himself. "I mean, I have to *think* about makeup and try to get inside a person's head—is that it?"

He squinted at me, for confirmation.

"I'm sorry?" he said, still second-guessing himself. "I didn't mean to . . ." And then, like it had just occurred to him that he held my career in his hands and he'd made a major gaffe, "I shouldn't have said anything," he mumbled, looking down. "Here—let me coat your face with the gel and we can put the mask on."

I could smell the flop sweat and the embarrassment coming off him, saw flashing in front of my eyes all the ways I could fuck up his career if he was wrong, or, hell, if he was right but spoke out of turn.

God. It was so stupid. This kid hadn't done anything wrong—he hadn't made any judgments regarding gay or straight—he'd just observed human behavior and had come to a conclusion. If there was nothing wrong with being gay, then there was nothing wrong with making the wrong guess, now was there?

And certainly nothing wrong with making the right one.

"It's okay," I said with a gentle smile. "I'm not . . ." The lie wouldn't come. "Out." I finished. "Not out. Maybe three people in the world know. Two."

"Three," Noah said behind me, and I met his eyes.

Yeah—I could see the hunger now, acknowledge that was how he'd been looking at me for the past weeks. He hadn't crowded me, hadn't forced my hand. I hadn't told him no, so he was just letting me know what he wanted.

It was starting to make my mouth dry and my heart hammer, what I knew he wanted.

"And now me," Junior said, like he was trying to keep it light. He started rubbing the gel on my face that would make removing the prosthetic mask and the glue a lot easier. "Don't worry. It'll stay that way. I just . . . you know. Carter and Levi, Simon, Anna—they're so out. You get used to an 'out' set. I way overstepped."

"You were human," I said, meaning it. "You're right. It shouldn't be a thing. If I'd been a stronger person back in the day, it wouldn't have been."

Noah was frowning at me, like that didn't completely match what he knew, but I wasn't going to talk about that now. I didn't care what Jillian had said. I didn't want to talk about that *ever*. When someone was *dead* you didn't get to have that argument with him, did you? When someone was *dead* you got to forgive him for any lingering resentment, for that little automatic whine every time you talked to the press about the girl you'd been seen with the night before. For the mad jealousy that crushed your chest when other people, braver people, posted their FB and Instagram photos of their husbands and their adopted children and their homes together and their perfect lives.

When someone was dead, you let that shit go, right? Because otherwise you'd be bitter about it, and hurt, that your life had been squashed down to the last nth of breath because the person who topped in bed didn't always make the best decisions in life, now did he.

"Okay, Mr. Montgomery—"

"Connor's still fine, Junior," I said, breathing my anger at Vinnie out. It had no place with this kid who'd caught *his* first big break on *Face Off* and his reward had been working this show.

"Connor," he mumbled. "Thanks. But now's when we put the mask on and do the makeup around it so, you know the drill . . ."

"Be vewy vewy qwiet," I said in my best Elmer Fudd. "And vewy vewy thtill."

"Yes, sir," Junior agreed, getting the werewolf prosthetic from the hairdresser's dummy. "Any last words?"

"I should have been a plastic surgeon?" I quipped, and I took my courtesy laugh from both of them as a blessing.

And then I shut up. I was good at it—hell, taping the YouTube selfie with no sound had proved that if anything had.

The shoot was going great—fantastic, even. I'd cut the loping scene, the sniffing scene, the roaring scene—all of it fun stuff, back to Acting 101: "How to be an animal." I mean, no lines, right? So the ultimate in expression—doubly intense, so you could see it through the mobile prosthetic—and body language and . . .

Well, fun.

Conklin called cut for the final bit, and I stopped my lope into the woods and turned back around on my good foot. I'd developed this way of standing like I was hip-cocked, but in reality? I was holding my left foot off the ground because the pain right now was burning a hole in my brain.

"Good shit, Connor—we're almost done. What I want now is one smooth take, from beginning to end. We don't do a lot of those shots in television, but I've got a good feeling about this. You game?"

I nodded and smiled. "Absolutely!" I said brightly. *Oh for fuck's sake, I need to take some goddamned Motrin and some turmeric and beg Noah or Junior to get me some motherfucking ice!* "Happy to do it!"

I limped back to my original mark—I couldn't help it—but Simon was talking to his cameraman and light man so they didn't notice.

Viv noticed. "Connor?" she asked quietly while she restrung some fake entrails I'd moved. "You okay?"

"Peachy," I said through gritted teeth. "This is the last take of the day. I can make it."

"Good." She looked at her brother in the corner of the set. "But I'm telling Noah to come help you back to the trailer when this is done. You're not walking too great."

I wondered if Noah had told her about my mountain bike mishap. Probably, because the two of them couldn't sit in the same room without giving each other affectionate and mountainous rations of pure-grade sibling shit. Those kinds of people did not hold back on things like, "Hey, I almost broke Connor Montgomery today!"

"I'll be fine," I said, making a conscious effort to relax my jaw. "Okay . . . here we go . . . mark."

I crouched at the mark and waited for Simon to call action.

Okay—lope, lope, lope, lope under the darkening sky, pause, sniff, scowl, growl, look around, lope . . . lope, lope, lope . . . sniff around the crime scene, growling, smell the handkerchief Brenda had dropped, the branch Carter touched, the tree Levi leaned against, growl . . . smell the fight scene with leftover body parts again— My girls! What has happened to my girls! Wind! Swift! Oh, girls, how could this monster have touched you! I threw my head back and *ran*, not loped, bending over as the CGI effects would change me into a wolf—

And my ankle gave out completely, my momentum and posture throwing my body forward in a spectacular roll as I let out a sound that defied description.

I ended up on my back, vision red with pain, tamping down on whimpers in my throat with everything I had.

"Connor?"

"Noah?" I still had my eyes closed.

"No, sir, it's Simon."

Oh hell. I opened my eyes. "Sorry," I apologized reflexively. "Is, uh, Noah nearby?"

Noah was not a trained actor, dancer, or stuntman—a buffalo would have made less noise through the carefully preserved fauna of the outdoor set. "Connor?" His voice pitched up in irritation. "Man, you should have said something!"

"Did we get the take?" I asked Simon, just as Noah hip-checked him to the side to peer over me.

Simon gave Noah a dirty look before turning back to me. "Uh, yeah—right down to that . . . well, really wonderful sound you made at the end. I mean, I think we're going to have the mixers see if we can merge that with a wolf howl—it could be iconic." He nodded manically. "I mean, that sound—that could be the show's *trademark*!"

I smiled weakly. "That's . . . uh, good to know." I was still on my back in the dirt. "Noah, could I have a hand up?"

"Here," said Simon, "let me—"

Noah ignored him, offering his crossed arms to help me up. We knew this drill—had, in fact, been doing versions of it since my tumble down the mountain—and I popped up easily—and then winced.

He caught my weight on his shoulder, and I relaxed into him.

"Fuck," I muttered.

Conklin crouched down by my ankle and started peeling away the prosthetics while I tried not to be a bigger baby.

"Don't forget to set those aside for Junior," I said. "And . . . you know, don't worry. It's—"

"Oh dear Lord—it's *purple!*" Conklin said, standing up and regarding me in horror. "Connor, what did you *do?*"

"I just . . . uh, took a tumble. It's been . . . you know . . . getting better. I swear. I'll be on it again on Monday—"

"You're going to the doctor's," Conklin said, sounding no-bullshit and take-charge.

"I've got him on speed dial," Noah muttered, giving Conklin an unfriendly look. "This time we're going in."

I was tired, and tired of hurting, and, oh God, Noah felt so good.

"Yeah," I mumbled, putting some more weight on Noah's shoulder. God, he felt like rocks and shoe leather—could probably carry my scrawny ass like I was a five-year-old. "That's fine. Just . . . here, help me to the trailer. Junior can take off the biggest pieces while you get the car."

Conklin got on my other side, and I let him sort of help, but the truth was, I could really only put my weight on Noah.

It just felt safer that way.

The set doctor came and looked at the ankle, then gave me a reproving look and told me I'd need X-rays. Conklin hovered the whole time, he and Noah competing for space like electrons in an unstable gas. I finally just grabbed Noah's hand and told him to

"*Sit down!*" so Conklin could walk around excitedly and talk with his hands about the phenomenal sound I'd just made.

"It *was* pretty spectacular," Noah confided as Conklin conferenced with the doctor. "Can't blame the guy for wanting to use it."

"I'm just glad I didn't scream like a horror-movie queen," I told him honestly. "That sound bite would compromise my manhood."

Conklin looked up sharply as the doc left the trailer. "Your manhood's intact, Connor. Is *that* why you didn't address this on the set before it went out from under you?"

I blushed, feeling like a kid. God, my dad had been quick to yell and quicker with the belt. "No, sir," I said quietly. "That wasn't it at all."

The guy had that head-swish/eyebrow combination thing—the one that made it so he didn't have to ask the obvious question. Yeah— he used it now.

I looked at his raised eyebrow when I answered, because I *am* twelve. "I . . . you know. I like it here." I smiled prettily, hoping the boyish charm would work.

Conklin's eyebrow could really defy some fuckin' gravity, I'm just saying. "Why would you think we wouldn't want you to stay?" He flailed big, capable hands. "I've got the writers working right now to make your part bigger—I practically had to *blow* Hunter Easton, but he's reworked most of the season for you."

"Kevin must have loved that," Noah whispered, and I glared at him. Conklin was still going off though, so we let him.

"I mean, I know we haven't done contracts yet but . . . but you're *Connor Montgomery!*"

I was tired of watching his eyebrows and his hands and that boundless energy. A month ago I'd been unable to get out of bed. Right now, I tilted my head back and closed my eyes. "Yeah—I'm Connor Montgomery. I'm the guy who had the mental breakdown on YouTube and left *Warlock Tea* because I was an asshole. Don't think I don't know that shit's gonna hurt my rep."

I opened my eyes to see Conklin staring at me. Suddenly his entire posture softened. "Uhm . . ." He closed his eyes and pinched the bridge of his nose. "I know why you left *Warlock Tea*," he said, shocking me badly.

"Film career," I said blithely. "I gave interviews."

"I knew Vinnie, Connor."

I stared at him, and he stared back, as though willing me to guess all that could mean. Oh God. I looked at Noah for a moment, because Noah had come to mean safety to me in the past weeks. Noah's head was cocked and one of his eyebrows was doing the same raised thing.

He was the one who asked the obvious question. "Biblically?"

Conklin flushed.

"Oh," I said, not sure what to do with the rush of *everything* that hit my chest. Vinnie hadn't always been strong—even after we'd committed, and moved into the apartment together. There had been times when I'd come back from a shoot and he'd needed to use a condom until his health screen came back. Not every time, or even a lot of the time. A handful of times. Few enough times for me to know he really did love me best. Many enough for me to know that wasn't easy for him to do.

"He told me what you did for him." Conklin couldn't make eye contact. "It was . . . it was hard for him. He, uh . . . didn't like . . ."

"Didn't like cheating," I said, because Conklin was wussing out. "It's okay. I knew it happened sometimes—not you specifically, of course, but . . ." I thought of the small box—the twelve pack—of condoms that Vinnie always kept fresh. I was never sure if it was because he was unsafe when he cheated, or because he just wanted to make double safe with me—but I didn't care.

"Con, uh . . ."

"Oh. Well, easy clean up."

"You know I love you."

"I know, Vinnie. Don't worry. I'm just glad to be home."

And I was—Vinnie had been my home.

"Well, just—you know. *I* know you're not a risk. *I* know why you left *Warlock Tea*. I know why you'd have a . . . God, Con. The way he talked about you—I'm surprised you didn't go stark-raving bonkers in public sooner. But then I guess we both know which one of you was stronger."

My ankle throbbed, and I scrubbed my face with my hands. Well, at least I knew why Conklin had been so creepy touchy with me—he felt like he knew me. He'd fucked my closet boyfriend.

But even then, I couldn't be that uncharitable. He'd felt close to Vinnie. And by default close to me.

And he'd just been really fucking human.

"Oh, Con . . . Simon?" Noah was trying to sound humble—and failing. "Uh . . . don't take this the wrong way but—"

"I'm gone," he said quietly. I didn't flinch from his hand on my shoulder. "I'll have Anna get Jillian the contract by Monday. Please stay. This show's so good with you."

"Thanks," I said automatically. "Yeah. Of course I'll stay."

And then he was gone, and I was alone with Noah.

"You knew?" And bless him, he didn't sound judgmental, not even a little.

"Like I said, not with who. It . . . I was gone a lot. Vinnie wasn't . . ."

"Strong," Noah filled in. "I get it. So, why *did* you leave *Warlock Tea?*"

I shook my head, not wanting to do this, not now. "Noah—" I all but begged.

"Got it. Let's get to the car and get you on some pain meds."

"No pain meds," I muttered. "RICE."

"All weekend," he said grimly, and then he squatted next to me so I could throw my arm around his shoulder. He straightened, and I pushed, and in a moment I was hopping across the trailer. We got to the steps, and Noah made me hold on to the doorframe so he could walk down and steady me as I hopped some more.

God, by the time I got to the car, I was sweating and pissed.

"You know what?" I bitched as he slid me into the backseat.

"You want me to sell your mountain bike?" he asked before shutting my door and getting into the front seat.

"No," I snarled, using my adrenaline. "I want to get better so I can ride that thing again. I'm going to ride it, and I'm going to *scream* down that goddamned hill, and I'm going to show it who the fuck is the fucking boss. *That's* what I'm going to do. And then I'm going to go down a bigger hill. I'm going to go down hills so steep I need a fucking parachute to get on the trail in the first place. I'm *tired* of this shit. I'm *tired* of things hurting. I'm *tired* of wanting to hide my head under a pillow and scream and cry and sleep. I'm fucking *tired* of pain. I'm going to make pain my *bitch*, and I'm going to fly down that fucking mountain with my hair on fire, screaming bloody murder all the— *Ouch*!"

There was a cattle guard in the driveway of the property we'd leased for the outdoor sets. Going over that fucking set of pipes almost made me throw up.

"Sorry about that," Noah said gently.

"Don't be sorry," I bitched. "Not your fault. I'm tired of pain, I just want to live my life without any fucking pain."

"Yeah, sure," he soothed. "But first, you've got to heal."

Neither of us were talking about the ankle, and both of us knew it.

"Yeah, fine," I muttered. "I'll fucking heal. I don't have to be gracious about it."

Noah laughed softly, and I knew what he was going to say before it came out of his mouth. "And we have the video to prove it!"

"Augh!"

I shut up and seethed for the rest of the trip.

By the time we were done with the X-rays and the bandaging and the brace fitting and, yes, the pain medication that I finally relented and agreed to take, I was too exhausted to seethe. I was too exhausted to *talk*. In fact, about the only thing I had the energy to do was to fold my arms in front of me, tuck my head in the corner of the door and the seat, and fall asleep. I woke up at the end of the forty-five minute drive, as Noah was parking the car.

He got out and opened the door for me, handing me the hated and dreaded crutches.

"Ugh."

"Yeah, well, get used to them. When you're not standing on the set, that's your default for the next two weeks."

I glared. "I can do water aerobics and weight lifting," I reminded him, and he rolled his eyes.

"Yeah. There's a pool at the Global—if you want I'll have Anna get you permission to go swim there in the mornings. Are we done being a diva who has to keep his body perfect now?"

"You seemed so sweet when we first met." I glared at him. "Who knew?"

"I'm a philosophy major, Connor. Sarcasm is our defense against the workforce disappointment."

"Ha." I started to hobble forward, letting him open the garage door for me. He followed me into the house, taking one of the crutches and holding my arm while I used the banister to make it up the stairs.

"Ha what?"

"You have the world's greatest job at the moment," I told him facetiously. "You get to watch me completely implode *and* shuttle me to exciting places like hotels and doctors' offices. You have nothing to complain about."

He took my arm over his shoulders as we cleared the landing, and held the crutches in his opposite hand. I leaned on him until we got into the bedroom.

"Can you pee standing up, or do you have to do number two?" he asked in all seriousness, and I . . .

I did not take that very well.

I collapsed on the bed, laughing my ass off.

"Number two? Oh my God—did you just ask me if I have to take a crap? Because—"

"Yeah, I get it—"

"I mean, I know the paparazzi can be intrusive sometimes—"

"Yeah, there was probably—"

"But, Jesus, Noah—not even Vinnie used to ask me if I had to take a crap!"

Noah rolled his eyes. "I'm sure he didn't. Vinnie was perfect and saintly in all things."

"No, he wasn't."

"Did I *mention* the *sarcasm*? Now do you have to go sit down and have private time for a while or what?"

I thought about it. "Naw," I said, suddenly sober. "Just let me pee and brush my teeth. I'll . . ." Fuck. "We need to buy one of those shower seats, don't we?"

Noah let out a sigh through his nose. "Yeah. I'll bring it tomorrow."

I tried not to whimper. I still had makeup and glue all over my face and my chest and my legs. "Good thing I shaved my legs," I mumbled, trying to find *something* good.

Noah was still thinking. "Here—tell you what. Go pee and brush your teeth and undress—I'll be right back." He handed me the crutches and disappeared.

By the time he got back, I was sitting on the john with a towel wrapped around my waist, feeling like I was about to get a proctology exam.

And then Noah rounded the corner, stripped to a tank top and boxers, a plastic stool in one hand.

I stared at him, feeling stupid. "Uh—"

"Relax," he said, quirking that full mouth to the side. "I'm not here to molest your pure virgin body—"

I snorted.

"—but that suit costs a fortune to dry clean."

"Why were you wearing the suit today?" I asked, distracted. "Weren't you wearing jeans and—"

"Conklin asked me to dress today—I shuttled a couple of people to the airport while you were in wardrobe and before you went to makeup."

A little part of me got all pissy at that—he was *mine* damn it—but now, wearing a towel while he was down to his skivvies, was probably not the time nor place to go all weird and possessive on him.

"Yeah, I forgot," I said. My eyes were getting a little glassy, taking him in. Dark-brown skin, all over. Viv had told me their mother had been part African American and their father was all Native American. Between their bone structure, skin tone, and gut-punching smiles, the two of them were doing the world a disservice by *not* being on screen.

He had stringy, knotty, mountain biker's muscles, and the surprising flash of pink over healing road rash on his wrists, his knees, on the side of his thighs. His knees were a little knobby—but his legs were muscular enough and that would probably go away with time—and his clavicle was pronounced and vulnerable. His neck—still thin from the vestiges of childhood—seemed impossibly long sticking out of the sweat-stained tank—but overall, he was rangy and loose-limbed, strong, and so, so heartbreakingly beautiful.

I wanted to run my palms over that magnificent skin to see if it was as warm to the touch of my hands as it was to the touch of my eyes.

It had been a long day for him too, and part of me wanted to just say, "Fuck it, Noah—take it all off—I definitely want to see you naked!"

But that seemed disrespectful somehow. He'd been so . . . so respectful. So kind. Coming on to him like a drunken whore was not where we were at right now.

But watching as he busied himself with the stool in the shower and getting the water temperature just right, it occurred to me that . . . oh God. Someday I'd really, really like to be.

A little draft in my nether regions warned me that my body was getting *really* excited at the possibility.

Noah stood back and grinned at me, looking . . . young. Young and proud of himself. "See there?" he asked, sweeping the shower curtain back. "Here, let me get your brace—" he dropped to the floor and started unhooking the Velcro "—and then you can get in."

I let him, because what was I going to say? *Hey, uh . . . I'm starting to lust after you in a big way, which is funny, because I haven't really thought about sex in a meaningful context going on fourteen months, and you know what? It's great that I can get a boner around you, but we've got to pretend that it's not happening, okay?*

No. I wasn't going to say that.

I didn't have to. Reluctantly, I dropped the towel, allowing Noah to support my weight while I swung my good leg into the tub—and my erection said it for me.

Noah waited until I was in the shower, the hot water pounding on my back, before he said anything.

"Well, at least I know you're happy to see me."

I hid my face in the washcloth and scrubbed. After a minute I needed to breathe, so I looked up and said, "Was there ever any doubt?"

Noah took the cloth from me and pumped some face wash on it, then started to scrub away all the gunk I'd missed. "No," he said softly, while I kept my eyes averted. "I know you're happy to see me, Connor."

He moved the cloth to my throat, his motions gentle.

"I . . . you know—"

"You can't right now," Noah filled in for me. "Shocked, yes, I am *shocked* that a debauched and wanton movie star would not want to have sex slightly more than a year after the love of his life died in a tragic accident."

"You say 'debauched' like I wasn't. I—" My voice dropped, because suddenly I didn't want him to know how bad it had been.

"Are you beating yourself up for taking a nap on the casting couch?" he asked, just the right amount of amusement in his voice.

"You don't *nap* on the casting couch," I said sullenly. "And yes, I would know."

"I am neither shocked nor disgusted," Noah said cheerfully. "You'll have to find something else to destroy"—he rubbed a knuckle over my clean wet cheek—"my faith in you."

I looked at him unhappily. "I've got nothin'." I was not sure where I was supposed to go with that.

"That's a lie." He sounded unhappy. "You've got *plenty*—you're just not letting anyone see it."

"What's that supposed to mean?"

He shook his head, the gentleness gone. "I'm going to get your ankles and legs. Let your bad ankle go limp, and I'm going to tell you which way I'm going to move it, okay?"

So the question just festered in my stomach while he scrubbed—very impersonally I might add—all of the body makeup and glue off.

Then he rinsed out the cloth, pumped some scented soap on it, and handed it to me. "I'm going to turn around now and let you get your privates. Tell me when you're done, and I'll wash your hair."

A part of me wanted to tease him—coward!—but he was being . . . considerate. And sweet.

I made short work of my privates and underarms and told him he could turn back.

"You're like a real Boy Scout." I smiled tiredly. Now that I no longer stank, my body was about to call it quits. "What, do you help little old ladies cross the street in your spare time?"

"Just trying to earn my spot next to Saint Vinnie," he said, and hurray, the sarcasm was back.

"He wasn't a saint," I told him, my voice stony. And then, with a flash of bitterness I was too weak to hold back, "And after that little talk with Conklin, you know it."

"Yeah, I was wondering when you were going to get pissed about that."

"Too late to get pissed." I'd meant the words lightly, but my voice had a tremor in it I thought I was over.

"Never too late to get pissed." He stretched to get a towel from the rack above the toilet, and I realized I could see right through his wet underwear. Part of me was like *Sweet! Look at that—he's uncircumcised!* And the other part of me was numb and indifferent.

I wasn't sure which part I wanted to win.

The towel around my shoulders snapped me out of it, and I dried off my own hair and creases. Noah wrapped his arm around my shoulders and hefted me up, and then, in a surprising show of strength, all but lifted me out of the tub. I leaned against him and closed my eyes.

"It's okay, you know," he said quietly, voice right next to my ear.

"What's okay?"

"You can be mad at him."

"I'm not."

"God's gonna hit you with lightning," he said, completely serious.

"Good," I retorted. "Will you take the press conference on that?"

He smoothed the damp hair back from my face and kissed my forehead—it was an intimate gesture, but curiously sexless. "I saw your press conference," he said. "After Vinnie died."

"I gave a press conference after Vinnie died?" I was genuinely surprised—I couldn't remember doing that.

Noah laughed without humor, and pressed his lips against my temple. We were wet and mostly naked, and humming like a live wire under a carpet was my dormant sex drive, but it was running on a sad, limp charge.

"They got you at your house—and you could see, in the background, that some of the curtains had been ripped down. And you—your eyes were sunk in, your cheeks were hollow. I've seen extras in zombie flicks look better. And you stood up and said, 'My f . . . my f . . . my *Vinnie* isn't coming home ever again.'"

Oh God. "All of Hollywood knows, doesn't it?"

"No." He shook his head. "Because all your passion was put into *not* saying the truth. Didn't leave us with anything else to believe."

"I'm so tired," I mumbled, sagging in his arms. Tired of hurting, tired of lying, tired of trying to keep it all together. "I've only been here a couple of weeks, and I'm exhausted."

"You know," he said, like it was no big deal, "maybe just come out to the set? Come out to Anna Maxwell, come out to Carter and Levi? Just give yourself permission to talk about him like you guys were a thing. See if you're not so tired then, okay?"

"Sure." Anything. "Just—"

"Bed."

He helped me into a pair of boxer shorts and for just a moment, as his hand skimmed my thigh, his touch didn't feel impersonal—and the flush of blood to my thighs and my groin didn't feel like exhaustion.

He made a little "heh" sound and then gave my ass an unmistakable caress before rubbing my bare back.

Then he helped me into bed and pulled the covers up to my chin.

"I really did use to be a slut," I told him mournfully, missing my sex drive for the first time in ever.

"I do not doubt it."

"I mean, in the good way too. I'd go down on you in a hot second, you know—"

"Before Saint Vinnie."

"You sound way too bitter for one so young," I said sagely, before bursting into giggles.

He stood, perhaps using super-special intuition to know that I was cooked and done. "I'm gonna crash in your guest room if that's okay." He put a hand on my shoulder, and that quickly the giggles were over.

"Could you stay in here for just a minute?" I pleaded, surprised at myself. "Just until I'm asleep?"

I felt his weight on the bed and his hand on my shoulder. "Sure," he said softly, reaching over to turn off the lamp.

His steady breathing, his hand, warm and reassuring, the knowledge that he'd be under my roof, just for a night.

Knowing he didn't judge me for being young and desperate in Hollywood.

Vinnie, I want him to stay all the time.

Yeah, sure, Con. That'll be good.

Can I do that and still miss you?
I don't know—can you?
I fell asleep still wondering.

CHAPTER EIGHT

The Ocean

Have you ever written in the sand?

You think that first wave is going to just eliminate *everything*, but it doesn't. No—there's scar tissue on an ephemeral tablet, little bumps and ridges and reminders that there was something important there, and just because it's gone *now* doesn't mean it didn't exist—

Oh! Oh! See what happened there? The next wave came and took it out for good. And all that's left is a blank canvas and what are you going to write on it now?

People in LA have sand castle contests, where they slave for hours to build fantastic creations—they have different kinds of sand/water mixes and they know how to cement the thing they want to build so it will last ... last ...

Until it dries out completely and crumbles.

Until the tide rushes in—take your pick.

The thing I learned about loving Vinnie for ten years was that every day could be the wave that washed the love away. You had to wake up *every day* and text or kiss or call or sneak over and surprise. You had to wake up *every day* and write that thing on the tablet of time to make sure that would be the day when your love was written on the sand.

But see, here's where the metaphor breaks down. Because you'd think that if love could be washed away so easily when we're alive, then the hurt—that would go away just as easily when the person is gone. But it's not that way at all. It's like their absence etches the love into bedrock with a power drill. One wave didn't wash it away. Ten waves didn't. Hell, nearly fourteen months of days just sort of cleaned it a little, made the edges nice and sharp and painful, so you sliced your heart on them every time you read your love.

But you wake up the next day anyway, and if you're lucky like me, you have a friend in the next room to help you get dressed and to pass the time with.

And then you wake up the next day—alone maybe—but your friend is still on the phone, texting to make sure you're getting your lame ass out of bed and asking if you want to go swimming later, even though it's his day off and he has no obligation whatsoever to haul you anywhere.

He does it because he's your friend.

And then you wake up the next day and it's easier to walk, but he takes you swimming before work anyway, and you have a pretty awesome day.

That night, you get a call from your agent saying you can keep having days like that—hell, you're even invited to Comic-Con next month with all your new friends for a panel—and she wants to know if your special friend is going to come along.

"Uh," I said, feeling stupid.

"He's welcome to," she said delicately. "I mean, you've got guest rooms in the beach house—in fact, I'll get someone to air the place out and stock it for you. You can have anybody you want there for the weekend before and drive down early that morning. Ask around—see who wants to. But Noah is definitely invited."

I almost laughed. "He is, is he?"

"Are you saying you don't want him to come?" she needled, and I gave it up.

"Of course I do." Awkward blushing. "He's . . . he's been awesome this last month. I . . ." I brightened. It didn't have to be intimate—and it didn't have to be all Hollywood, either. "I'll ask his sister and her boyfriend—can we get passes for them for the week? And we can go for the week too—"

"You're gonna get mobbed," she said frankly.

"You think? Because I'm not—"

"Baby, I'll get your friends passes, I will. But if you're going to try to cruise the vending rooms and go to the panels, you're going to need at least six Noah's to block for you. You're doing two panels—one for *Jupiter Seven* and one for *Wolf's Landing*. How are you not seeing this?"

"*Jupiter Seven*?" I had to scramble for a moment. Oh God, yeah. I'd just come back from filming the day before Vinnie had gone to that party. "Oh Jesus. Jillian—haven't I had all sorts of promo shit I'm supposed to do?"

"I put it off a little," she conceded. "You have an interview the week before Comic-Con—they're flying up there. But the interview is in *Vogue*—do you hear what I'm saying? Sugar britches, you're too big to go be a kid there again."

I swallowed. "Well, you know, Vinnie and I—" From my first role in *Warlock Tea*, we'd gotten passes to Comic-Con. That had been his birthday week, and we'd bought the shit out of vendors to indulge him, and talked to the fans up close and personal to indulge *me*— God, we'd loved that shit.

"Yeah." Jilly knew. "It's tradition. But some traditions you lose because they're bad, and some you lose because it's no longer their time."

I shrugged, and like that, I gave in. "I guess I just got used to up here," I said, remembering that one sweet little clerk's admission that the chamber of commerce had worked out some sort of agreement about not bothering the Hollywood people. "It's nice—even the press is low octane."

"Well, that's why you should spend as much time as possible on your own turf," she cautioned. "But I'll set your friends up with passes anyway."

"I'm going to spend time in the signing room after the panel, right?"

"Yeah, yeah."

There was a pause, because really, that's all the business we had to talk about, and then she said, "So, is he still just a friend?"

I sighed. "Jilly—"

"Yeah. Hasn't been long enough."

"No."

"But don't write him off, okay?" She sounded anxious, and I hoped my laugh reassured her.

"Jilly, the minute I am ready, he's going to be the first to know."

"Really?" she cooed, like it was a foregone conclusion.

I realized it wasn't. Not at all. Noah was gruff and impatient and sarcastic—and he was also kind and capable and sexy as all hell. If he didn't have men banging down his door, then he was hanging out with the wrong men.

Or the wrong *man*.

Oh God. If I wanted to be fair to him, I had to say something. Tell him . . .

What?

That it would be all right if he dated while I waited for my heart to put itself back together? That I was just fine with him going out and fucking half the known universe while I pined after my dead lover? Yeah, that's good. Way to be a man, Connor—just give the guy up—

Don't be an asshole, Connor. Jesus, can't you fucking hope?

Way to talk, Vinnie. You're gone *if you hadn't noticed. You get no say,* none *in how I conduct my love life.*

Be real, Con. I mean, seriously—I am totally *dictating your love life right now. If I grabbed you by the balls and hauled you to that dance place and forced you to get drunk and fuck strangers, you'd totally let me do that!*

I actually recoiled, physically and mentally, from that idea.

"What?" Jilly was saying on the phone line, while I had this mental knock-down, drag-out with a ghost. "What is going on in your head?"

"I should talk to Noah," I said from a long ways away. "I should tell him not to wait for—"

"Don't you dare," she snarled, so vehemently I flipped Vinnie off and concentrated on her voice over the phone. "Don't you go and break that boy's heart and ruin your chance at having a good guy at your side and—"

"I wouldn't be breaking his heart." I believed that. "Jilly—he doesn't need me. I am *such* a liability—"

"Shut up," she said thickly. "Please. Connor, I scraped you off your floor; I begged, bribed, and blew people in the press to leave you the fuck alone; and I'd do it again, I'd do it twice—and I haven't asked for anything but your happiness. Now do me a fucking favor and give the happiness time to take, okay?"

I sighed. "Yeah. Sure. I don't know what you think he's—"

"He's everything Vinnie wasn't," she said, and I sucked in a razor-blade breath.

"What did you—"

"You know it's true," she retorted. "He's strong, he's self-sufficient, there's not a vain bone in his body. He would make you first, and honey, Vinnie couldn't do that. Not ever."

I thought of Simon Conklin and closed my eyes.

"Vinnie slept with my director," I admitted like it was dragged out of me with a tow truck and a chain.

"*See!*" she crowed. "I knew he did that—I knew he wasn't faithful. But *you*—not once did I walk into your trailer and think, 'Someone else has been here blowing Connor.' Your heart is just too fucking true for this business. You need someone who gets that about you, okay?"

I thought of the hurt on Noah's face if I did what ghost-Vinnie had said and charged down to the bar to get drunk, to get laid, to break his heart.

"Okay," I said, just to make that image of hurt and betrayal go away. I knew what that felt like—I wouldn't inflict it on Noah for the world. "I'll wait," I agreed after a moment. "I'll wait and see how it goes."

She let out a breath that did *not* sound like it had smoke in it, and we spent the next fifteen minutes talking about her kids—who were doing better, actually. When she rang off, I looked outside at the bright nine o'clock over the sound, and wondered again about that island.

And enjoyed the feeling of the ocean in my lungs, of giant trees, and of the breeze that cycled through them.

See, Vinnie. I don't have to do everything you say. I don't have to go out and be a destructive douche-monkey because you said so.

Yeah, Con. You're a real saint.

No, Vinnie, that was your department.

I stood and stretched and decided to go upstairs and turn on the television. I wasn't sure when my conversations with Vinnie had taken on the tincture of the sulks before a fight, but one of the only good things about his departure was that I didn't have to live through those silences anymore.

I could walk away, eat some ice cream, and shotgun *Daredevil* on Netflix.

And ignore the acid building up in my chest just waiting to be spit out.

That weekend, after we were done swimming two hours' worth of laps side by side, Noah asked me to his family's house a week from Sunday—and I was stunned.

"You want me there?" I asked for the umpteenth time, smoothing my wet hair back from my forehead. The Global had an Olympic-sized pool, but since we went there so very early, it was pretty deserted. "For . . . you know. For real?"

"Yeah, Connor. My sister and I talk about you all the time—you think Dad and Gran and the girls don't want to meet you?"

"Ky and Trina," I said, because I had gathered in pretty much all he'd had to say about his family. "Your father is Samuel and your grandma is Helena and your dad has added on to your little family shack about six times so everyone has a room and it's practically a mansion. And next door"—my voice dropped respectfully—"is where your friend Sharra lived, the one who broke your heart and taught you how to be kind, and—"

He shut me up with a splash. "Jesus, you're a sap. I've got a family, and yes, they're up in my business and that means up in your business. It's Gran's birthday, and I didn't want to leave you alone Sunday. I thought you might like to come."

Well, on the one hand it was pity, which was sort of embarrassing. On the other hand, who cared?

I was going to go meet someone's family. I hadn't been so excited since the last Christmas Vinnie's family had come to visit, and I had pretended to be part of *them* for a few weeks.

"Yeah, sure." I sounded pathetically grateful, but I didn't care.

Of course, Noah waited until we were in the locker rooms, coming out of the showers, and I was vulnerable and embarrassed and trying so hard not to check out his naked body when he wasn't looking, to drop the other shoe.

"So," he said to my turned back, "there's something I didn't mention."

"What?" I was surprised enough to turn around and face him. *He* was in cargo shorts and a hoodie. I, uh, was not.

He didn't reply. Instead, he took a deep breath, widened his eyes, and raked my naked body up and down with his eyes, a slow hungry smile subtly lighting up his face.

I was unprepared for the blush that swept up—and *down*—my body.

That smile turned not so subtle.

"That sight never gets old," he said, and I covered my face with my hands.

His chuckle told me that now he had an excuse not to look me in the eyes. My cock started to wake up, as though aware it was the center of attention for the first time in a while. "I should get dressed," I mumbled and turned to get my boxers.

I dropped them, because I *am* a walking porn movie, and as I bent down I heard Noah's strangled voice.

"No, don't." He took a deep breath. "It'll just make it worse."

Very slowly I stood up, and I felt his warmth at my back, and the roughness of laundered cotton. He shifted, crouching down, and his hands appeared in front of my feet as he grabbed the offending boxers and offered them to me to step into.

"Is this really—" My voice froze. His cheek, barely stubbled, grazed my backside, and I felt a puff of air. "*Necessary?*" I squeaked.

My cock was well and truly getting hard, and I reached down and tapped it with a finger to make sure it was, well, *mine*.

Behind me, Noah said, "Step into the boxer shorts, or I will take you right here."

Me, face forward against the locker, Noah spreading my ass cheeks, tongue up my hole, then thrusting into me sweet, so sweet, thick and long and huge as I screamed in release . . .

I took a painful step into my underwear, and then another. Noah's lips grazed my left cheek purposefully and trailed up, up, as he adjusted my underwear into place. He ended with a kiss to the back of my neck, beneath my hair, and his arms wrapped around my waist, pulling me against that long body.

"Good choice," he murmured in my ear.

"They'd . . . they'd never let us in the pool again," I said weakly and was rewarded by his gruff chuckle.

"It would be worth it." He traced my ear with his mouth as he spoke. "But you're not ready."

We both heard someone coming into the hotel changing rooms, and he released me so quickly I stumbled forward. I used the move to grab my shorts, and I dressed in mortified silence, aware that two of the hotel's occupants were using another bank of lockers to dress.

I turned to Noah as soon as I could, a child's smile on my face because I was so desperate to please.

He covered his eyes with his hand.

"Pit stop, Connor. And a comb. And product. And a razor if you're going into makeup today. Any of this ring a bell?"

I blinked slowly. "Yeah," I said, nodding. "Of course."

Of course I'd forgotten all of those things because Noah Dakers had put his mouth on my skin, had caressed me intimately, and my sex drive, which had been the slumbering giant in my loins, was suddenly looking around and ready to play.

Twelve years ago, it had been a happy child sort of giant, and it would have played with anyone. Eleven years ago, it'd been content to settle down with Vinnie and only play with one person, forever.

Right now, it was eyeballing Noah as the only friend it'd ever wanted, and I wondered how many times I was going to have to take it in hand before our, erm, titans clashed, so to speak.

Because they had to. They just had to. That caress had been a promise. Hell, that *threat* had been a promise, and my body had been betrayed so badly in the last year. I needed those promises kept.

And it wasn't until I was shaving that I remembered what had prompted that whole episode in the first place.

"Uh, Noah?" I asked while dragging the razor down my cheek. "What was the thing you were going to mention—the catch behind visiting your family?"

He grunted. "Give me the razor," he ordered, and I did. He turned me toward him and started to shave me, neatly, methodically, and impersonally.

My entire body was blushing with the first stripe down my face.

"Why are you shaving me?" I asked, lips as still as I could keep them.

His eyes went to half-mast and his full lips pulled faintly back. "'Cause it's sexy as hell," he said throatily. He rinsed the razor and started again. "Also, because you're less likely to cut yourself if I'm doing it while I talk to you. So, this family thing—my mom is going to be there."

I frowned. I'd *pumped* him for information; this statement was several kinds of wrong.

"But I thought she'd—"

"Left. Yes, I know. Me too. And I was totally fine with that. But apparently she wrote Ky a letter—"

"The youngest one? Man, that's shady."

"Listen to you, talking all street. Yes, it's shady. And emotionally manipulative. And generally just not . . . not promising for a reunion. So I'd already asked if you could come, because Gran is teaching the girls how to cook, and I'm one hundred percent for feeding you some more, but then Ky sprang this on everyone—"

"Well, if it's going to be awk—"

"And I said fuck it," Noah finished with a hard glance that shut me right up. "If she doesn't like my friends, then she shouldn't be there. So, there you have it. Don't worry—if God is on our side, she won't show up. If she *does* show up, well, I was planning to take you to all the good spots on our property anyway, and that should keep us out of her hair for the most part."

He'd finished shaving me and was holding a towel to my face. I captured his hands as they worked on either cheek.

"Why didn't you tell me?" I asked, feeling absurdly hurt. "I . . . I mean, I'm not so solipsistic I wouldn't want to know."

He rolled his eyes and tapped my nose gently. "Last night, Connor. *Last night* I asked if you could come. *This morning* Ky sprang her little surprise. So see? You still trump the family drama."

He swallowed, and we had one of those rare moments in which he seemed to need me for something. "I'd really like you to come."

I smiled uncertainly, his hands still trapped on my cheeks. "I, uh." I smiled again. "I used to go over to Vinnie's house for Christmas. We put all our stuff into his place, and all our Christmas decorations too—it looked all kitschy and fun—mine was the open living space, you know? All comfort, no color. But he'd have his parents to his house and him and me . . ." I blushed against the towel. "We pretended I was just a friend, and the house was full up, so we'd sleep in his bedroom. And we didn't have sex, because—"

"People in the house is awkward," Noah said, nodding emphatically.

"Right? But we . . . I got to pretend they were mine," I told him.

He dropped one of his hands and kissed my cheek. "My dad and gran? They'll be your family if you want," he promised, so serious I *had* to love him, just for that. "They . . . they still have Thanksgiving with Sharra's folks, so they can see the girls grow. They'll love you."

Oh, I could almost believe it.

I stepped away from him and grabbed my moisturizer. I applied it while I checked my carefully tousled hair in the mirror to see if it had enough product.

"That's sweet, Noah," I said, putting that distance in my voice I'd been so good at maintaining. "It's sweet, but . . ."

I couldn't finish that sentence. I turned toward the locker instead so I could put my toiletry kit in my gym bag.

He was at my side in a moment, his hand burning through my sweatshirt. "But what?"

"Man, Noah, I'm . . . I look good on screen, but obviously nobody in real life is going to . . ." Be my family. Love me for real. "I'm not that good a bet," I finished, and then I slung my bag over my shoulder and stalked out, beating him to the car.

We were both silent during the drive. He took us on a detour to the Stomping Grounds, and made me wait in the car while he got us coffee and sandwiches.

He came out with the cups and the bag, which he handed to me, and once I started drinking, he started talking.

"You have *got* to tell me about your family."

I swallowed—and dodged. "What about them? Mother, father, four sisters."

"Wow. I did not even know that. What do they think about your career?"

"They think that it gets them a set amount of money every year to ensure they never open their mouths about why I got kicked out of school."

Noah drove off the road.

On purpose—I mean, he picked a great place to park on the side—but he literally drove off the road that led to the studio and put the car into park before turning to look me in the eyes.

"And why did you get kicked out of school?" he asked, like I was trying his patience.

I took a sip of coffee and stared idly out the side window. Fog. It was misty today, and the earth smelled of rushes and salt water, and I suddenly wished I were out in that mist and all alone.

"I was the school mascot," I said. "You know. The drama queer who wore the big stupid outfit?"

"What were you?" he asked, and that was very tricky. I almost met his gaze so I could flash a smile.

"A Trojan," I said, completely deadpan.

He snickered. "Please tell me that's the truth."

"I shit you not. The Cosgrove Trojans—'cause Trojans cum in the grove, get it?"

"I assumed there was a dirty pun in there somewhere," he said. Wow. His sarcasm really *didn't* ever turn off.

"Yeah. Well, in this case, the dirty pun was in my mouth—and it belonged to the point guard on the basketball team. And we were behind the bleachers at a game—"

"The big game?" he asked, voice dry.

"Who the hell cared? Lance Quinlan was letting me *blow him*—it was the most glorious night of my life."

"Until?" It was like he knew where this was going.

"Until the bleachers got moved during the half and the whole school saw him give me a facial."

Noah laughed like the sound was dragged out of him with a tow chain attached to a garbage scow. "Ho-lee *shit*."

"Yeah," I said, finding my humor. Vinnie had laughed at this story until he'd peed. "It was . . . well, spectacular. And so was my father, throwing me out of the house. And none of my friends' parents would let me sleep on their couches. I literally packed a suitcase, grabbed my wallet—I had about three years' worth of mowing lawns and babysitting that I'd been planning to use to get me to LA anyway—and jumped in a truck with the first asshole to give me a ride."

I grunted. And I'd turned my first trick. Because, you know, it's what whores did.

"Why was he an asshole?" Noah asked quietly.

"God, Noah." I felt more naked than I had in the changing rooms. "Isn't it enough? You know my parents take money to not talk to the press. You know Vinnie wasn't faithful . . . I mean . . . you used to look at me like I was a movie star. It sure would be nice if you could—"

"I see a man," he said, and I was forced to look at him after all. He reached into the backseat and stroked my cheek with his knuckle. "A really good-looking man." He smiled kindly. "But a man. And nothing you've told me—not about Vinnie, not about your parents, not about being young and broke and hungry—none of it makes me lo . . . li . . . care about you less."

I opened my mouth to tell him not to do this to himself, when he reminded me of something I'd forgotten.

"Besides," he said, making sure he had my attention, "you still haven't told me why you left *Warlock Tea*."

I broke eye contact with him and stared out into the beckoning fog. "We're going to be late," I said, not stubbornly, but he knew.

"Someday," he said confidently.

And why wouldn't he be confident? So far, I was proving to be stunningly undedicated to grieving the rest of my life away cold and alone and unloved.

Vinnie, will you forgive me for moving on?

I don't know, Connor—will you forgive me for being weak?

You weren't weak.

Lying is a shitty way to forgive someone, Connor. No. *I don't forgive you.*

Vinnie!

Tell me the fucking truth, asshole, and you can have whatever your little heart needs to be happy.

Shut up.

Gladly. You're the one who talks to me, *remember?*

I can't believe I miss you.

I can't believe you miss me either. I almost ruined your career twice, I was unfaithful, I didn't have the balls to come out to my family or the press—I can't believe you loved me at all!

I did. Oh God, Vinnie, don't say that, baby—I loved you. I loved you so much. Don't make me talk about—

I'm not answering you right now. The Connor I *loved had backbone. He fought for roles, he made Jilly take me on as a client. He bullied me into rehab, twice. This guy—he's tired and sad. How can I love you like this?*

Noah loves me.

He'd been trying so hard not to say it, but I hadn't had the heart to stop him completely.

And Vinnie had no answer to that. I guess there *was* no answer to the fact that Noah loved me weak and Vinnie couldn't love me enough, even when I was strong.

CHAPTER NINE

ANYTHING THAT DRAWS ATTENTION TO YOUR MOUTH IS A GOOD THING

G od, that was a long week. Part of it was that I was looking forward to meeting Noah's family—and quarreling with ghost-Vinnie about it the whole time. And part of it was work. The writers—who had been in full fighting trim to begin with but now had Hunter Easton and Kevin Hussain totally on board with the new cast additions—decided to sacrifice Swift and Wind so they could be on a spin-off show (where I'd make guest appearances, of course), and *I* got to be the one who killed them.

I looked at my pages that morning after Noah and I arrived on the set and then looked up at Lissa and Brenda. "I rip your throats out?" I practically whimpered. "I have to *rip your throats out*?"

Lissa giggled like the little blonde minx she was. "It's okay, Connor. See—our throats regenerate. It's symbolic. You're joining the Wolf's Landing pack, and since we betrayed you, you have to excise us from *your* pack. Don't worry. It'll totally all be CGI—you don't have to hit us at all for real or anything."

Brenda patted my shoulder. "Like you'd hit *anybody*," she laughed. "Oh my God—I mean, you have a rep as a nice guy, Connor, but I don't know if I've *ever* worked with such a *nice guy*."

I smiled at them both. "You guys have been a riot," I told them— because they had. The week before, we'd finished this wrought, dramatic scene when I discovered they'd betrayed me with a rival pack from our own timeline. Simon had called "Cut!" and there I'd been, spittle flying out of my mouth, chest heaving, so totally in character I practically needed to hit something. Brenda and Lissa had looked at me in the silence that followed "Cut"—and then looked at each other and started making out.

The entire set had cracked up—including me!—and they'd both jumped on me and hugged me.

"Jesus, you get intense," Lissa had said at the time. "You just need a good mauling to help walk that off!"

I'd laughed so hard—working with the two of them had been a balm to my soul. As much as I was going to enjoy working with the regulars and becoming enmeshed in the *Wolf's Landing* milieu, I was going to miss them.

"Yeah," Lissa said now. "Just remember that sometimes you need to be hugged after doing the rough stuff, okay?" She winked. "We'll try to have Noah standing by after you have to rip our throats out. He can help you out."

I stared at her, my mouth opening and closing like a lizard's. "Uh . . ."

She looked around and both of them moved their heads in close to mine. "What?" Brenda asked. "You didn't want anybody to know you guys are a thing?"

"We're . . . uh . . ." I paused. "We're not sleeping together?" Because hell*o*.

Both of them put their hands to their chests and made that "Aw . . ." sound that girls can do with perfect sincerity.

"Isn't that just the—"

"Oh my God, could he be any—"

"Sweetest—"

"Such a *doll*!"

I looked over at Noah, who had long since stopped pretending to play with his phone.

"Are you hearing this?" I asked, somewhat at a loss.

"Yes. Those nice girls think I should sleep with Connor Montgomery. I like this plan."

I rolled my eyes. "Of course you do."

He raised his eyebrows, daring me, I think, to say "I'm not ga-ay!" or something else appropriately weenie for this moment.

Then I looked back at the girls, who had nothing on their faces but friendliness and curiosity. "He is pretty hot." I felt a blush creep up my neck. "Let's just say he's on my list of one."

They sobered, and Lissa patted my knee. "You don't have to say it, Connor," she told me softly. "We can sort of guess who your last boyfriend might have been."

Brenda made an uncomfortable noise, and we all looked at her. "Lissa didn't know this until after she hit on you, but you guys used to go to my favorite coffee shop . . ."

Lissa cleared her throat meaningfully, and Brenda rolled her eyes.

"Okay, I was the *barista* at *your* favorite coffee shop, right before you got *Warlock Tea*."

I blinked, ashamed that I couldn't remember her. "I'm so so—"

"No, don't even. I lost sixty pounds, dyed my hair, got contacts—my own mother doesn't recognize me. I'm just saying: you guys weren't so careful back then. I saw you holding hands. Once I saw him kiss your cheek. You were . . . really in love."

That blush washed over my face and faded, leaving my hands and cheeks cold. "We were." I gave her a lying smile. "And apparently we were lucky that story didn't break years ago."

Vinnie, we weren't fooling anyone.

That's not true, Connor. I was obviously fooling myself.

At that moment we were called into makeup. Noah came too, to help me run lines like he always did. But my stomach was jittery and uncertain, just from that very matter-of-fact acknowledgment that me and Noah were a thing *before* we were a thing. My inner Vinnie voice was getting pretty bitchy about it too, which probably explained what happened on the set.

"You . . ." Slade's (my) voice threatened to break. "You went to another pack? Both of you?"

Swift crouched by our campfire, her eyes wounded. "We were afraid. Slade, this world, it's so different, and you were so lost—"

"You didn't . . . you didn't ask!" Slade (I) felt a knife in his vitals. Betrayal. All we'd ever asked for was loyalty. "I . . . I worked for you! I *fought* for you! I *killed* for you! And you couldn't . . . you couldn't talk to me? Even to ask? You're just . . . just *leaving* me?"

"You couldn't hack it!" Wind cried shrilly. "We got dumped in this stupid alternative dimension, and you fell apart!"

"I was keeping us together!" we snarled. Spittle flew from Slade's (my) mouth, but we were too angry, too wounded, to care. "I . . . I sold my fucking *soul* to protect you two—"

"We didn't know that!" Swift shouted. "We didn't know! How could we know—"

"You could have asked." I wanted to fall to my knees and rend my hair—but *I*, Connor, knew that I'd be out of the shot. "You could have . . ."

"Slade," Wind whispered. "It's too late. You have to cut us loose."

Oh, I'd loved her. She'd been my mate, my playmate, my friend. She'd been my hope in this strange place and my memory of good times, stable times in the past.

"I could have forgiven you anything," I said quietly. "*ANYTHING!*"

Slade (I) whirled and spread our claws and swiped with all the power in our body. Wind fell to the ground, and Swift looked at me . . .

And screamed.

"Cut!"

Nobody moved.

"Cut!"

Wind—Brenda—stood gingerly up from the pad she'd fallen on, and Slade (I) looked at her in horror. Had I hit her? I hadn't . . . had I . . . I'd been so . . .

She smiled at me, eyes large and bemused. "God, Connor. That was . . . damn."

My eyes cut to Swift . . . Lissa . . . oh God . . . and she was nodding excitedly.

I was suffused with a terrible sense of dislocation. I (Slade) had been betrayed. I (Slade) had screamed and lashed out and hurt the thing that hurt us. I (Slade) was still . . .

Bleeding.

I swallowed, and the pain didn't go away.

I swallowed again.

"Connor?" Simon Conklin called from up in the chair. "You good man? That was a great take—we don't need that again. In fact, that's a wrap. You okay?"

I nodded and tried to deal with the fact that I was Connor—and I was still in pain.

"I, uh . . ."

"He needs to walk it off," Noah said from off set, and his voice grounded me. "C'mon man."

His footsteps sounded loud and portentous, but his hand, wrapping around my biceps, was another thing that brought me back to myself.

And to that terrible, terrible pain in my chest, that emotional evisceration that I'd been trying so hard to keep from feeling.

I followed him blindly, off the soundstage, around the corner, to the space between my trailer and the girls'.

"I . . ." I wanted to say I was okay, but my vision wasn't solid yet. I couldn't see the girls anymore. I couldn't see Noah. I couldn't see this cold and shady spot with the trees arching overhead.

All I could see was . . .

Vinnie, looking at the box of condoms, guilty. Vinnie, stoned and tearful, tackling me for the Percocet I was flushing down the toilet. Vinnie, begging me to stay, not to go back to the shoot, begging me to give up my job when I'd worked so hard to get it. Vinnie, telling Jillian that it was okay, we'd hide ourselves, hide our lives, hide our love, because he was afraid to tell his parents and she didn't think we could make it. Vinnie, that second time at rehab, apologetic and resolute, and he'd done it, hadn't he? He'd gone clean and sober for three years and Vinnie . . . oh God no. *Vinnie . . .* Don't make me remember. *Vinnie . . .* NO NO NO NO—

Vinnie, blue face reconstructed, body covered by a sheet, cold and dead in the morgue, where I'd come to identify him, because I was the one in his wallet, in his license, in his life . . .

Vinnie, in a box I wasn't allowed to carry, being buried when he'd told me he wanted cremation, at a ceremony I'd had nothing to do with, because his parents didn't know.

"I . . ." I tried again, but Noah wasn't there. The trailers weren't there. It was just Vinnie, all the times he'd let me down, all the times I hadn't gotten angry because . . .

"I'd forgive you!" I told him. "I'd forgive you. I'd forgive you anything. I would have forgiven you anything, I swear, I swear—"

"Except dying."

God help me, I'm not sure whose voice it was.

"*Vinnie, you bastard, how could you*!" I screamed it, probably scared the fucking birds, but I didn't care.

Because Noah—*Noah*—put his arms around me and rocked me as I sobbed, gibbered against his shoulder, and ranted at the ghost of the guy who'd betrayed me in the worst way of all.

Eventually Noah took me into the trailer and took my makeup off gently, giving all the prosthetics to Viv to give to Junior. He had Viv block for us, telling Conklin and the girls—crap, I don't know what she told them. For all I know, she said I had virulent explosive diarrhea or something, but whatever it was, it worked.

Noah hustled me into the back of the car and drove me home.

It was late June—the sky wouldn't darken until almost ten o'clock—but Noah didn't give a shit. He took me upstairs, literally undressed me, and thrust me into the shower.

Then he hauled me out and wrapped me in a bathrobe and put me on the bed. I don't know if I'd said a word since the meltdown at the trailer, but it didn't matter. He was there—hard chest, dark eyes, capable hands—and that solid presence just seemed to fill in all the spaces that I usually filled with talk, or even the talking in my own head.

I finally spoke when he thrust a bowl of soup into my hands and turned on the television. He was seated in a chair next to the bed, leaning on his elbows, pretending great interest in the movie on TNT.

"Noah?"

"Yeah?"

"If I eat my soup, will you sit next to me in the bed?"

His hand was warm and reassuring on my thigh.

"Yeah. But eat the soup or it'll spill."

"Yeah, okay."

I did as ordered and then set the bowl on the nightstand and scooted over. Noah stood up and stripped off his shorts and sweatshirt, pulled down the covers, and crawled into bed next to me.

"It's only seven o'clock," I said, laughing hollowly. "I mean, me, I can see, I'm obviously a basket case, but shouldn't you be out dancing or some—"

"Shut up, Connor."

"Why?"

"I think it's perfectly obvious the only place—and I do mean the *only* place—that I want to be is right here with you."

He held out his arm, and I scooted back to him, my head on his chest, his arm over my shoulders. I shuddered a couple of times, like you do when you've been so, so cold, and you're getting used to being warm again.

I probed the empty cavern in my chest. "I . . ."

"What?" he asked, kissing my forehead.

"I am so . . . *so* . . . *angry* at him," I finished, feeling shock and wonder for even being able to say it.

"I don't blame you," he said with a little snort. "I'd be pissed too."

"But he . . . I wasn't angry with him when he was alive!" I protested. "That stuff—the cheating, the career, the rehab—"

"Rehab?"

Well shit. "That's why I left *Warlock Tea*," I confessed, because why not? Noah knew the worst of it—of *me*—now. "It was also why I didn't sign on to do Marvel Cinematic Universe—"

"Seriously? Who were you going to be?"

I grunted. "Bucky."

"Now that's a real shame."

"The guy they got is better," I said, meaning it. "He's got this intensity I don't have."

"Didn't. Didn't have. Whatever you thought you didn't have five years ago, you've got it now. But, rehab?"

"Yeah. I . . . I mean, it's what you do, right? You see people in Hollywood crumble all the time. You see their relationships detonate. Because human beings are human. You're surrounded by what's fake and what's beautiful, and you can't tell which is which. But real—real goes to bat for you. Real . . . real leaves *Warlock Tea* to do movies because Vinnie needed me. Real forgives because . . ." I shook my head. "But *see*—I'm not even mad at all that. I could have lived my entire life and forgiven him for all of that—"

"But he had to be there with you."

I closed my eyes, too spent to deny it. "Yeah. It was the one thing I asked really. That no matter what else happened, it would be the two of us."

"I'm sorry, Connor." And he meant it. Here he was, holding me, but he was sincere.

I turned my head on his chest so I could see his face. "About what?"

I dreaded what he'd say. I dreaded hearing that I was weak for letting Vinnie be weak. I dreaded hearing someone telling me that I was too good for Vinnie, because *God*, for all his faults, I'd loved him so much.

"That you didn't get to spend the rest of your life with the man you loved."

And oh God. He didn't judge me. He didn't judge Vinnie. He just . . .

Understood.

I reached out and rubbed the bottom of his full mouth with my thumb.

"*You*," I said seriously, "are a force to be reckoned with."

He smiled a little, and I expected sarcasm.

He took my breath away instead.

"I will never cheat on you," he said. "And I will never need rehab. I like my job driving you around—we could put you in the front seat and call me your personal assistant, and I would not have a problem being by your side wherever you go. I don't want to be an actor, but I sure do love watching other people do it, so that would not be a problem. So I can pretty much promise to be everything you need in a man and never got before. But there is one thing I cannot promise, and I'm not even going to try."

He stared at me, hard, until I looked away.

"Everybody dies," I said into his shoulder.

"Everybody dies," he confirmed, stroking my hair back from my face. "The only thing I *can* promise in that area is that if you lose me like you lost Vinnie, you'll be strong enough to survive it."

Vinnie, did you hear that? I'm strong enough to survive you.
I knew you were, Connor.
Don't go yet.
I'll always be here. But you've got someone else now.
I can love you too.
Are you sure?

I fell asleep on Noah's chest and slept hard for the entire night. The next morning I woke up, naked under my bathrobe, and alone.

But I could hear Noah in the shower.

I yawned and rolled over on my back to stretch, the bathrobe falling away and leaving my skin silky under the soft sheets. Ugh—I had creases on my skin from the robe, and I struggled to kick it off under the covers, not wanting to get up just yet. It fell over the edge, and I went back to stretching, suddenly conscious of my body in a way I hadn't been in a while.

Oh my God, I had *nipples*, and they were rubbing up against the sheets and getting hard and pearly.

My naked bottom was wriggling against the sheets too, and my thighs and my groin were growing heavy.

My cock felt every rasp of cotton against it, and every nerve ending in my body woke up and stretched along with me.

Oh God.

I was *alive*, and my body felt sexy and *alive* and suddenly my skin wanted to celebrate too!

I ran my hand down my chest and sighed when I squeezed my pecs. Oh wow—I had such sensitive nipples, Vinnie had once gotten me off just nibbling on them alone.

I pinched them to see if that still held.

Oh man. Yes. *Yes*, my nipples were still sensitive, and I rocked my hips up and down, undulating under the covers because it all felt so good. One hand stayed up at my nipples, and the other hand moved down my abdomen, stroking, teasing—nothing was vital, nothing was urgent, I could take my time. I rubbed the crown of my cock, shuddering at the little spurt of pre-cum and bringing it to my tongue to taste.

Oh . . . yes. I'd forgotten that. I'd forgotten I liked the taste of cum.

I closed my eyes and went back to playing with myself, but I opened my eyes when the covers were suddenly ripped away. I gazed up at Noah, mouth parted slightly, a combination of sex and embarrassment washing a flush up from my thighs to my throat.

"I saw you," he said, bending over so he could run his finger along my lips. "You were tasting yourself?"

I smiled shyly and looked away.

"Yeah."

He bent and touched his mouth to mine, licking at the seam of my lips in strong strokes, but I refused to part.

"What's wrong?" he asked.

"I haven't brushed my teeth," I told him, embarrassed.

He backed up enough to scowl. "Connor, so help me, if you get stupid about this I will get you hard and wrap a ring around your cock and not let you come for an *hour*."

My cock tightened against my stomach and spurted a little more pre-cum out, and my entire body went on high alert.

I licked my lips, suddenly needing that domination, those sensual threats, that *purpose* and hard hand with everything in my body.

"Are you going to plug me too?" I asked, just to be sure.

His lips curved wryly. "Do you have one?"

I sort of drooped. "No." Because you don't pack sex toys when you're not thinking about sex.

"We'll change that," he promised, and my eyes rolled back in my head.

"Nungh."

He laughed wickedly and then wrapped one hand around my cock while he took possession of my mouth. Morning breath or not, he swept inside, dominated, took me fully when I hadn't known I'd been going to give.

It didn't matter.

I gave him everything.

His touch on my skin was an explosion of color, his mouth on mine sang the perfect chord. Clean male filled my lungs like the smell of redwoods and ocean, and he tasted . . .

Augh!

So good! I flailed my hands, trying to glut myself on his skin, but he seized them in his other hand and held them over my head for a moment.

One hand on my cock, one hand securing my wrists, and I was stretched out beneath him, willing, helpless, frantic, and needy.

Oh my gracious God, sex was a *thing*.

"Connor," he said sharply, getting my attention.

I had no words. I writhed beneath him—but not too wildly, or he might let go of my cock.

"*Connor*!"

"Yeah?" I asked breathily. Words. Words. *Cock ass suck stroke rim fuck CUM!*

"You need to listen, okay?"

I nodded, mesmerized. Kid—I'd thought he was a kid, right? I'd jump off a cliff if he talked to me in that voice.

I'd soar.

"This time is for you," he told me. "Don't worry 'bout me. This time—all you."

I whimpered. I wanted to taste him. I wanted his cock filling my throat, I wanted my tongue up his asshole, and his cock in mine. Oh God . . . I wanted—

"For you," he repeated. "Lay still. Let me. I'll take care of you, Connor. I promise."

I nodded, trembling, and I struggled a little against his clasp on my wrists.

"I'm going to let them go now," he whispered, next to my ear. "And I want you to touch your nipples. That was so pretty, your hands on your nipples. Did you pinch them?"

I whined.

"I want you to pinch them and play with them. I'll do the rest."

"Okay."

"Good. Now one word, okay?"

"Anything."

"Say 'please.'"

I all but melted into the bed. "Please, Noah, would you—"

He sealed his lips to mine again, and let go of my wrists. I kept them there, above my head in spite of his direction, because for the moment, I was overwhelmed.

The kiss went on and on, until my entire world became the heat of Noah's mouth, the taste of his tongue thrusting against mine, the slick of his chest against me. He kept a light grip on my cock, not hard enough to stroke, mostly just hard enough to tease, to keep me from forgetting: this was going somewhere.

His free hand buried itself in my hair, tugging, positioning my head until my throat was exposed, my chest stretched out, and I was more vulnerable than I'd ever been in my life.

I was shaking so hard. I couldn't remember ever trembling during sex, ever *needing* so damned much from a touch on my cock, from a kiss.

"Shh . . ." he whispered in my ear. "I promised. I'll take care of you."

I nodded, and he kissed down my throat, nibbling on my Adam's apple, licking along my clavicle, scraping his teeth lightly between my pecs.

"Please, Noah," I whispered, wanted him to stop there. His tongue . . . his teeth . . .

When he clamped his mouth over my nipple and sucked hard, I let out a sob.

"Yes . . . yes . . . oh God . . ."

He suckled and nipped, and my hips thrust in rhythm, unfulfilled. My cock batted uselessly against the soft cage of his cupped hand.

I keened high in my throat, close, too close, and he moved back suddenly and licked my other nipple.

Then started kissing down my stomach.

"Noah!"

He looked up and caught my eyes. "Put your hands on yourself, Connor."

Oh right. Thank you, thank you, God, thank you, *Noah*, for giving me something to do. I was thrashing, I was *mindless*, and at the touch of my fingers against my own skin, I calmed and began to tease myself, pulling rhythmically, pinching tight. Breathless little sobs still issued from my throat, but Noah didn't mind them, so I didn't.

Instead, he grasped my cock tightly, and his breath puffed against the wet, dripping head.

Slowly, so damned slowly, he stretched out his tongue and licked, the rough surface scraping my cockhead deliberately.

My sobs turned into a concentrated moan, and I moved one hand toward his head.

He stopped me with a scowl, and I put my hand back where it belonged.

And then he licked my cock again and stroked up.

And again. And again. And again.

"Noah," I whimpered. "Please . . ."

"Say it," he whispered harshly, breath teasing the wet skin.

"Suck my cock . . . please . . . tug my balls, tease my hole . . ."

"Hold still," he ordered. "Keep your hands where they are."

"Yes . . ." I begged. "*Yes!*"

He lowered his head quickly and sucked me all the way in to the back of his throat, and the world behind my eyes blew up in a technicolor blast. My hips arched because they *had* to, and my hands pinched my own nipples hard enough to hurt.

He let me fall out of his mouth just long enough for me to feel air, and then engulfed my prick again, and again, and again, and again.

I chanted in time, "Fuck, fuck, fuck, fuck, fuck . . ." Because it was all I had: it was all the wonder, the explosion of pleasure, the overwhelming of all the nerve endings that made my eyes burn with sensual saturation.

I kept one hand on my chest, but the other one . . . I had to touch him, I had to massage his scalp under that wonderfully soft, glossy, curly hair. It stretched long as I tugged, getting close to his shoulders, and I wanted to pet it more, pet it forever, feel the heat of his skin underneath.

But his mouth was moving urgently, and his grip on the base of my cock felt so exquisite, I wasn't going to last long, and, oh God, I wanted it to last forever, but I needed . . . needed . . . needed . . .

I thrust hard into his mouth, and he squeezed me hard back, and I propped one knee up, spreading my thighs in open invitation.

He switched hands on my cock, and slid his spit-slickened fingers down the crease of my thigh, probing, not gently, the tight clench of my buttocks.

He pulled back his head and gripped me hard. "I can't touch you there if you don't relax," he growled, and that meant I had to trust him, yes it did. I had to relax my muscles, open to him truly, let him touch me in my favorite, tender, forbidden spot.

I sighed, my hands stilling, and concentrated all my furor inward, making myself loose, limp, easing my ass cheeks apart and—

Oh my God!

He thrust a finger inside while bobbing his head down so far I lodged in the back of his throat, and then he pulled back on both ends and then thrust forward, and once, twice, three more times and—

I screamed.

Oh God, I screamed in orgasm, sobs ripping open my throat, my chest, my *skin*. Fire raced down my veins, through my heart, stopping the air in my lungs for a moment as the enormity of climax rushed up through my throat. I beat a savage tattoo with my fists on either side of me, unable to keep my hands on my flesh, unable to touch Noah for fear of pounding on *him*, of hurting *him*.

He let go of my cock to seize the hand closest to his ass, and tug it to his chest.

That's when I groaned, deep and hard, from my toes as the climax roared through my entire body. Cum charged up my cock and filled his mouth until he couldn't swallow, running down his chin, smearing his cheek.

Oh Jesus, never in my *life* had I come so hard.

And then I was empty, lost in that daze that comes after sex, adrift and uncertain. He'd . . . serviced me. What now?

He stood up for a moment and mumbled, "Fuck it," and pulled the towel from around his waist and started using it to clean up the mess on my thighs, and then on the bed.

I stared at him in dismay—he was *fully* erect, his foreskin retracted to leave his cockhead shiny and bloated. While he bent over the bed to tend to me, I reached out and stroked him with wonder.

He hissed and held still, closing his eyes. "Sure you want to—"

I wrapped my fingers around him—they couldn't entirely touch—and stroked slowly from base to tip and back again. The muscles in his legs trembled, and I scooted over and tugged him gently.

Awkwardly, because I wasn't letting go, he pushed himself up onto the bed and lay with his head near my knees and his cock even with my chest. I rolled to my side and started to stroke him off with one hand, while with my other hand, I simply . . . stroked *him*. Palmed the smooth dark skin of his hips, his thighs, his muscular ass. I filled my hands up with the touch of another man, and with every pass I shuddered and got harder.

I opened my mouth and stretched out my tongue to touch his cock, but he reached down and grabbed my hair.

"Connor," he said sharply, "aren't you even going to ask?"

I shook my head. "No." *Vinnie and me and the condoms, and yes condom meant he'd cheated and no condom meant he hadn't*—I wasn't going to ask. Yes, I was risking my health, but God, after thinking I was dead for the better part of a year? I didn't care.

I thrust my head forward, and Noah grunted, locking my head in place with his hand knotted in my hair. "I'm clear," he said, irritated. "I know *you're* clear." Well, yes—trips to the doctor's office, it came out. "But you can't do this with anyone else without asking!"

I scowled at him. "I'm not doing this with anyone else," I snapped, stung by the very idea. "I'm only doing this with you."

His mouth parted, and the hard, commanding thing he'd done with his face to keep me from self-destructing slipped completely away. His hand in my hair softened, caressed me, and slid to my cheek, which he stroked.

"I'm only doing this with you too," he said. "Suck my cock as much as you want, sweetheart, I'm not going to stop you."

I clung to it, one hand around the shaft, one hand cupping his balls, fondling, and lowered my head, stuffing it as far back into my mouth as I could get it.

He moaned, and the sound anchored me. I wanted *more* of that sound, so I pushed my head forward another inch, another, until my nose touched his coarse, curly hair and I couldn't breathe. He tugged gently on me, and I backed off, and then thrust forward again, and again, and again.

He groaned, and he was ramped so high, I could tell he was close. But when he took my cock back into his mouth, I was surprised at how close *I* was, how badly I wanted him all over again. I propped my knee up, inviting him again, and this time I was relaxed and needy. His wet fingers skated over my asshole, and then probed, and then thrust, and to my shame I let him drop out of my mouth because I was shaking too hard to hold him.

"Noah," I panted, stunned by how much I needed him again. "God, Noah . . . could you . . . I'm going to—"

I wasn't usually this inconsiderate, damn it. I tried, grabbing his cock again, just stroking, but he spat on his hand and thrust another finger up my backside and I was lost. I squeezed him sporadically, licked him when I could, but I was filled, not entirely, but enough, enough to remember the taste of possession, to crave it, to need it from *this man* who was stretching me almost to the point of pain.

"Noah . . ." I sobbed. "Oh God . . ."

He pulled back enough to say, "Shh . . . I've still got you." And then he thrust his head forward and his three fingers to the hilt, until it hurt—

And I came. I shot cum until I cried out, tender, and he pulled away, leaving me limp and still twitching, his cock leaking pre-cum onto my face as I lay helpless.

"Connor, hold still." His hand, covered in spit and cum, moved down and grasped his own shaft. Up close, I watched him squeeze himself, stroke himself, his head leaking more and more pre-cum onto my cheek, my lips, my chin. I closed my eyes and stuck out my tongue and waited, listening to his breathing, his gasps, the irritated grunts he made as he got closer, and closer and—

"*Coming!*"

I felt it shooting across my cheek, striping my tongue, falling across my eyes. Thank God they were shut.

Again, and more, until my face was dripping, and still I swallowed, licking around my mouth, my chin, tasting as much of it as I could.

His whole body went limp as the last of the orgasm twitched out, and then he scooted around on the bed. The roughness of the towel on my face practically lulled me to sleep.

"Good?" he asked gently.

"Yeah," I said, eyes still closed. "So good."

"Glad to hear it." The towel swiped my eyes a couple more times for good measure, and then his mouth slanted over mine, and I opened for him.

He possessed me easily, like I'd always been his, and I kissed him slowly, desultorily, until I fell back asleep, naked and sweaty, and still coated in cum, both his and mine.

And oddly weightless, dreamy, floating in an unfamiliar space.

Oh God.

Vinnie, I'm sorry. Please tell me it's okay.

But he didn't reply.

Vinnie, I sort of remember this. I remember feeling like this with you. Is that okay, Vinnie? Please—I need to know!

If Vinnie stayed to watch me come in another man's arms, he wasn't around to answer me when I needed him most.

Bastard.

Well, fuck.

Just as well. Noah was rangy, but his chest was wide, and there was really only enough room in the bed for two.

CHAPTER TEN

SOME THINGS ARE TRUE WHETHER YOU BELIEVE THEM OR NOT

I woke up to a note on the bed: *Gone to get doughnuts (now that we've glazed a few). If you have a preference, text me.*

I blinked and thought about it. Pulled out my phone and texted, *Savory with sweet? It's almost noon.* Then, *Thank you.*

Yeah, okay. And coffee.

Excellent. I'll shower.

Wait until I get home.

I stared at the text, not sure what that meant.

Then: *Yes, I'm being a dominating sexy pervert. Do you mind?*

I smiled slowly, blushing down to my toes.

No. I don't mind. Any other orders?

Any plans for the day?

I thought about it. Mostly, my plans had been to sleep in and get something to bring to his family's house the next day.

Birthday shopping for your gran?

You are a very nice man. We'll get something tomorrow on the way. I'll ask her what she wants when I stop and get clothes.

I paused for a moment, mouth dry.

Connor? Is that okay?

He was staying the night again. In my bed. I tried to talk to Vinnie in my head to see if that was okay, but all I got was static.

Connor?

Is fine, I typed. *Is awesome!* That last one was stretching it—I couldn't decide, really, if it was awesome or heinous or something in between. But Noah . . . Noah deserved "awesome."

The phone rang in my hand, and I answered it warily. "What?"

"This isn't going to work if you try to 'act' your way through the stuff you don't know," he said crisply.

I grunted. "I actually really do want you to stay the night." Something in me settled—I was speaking the truth. I ignored the sulky, unfinished business that was Vinnie glaring at me from the corner of my mind. "Again. I just hadn't thought about it, and it took me a minute."

"Okay, then," he said, and I had to smile.

"Okay, then," I told him softly. "How close are you? Because I really do want to shower."

He laughed. "Yeah, okay. The leaving the sex toy on the counter while you were in the shower was the idea, but we don't have to do that."

"You didn't invite me with you to shop?" I mock whined.

What he said next wasn't playful, and it wasn't funny, and it was, in fact, the thing that would make or break us, right out there on the table.

"Baby, you are *not* out. It's one thing for *me* to shop—the whole town knows I'm gay. But if you and I walk into Red Hot Bluewater together, you are going to be in the tabloids whether you plan it or not!"

Oh. Oh yeah. He was right. The whole world had not reshaped itself because I had my little tantrum at Vinnie. I was still a closeted actor, and I still had a choice to make.

"Connor? You there?"

"Yeah," I said, feeling curiously empty. "Yeah. Just—"

"You are not coming out for me," he said flatly.

Well, of course not. It was too soon. It was "Gee, aren't we lucky I hadn't called out Vinnie's name in orgasm!" too soon.

But I hadn't—so coming out wasn't beyond the realm of possibility.

"No," I said, still . . . vacant. "No—not for you." I remembered everything that Jillian had been trying to say, her last day here, during our last phone call. "Just . . . just for me." The truth—it was happening. "It's an idea, okay?"

"Well, wait until I get back to talk about it some more."

He hung up and left me alone with Vinnie and the elephant penis in the room. I had permission from my agent now—but even if I hadn't? There was nobody else whose career hinged on this stupid personal fact—nobody but me.

Connor! My parents! What will they think?

Vinnie, who cares? I'm not going to go explicit with our sex lives. I'm just going to come out. Oh God, really? I was going to come out? I could come out, right?

But people will know!

People KNOW! "People know, Vinnie! Everybody you cheated on me with—they knew. Simon Conklin—he knows. The barista at our first coffee shop—she fucking knows and now she's someone the press gives a shit about. People fucking *know!*"

Don't yell!

I was more than yelling. I was yelling out loud, not in my head. I'd thought I was done with the anger, but apparently it had lived too long, too deep, for me to be done with it.

I'm pissed! Damn it, if you had lived, I would have fucking done it for you, as long as you needed me to. But you didn't *live, did you? You fucking* died *on me, and guess what?*

You can do anything you want now, can't you! No matter how many people you hurt—

I'm not telling your parents about us, Vinnie. I'm telling the world about me.

And then I got out of bed, still covered in Noah's cum, and stalked to the bathroom.

Pretty proud of yourself, aren't you! You fucked some other guy now, got back at me for—

Stop it right there. Noah and me—we've got nothing to do with you and me.

He's a boy.

He's more a man than you ever were.

I ignored the wounded silence in my head and turned on the shower. It was true. Noah—he was as self-possessed a person as I'd ever seen. He didn't need to prove a damned thing. When he'd held me down, given me orders, it was because he had a plan—and I . . . hadn't. I'd been lost and flailing and uncertain—I'd damned near forgotten how to have sex, and once I used to think it was the *only* thing I could do.

But Noah had never lied about himself, didn't become someone else for a living, wouldn't know how to be anyone *but* Noah Dakers if he tried. You couldn't master someone else if you hadn't mastered yourself—wasn't that how the saying went?

Well, Noah had obviously mastered himself—and I didn't know if I ever would.

Not with that much certainty—it wasn't in my nature. I wanted to please people so badly—didn't most actors? And when I became somebody on the set, on the screen, could I really do that if the barrier between myself and a character was hard and fast?

No. That's why I'd called Vinnie every night when I'd been away—I'd needed to remind myself of who I was.

And that's why Vinnie had been so lost on his own—because I hadn't been there to remind him either. He'd come out of a role just as confused, just as disassociated as I'd been, and there hadn't been a soul on the set he could trust.

It was a horrible thing to do to ourselves, Vinnie.

I held my face to the spray so I didn't have to think about how badly we'd both needed somebody, how hard we'd made it on ourselves because we couldn't have that person on the set, couldn't have a PA or a friend or anybody to just walk up to us with a tissue and some coffee and remind us what it was like to eat, drink, and poop as real people and not the person doing lines on stage.

Yeah. It was.

And he didn't have to say anything more. It was so much easier to find a fuck buddy than a friend you could trust, wasn't it? So much easier to swear a guy to secrecy when you were pounding his ass. And Hollywood didn't out each other—we kept each other's big gay secrets if we were part of the big gay population. Simon Conklin may have been out himself, but he wouldn't have outed Vinnie to anybody if he hadn't known I'd been part of it.

The water was scalding, and I turned my back to it, let it parboil me into some semblance of normal.

I want to be out, Vinnie. I don't want to live the next ten years of my life afraid of who's going to see me and my lover in public. I'm working on an out set, with out actors, and an out director. I'd seen Carter and Levi the day before, eating their lunch on a corner of the set. Levi had been frowning as Carter popped a mushroom in his mouth, and Carter had been going on and on about the hummus. Finally, Levi—dark, brooding Levi Pritchard—had deigned to chew, and you could see when the taste kicked in.

And the smile he'd given Carter in return—it had brightened the set.

Such a small moment—intimate but not dirty, not secret. And they'd had it because they were living in the sunshine. Yeah, sure— Levi might not get another gig after this one. But he might. Or he might just follow Carter around as Carter's star rose higher and higher.

That was their decision and nobody else's.

And they didn't have to change it based on what the world thought about their relationship—it was *their* relationship. Telling the world just let them have it in peace.

The water turned cold, and I reached behind me and shut it off— but I wasn't ready to get out yet.

"Connor?"

Noah's voice from inside the bathroom startled me.

"Sorry," I mumbled, sticking my head out of the curtain. "I was thinking."

"Yeah?" he peered at me, concerned, and then he grabbed a clean towel and thrust it at me. "What about?"

I took the towel and wrapped it around my waist shivering a little.

"About doing the thing that I don't want to do so I can do the things that I do want to do," I said, climbing out of the tub with my body but my mind was still elsewhere.

He walked up to me, dripping skin and all, and wrapped another towel tightly around my shoulders. "Stop," he said into my ear. "You've already done some of that this weekend. Leave the rest of it for later."

I leaned back into his arms. "I really want to go shopping with you again." I closed my eyes, excited by being naked and held by a man. "I want you to grab my hand and kiss me on the cheek and nag me about my spending and—"

"Yeah," he murmured, nuzzling my temple. "That'd be nice."

"So I have to—"

"Not worry about it right now. C'mon down and get brunch, okay? You haven't eaten yet and you've had a big morning. Simple things, Connor. Simple things get you from one step to the next."

He let go of me and walked out of the bathroom, and I brushed my teeth and combed my hair and applied moisturizer while the air dried me completely off. Finally I was ready to wrap the towel around my waist and venture into the bedroom, and I laughed a little at what I saw on the hastily straightened comforter.

Yoga pants—and that horrible T-shirt he'd bought me after Jillian had broken into tears and made the "clown cum rag."

You know that was our *thing,* Vinnie said bitchily from a corner of my mind.

It's a good thing, Vinnie. It can be something I do with him too.

'Cause I just wasn't that special, was I.

I sighed and picked up the T-shirt.

You were. You really were. But so was I. And I want to wear the fucking T-shirt.

And yeah, there was a pouty silence in my head, but by the time I finished with the boxer shorts and the yoga pants, even that had faded.

I was going to spend a day in with Noah, my new lover.

Vinnie really had nothing nice to say about that, so it was just as good he kept quiet, wasn't it?

Noah had opened the back door and set the pastries and a couple of cowboy sandwiches on the small glass-topped table on the patio, along with the milk and a few glasses as well as napkins. I knew that the service (or, well, his grandmother who only came when I was out) kept the patio and the table clean, and the chairs aired out and dust-free, but I'd been gone so often I hadn't had much chance to use them.

Today was warmish—high seventies—but Noah had laid a hoodie on the back of my seat anyway, which I put on before I sat down in the shade.

"Wow," I said, smiling at the spread. "Al fresco. Awesome."

He twisted his full mouth, and I had a flash to where that mouth had been two hours ago. "You know, so you don't feel trapped."

"Oh!" I reached over and grabbed his hand. "Oh no. No, Noah—no. I'm . . . I'm not feeling trapped. Not by you—not by what happened." I blushed. Inane. "Not by making love. I mean . . . you know." I smiled winningly. "I'd like to do that *again*."

He laughed and laced our fingers together. "Good." He kissed my knuckles.

"I . . ." I grimaced. "See, I wanted to come out. And Jillian wasn't sure my career could take it—and, you know, ten years ago, five years ago—"

"You had to be sort of a superstar, or someone with a track record. I get it."

I nodded. He'd pulled his glossy, curly hair back into sort of a man bun before he'd gone out, and I wanted it down again. I wanted to play with it, now that I had the right, but it wasn't the time.

"And Vinnie—he *really* didn't want to come out. Because that would mean his family would know."

Noah closed his eyes. "Connor—"

"I'm not going to lie forever," I said quietly, because I could see it now, flashing before his eyes, his entire life held captive by the fear of a dead man.

He opened his eyes and gave a relieved nod. "Good."

"There's a thousand things I can say, a thousand ways I could spin it for the press, so that Vinnie's name doesn't have to be mentioned. And speculation can remain just that—"

"But that's not *fair*!" Noah burst out, letting go of my hands and standing up.

I smiled uncertainly. "To—?"

"To *you*! Damn it— You . . . you were *mourning* for a *year* alone. You were . . . two months ago, you could barely say his name because you were so afraid someone might guess what he was to you. I mean, *Connor*! You have to know coming back from that sort of thing— that's *hard*. Don't you want people to know how strong you are?"

My mouth went slack, and I felt my face light up, like sunshine. "You think I'm strong?"

Noah had been pacing, and he came to kneel at my feet. "Yes," he said, like he was talking to a child. "Yes, baby, I think you're fucking strong. You didn't start your career once—by my count, this was your fourth try. You held a relationship together when it probably should have disintegrated after the first fuck. You held a *man* together by the sheer stinking strength of your love. Of *course* I think you're strong. But I've heard the gossip—same as you've imagined it. People see that video, and they think you're a drunk. They see the track record, and they think you're a flake. And everything I've seen from you shows me that you—you're a *hero*. Don't you want the world to know who you really are?"

I thought about it. "I don't know . . . I guess if I'd wanted *that*, I wouldn't have become an actor."

He stared at me, openmouthed, as though he couldn't figure out what the words meant.

"Connor, what's wrong with who you are?"

I tried to give him an answer—something insouciant, light, something that would wash the statement away. In the end, I just shook my head and turned toward lunch.

I really was hungry. "So . . . doughnuts for appetizers or breakfast?"

He stood and grasped my chin, making me face him. "Connor Mazynsky, there is nothing wrong with who you are."

My sunshine smile returned, and I bit my lower lip to keep it from stretching to goof-ball limits on my face. "Not when you look at me like that there isn't," I confessed, and then I couldn't look at him anymore. I decided savory for the meal, and sweet pastry for dessert. I grabbed one of the cheese and sausage croissants and blew on it a little, sank my teeth in, and closed my eyes.

"This is really lovely," I said after some chewing and swallowing. Noah was still staring at me, face inscrutable, so I fixed my attention on what I'd come to think of as "my island."

It always looked so peaceful. I bet there was someone out there who could swim that distance, right? Maybe a wet suit, or chicken fat or something for insulation. Maybe a boat? Yeah . . . but swimming seemed personal. There were fish under the water—swimming made you one with the fish.

"Connor?" Noah was saying, and the tone of his voice was at "I've called your name three times and you were in la-la land" timbre.

"Sorry," I said, licking my fingers. I seemed to have finished my croissant.

"Where were you, man?"

I looked back out at my island. "I bet I could swim there," I said, nodding.

"No, you couldn't," he said, like it was a flat-out impossibility.

"No, seriously—a wet suit, some insulation—"

"The water is fifty-eight degrees on a good day. If you jumped in and screamed your way out, you *still* wouldn't see your balls for days."

I jerked back involuntarily. "I just rediscovered my balls," I said, wanting to cup my hands in front of them. "I would like them not to disappear."

"Then stop focusing on the island and listen to me *here*. Connor, why are you disappearing from me?"

I took a deep breath, the kind you use to center yourself in yoga, and tried to put together the threads pulling my brain to that peaceful, isolated little spot of redwood heaven.

"I'm not that strong," I said apologetically. "You looked at me and thought I was strong, and I could list all the ways I'm not, but that wouldn't help. Because the thing is, I still want to come out. And I want to do it and keep Vinnie's name out of it. His family—" I closed my eyes, and I could hear them, kids calling to each other, brothers and sisters and in-laws all telling jokes in the kitchen.

I kept my eyes closed and said, "I'm in the movies, Noah. They're as close to a movie family as you'll get. And . . ." they hadn't called me for Christmas, or Vinnie's birthday last July, or after the funeral at all. "Maybe they don't know about their son, but they've got this picture of him. I know—" cheating and rehab and weakness oh my! "—*so* many bad things that would rip apart that picture. So I need to come out, and I need to do it in a way that doesn't hurt them. But I want to . . ." I shuddered, in the good, ecstatic way. "I want to . . . have a lover who's proud to be mine." I gave him a watery smile. "And I can't do that in the shadows."

"And I told you that you didn't need to do it right now," he said softly. "I meant that. If we just stop talking about it, will you come back from the island today?"

I nodded and took one of the doughnuts, because that was my dessert. I nibbled on it experimentally, and it was *really* yummy, so I took a small bite and let it melt on my tongue.

"These are really good. Where'd you get them?"

"This place that just opened up—Cookie Crumbles—got a real 'rainbow vibration' from the owner, if you know what I mean."

Huh. "Yeah, well, this whole town is under the rainbow. I'm not even looking that shit in the mouth. But we'll definitely have to go back to his place—I can totally stand it."

"Good—so civilized conversation progressing nicely. What else do you want to do with your day?"

I thought about it. "Maybe a bike ride," I said after a moment of pointedly *not* looking at the island. "Not too far—twenty miles maybe? And then we can come back and . . ."

Noah's laugh was evil. "Do stuff that would make it hard to ride a bike after." He nodded and raised his eyebrows.

I blushed. "Pretty much exactly."

He leaned forward and brushed my cheek with his thumb. "You blush so pretty," he said, like a wondering little kid. "I mean—how does that keep happening?"

I shrugged. "I don't know—I didn't used to blush with Vinnie . . ." I thought about it, hard. "Not even back at the beginning."

"So just me, huh?"

I bit my lip and looked away. "It's just . . ." I shrugged. "You're . . . a really decent person. When we first met, and you were all fanboi, I thought, 'Oh, what a nice kid.' And I wanted really badly to keep that . . . that new-movie-star gloss on, you know? So you would always think I was . . . Connor Montgomery, movie star!"

"You think I don't have my—"

"Your slutty college days?" I said dryly. "That's not turning tricks to make rent, Noah. Or paying off your parents or . . . any of the other things we just agreed not to talk about. That's . . ." I shrugged, uncomfortable. "That's what growing up should be like. So no. You sleeping around in college didn't make me think any less of you. So it matters what you think of me. And . . . I just keep being afraid that the next thing out of my mouth is going to be the one that lets you down."

He looked at me soberly, taking me serious in a way I wasn't sure anyone else in my life ever had. "Remember what you said last night, about Vinnie?"

So many things about Vinnie . . . "That he did the one thing I couldn't forgive?"

Noah nodded. "He left you. I get . . . I get that you're still healing. And I get that I might be your healing guy and it might not last beyond that."

I opened my mouth to contradict him, but he didn't let me.

"But right now, think of me for you like you were for Vinnie. The only thing you could do that I couldn't forgive would be to leave without giving us a chance. And even then . . . if there was anything left of my heart . . . I might put it together if you came back and asked."

I stared at him, shaken by that much . . . raw emotion radiating from his eyes, his hands on mine, the tension at his mouth. Oh God . . .

Vinnie, I can't—

Coward.

Vinnie, you're still in my head—

But not in your bed, asshole. Give him something.

Noah smiled then, and patted my cheek gently. "I'm going to let you contemplate your island for a few minutes," he offered. "I'll be back when the dishes are done, and we'll see about that bike ride."

But I couldn't look at my island after that. I stared after him, and tried to come up with words that would do justice to the words he'd given *me*.

I had no words—none. Only this sudden warmth when I hadn't realized I was cold, and this sudden need to *do* something for him, because he'd just offered so much to me.

I stood up restlessly and thought one last wistful time about jumping in the water and trying to swim, and then walked into the kitchen. Noah was throwing away napkins and putting the leftover pastries back in the box, his movements loose and unhurried.

He *was* the real deal. He'd given me everything he had to make sure I knew I could lean on him for strength—and then relaxed and hoped I'd take it when I needed it.

Oh, little did he know.

I *always* needed it.

Carefully, because he moved with efficiency, I slid behind him and wrapped my arms around his waist, resting my cheek against his neck.

"Mmm . . ." His voice rumbled through his chest.

"You'll never be just my healing guy," I said after a moment. "You are . . . so much more than that."

He dried his hands on a dish towel and turned around to hold me against his chest.

"I didn't need to hear that today," he said kindly.

"I really needed to say it." I didn't want to look at him, into those all-too-perceptive eyes.

"Then I'm not going to complain. Do you still want that bike ride?" he asked.

I tilted my head back, and he played with the hair around my hairline. "Oh yes." I looked forward to being on a bike with him again. "I . . . I've always loved it, but I've never been able to find company."

His smile was contented like a cat's. "So *not* something that you and Vinnie . . ."

I rolled my eyes. "No, not something that Vinnie and I used to do."

"Then I'm all for it."

Noah refused to take me mountain biking this day—we had to stick to the roads and the easy trails, no off-roading or risk taking for me.

I got the feeling he was expecting me to do something that would jinx what we both knew was going to happen that night.

But because Noah was a *stellar* lover and a fantastic human being, I didn't have to think about what was going to happen that night. I concentrated on the forest as the bike wound in and out. I concentrated on the flatlands running the edge of the sound, or on the beauty of a gorge we crossed, hugging the side of the bridge like limpets, afraid two cars would need to use the bridge with us.

Noah took me to a lookout, the plateau of a tiny mountain that embraced the sound, the hamlet of Bluewater Bay, and the awesome backdrop of Mount Olympus in one majestic panorama. I must have stood there for half an hour, glutting my vision on my new home.

From this angle, my island was much smaller but just as mysterious, and I couldn't see my house at all.

Still, I stared out there, thinking about my obsession with the place. It was small, but if I reached out and touched it . . . right there . . . I could hold it in my hand.

"What do you see there?" Noah asked quietly. He could tell where I was looking, I guess.

I flushed and struggled for words. What did I think was there? Vinnie, wearing ragged jeans and a flannel shirt, stocking a cabin with firewood, smiling and saying, "I've been waiting for you here!"? Vinnie had hated the Pacific Northwest. Hell, Vinnie had hated the ocean north of Monterey.

Was I going to see his family, there on Christmas Day, all happy and smiling and offering me a place by the tree and some hot cocoa? His mom, Denise; his father, David; and his grown brother and sisters? Would I see his nieces and nephews playing by the tree, all seven of them? Would I get to be "Vinnie's friend Connor" again?

"Uncle Connor," I mumbled to myself. I should have been Uncle Connor.

No, I didn't want to see Vinnie's family on that island. Come to think about it, I didn't want to see Vinnie, either.

What would I see?

Unconsciously I looked at Noah.

"You'd be on that island," I said, smiling at the thought. He probably rocked the plaid shirt/jeans and waffle-stomper look. There was something rugged about him in spite of his youth and his ranginess and that sarcastic wit. If anyone could *do* a small cabin on an island, Noah could.

But right now, Noah was looking at me uneasily. "I'll be wherever you are," he said, and I was suddenly in the real world and not the ghost world of people who weren't real, walking about on the San Juan Islands in the mist.

"Then maybe we'll take a boat out there one day and see," I said lightly, trying not to obsess anymore.

Noah nodded suspiciously and pulled two energy bars out of the pack at his waist. He handed me one, and gestured to the water bottle attached to my bike. I grabbed it, and together we shared a snack.

"Good thing you thought of these," I said, after we'd downed them. "We would have been starving when we got back."

"We'll still be starving," he said glumly. "So we don't have any more time for me to worry about what's going on in that pointy little head of yours."

"Nothing!" I defended. "Nothing is—"

Noah shook his head. "We'll take a boat out to the island, Connor, and we'll see whatever's there. But stop obsessing about it. There's something going on," he tapped the center of my helmet, "right in here that makes me *very* uneasy."

I grinned. "Nothing's happening up there," I promised him. "That's usually the problem. Now let's go back—I can make us dinner!" With that I turned the bike around on the small service road and coasted back down.

It didn't come up during dinner, and when we were done, we spent an hour on the couch, flipping through the channels for the shows on summer hiatus.

"Look, there's our baby," I said, pausing on *Wolf's Landing*. "Ooh—it's back in the first episode, before whatserface got replaced by Amelia."

"Have you worked with her yet?" Noah asked curiously.

I shrugged. "Not so much—she seems okay."

"I'm waiting to see that new director on set—Rafael something. He's supposed to be hot shit."

I grimaced. "Yeah. Ah, the young, the cocky, the absolutely sure that camera angle hasn't been done a thousand times before."

Noah chuckled. "Yeah, well, it's all been done a thousand times before—it's up to the individuals to make it seem like they *discovered* that idea, right?"

I thought of stories told about the late, great Kim Manners, and how he'd literally lain down on the ground to film a shot from the actors' feet on up.

"Yeah," I said thoughtfully. "Make the individual touch matter, right?"

Noah was smiling, that wicked smile he'd had this morning when he'd caught me feeling myself up. "Speaking of individual touch," he said gruffly. "You need to go shower."

He'd showered while I'd started dinner, and I stretched self-consciously. "Yeah . . . yeah—I'm sorry, do I offend?"

He shook his head. "No, Connor. I just . . . left some things up there. I think you need to take a look at them before you clean up."

I started to squirm, remembering that he'd dominated me that morning, and that he was probably going to keep doing it until I said stop.

I didn't want to say stop. So long, I'd been waiting for someone to tell me what to do. *Noah* could tell me what to do.

"Uh, okay." I found that everything down south had clenched, was aching, because of the things that may or may not be upstairs waiting for me. Oh man—I could hardly take a real kiss! "Uh, you know it's been a while, right?"

Noah nodded soberly. "Yeah, sweetheart. That's why the things. You're going to need some help, I think, not to rocket off the bed."

I smiled, feeling light and airy and . . . pliable. "Okay, Noah. You're the boss here."

He looked startled, like I'd maybe said or done something important without realizing it, but I couldn't stay and figure out what.

He'd given me an order. I needed to follow it. I loved it when life was simple.

CHAPTER ELEVEN

IT WASN'T SO EASY,
THAT THING I JUST DID

I let the water run and then turned to the counter, more twitchy than curious. He'd left a note on top of the three boxes balanced there: *Choose your favorites. I just want you ready.*

Choose my favorites?

He'd raided the sex-toy shop like a *boss*.

The plug set was graduated—and I could see his thinking there. *Noah* was pretty big—he didn't want to hurt me, and it had been a year. There was also a dildo, bigger than the plugs but smaller than Noah, and two cock rings—one rubber, one leather—and that was just what he'd set out on the counter. In the little boutique bag on the back of the toilet seat he had everything from nipple clamps to handcuffs to blindfolds to paddles and ticklers—Jesus, Noah, how many times were we going to have sex tonight?

I stepped into the water and started to wash, practically panicking from all of the possibilities. A thousand scenarios, all of them overwrought, overstaged, and kinky as hell, filtered behind my eyes like a porn film on Super 8.

Vinnie, have you seen this shit?

Yes, Connor, I've seen it and used it.

Oh.

My hands were shaking by the time I got out of the shower, and when I picked up one of the boxes, Noah's voice from the next room surprised me into dropping it. "Don't overthink that shit! That's for later if we get there."

"Get out of my brain!"

I must have sounded a little panicked, because he opened the door and fixed me with those fathomless eyes. "I could hear you stressing from downstairs—it's weird. It's like radar. Now calm down, make a decision, choose a plug, forget about the cock ring and the other stuff—think of it as sort of a gift. You didn't pack any sex stuff because you thought sex was dead. This is a welcome-back-to-your-sex-life present—but we're not going to use it all tonight, or even ever."

I looked at the bag again, feeling both relieved and disappointed. "Not ever?" I reached in and pulled out the butt plug with the flogger tail. "'Cause this is sort of cool—I've never seen one of these."

Noah rolled his eyes. "No, you were too busy trying to land roles, Mr. I'm-a-Hollywood-slut. You have seen *nothing* like horny until you've been in a college dorm room with a bunch of repressed jocks who want to go college-try-bi."

My mouth fell open, and I gave a dismayed little gasp. "You mean . . . I have to *study* to have sex again?"

Noah started to laugh, and he opened the door fully and came into the bathroom, wearing nothing but his boxer shorts. Without asking permission, he slid in behind me, so we were both facing the mirror, and he smoothed his rough, pink-palmed hands down my light-brown shoulders.

"Calm down," he said throatily, breath tickling my ear. "There is no studying. There is no test at the end. Connor, there is really just you and me."

His hands, my shoulders—that was really all it took. My bones melted, muscles spreading in pools, as I allowed him to take over.

"There is a you and me," I said, partly to make sure.

"You're going to doubt that now?" He ran his lips from my ear to my shoulder blade, via the side of my neck.

"No," I sighed. No doubting, just doing. Was that why I'd been so good at sex? I hadn't seen what happened after the last come?

He ran his hands firmly over my moist skin, kissing, touching, nibbling. I watched in the mirror as his brown fingers pinched my nipples, soft, hard, *harder*, until I keened and wrapped my hand around my cock.

He pulled it away.

"Open the box with the three," he said, and because he asked me to, my hands hardly trembled.

They were bubblegum pink.

"Lube the small one," he whispered.

I did, the clear lubricant dripping slowly down the pointed end. He took the base from me carefully, and his hand disappeared from the mirror. A breath later, the tip of the plug traced its careful way down my crease, dipping for a moment into my pucker, then poking the base of my balls.

"Tease," I whispered. Then, "Oh!"

While I'd been talking, he'd slid it right back up and home.

I clenched around it and whined—it was small, the width of the widest part *maybe* the width of his thumb. Just enough to feel—but not enough to fill.

"You *have* done this before," he chuckled. He tugged on it until the bulb kissed my rim, and then pushed it back. And then again, and then back. My cock ached, flopping wetly against my thigh. I leaned forward, resting my hands on the side of the sink and thrusting my ass out, unconsciously begging for more.

"Noah . . ." It was a plea.

"Lube the second one," he ordered. He played with the first one the whole time—and my hands shook so hard I almost dropped the lube and the plug.

He let go of the thing in my ass long enough to rescue the second plug, and I retrieved the lube from the sink.

"Hold on," he murmured, and tugged the small one out.

I gasped and whined, because I was *so* much more sensitive after all his playing than I'd been at the beginning, and then, while I was still breathing hard, he popped the second one in.

"Nungh!"

"Good." He was laughing at me—and I didn't care. I was at his mercy, yes, but he was taking care of me that way. It's the only reason to put your pleasure in someone else's hands—if you know they'll use their hands to stroke that pleasure into ecstasy.

I clenched around this one and whimpered again. Bigger—I could feel it, but still not enough. I stuck my ass out and rocked back and forth, needing so hard, so bad, that I wasn't sure I could make it.

"Connor!" Noah popped me sharply in the back of the thigh, and I stopped rocking.

"Sorry," I mumbled.

"No, baby, don't be sorry." Noah rubbed my bottom, easing the sting. "Just focus for me, okay?"

I nodded, finding my center, finding peace. He didn't tease me with this one, just pulled it out slowly. I gave a hard shudder, moaning into the cave of my body as I leaned over the sink, but I managed to keep it together. The long stroke of his hand helped.

"Here," he murmured. "Stand up. I need to use the sink."

I stood up, feeling empty, deprived, and watched him as he rinsed the plug off in hot water and antibacterial soap, and then . . . lubed it again?

He smiled sleepily at me and dropped his boxers to the floor. Then, while I was staring at his cock—which looked just as good as it had looked this morning, and just as alien, as though I'd never seen one before—he arched his back, and moved the hand with the plug behind him.

I stared at him, my mouth open, my body flushed and ripe and aching, as he thrust the plug slowly in his backside. His lips parted, his face grew lax, and then his entire body slackened, probably when it slipped into place.

His eyes met mine in the mirror, sultry and debauched, and I was aroused beyond words.

"You . . . you . . ."

"I like the way it feels." He sounded so replete that I moved my hand to my cock, just to join him in that place. He knocked my hand away and rolled his half-hooded eyes. "Now one more, and we'll go into the bedroom, okay?"

I nodded, but my hands shook too badly to even pull the plug out of the plastic nest. He took it from me slowly, and I saw the tremor in his hands too. He wasn't shaking badly enough for him to drop things, but I was reassured, somehow, to know he was aroused, and it was hard to wait, and that this moment wasn't easy either.

His warm palm in the small of my back soothed me, and he took the lubed plug and thrust it slowly inside.

"Aaah . . ." I remembered this, the burn, the stretch, that strangely peaceful headspace you had to put yourself in to accommodate it. "Oooohhh . . ." And it was in, and I was full, full and shaking with it. Noah wrapped his arms around my shoulders then, covering my nakedness, filling me with heat. He buried his nose in the hair at my nape, and his arms tightened convulsively, just as I noticed his cock, pressed against my right cheek, granite hard and slicker than the plug in my asshole.

"I," he breathed, "am so ready to fuck you. Can we make it to the bed, or should I do it right here, where you can watch me?"

I dragged my eyes to the mirror, saw the darkness of his skin had grown even darker with a sex flush, and that my throat had washed purple with the same. We looked debauched, both of us, like we'd been fucking all night, and would fuck some more, and would sleep in each other's cum and wake up smelling of sex with throats raw from screaming.

I closed my eyes and shuddered. "Bed," I managed. It was probably the only decision I was capable of making right now.

He reached down and, to my surprised, grabbed my cock and tugged. The touch was sensual, but the idea of it was so comic I actually came down from my peak a little.

"Are we doing that now?" I asked, allowing myself to be led.

"I'd put a leash on it and take you out in public," he threatened.

I had to laugh. "You hate people looking at you!" He did—he was so good at being self-effacing, at kicking back with his phone and simply watching the world and allowing it to amuse him.

He squeezed me and gave a tug sharp enough to make me moan. When I opened my eyes, he was close, looking deep inside my heart. "Connor, if you are naked, your ass spread with a plug bigger than this one, and a leash wrapped around your balls as I parade you in front of the world for all to see, do you really think they're going to be looking at me?"

My vision washed black, and my knees trembled. Noah caught me and helped me sit down on the bed—which was a mistake because the plug was driven in particularly deep.

"Oh my *God*!" That quickly, I was a breath away from coming.

"Shh . . . shh . . ." He ran his hands all over my body, not arousing, calming while keeping the desire stoked. I slumped on the turned-down bed until he pushed me back and shoved a pillow under my hips, then spread my thighs and propped up my knees.

I was laid out for him to use, and if I'd had any room in me for doubt, I'd be terrified. I'd never trusted Vinnie like this, had *never* given someone power over me like this. But I needed . . . oh God.

Tears leaked out the corners of my eyes, my desire for possession was so acute.

I probably could have come just from *imagining* his mouth on my cock, but he could tell—I was too close to dick with, too close even to blow.

"Are you ready?" he asked, tugging slightly on the plug.

"God, yes," I all-but-sobbed.

"One rule."

"Please . . ."

"Don't hold back," he ordered, and then yanked the plug out and slid his cock home.

I screamed, loud and breathlessly as he found his seat, and then louder as he rocked his hips back. "*Noah*!"

"I'm fucking you!" He hammered inside of me with no reserve, no inhibitions, just the hard, furious fucking of someone who has been on edge entirely too long.

"God, yes!" I screamed the words, and he responded by fucking me harder. He said not to hold back, and I didn't. Oh my *God*, I had forgotten this! I was high, I was *soaring*, my body shrieking on the peak of orgasm in that breathless gasp before the weightless plummet down. I wrapped my legs around his hips, clutched at his shoulders, and *held on*.

My body washed hot and cold, and I was forced to close my eyes, because the expression on Noah's face—fierce, relentless, surfing the ragged edge of climax and insanity, was too close a mirror for what I felt.

And I—I was without brakes. I pounded his ass with my heels, scraped his shoulders with my fingernails, and the racket— God, I would not stop.

"Fuck . . . fuck . . . fuck . . . Oh Noah . . . So close . . . I've got to . . . Please, can you make me—"

"You can do it, Connor. C'mon, baby . . . c'mon . . . I need to feel you clench . . . need to feel you so tight . . . Can you come for me? C'mon, *come* for me!"

He sat back on his knees and shoved my thighs up. "Grab your dick, damn it. Let's go!"

Oh! Just that little bit of control, that did it, the exquisite pressure of my own fist, jacking my cock, and Noah's relentless fucking . . .

This time I screamed so loud my voice cracked, and I felt it, boiling up from all points south, my stretched asshole, my tingling taint, my hard, tender balls, and my cock, *mine*, which was alive and bucking in my fist. Stroke, stroke, stroke, the tightening of my thumb and forefinger around my crown, the combination of heat and friction ramping the pleasure to unbearable levels.

"*Noah!*"

My voice broke as I came, hot and urgent, the semen spurting between us. *We can wear it on our skin*, I thought dreamily, just as Noah roared, and rutted feverishly inside of me, locked in place by the clenching of my ass.

I could feel him, the spurting of his cock, the heat of his cum inside me. I'd forgotten that feeling, that alive feeling of holding another person inside of you, of having their fluid leaking from your body.

My eyes closed, with Noah's cock still lodged solidly up my ass, and I started drifting.

His kisses on my face pulled me back—mostly. "Con?"

"Yeah."

"'Kay. Making sure you're still here."

"Is hard," I confessed vaguely. "So . . . loose." Not just the rim of my ass, which was beginning to leak cum around Noah's girth, but my body, my mind—everything.

Noah puffed laughter and kissed me soundly. I focused on *that*: his heat, his body, the merging of the two of us. Those things I could get a handle on.

"I've got to move," he said after a moment, and I realized he was clenching and unclenching his ass—pretty much like I still was because, well, there was something *in* there.

I made a sound of disappointment and relief as he slid out, and then I rolled over to my side to watch him walk toward the bathroom.

"Can I see?" I slurred, the desire to watch him play with himself— even at the end of lovemaking—surprisingly strong.

He looked at me over his shoulder and propped one hand on the doorframe. "Aren't you feeling kinky." He winked.

"It's just . . ." Vinnie hadn't liked bottoming. He'd let me top, but even though I'd tried—had, in fact, done the things with the plugs and the stretching and the kindness—he'd never really relaxed into it. I mean, I got it. Being gay was not equivalent with loving anal, but I just *loved* it so much. I'd wanted to give him that same high. Knowing that Noah loved it too—without shame or inhibition or stigma about being a "top" and so not wanting his ass played with—that did something hot and melty to my insides. "Sexy," I finished weakly, watching as he slid his hand down his backside.

The hot pink of the plug stood out in vibrant contrast to Noah's almost black skin, and he paused his hand right at the little pull loop at the base. With a shudder, he tapped the plug, putting on a show for me.

I couldn't look away.

He tapped the plug again, and let out a breathless moan, and my spaghetti muscles did the unthinkable and propelled me out of bed.

"Let me," I pleaded, drawn to the long line of his back, the otter-sleek muscles of his legs and thighs.

"Sure," he breathed. He leaned against the wall and thrust his ass out a little more, and I touched the plug gently, almost afraid.

This could hurt.

He shuddered, and groaned and bit into his biceps, and I dropped my hand.

"Killing me, Connor. Don't tease!"

"Oh! Yeah— Okay!" I grasped the plug again and tugged with some force, making him moan into his shoulder. Out, out, out, until the widest part was wedged solidly in the circle of his sphincter. I looked down at it, marveling. He was bigger than the plug and he fit inside *me*—did he like to look at it, like a human magic trick? Watch me fit a human inside of this human?

His fist hit the doorframe with a frustrated *thump*. "Connor . . ."

I let go, and the plug sucked right back in.

"Augh!"

I squatted down behind him—probably ugly naked, with his cum running down my backside and down my thighs, but I didn't care. Using one hand on his hip to steady myself, I grabbed it again and pulled out slowly, slowly, slowly, knowing he was stretched now, wide, wide enough?

The plug popped out, and I nudged his elbow with the back of my hand. "Put this in the sink, willya?"

"Yeah but—"

I licked his stretched asshole, and he took it from me. I heard the thing drop into the sink with a clatter.

"Connor?" He whined my name; there was something he needed.

I licked again, and again, and reached around front and ran a tentative finger around his cock.

Like mine, it was getting hard again.

He grunted and thrust back against my tongue, and I blessed him for getting the good lube—not flavored but not slimy either. In fact, it was tangy, a little like cum, and I didn't mind imagining that it was *my* cum I was tasting, because I'd just taken him, and needed to taste him again.

"Do it," Noah ordered, his voice far away. "C'mon, Connor, do it."

My cock throbbed to the command in his voice. I grabbed his hips and hauled myself up, then smoothed my hands down his back. I pressed my whole body along the length of his and nuzzled his ear. "Yeah?"

"Please," he whispered, begging and ordering in the same breath.

I shuddered. He could not know what that did to me, to be told what to do, to be needed, to be wanted so badly.

His hole clenched, wet and tight, around my cockhead as I breached his entrance, and then it clamped down, sucking me in, tighter, deeper, until I was plastered against his back, spreading his ass cheeks so I could get closer, closer . . .

I wrapped my arms around his slender waist, and welcomed the weight of one of his hands, holding me to him, stroking my wrists with his thumb.

"Good?" His voice was strained, breathy.

I half sobbed, wiping my cheek against his shoulder blade and pulling my hips back. "Yes ... God, so good. I need ..."

"Move, baby. I want it too."

I snapped my hips forward, and the sound he made was filthy and, the shudder that rocked his body resonated deep in my balls.

"Oooooh ..."

I pulled back until I stretched him, and then—

"Ooooh ..."

Slow. I'd just climaxed; my body could take it slow, right? I moved slowly, powerfully, feeling like every pump was so deep he could press his stomach and feel my cock pressing back. Slow. Slow. Slow.

Noah let go of my wrist and started thrusting back, *hard*, every time I thrust forward.

"You enjoying this?" he panted.

"God yes!"

"You like going slow?"

I whimpered. It was hard.

"You wanna, I dunno, *fuck me hard and fast*?"

"*Oh my God, yes!*"

The fucking magnificent power! I clenched one hand on his hip and reached up and grabbed that soft, glossy hair, pulling his head back as he thrust out his behind. And then I hung on for the ride.

"*Faster, Connor, harder! Oh fuck, oh fuck, that's it, hit that, hit that, hit that c'mon, Connor, you fuck me so fucking good!*"

He howled that last word, and his arms gave out, his face pressed against the wall, his body clenching so tightly around my dick I couldn't move, probably couldn't pull all the way out if I'd wanted to. I stayed inside him, rutting, trying so hard to just catch that spot, that one place on my cock, that ... that ...

Noah cried out. "*Right there!*" and apparently that was the spot for both of us.

My body rolled forward, clenching to Noah's, and I let go of his hair and hip so I could grab his shoulders and hold on for one long, bone-rattling come.

I collapsed against him, the semen from my second climax easing my passage out of his backside. Messy. We were both messy, outside and in, sweaty, covered in fluids, and I didn't care. I wrapped my arms around his waist again, wanting to roll in him.

"Wanna shower?" he asked, words muffled against the wall.

"No."

He laughed and pushed off the wall enough to turn and hold me. I laid my head against his chest and listened to his heart thumping, strong, sure, and slowing down from what must have been a hell of a gallop.

"No? That's sort of dirty," he teased.

"I like dirty," I mumbled. I was surprised my knees could still hold me. "I like sexy, filthy, dirty you all over and in me."

He quivered all over and gathered me tighter. "Talking like *that* will get you fucked again, and that might kill us both."

I looked up at him, so mellow all I could do was smile. "Can we go together?" I asked soberly. It was all I asked.

He startled, as though he'd just realized what he'd done with his careless hyperbole. Then he kissed my forehead, as though in benediction.

"Yeah," he promised. "If at all possible, we can go together."

"'Kay," I said, half-asleep on my feet. "Let's do that."

He steered me to bed then, still dripping on both ends, and slid me between the sheets. He kissed my temple and told me he'd be back after he took a piss and cleaned the jizz off the wall.

I giggled at that, and was still giggling when he came back to bed. I groped him without finesse just to make sure, and my fingertips came back sticky.

"No, you big baby," he muttered, laughing. "I didn't wash."

"Good."

I didn't want to talk anymore, not to Noah, not to Vinnie. *Especially* not to Vinnie. Perfect. I couldn't remember, not once, feeling this perfect after sex.

This was why men fell asleep when they came. They wanted to remember life this way.

CHAPTER TWELVE

WE'LL ALWAYS HAVE PARIS

Sometime in the night, Noah rolled over and simply took me, thrusting into my body gently until we both grunted and spent what little our bodies had left.

He fell asleep immediately, but I lingered on the edge, thinking, *Noah. Noah is inside me.* I could see him, sort of a dazzling light around a warm, solid darkness at my back. I remembered when Vinnie had done this, and I'd always been confused—mostly asleep and in the dark, Vinnie had been a cock, a hand, hips slapping against my ass, but not a person.

Noah was *Noah.*

He was different.

I woke up to the smell of body wash and steam coming from the bathroom—and bacon and potatoes coming from downstairs.

Noah's here.

The thought shot me out of bed and into the shower—which was still warm—and I scrubbed quickly and carefully.

Yeah. Riding a bicycle was not going to be on the agenda today.

Ass, asshole, inner thighs, outer thighs, biceps, triceps, stomach muscles—Jesus, and I was in shape! It all ached, as though I'd spent the night flexing in a killer session of Pilates instead of getting laid.

My rim was sensitized—the slightest touch made my body sing, and then all those sore parts groaned in unison. *Holy God, man, give us a break! You can't fuck all weekend!*

Wanna make a bet?

But I wasn't so gone into sexy-sexy land that I didn't remember I had some family obligations.

I had to buy Noah's grandmother a present, and show up at a birthday party. I had to meet Noah's little sisters and his father and sit at their table and be charming and hopefully not phony even a little and make them like me for *me*, not the movie star but for *Connor*, the real person.

It was sort of daunting and a little bit exhilarating.

I was going to meet Noah's family as a boyfriend.

Noah was right—for all of the things I claimed to have done, when it came right down to it, I had very little on my résumé.

Wait—I *was* going to meet them as a boyfriend, right?

"Noah?" I asked a few minutes later, coming down the stairs dressed and finger-fluffing my hair. "What are we?"

"What?" Noah stuck his head out of the kitchen so he could see me. "No product today?" To make sure.

"Shit— Wait— I'll go—"

"No, that's fine. You look sort of adorable without it. What was the question?"

"What are we?"

Noah looked up and to the right, then to the left, like he was searching his files for the appropriate context. "Men?"

"No!"

"*Gay* men?"

"No— I mean *yes* but that's not what I'm asking."

"Then help me out here, baby, I'm lost."

He was wearing a plain white chef's apron over his T-shirt and cargo shorts. He looked like he lived here—anything but lost.

"Are you burning my bacon?"

"No, because it's all cooked, and even *that* sounds dirty after last night." He grinned, all sexy, and I walked right into his arms and kissed him. Mmm . . . yeah. That hadn't changed either. Still good.

He pulled back and grimaced. "And *you* are a distraction. What were you asking me again?"

I turned toward the kitchen and the giant piles of potatoes, bacon, eggs, and toast on the table.

"Holy God. Are we having the whole cast for breakfast?"

Noah pinkened. "Uh—actually—"

"We have *company*?"

"Well, Viv texted. She and Cheddar broke up, and she didn't have a gift either, and I told her to come by and we'd eat, and then go get something from town."

"Viv broke up with Cheddar?" I asked, sort of sad. "I mean . . . she seemed so in love with him—I had hopes!"

Noah's smile made his cheeks apple. "The other way around. But *you* are a *romantic*!" he said, like he'd discovered I was a doctor in my spare time. "That is *amazing*. I love that!"

"But—" I flailed my arms. "But *why*?"

He grew serious for a moment. "Because Cheddar was right, hon. He's small-town boy with a very teeny brain. Viv . . . she's going to be . . . God. Anything. She's going to cure cancer or run for office or something."

All of the banter and the joy faded from my morning.

"So, can we eat breakfast or do we have to wait for her?" I asked brightly.

"Wait, what did you mean, 'What are we?'"

"Nothing—not important." I slid out of his arms and trotted to the table. The eggs were a combination of runny and burnt, the bacon was *definitely* burnt, and the potatoes were burnt on one side and hard on the other.

Suddenly I didn't have to worry about keeping my happy face on—I had to worry about keeping my "Looks yummy, hon, can't wait to eat!" face on.

"Mmm . . ." I said, keeping my lips together and my eyes wide. "Looks—"

"Like crap," he said baldly. "What just happened here?"

I grimaced. "We learned you can't cook eggs."

"No—before that. You said, 'What are we?' Let's start there."

I selected a slice of bacon that didn't look too burnt and opened my mouth.

"Don't eat that!" he snapped, yanking it out of my fingers. "It did *not* look that bad when I put it on the table."

"No, it's fine!" I lied, desperate for something—anything—to put this day back where it had been when I'd come down the stairs.

"Connor, put the bacon down," Noah commanded, and he had his game face on.

Just like that we were back in bed, and I was primed to do what he told me.

I put the bacon down, and then rolled my eyes at myself. "Yes, *sir*."

"Don't be a smartass. Let's go back to 'What are we?' What *are* we?"

I'd balanced the bacon on top of the mound of burnt potatoes. As I stared at it, it broke in half and tumbled down to the base of hash-black mountain.

"Are we . . . boyfriends?" I asked. "Is that how you're going to introduce me to your family?"

"Was going to, yes. Is that a problem?"

I glanced up and met his eyes, smiling wistfully. "No," I said after a moment. "No."

Noah nodded slowly. "Then why'd the happy go out of our day, baby? What's the problem?"

"You're just like your sister." My voice wobbled. "You could . . . cure cancer or . . . run for office or something. It was a nice fantasy—that you'd be okay being my driver or PA or whatever—but you're going to get bored."

He sighed and moved around the table. Once again we were groin to groin, and this time he framed my face with his hands and kissed me. I responded, because how could I not?

He pulled back. "Of course I'll get bored." He paused while my heart shriveled. "But I've got faith I'll find something else to do. Day trading? Writing? Sure. I've got half of the Great American Screenplay in my dresser drawer—why not? But that's the thing. You and me, we can keep busy. But we can keep each other busy too, so I don't think it's going to be a problem."

Some of the sunshine seeped into the day again. "Okay," I said, that same wistful smile creeping back. I looked at the failed breakfast on the table and shook my head. "You did so well with the veggies when you heated the lasagna that one night. What the hell happened?"

He kissed me again, until I melted into his chest. Each individual muscle group in my back and neck dissolved into goo, and my heart started to thaw again, after that frozen instant of panic.

"I got distracted." He rubbed the top of my head with his chin. "Because I was happy."

I tilted my head back and smiled better this time. "You were happy?"

He nodded. "Still am. But, baby, we've got to get you to your stylist at work—your roots are totally showing."

I gasped and covered the top of my head with my hand. "Oh fuck—you're so goddamned tall!"

He laughed—but he didn't let go. In fact, that's where we were standing when there was a knock at the door.

"Fuck," Noah muttered. "She can't see this disaster—she'll never let me live it down!"

My day was happy again. I stood and kissed his cheek. "Okay—you throw that crap away, and I'll distract her. We can go get those doughnut things that turned me on the other day."

He narrowed his eyes like he was going to argue about being turned on by a pastry, but I smacked his ass and trotted toward the door.

Viv looked . . . sad, when I let her in, and without thinking I opened my arms. She burrowed in, and I remembered those moments with Jillian. Hugging girls tight was nice—they were soft and they smelled *really* good, and girls like Viv didn't seem to have a problem at all with holding tight and trusting you'd hold them back.

"How you doin', sweetheart?" I asked semiplayfully, and she nodded against me. "Not so good?" I'd never touched hair like hers, with those amazing corkscrews and tiny curls, but I stroked her head, careful not to tangle, and then half laughed.

"What?" she asked, still jammed against my chest.

"Your hair," I said in wonder. "It is *so soft*."

She pulled back then and smiled at me, her eyes red-rimmed but her soul intact. "Yeah?"

I nodded. "Your brother's is too, but it's . . ."

"Slimy," she said with sibling disgust.

I shook my head. "No, smooth but—"

"You have no idea how much shit he puts in it so it does that."

I frowned. "I didn't see anything on the counter—"

"No. No, you've got no idea. He probably keeps it in his overnight bag. He is a vain motherfucker, and you should know that about him."

I laughed. He was vain, and cooking was something he had to concentrate on. Oh, thank God. "It's so good to know he's not perfect," I said, meaning it.

She raised an eyebrow at me, looking as skeptical as a three-year-old about broccoli. "God, are *you* in for disappointment." In the background, some of the clatter from the kitchen escalated, and she tried to look around my shoulder. "What's that noise? Shouldn't we be going in for breakfast?"

"He's cleaning up from dinner," I said with a straight face. "We decided to go for coffee and doughnuts."

"Oh, thank God." She sniffled a little and stepped back. I found a box of Kleenex on the mantel and handed it to her. "He's a horrible cook. I mean, Gran taught him how to make side dishes but anything else he tries, he destroys."

Oh lordie—she was more than dear, she was a gift from the gods. I took the Kleenex from her and carefully wiped under her eyes and made her blow her nose.

"You and I are going to have long talks," I told her, my morning happy completely returned. "And you are going to tell me all the ways in which he isn't perfect."

She looked at me sideways. "Why is this important?"

"Because I believe in happy endings," I said soberly, and hello, Vinnie's almost-forgotten psycho cow. She burst back into tears again, and I was still cleaning her up when Noah ran back in.

Well, at least I knew I wasn't the only one who wasn't perfect.

We stopped at the kite store, at Noah's direction, one of those places full of beautiful bright rainbow wind twirlies.

"Oh . . ." Viv complained as we looked around the store. "Noah . . . No. Just—"

"Gran loves them," he said. "And watch—he can pick kitsch out of a designer boutique. It's insane—it's like a superpower."

I ignored the heathens. "Look at this!" I called from the corner of the store. I held it up and watched both sets of brown eyes widen. "It's great, isn't it?"

A bear—with arms that caught the wind—flailed and chased a hunter. As the bear's arms spun, the hunter's pants fell down and pulled up and fell down. You know—'cause he was bare-assed, shitting in the woods and now he was being chased by a bear?

I loved it.

Delighted, I spun the arms around as fast as I could and *bloop-whoop-bloop*, there went the poor hunter's trousers.

I looked up at Viv and Noah, nodding excitedly. "What do you think?"

"It's hideous!" Viv squawked, and I sort of deflated.

"Really?" Couldn't they see it was wonderful? The woodwork was perfect, and it spun like a dream, and *bloop-whoop-bloop*, his pants just wouldn't stay up.

"Hideously *awesome*," Viv said, and when I looked up she was rubbing her side as Noah set something down quickly in front of him.

"Are you okay?"

"Gas," she muttered. "Because I haven't eaten yet. It's great, Connor. I think you actually picked the one thing Gran will love the best."

I nodded at Noah, looking for approval, but he was sort of staring at me, jaw slack, eyes wide and limpid.

"It's great, right?"

"Yeah," he said weakly. "She's right: you're the only one who could have picked it out."

I bought it, and Viv picked out the bag—something sort of boring with a pale pink bow and cream-colored paper that looked really expensive—but the windmill fit right in. We went to get coffee, and I was practically dancing in excitement.

"So, what's she like? I mean, Noah says she's sweet, and she taught him how to cook, and you guys decorated the house just great, so I know she's got good taste—"

Viv burst out coughing.

"Are you okay?"

"Oh yeah, but you're making me dizzy with all that bouncing. Noah . . ."

Noah nodded, and looked at me, crooking his finger. "C'mere, baby," he said softly, and I walked into his space. He didn't put his hands on my hips or my shoulders, and I fidgeted, wondering why.

"Do you want to be out here?" he asked and for a moment my mind went blank.

"I'd forgotten I wasn't out already," I said, feeling stupid.

He nodded. "I will touch you in public all you want. Just . . ."

My choice. He couldn't tell me what to do here—it had to be my choice.

Well, I was no longer bouncing. But I really needed to touch him. I grabbed his hand and turned back around, and pretended like I hadn't just taken steps to slide my world sideways.

"Okay," I said, "so coffee?"

"Yeah," Viv said, "and food maybe. Noah, next time you invite a girl over for breakfast, let Connor cook."

About an hour later, Noah negotiated the big town car down a tiny country road that was probably designed to handle pickup trucks and cows—and the pickup trucks were an afterthought. The terrain varied from green meadows to trees to wide plains with a sweeping view of the bay, and I wondered who lived out here and why. How did they make their living, and where were the houses? Were the houses out here, and I just wasn't seeing them? I'd seen a couple of offshoots of this road, and I figured there *must* be houses—because I'd also seen little clusters of mailboxes, grouping together for comfort.

The car jounced over a particularly hard rut, and I yelped as my head hit the side of the car. "Jesus!"

Noah grimaced and looked over at me. "Sorry, Con. Man, this road gets worse and worse—and Dad keeps saying he's gonna gravel it over, and he keeps forgetting."

"It's the money," Viv said apologetically from the back. "He doesn't want you to—"

"God*damn it*!" Noah smacked his palm against the steering wheel. "I knew it. I told him I make decent money, but—"

"But you're paying off student loans, and he knows *that*," Viv said pertly. "Don't worry—between me and Gran, we've got enough. He says he's calling the gravel people tomorrow, and then collecting from the neighbors. He's got to—you're going to rip the chassis out of this thing, and I don't think the production people are gonna give you a new one."

Viv had left her car—a tiny yellow Prius—at my house, and I wondered how she'd even gotten it down this road. Then it hit me—she'd been coming from Cheddar's place. She'd said that at the coffee shop, that she'd left a bunch of her stuff there, and she didn't have the heart to go get it now that he'd broken it off with her.

Poor noble bastard. I wish I had his balls.

But we'd already established that I didn't—I'd shot my wad holding my boyfriend's hand as we walked down the boardwalk. Nobody had looked at us twice, nobody had shouted, "Oh my God! Connor Montgomery is gay!" But that was because we were in Bluewater Bay. I'm pretty sure if we set foot in Seattle or Tacoma or anywhere but here, we'd be doomed.

I started making plans to call Jillian right then and there.

The rutted road finally came to an end right where a concrete driveway started, and I rolled down the window so I could get a good look at the house.

It didn't disappoint.

A two-story farmhouse, with turrets and archways over every window, it was painted barn red with blue and yellow trim. On the front lawn whirled, twirled, twisted, and spun pretty much every wind ornament I *hadn't* gotten at the kite store—most of them rainbow. All of them blurred with motion from the breeze that swept right off the sound in the distance and across the marsh grasses that covered the small hill.

"Oh, Noah." I was helplessly enchanted. "I love it here."

"I knew you would," Noah said, while behind us Viv said, "I don't believe this."

I looked back over my shoulder. "You don't love your house?"

She shook her head. "My whole childhood I wanted a normal house, like all the normal kids."

My shoulders slumped a little. "I lived in that house," I told her. "I got kicked out of it too." For the first time in a while I thought of my mother. Dad had been the one to sign the contract—but did Mom think of me? Even a little?

"That sucks," she muttered. "I'm sorry."

"Don't be." I shrugged. "Just . . ." I looked at the house again, now taking up all of the view in the front. "Just be happy you live here."

Noah parked the car in a carport, a nice one attached to the house. He went to open the door there, and my face fell.

"What?"

"I don't know," I said, thinking. "I guess I wanted to go through the front."

He laughed and seized my chin, and abruptly I realized I'd been surrounded by his smell for three days, and that I wanted to be closer to him, surrounded by sweat and minty body wash and something dark and rum-like.

He kissed me, hard and open, while his sister slid into the door behind us.

He finished, and I was left, boggled, staring at him in total stupid. "What did you just do to me?"

"Hopefully I relaxed you. This is my dad, my grandma, and some woman I haven't seen in thirteen years. I know you think life is a movie script, but trust me, these are *not* movie people."

"Huh . . ." I thought about that while he led the way into the house. "I thought all people were movie people."

Noah rolled his eyes, and I ignored him. I was too busy looking around at what was about to be my favorite place in the world.

Oh my God.

The hallway was purple, the doorjambs were cream-colored, and the living room was royal blue with gold accents on the walls. I looked up the staircase immediately to my left, and saw that the newel post and railing were painted every color in the rainbow, and the first door I could see was ruby red.

The wall bracketing the staircase was goldenrod yellow.

"Noah?" I felt like I had when I was five, and my parents had taken me to see my first Disney movie in the theater. My mom had been pregnant with my little sister and had gone to the bathroom about six times, but it didn't matter. For an hour and a half, me and that redheaded hussy had dreamed about Prince Eric with the same heartrending passion, and I'd been the happiest boy in the world.

Vinnie had looked just like him.

"What?" Noah said distractedly as he pulled me along behind him.

"You live in the *Wonka* house!"

Noah stopped short and I ploughed into the back of him.

"I live *where*?"

"Like Willy Wonka's factory?" I said, still in awe. "You know, 'The Candy Man Can'?"

Noah closed his mouth with an effort. "You're right," he muttered. "Every family *is* a movie family. Dad! Gran! Get out here and meet Connor before panic kicks his brain right out the front door, okay?"

He pulled me past the staircase and into the living room just in time for a hobbit and a giant to approach.

I let out a choked sound of laughter, and he shook his head sternly.

"Connor, this is my father, Samuel—"

"Nice to meet you, son," said the giant.

I smiled at him from my lowly height of five foot ten and wondered if the air was thinner up there. He was taller than *Noah*, which was saying something, and he was built like a farm truck to boot. His buzz-cut graying hair framed a square face with a long jaw, and his eyes were almond-shaped instead of Noah's and Viv's rounder versions—but there was no mistaking he had a hand in their genetic makeup.

Especially when he smiled sweetly, his eyebrows raised, like he was expecting any weirdness or psycho cows I might throw at him. It reassured me, like it was meant to.

"Nice to meet you, sir." I smiled prettily. I wasn't trying to flirt, I was just trying to *impress* this really big man who might or might not guess what his baby boy had been doing to me all night.

"Good to meet you—for the last month, you're all we've heard about, isn't that right Mom?"

The hobbit came forward, a tiny brown woman, pudgy in all the places, with gray hair cut straight at her shoulder and so many wrinkles around her eyes that I was surprised she could see.

"Oh, he *is* pretty, Noah," she said in delight. "That was the first thing he mentioned—that you were as pretty in person as you were on the screen."

I blushed. "Well, ma'am, a highly trained bunch of stylists put hours into that—I'll be sure to compliment their work."

I was trying to be charmingly self-deprecating, but nobody laughed.

"And the second thing he mentioned," she continued, as though I hadn't spoken, "was that you were even more beautiful on the inside."

I had nothing for that one, no way to respond.

I shifted my weight from one foot to the next and smiled uncertainly. "Well, uh, that was really sweet," I said, my voice losing its glib edge. "Noah has been exceedingly kind this last month. I . . . I would have been lost without him."

"That's good to hear," Samuel said, that killer Noah-smile sort of blowing my mind in his wider, stronger, red-brown face. "It means he was raised right."

I swallowed, hearing my father talking about how I had to be stronger so people would know I was raised right, and how I had to be less dreamy so he wouldn't be ashamed of me.

"I've never heard that about kindness, sir," I said, naked in front of these people in just a few words. "I think that's really wonderful."

Noah's hand in the small of my back gave me strength and some vestiges of grace.

"Where're the girls?" he asked. "All I've heard all week was how much they wanted to meet Connor—where'd they go?"

Samuel's pleasant expression faded. "Their mother is with them upstairs," he said darkly, and he met Noah's eyes like Noah was a grown-up. "She brought makeup and such."

Noah grunted. "I didn't see an extra car outside—"

"She had some man in a truck drop her off." Samuel sounded disgusted and skeptical. "She swore the guy would be back in two hours, so, by my count, she's got an hour left."

Both men shook their heads at the same time, and Viv crossed her arms in front of her and made a little *humph* sound. Well, whoever this woman was, and whatever her reason for leaving the family, it was clear she'd have her work cut out for her impressing the senior members.

"Is it okay if I take Connor out and around? Show him the copse of redwoods and the inlet and stuff?"

"Sure," Samuel said, nodding. "Be back in the last fifteen minutes, and you can say you've done your bit. Viv, do you want to—"

"I'll go with Noah and Connor, Dad," she said quickly.

"Are you sure? And where's Cheddar? We were looking forward to seeing—"

Viv burst into tears again, and Samuel groaned like a man who was used to dealing with young women in tears. "Okay," he said, grabbing a tissue. "You and Noah and Connor go talk about that. Gran and I will finish lunch."

"Let me give you cookies on your way out," Gran insisted. She pinned me with a gimlet gaze from her tiny brown eyes. "You especially—you're too skinny."

"I won't be if I stay here long," I said, smiling.

She sniffed. "You're still grieving the weight away," she observed, blowing my mind. "Let go of the sadness; maybe you can keep some of the fat."

I gaped and caught Noah's eyes. He shrugged, and gestured me to follow her into the kitchen. There were at least five-dozen cookies cooling on two plates on the kitchen counter, and she pulled out a Ziploc bag and filled it.

"Make sure you eat your share." She glared at me.

"Of course, ma'am," I said, smiling at the thought. I'd just been *ordered* to eat *cookies*. How wonderful was that? She was tiny and plump and doll-like and . . . and human.

I'd forgotten what that was like, and I suddenly flashed to my own mother as I was leaving the house before the game that night. *Make sure you eat dinner!*

Such a simple thing, caring. I wonder when she'd shut it off— or was it like grieving? Did she cry the next morning like I cried for Vinnie? Did she and the little kids miss me? Did they spend months not able to say my name? Did my money pay for my sisters' college? That was nice to think about—I liked that idea.

"Hey," Noah said, tugging me out the door.

"Yeah?" I surfaced from my last night as Connor Mazynsky. "What?"

"Where'd you go?" He pulled me sideways, and I realized there was a little path from the grassland leading toward a stand of trees—a miniforest, really—that extended to the west toward the edge of the sound.

I looked behind me and saw Viv wandering dispiritedly behind us, a stick in her hand that she used to swing at the grasses blowing across the path.

"Nowhere," I lied, wishing I could make her pain better. What could I say? It would fade? Well, yes and no. It didn't so much fade as become veiled with more life than just the pain. You just never knew when a veil would get torn away, and there it would be, bright as always.

"Connor?"

"What's the last thing you remember about your mom?" I asked, because today was not supposed to be about me.

Noah didn't even have to think about it. "Dad caught her cheating for the umpteenth time," he said flatly. "He never yelled—she did that. He just suggested—every time—that she may want to simply find another life. She didn't seem to like this one. I heard him those last couple of years—and it started to sink in, you know? She was good with the birthdays and the big things—she loved us—but Gran did the day-to-day watching and the checking the homework and the cooking the meals and cleaning. Dad was building his business—you might not have seen the lean-to in front of the carport, but it's a treasure trove of tools of all sorts, and he's got the skills to use those. Anyway, she just . . . just didn't want the day-to-day. She wanted something different, something bigger. And it was like . . . every kid was her attempt to fit into this life, right here. So Dad caught her—I think just the usual stuff, coming home late with sex written everywhere—and I heard them talking the night before. And the next morning, before school, she was downstairs instead of sleeping. She kissed every one of us, and cried, and said she was going to live somewhere else, but she'd call us when she could."

I blinked. "And that was it?"

"She did call for the first couple of years. But it's hard to stay connected when you're just a voice on the phone." He held his hand out and caught the edges of the brush with his palm. "I mean, she tried—she wrote cards and stuff. But . . . I don't know. We all pretty much knew who she was in our lives. There weren't any surprises, right?"

Huh. "You're not bitter?"

Noah thought about it. "I came out to Dad about two months after she left. It was sort of a test, right? To see if he'd reject me, to make sure me and the girls were safe, putting all our faith in him and Gran."

I remembered that story. "He totally passed."

"A-plus parent, yup. And Gran's a little spacey, and she cooks with cheese and lard—"

"Oh God."

"She's making a salad just for you—I begged her. But yeah. A-plus Dad, B-plus Gran, I mean, that's the honor roll in parenting right there. Just because Mom dropped out of the course, that doesn't mean it's not worth taking."

I half laughed. "Oh *there's* the philosophy major at work."

"Yeah." He *didn't* laugh. "So where were you?"

"God, you're tenacious."

"Connor!"

We were drawing near the redwoods now, and they provided a break from the wind. As we stepped past the first tree, it was like we'd taken a step into . . . Well, we had giants and hobbit-gnomes and Noah.

The hero too good to be true.

"I'm in Middle-earth," I said with a happy smile, and then I grabbed his hand and drew him further into the woods.

"You are not!" he protested—but he let himself be dragged.

"I am. Your family is magic, you live in a hobbit hole, and you're too good to be—"

Noah pulled me into his arms and kissed me.

—*true!* I thought, opening for him, intoxicated by this family, by the beautiful home, by the wind coming off the ocean into the redwoods.

Then he broke off the kiss and held my chin. "Connor, what's wrong?"

"Noah? Noah, if you guys are having sex against a tree or something, warn me, otherwise, I'm pretty much your shadow."

I smiled brightly and kissed him on the cheek, and then turned to Viv. "C'mere, our beautiful Princess Vivienne—lead me through this magical land."

She let out a long-suffering sigh. "Give me a goddamned cookie." She glared at her brother. "Noah? Really? Of all the people you could have picked, you had to pick one just like—"

"I am *not* in love with my grandmother!" he snapped.

"Thank God!" I said, and Noah shoved a cookie in my mouth.

Oh my heavens—soft cinnamon sugar cookies are . . .

"I'm melthing," I moaned, swallowing in little teeny increments, the better to savor the cookie.

"This is so not going how I pictured it," Noah muttered.

I swallowed the rest of the first bite. "That's because you're not eating your cookie! Now someone take me for a walk or we'll be here all day!"

Noah humored me—that's really the best way you could put it. I just . . . I saw this family, troubles and all, and wanted their troubles to be mine. I wanted to belong to someone who would collect rainbow windmills and fill their yard with them. I wanted to belong to someone who would tell his gay son that he still loved him, and then prove it by not changing a damned thing about that kid's life.

I wanted to be like Noah and Viv, who knew that a relationship—even a bad one—might not be forever, but who still didn't have a concept of what the bad kind of forever might be.

It was like acting. For an afternoon, I got to have someone else's TV-perfect life, and I wasn't going to ruin that with fears of . . . well, everything.

So I got Noah and Viv to take me through their little forest and show me the ravine they used to swing across (before the youngest broke her leg—something I could tell Noah still felt bad about) and the little tributary that flowed down to the sound.

We walked the beach along the redwood stand, and they marked out the property by their line of sight. He pointed out Sharra's house, as though it were the most natural thing in the world, and I pictured him as a gangly child with outsized hands and feet, and wild hair, running through the woods with a little girl who—by his description—had been as dark-skinned as he was, with tightly bound braids tied at the end by rainbow-colored rubber bands.

Had she dreamed about an island? Was that why she'd gone swimming?

I didn't ask.

I took the afternoon as a gift, and for the next hour and a half, it gave. At the end, Noah and I walked through the woods holding hands like real lovers, and Viv walked ahead moodily, lost in her own thoughts and hopefully some peace from whatever had gone down with her and Cheddar that morning.

We watched as she stepped into the brightness of the meadow, and then Noah tightened his hold on my hand and hauled me behind a tree.

"Wha—"

He kissed me hard and thoroughly—deep and carnal, backing me against the tree and shoving his groin up against mine in a show of no-bullshit that almost shocked me out of my happy little round of self-deception.

I moaned, breathless and growing harder by the second in my shorts, and bucked up against him. He pulled back, biting my lip sharply enough to sting, and tangled his fingers in my hair.

"What. Is. Wrong?" He made each word distinct.

I swallowed and looked away.

"Connor—"

"Please," I said, smiling but not looking at him. "Please. I haven't been able to play make-believe in so long . . . let me just . . . believe that life can be this easy, okay?"

Connor—

Not you too.

You don't need to make believe with him.

Just— Can we just not? Do we have to talk about everything?

You can be real with him.

I don't remember how.

Because, God help us both, Vinnie and I had spent an awful lot of goddamned time in the kitschy house, *his* house, pretending we lived together, and that we had a future as a couple. We planned—and sometimes even took—vacations together, and talked about families and children.

But we weren't out, not to his parents, not to Hollywood, not even to friends.

It was all make-believe.

I was so good at it, I'd forgotten how much of it I'd done.

"It's real," Noah said, and for a moment he looked stricken.

I framed his face with my hands, the stubble teasing my palms, bringing me back to myself as I hadn't been since that morning, when I'd stared at the piece of burnt bacon and wondered how this had become my life.

"Yes," I lied. "Sure."

He shook his head, his eyes shiny. "Connor, I am going to prove to you that—"

"Shh—" A weekend. Friday I'd lost my shit. Saturday I'd found it. Couldn't I have a day just to hold it and figure out what made it mine?

"No," he snapped. "I will not hush. Did you just hush me?"

Oh God—he was just so dear. I kissed him because I had to, and when I pulled away my eyes were shiny too. "Well," I said, "you're bossy."

"You bet your tight white ass I'm bossy," he muttered. "And this is not the end of this conversation."

"Course it's not." I smiled at him, grabbing his hand and tugging, feeling oddly capsized because my heart was light and heavy at once.

"When we get home alone—"

"Yeah?" I grinned cheekily. "Do you have plans for us home alone? 'Cause I'd like to hear those plans, oh yes, I would!"

He growled and lunged, probably to haul me up against him and have another forceful little talk, but I dodged out of his reach and into the light.

"God, you're slow for someone so young," I taunted over my shoulder, and this time he *did* catch me, but by now we were playing, and I turned my laughing face up to his for another kiss.

"Oh my God. Noah, you're *gay*?"

We both froze, and Noah's face assumed the countenance of a stone mountain.

"I told you that when I was fourteen, Annette," he said, swallowing. I rubbed his cheek again, softly, betting he wished we could still make believe. Then I turned to meet his mother.

"Well, I told you—"

"No son of yours would be gay," he said, voice hard. "I hear you. I'm not your son. Didn't want to be then, still don't want to be now."

The woman scowling at him must have been stunning once. She had a round face with round, limpid eyes and full lips. She'd skull-trimmed her hair—but I could still see the occasional gray stubble—and worn lipstick bright and red, which she could get away with since her skin tone was more dark than light. Her lashes were long and black and curling, and her makeup was perfectly Egyptian, highlighting those eyes and making them look sleepy and seductive— from a distance, she might have been thirty.

Close up, I could see the deep lines by her eyes, and the ones around her lips. I could smell the cigarettes, and her mouth had that drawn-in look that smokers get when they smoke too much for too long.

The skin under her chin was a little saggy, as though she'd been dried out by life.

"Well, maybe that was a little harsh," she said, pulling the corners of that once-lush mouth up into what looked to be a conciliatory gesture. "It's just a bit of a shock."

"Annette, this is Connor Mazynsky," he said.

"I thought the girls said his name was something else," she muttered to herself. "Something famous. Connor—"

Her eyes widened, and her mouth made a little O.

"Good try," I said, because it had been.

"I was so hoping this wasn't going to be an issue," he said.

But I knew, even as she focused on my face with a patently false smile, that it would be.

And that I would have come anyway.

"Connor *Montgomery*," she said, looking like she'd seen the holy angel of avarice himself. "*That's* who you are. And you're gay too, like my son?"

"I hope so," I replied cheerfully, "given we were just necking in the woods!"

"Oh my." Her lips pursed in a feline smile. "The things you know that other people wish you didn't."

I shrugged and made my plan right there. "Who's not going to know? I'm interviewing with a major blog next week—my agent and I have planned my coming out for months."

Noah's grip on my hand tightened painfully, but I couldn't look at him or she wouldn't buy it.

"Really," she said, incredulity dripping from her tone.

"Ma'am, if I'm sleeping with your son, making him keep our relationship in the closet would be a really shitty thing to do to him, wouldn't it? I mean, you never know when some unscrupulous slime-bag is going to come around and try to pressure his family into giving up the secret, or put the screws to Noah and me to pay up to keep quiet. I mean, there are *so many* unpleasant people in the world who would take a nice family like this and just fuck them over because of who little Connor Mazynsky likes to kiss. That would be a real fucking shame, wouldn't it?" My voice grew harder by the second; make-believe time was officially over.

"Yes, sir," she sneered. "That would be a real shame." She summoned up a bright smile for her son. "I mean, I'm trying to get back in with the family, aren't I? I wouldn't want anything to hurt them, right?"

"I certainly hope not." I kept my eyes locked on hers until she dropped her eyes resentfully. She was wearing a tight shirt—much like Viv's, actually, but hers was whiter and thinner, and she was wearing Daisy Dukes to go with it. Her sandals were the flashy kind with the bright baubles on the toe strap, and she studied those twinkling bright stones and her bright-red toenails for a moment while the silence lingered.

"Annette," Noah broke the silence—but not her absorption in her feet. "Did you have anything else you wanted to say besides, 'Oh my God, you're gay!' and 'How can I blackmail your boyfriend?'"

The mutinous set to her mouth softened, and she looked up at him with what seemed to be an earnest desire to connect. "I . . . I honestly just wanted to say hi," she murmured, as though wondering how it could have all gone so wrong.

"Maybe start with saying hi." He was so angry. "Try that if you come back in another fourteen years."

He grabbed my hand then and pulled me around her and through the waist-high grasses that flanked the path.

"Noah!" she called out, and the desperation in her voice made *me* stop, so I jerked on his arm hard enough that he turned around in irritation.

"*What*?"

"I . . . I'm coming next weekend too." Her voice quavered. "Can you give me another chance?"

"That depends on if you can keep your mouth shut long enough for Connor to come out in his own time," he snarled, and the look he cast me was so remorseful I shrugged. I'd been thinking about it anyway, right?

"Look, I'm sorry. I've been living hand-to-mouth for so long. I mean, I thought I could make a living singing, but it's hard—"

"So you figured a quick and easy grift would be the way to go?" he asked, still outraged.

"I've done worse," I reminded him, sotto voce, and he gave me one of those Connor-so-help-me looks that I was coming to treasure.

"Well, he's got money, hon!" she protested. "Man, look at his shoes—he's *rolling* in that shit, and all he does is stand up in front of a camera and—"

"*Don't* you even *talk* about what he does!" Noah shouted. "Not another fucking word. I've *seen* what he does, and how *dare* you walk into my life after fourteen years and just start casting judgments and making these lame-assed assumptions—"

"I'm sorry," she said through ugly tears. "I'm sorry, Noah, I'm sorry. I'm trying here—"

"*Well go try somewhere else!*"

His words shocked us all, maybe me the most, because he'd been yelling so loud his voice cracked. I hadn't seen him lose control—not once. Not *ever*.

But now, he was lost, adrift in his own turbulent ocean, and maybe now, he needed me.

"Noah," I said softly, grabbing both hands.

"We gotta—"

"Shh," I mocked, smiling just a little.

"Connor, what she said about you—"

"Doesn't matter."

In the following silence, we could hear her sobs—contrite, I think, but then how should I know?

"How am I supposed to—"

"Just don't leave it like this," I said. "You never know when it's the end. If you're lucky, you leave it good."

Vinnie's kiss on the cheek as I settled in to a long jet-lag catnap. His hand in my hair, stroking. "God, it's good to have you home, Con. No more movies for a while, okay?"

"Yeah, Vinnie. I'll come to your next shoot if you want."

"Yeah. I really need you around, you know?"

I took his hand and kissed the knuckles. "Me too."

"Back soon."

Noah closed his eyes, and I could see the dampness on the lashes. "Yeah," he said, voice thick. "You'd know."

He looked up. "Annette?"

"Y-y-yeah?"

"Connor's going to be with me next Sunday too. If you're coming back then, you'd better figure out how to make a better impression."

We all heard a broken engine with a bad muffler pulling up along the rutted road in front of the driveway. Annette looked to the beat up F-150 and then back at us.

"That's Angus. I need to—"

"Annette?"

"Sure, okay," she agreed, flashing a confused, angry glance at me. "I'll . . . I'll learn how to get along—"

"And?" he warned.

"And I'll keep my mouth shut," she finished, obviously resentful as fuck. "But I can't promise much, Noah—"

"There's some fucking news."

"I mean, I've got friends, I'm going to talk—"

"Go to the press, and you'll never see me, or Viv, again. Ever." Viv had been long gone by the time we'd come out of the woods—I wondered if her encounter had gone any better.

"If nothing else," I added, "their jobs are on the line. They signed nondisclosure agreements, and Noah is technically on the clock."

That was a total lie. He'd told me he got to keep the car because it made being at my beck and call easier, but he billed them his hours and showed them his mileage from when he was actually on duty.

But Annette must have bought it, because she nodded, looking vulnerable and put-upon, and then dashed through the fields for the driveway.

Noah and I watched her go, and then Noah wrapped me up in his arms tight, so tight, for a moment I didn't think I could breathe, but that was just fine.

He let go and grabbed my hand. I followed him, but with my other hand I pulled out my cell phone.

"What are you doing?"

"What do you think?" I stared at him, surprised he'd have to ask. "Calling Jillian."

"Baby, no."

"Jilly?"

"Con?" Jilly slurred over the phone. "Everything okay?"

"Were you *napping*?" I asked, horrified. Jilly didn't nap like I didn't do my own roots.

"Yeah. Well, me and my kids had a long talk last night. You get to nap when you don't sleep until dawn."

"Oh. As long as it's important," I said, meaning it. Noah steered me around a rock, and I glanced at him gratefully.

Then I tripped as he tried to steer me around another one, and decided to stand still. "Go," I told him, but he shook his head no.

"What was that?" Jilly asked, sounding like she was waking up.

"Look, Jilly—you know that interview I'm doing for *Vogue*?"

"Yeah?"

"Do they have a blog?"

"Uh, yeah . . ."

"And can they be here tomorrow?"

"Connor, are you—"

"Yeah. Make sure they're at the studio tomorrow, where we held our press conference. We'll do a quickie interview in there, and we can do the longer magazine spread when they're ready. Could you tell the producers too? I mean, I don't think it's a furry deal—"

"No," she assured me. "It's not. It's your dream setup if you really want to do this."

I studied Noah, whose eyes were still red from an encounter with his mother that nobody could have prepared him for.

"I'm terrified," I admitted honestly, because I owed him that. He wrapped his arm around my shoulders, and I leaned. "Scared shitless. But . . . but Noah's family could be under a whole lot of pressure if I don't handle this right. If I come out, make it a small announcement, have it hit the internet through one legitimate news source, it could be like Quinto and Bomer and everyone else who came out way the fuck before I did, you know?"

"Yeah, baby. It's time. It'll be . . ."

"Don't say easy," I warned. After years of hiding? No.

"No," she conceded. "And not painless either. But it'll be better, Connor. I hate to make promises about this shit, you know it, but—"

"Better." I took it and held on tight. "Better."

"Better."

There was silence then, and we all, I think, absorbed the implications of what was charging down the time stream. And then I remembered my priorities.

"And Jilly, I'm going to need someone early to do my roots. Noah says you can totally see my natural color."

She swore. "What's that kid's name? The one who smoothed over your road rash?"

"Junior."

"Yeah, him. I'll text you with the time he'll stop by. Good call, by the way."

I grunted. "Well, you know, can't go showing your property when it's not up to spec."

She laughed for a moment, then sobered. "Love you, Con."

"Love you back, Jilly."

We both ended the call, and I looked at Noah and gestured forward. "Lead on, my white knight—" Noah snorted at the obvious flaw in the image. "Okay, knight on a white charger—"

And *now* he laughed like a twelve-year-old boy.

"Yeah, I'll put you on my charger!" I grumbled. "Just lead on. And feed me a cookie—we still have a few and your grandmother has put the fear of cookies in me."

Noah kept laughing, and I munched on the last cookie while I tried to figure out how what I'd said came out dirty.

Noah's younger sisters, Ky and Trina, didn't mention their mother once during lunch. But they *did* show a whole lot of interest in me.

"Did they have real monsters in that *Jupiter* movie?" Ky asked, still mostly child at fourteen, her dark eyes round and wide like Noah's and Viv's.

"Some of it was people in makeup," I told her honestly. "And some of it was CGI, and some of it was like *Jaws*—you've seen the fake shark?"

Both girls nodded. They wore their hair scraped from their oval faces, the tight curls fighting for freedom until they met the elastic band and exploded into Viv's ringlets on the crowns of their heads. Trina was a little taller, and Ky was a little rounder, and Ky still had braces while Trina was fighting the indignity of acne—but there was no denying that they were sisters, or that once they cleared the horrors of adolescence, they'd both be stunners like the rest of their family.

"But how did you talk to them?" Ky persisted. She was the most vocal, which explained why she'd had the guts to have a conversation and a whole relationship with Annette that the rest of the family had been kept in the dark about. Fearless, this one—and she appeared to be certain that she was as adult as the rest of them.

"Well, mostly there was a ball on a stick," I told her, smiling. "They held it and moved it where the Jupiter monsters were going to be, and I spoke to the ball—"

"But you didn't *act* like you were talking to the ball!" Trina burst out passionately. "I saw the trailer!" Oh, not for the first time, I really wished there were such things as Jupiter monsters and werewolves.

"Yeah," I said simply, "but that's why it's acting. Because in my *head* there's a Jupiter monster, and in my *heart* I'm talking to a Jupiter monster, but my *eyes* actually see a ping-pong ball painted fluorescent green."

"Why green?" Ky took a drink of milk while I answered, and worked on some truly tremendous spaghetti in a homemade sauce that Gran (she wouldn't let me call her Helena) had apparently been working on all day.

"Because they use a special shade of green that makes it easier to erase from the shot, so they can put the CGI monster in," I told her, and both girls looked at each other and shook their heads.

"Who'd want to be an actor?" Trina asked practically. "*I* want to draw the monsters!"

Noah, Viv, Samuel, and Gran all laughed indulgently.

"You keep working at it," Noah said in complete familial support. "Maybe someday you will."

"Well *I* don't want to be in Hollywood at *all*," Ky said wisely. "No offense, Mr. Montgomery, but I don't think I could talk to a *ball*."

"It's demeaning," I confirmed, and Noah's hand on my knee let me know that *he* didn't think so, and that's all I needed to know.

The girls excused themselves and cleared their plates, and Samuel took another piece of garlic bread and waited for them to leave.

"So, you two talked to your mother?" he asked, looking at Noah and Viv.

"I told her to fuck off," Viv said bluntly, and Samuel grimaced.

"Darlin'—"

"No. I'm not in the mood for her today. I may never be in the mood for her. She came at me with the big hug and the 'baby girl' and I said, 'I'm Dad's baby girl, and don't talk to me.'" Viv shrugged. "She let it stay at that—I think Noah was her big fish anyway."

Noah rolled his eyes and muttered, "And then she tried to blackmail me."

There were gasps, and the story came out, and then everybody realized that *I* was coming out, and I—

Stood up and started to clear the table, because I didn't want to talk about it anymore.

I made it to the kitchen and was rinsing dishes in the big farm sink when Noah's grandmother came in to help me.

The kitchen was done in orange and green—and the tile was bright sunshine yellow. There were prints on the walls, van Gogh actually, to match, and I wondered if they'd let me come over and just sit in this kitchen after Noah gave up on me for good.

"You're acting like this isn't a big deal," she said quietly, pulling plates out of the rinse basin and stacking them in the rack. "It's a big deal for a twelve-year-old kid who only needs to tell his father—why isn't it a big deal for a grown man who has to tell half the civilized world?"

"It shouldn't be," I murmured, starting in on the silverware. "I mean . . . who cares who I sleep with—in the movies, I always get the girl, right?"

She didn't laugh. Why did I want to love these people so much if nobody laughed at my jokes? "It's a big deal—and you're doing it for someone you've known for a month and a half."

I sighed and pulled my hands out of the dishwater before I got to a knife or something that could hurt me.

"I'm doing this for the guy I knew for ten years," I said to the wall behind the sink. It had been washed so often it was a lighter green than the rest of the room. "Because . . . because you can talk all the time about how it shouldn't matter what the world thinks—but it . . . it hurts things when you lie all the time. It hurts the person you're with. It hurts the thing between you. It's . . . it's hard enough having a thing. That thing is so fragile. Viv and Cheddar. Noah's mom and dad—their things should have worked. There's not a single good reason for them to not be together. But they're not. They won't be. Lying to the world is a huge reason for people to not be together. It's just time I took it off the table, you know?"

She'd reached for a towel while I was talking, and she handed it to me in the silence that followed. I dried my hands automatically and then looked at the towel.

"I'm not done," I said in surprise.

"Yes, you are." She regarded me soberly. "We're going to open my present, and we're going to have cookies and ice cream."

"You clean *my* house all the time," I said, trying one more time for the joke.

"Bend down," she ordered, and I did. She reached up and put her hands on my cheeks and looked me in the eyes. "You don't have to entertain us," she said, scowling. "You don't have to be funny. You don't have to be the good boy. You're good enough for Noah—that's really all that matters."

My eyes burned. "I'm the good boy?" I said wistfully. I'd never been the good boy as a child—I'd been a dreamer, and a slacker, and the kid who went for drama and not sports.

Her hands on my cheeks grew gentle. "Yeah." She nodded. "You're already the good boy. Go sit in the living room and charm Ky and Trina some more. Don't listen when they say they don't want to be actors. They're just trying to be—"

"Smart," I said dryly.

She didn't laugh, and I straightened up and sighed.

"Are you sure you don't want me to—"

"Gran! Con! Get in here! It's present time."

"During the week, we clean other people's houses to feed our family," Gran said matter-of-factly. "During the weekend, our family comes first."

"I like that," I said, and gestured her out of the kitchen.

She laughed like a child when she saw the lawn ornament, and I glowed under that much delight. When Noah said I'd picked it out, she actually graced me with a huge, ear-to-ear smile. "Of course. He's got the heart for this."

The rest of the afternoon was a blur of people telling excited stories in the living room, and of eating more cookies, but this time with ice cream.

Noah finally called time around five o'clock, saying that I had a big day tomorrow. Viv was staying the night with her family—her gran would drop her off when she visited to clean the house.

"Oh God," I muttered, as we climbed into the car.

"What?"

"We need to change the sheets in the morning."

"Oh God," Noah said, his eyes growing enormous. Somehow it was reassuring that he had the same inhibitions. "Absolutely. And definitely break out the air freshener."

I grinned at him, content for a moment, and then he took a spear to my little bubble of happy.

"You don't have to, you know."

"Don't have to what?"

"The interview tomorrow."

Oh. "Noah?"

"Yeah?"

"Can we not talk about it?"

"Baby—"

"Look, it's no big—"

"Do *not* lie to me!" he snapped angrily.

I retreated into wounded silence.

Vinnie—

I have nothing to say about this.

I'm just so tired.

You promised my parents didn't have to know.

We're not kids anymore, Vinnie!

Sure we are. You're a needy child who just melted over a woman who likes toys and gave you cookies.

I just need—

Whatever. Talk to your new lover. He's got the fucking say, right?

"Connor, talk to me."

I turned my head and was almost surprised to see Noah driving. Who was I talking to again?

"Noah, I . . . My head is so screwed up by lying about this shit for so long. If I'm going to fix it, I need to do this one lousy fucking thing to start making it right."

He steered one-handed for a moment and reached across the console to grab my hand. "I'll be right there," he said softly, and I squeezed.

It was a nice thought, but I didn't have the heart to tell him that for this thing, I was going to have to be totally and completely alone.

CHAPTER THIRTEEN

TOMORROW THEY MAY WRAP
FISHES IN IT

J unior was actually waiting for us at my rental so he could do my
roots that night. Noah was both amazed and offended on Junior's
behalf.

"Now see—if you'd given them a *day*, Junior could have done
them after you were done shooting, but no. You had to change your
life in a weekend, didn't you?"

"I was probably going to do it the week before Comic-Con if it
makes any difference," I retorted. "Because seriously, you're the only
one so tall you can look down and see where they're growing out right
now, and because they're going to fancy me up and have me pose
naked in the wilderness or some shit. But you had to point out that
they're growing and now we're stuck."

"You're Nine-G, right Connor?" Junior asked, pulling out his
magic kit of special super-whoopty hair color that was apparently
better than what they sold in stores. The colors went by codes, but
I recognized the ash blond that had been used on me since *Warlock
Tea*. "And Noah was right—I can totally see your part. We would have
fixed this tomorrow if you hadn't called us in early."

I sighed and stared out the kitchen window, trying not to chafe at
the plastic drape wrapped around my shoulders. "Sorry, Junior."

He winked. "No worries."

"Have you ever thought of getting it done closer to your real
color?" Noah asked, comparing the sample lock from the kit to my
hair in its non-product-enhanced glory with a skeptical eye.

"They don't have a box here for beige hair," I told him pragmatically.
"And yes, Junior—Nine-G is what they usually give me."

"*Beige?*" Noah was so cute when he got all defensive for me.

"Yeah, the romance books call it 'sandy blond.' It's beige. I don't care. I have cheekbones, a chin, and my lips are still mine—I'm calling it a win."

"And an awesome tan for someone living in this part of the country," Noah chided with raised eyebrows.

"I got my tan from the same place you got yours, Mr. Dakers," I said primly. "Good genes. Now get out of Junior's way and let him work."

"Yeah, it would be a real shame if you ended up with your hair colored *sandy* blond instead of *Nine-fucking-G*."

I smirked and conceded—he was the king of snark, and bless him, he was doing this for me.

That night, after Junior had left and my hair was all rinsed, he kissed me.

Forever, he kissed me.

We necked on the couch like teenagers, while *Night at the Museum* played in the background, and I groaned against him, because my body was craving possession all over again.

He didn't give me what I wanted—he gave me what I needed.

More kissing, more grinding, until he shoved down our boxers and we were skin to skin. I thought he would grab both our cocks in one hand—which sounds erotic as hell, but if one or both parties are well endowed can just get awkward—but he didn't. Instead he cupped my bottom and pulled me up, until I was straddling him, then he reached his long arm around my ass and kneaded, kneaded, his fingers grazing my crease, tickling my taint, barely stroking my balls.

I collapsed against him, grinding our cocks together, and he continued to knead, and to tease, until I groaned in frustration.

"Grab us, baby," he ordered. "I've got your back."

I tried to laugh at the pun, but he slid a dry finger just inside my pucker, and I grunted instead. I sat up and grasped us, one in each hand, and it was the *weirdest* thing. Him and me, our pleasure tied together by my little rabbit brain trying to stroke us in time. But every squeeze of my hand made me groan and every time I passed a thumb over our cockheads, he'd rut up against me.

And the whole time, his finger was getting braver, sliding farther in and farther out, and the dry burn was enough, the stretch just enough, until what I'd thought would be a tease, a terrible, unfulfilled promise of orgasm, was suddenly *right there*.

I spilled over, gently at first, and then in torrents as climax crashed my surprised nerve endings. My cum spurted, hot and slick, over his cock and I played in it, sliding my fist harder along the slippery length. He stopped finger-fucking my ass and just *grabbed* it, arching his head back and coming until my hand squelched in the mess.

"Shit," I muttered, pulling my T-shirt up and off and trying to wipe us both off before it trickled onto the couch.

"What?" Oh, he looked insufferably pleased with himself.

"Noah, the couch doesn't have sheets. Man, how are we going to clean this up if we get anything on it?"

His hooded eyes popped open, and I got to spend the next fifteen minutes doing something I'd never had to do before: clean up evidence of sex so a family member didn't see.

When we fell into bed, tired and happy, I thought that maybe I could live without that part of being a family member.

And I also thought that, if this was my last night as a man in the closet, I'd just given myself a really good reason to come out of it.

The trailer on the lot hadn't changed much from the first day I'd visited, but this time there were fewer of us there. Anna and Simon were standing off camera, looking bored and like they needed to get to their day's work, and Noah was in his usual place, resting his elbows on his knees, watching me like a hawk.

The photographer who had taken some shots of me outside was now our videographer, and he was standing behind a tripod, looking as bored as Anna and Simon. Well, it wasn't as exciting as the photo shoot, I guess, where he'd been squatting and getting close-ups so the effect was of the trees above my head and me looking heroic and shit. Vinnie used to say it was a good way to look for cliffhangers, and we'd both gotten good at blowing our noses and trimming there to make sure nobody got our boogers on camera.

So that was done—I was on camera, shade Nine-G roots and all—and now I had to talk to Suzanne Sylvano, up-and-coming blog reviewer who was *really* not dressed for the Pacific Northwest.

"So," she said, crossing one elegant leg over the other, exposing some serious thigh in her super-short business skirt, "we were supposed to meet in a few weeks, right?"

"Right," I said, "the week before Comic-Con—but I realized I didn't want to wait that long."

She threw back her head and laughed—too loud and too long for no joke at all—and batted her extra-long lashes at me. A pretty woman—in her early thirties—with a mane of red hair and apparently shark jaws primed for man-meat.

"What was so urgent you just had to have it on the blog?" She finished each sentence with a charming smile—I could almost hear the little *ding* when her teeth glinted at the camera.

"It's really not urgent," I said. And then I launched into the party line. "I'm working on a really great set and have been for the last five weeks. The cast and crew have been so accepting, and I've really enjoyed being back in the rush of things. But meeting new people after so long, I sort of realized how much of myself I've kept from the world, and it makes it difficult to have an honest relationship with all these great new people, you know?"

Suzanne Sylvano nodded sympathetically, but I could tell by the way she licked her lips and touched her hair that this was still going to rock her world in the bad way.

"So, what is it that you think fans need to know?" she asked coyly.

"It's not a big deal." I corrected myself: "At least it shouldn't be—but I'm a grown-up enough about the media to know it could be if it's in the hands of the wrong people." I looked at her trustingly, to indicate that *she*, Suzanne Sylvano, was the *right* person, and not just some random blog reporter Jilly snagged by the scruff of the neck so we could have the media upper hand.

And *that* seemed to pull her off the "maybe I can bag a movie star" train. Her body language turned completely professional—she stopped making eyes at the cameraman, stopped making eyes at me. She looked me in the face and nodded, as though she was the person who could do justice to the story.

"I'm in the beginning of a new relationship," I said plainly. "With a man—and I'm so very tired of hiding who I date, and whom I see privately. The world is changing—mostly because a lot of actors have come out before me. It was time I became one of the people that made being gay a fact of life and not a headline or a sensation. It's just who I am, that's all."

"Oh," she said into the suddenly silent room.

I maintained a polite listening smile, waiting for her next question, and she sort of gaped at me. "I . . . I had no idea that's what you wanted to say to the press," she floundered. "What made you decide to come out now?"

I suppressed a sigh. Yeah. Maybe giving Jilly the teeniest bit of notice might have helped.

"It was the right place and the right time," I said brightly.

Suzanne Sylvano took a deep breath, and her eyes sharpened. "Wouldn't it have been a better place and time before Vinnie Walker died?"

My jaw tightened. Oh yeah. Here it came. "Vinnie knew I was gay," I said. "And he knew my reasons for staying in the closet."

"Which were?" She leaned forward, her eyes narrowed, and oh yeah, it had to be splashed in her face, but she finally smelled the blood.

"Personal," I said smoothly.

She made a sound of impatience. "Are you trying to tell me that hiding your relationship with Vinnie Walker wasn't a primary reason for keeping silent?"

Oh, she was beautifully inept at her job. "Are you trying to tell me that a live actor has just outed himself on your blog and you've got nothing better to do than try to get him to out his dead friend?"

Her mouth snapped shut, and her eyebrows shot up, and the man-hungry young woman disappeared and the barracuda was fully in place. Fifteen minutes—we'd given her fifteen minutes for the scoop of the month.

I had ten more minutes of fencing to do.

In the end, it was done—the piece was scheduled to hit the vlog on a 3 p.m. deadline, and the now-angry vlogger—and her amused photographer—backed their way out of the trailer.

I stood up from the two chairs we'd used for the interview and started putting them back in Anna's workstation, where they belonged.

"Uh," I said, smiling hesitantly, "thanks for letting us have the room and stuff. I know it was short notice, but it was really nice of you to let me—"

"Oh my God," Anna said, looking at me from shiny eyes. "Connor, that was great!"

"Why, because it was a day late and a dollar short?" I said bitterly.

"No." Simon's voice lowered. "I . . . I know a little bit about how long you've been waiting to do that, Con. That was . . . really classy."

"Except for my roots," I said ruefully. "That was a rush job."

I finished putting the chairs back and smiled briefly at them both and then looked to where Noah stood by the door.

"So, the soundstage in ten, right?"

"Makeup first," Simon said, his eyebrows drawn together like he was worried. "Are you sure you don't want to—"

"I'll see you there."

Five more steps to where Noah was, four, three—he opened the door and let me precede him, but I knew he'd follow me. We walked quietly through the lot, shoulder to shoulder—but not toward makeup, toward my trailer.

"Well done," he said, after a few moments of listening to our footsteps.

"I—"

"I especially like how you handled the questions about Vinnie. All ten minutes of them."

I grimaced. "Stupid twat."

"Ouch!" Noah laughed, and I instantly hated myself.

"That was horrible. I totally apologize. I hate even *thinking* that word. But 'Are you seriously telling me Vince Walker wasn't gay?'—I mean . . . *dude*."

"Yeah, but your answer, man: 'Vinnie and I had no secrets from each other.'" He shook his head. "You really think the world's going to buy that?"

"No," I said glumly. "The fanfic sites are going to explode. But that's okay—let them speculate. What really matters is that it's not hanging over *me* anymore, right?"

We got to my trailer, and I opened the door with shaking, cold-sweaty hands. Noah followed me into the standard space—a couch and a few chairs made cozy with a throw rug Vinnie had given me for *Warlock Tea* and I'd carried with me to every shoot since.

I stood in the middle of the space, looking vaguely around, and then Noah grabbed my shoulder and pulled me into his arms.

Oh my Lord . . . that. *That* was what I needed.

I clung to him, shaking, all of the nerves, the sadness, the irritation at having to make something that was personal and mine public because otherwise I'd never be able to own it . . .

Vinnie, I'm out.

And I'm still in.

The voice in my head was curiously flat.

That's what you wanted, right?

Right. The world never has to know the real me.

I knew you. I loved you. You always said that was enough.

I think we've established I was always a selfish prick. Don't throw it in my face now.

I recoiled from the wounded bitterness in Vinnie's voice, and clung to Noah instead.

"How bad's it gonna get?" Noah asked somberly.

"I have no idea," I mumbled. "It could be nothing. It could be a few calls for some exclusives and the press conference from the first day all over again. It could be *The National Enquirer* haunting my shrubbery for a picture of your ass. I honestly have no idea— What?"

"Really?" he asked, eyes wide, a delighted smirk twisting his mouth. "You think I'm that sexy? Could I get my ass on the cover? That would be awesome!"

"Shut up."

"No, seriously—we could totally capitalize on this thing. They want a piece of us, let's give it to them. Can I keep a vlog and talk about how you never top?"

"Shut up. I will fucking top you right now," I threatened, and he let out a roaring laugh that shook through my body as he held me—and bled out the last of the shaking, rambling nerves that had racked me since I'd crawled out of bed that morning and refused breakfast.

"Yeah, I'd let you top," he patronized, rubbing his chin on the crown of my head.

"Thank you," I whispered, suddenly not able to laugh or speculate, even a little.

"For what?"

"For not caring that the world's going to be up our ass like an ugly bug."

"Con?"

"Yeah?"

"You know I love you, right?"

I shuddered and clung to him harder. "You know what's in my heart, right?" I asked, the word looming like a big wall of infidelity, the last landmark of a ten-year relationship, the one thing that had made Vinnie and me special.

"A whole lot of sadness for the last guy who loved you," Noah said wisely.

"And a little bit of joy for the guy who loves me now," I told him, hoping it was a gift. I leaned my head against his shoulder. "I won't always be broken, Noah. I . . . I'm not at a great place for promises, but I want to keep that one."

"Connor?"

I looked at him. "What?"

"I'll love you if you can't."

"Can't keep the promise?"

"Can't love me like you loved Vinnie."

That broke me. "I will," I whispered, wiping my eyes. "I already do."

But I couldn't say the word. Not right now. Not when the fallout of what I'd just done had yet to rain down.

And even if it didn't rain down, I still needed to walk through the rain of regret for not having done it sooner, for not having forced Vinnie's hand, for not having said, straight out, "I'm not living in the closet, Vinnie. You do what you want but I'm going to have a little faith."

Oh God. How much more real this last year would have been if it had been real for the rest of the world too.

I didn't say any of that to Noah, though. I just took what he was offering and held on, for a minute, and another, and another, until Viv knocked on the door and told me it was time to report to makeup.

Carter and Levi were in the makeup trailer, which surprised me, because we were still not supposed to know the other existed in this world, and we didn't have a scene together for another week.

Carter was wearing a bright, golden-boy smile, and behind me Noah said, "Oh no . . ."

"Oh no what?" I looked at Noah, my vision clinging, because at this point he was my safe haven.

"Conklin told him."

"Of course he did," Carter said. "Congratulations! You must be really proud!"

"No," I said, shaking my head and settling down in my chair. "It was no big deal."

"It was plenty big a deal." Levi Pritchard was dark and growly in person just like on screen. For some reason I trusted that more.

"You guys did it first," I said, trying to make that sound supportive and modest. Even Levi smiled, so I must have succeeded.

"Yeah, we did," Carter said. "But why did *you*? I mean, we like you here, but you can still shoot films in the hiatus, and this could limit your roles."

I shrugged. "Most of the directors I like to work with won't care, and not getting another movie role won't kill me. As long as I can keep working *somewhere*, I'll be fine." Oh God. I *loved* movie shoots. I *loved* being an action hero, running to stop the bad guy, driving the fast car with manic desperation. I liked the more in-depth character stuff you got to do in a television show, but . . .

But I wasn't going to show uncertainty, not here. Not in front of other actors. Not where people could see. Noah knew. It was enough.

I stopped lying then, and gave these nice men some of the truth. "And I'm seeing someone—it's going to make his life hard enough, me just being in the public eye. It would be great if he didn't have to worry about being in the closet with me too."

Levi nodded, arms crossed in front of his chest, like he found that acceptable. Carter's boyish enthusiasm never dimmed.

"Well, that's great. If you need help with the paparazzi or the papers or bloggers, just let me know—Levi and I have some pointers. I mean, you don't *need* to milk it if you don't want to, but there can be some very nice publicity perks if you want them."

Yes, I'd seen. Their courtship was famous—their marriage celebrated—and the fact that neither of them shied away from the world knowing was . . .

Extremely brave.

But, also, not me.

"Thanks guys," I said, smiling quietly. "That's really generous."

Junior was suddenly standing between me and Carter and Levi, and they said good-bye and left the trailer. I breathed a sigh of relief, and thought I was doing really well until Junior tucked a bib into my white T-shirt and started sponging on foundation.

"They're really nice," he said, as though I'd said they weren't.

"Yeah, I know. That was kind."

"I mean, I know they come on a little strong but—"

"No, I get it. They're the alpha dogs here, Junior. They were welcoming me into the gay pack, it was sweet."

Junior let out a breath and kept sponging foundation. "Look, I know you're a really good actor on the soundstage, Mr. Montgomery, but here in my chair? It's like looking through glass. You needed them both the hell out of your space so you can pretend this morning didn't happen."

I closed my eyes so he could get my lids. "Junior, do you and your girlfriend need anything for your house? Engagement ring? Car? Honeymoon fund?"

He laughed a little. "Antique satin," he said promptly. "She wants to make this wedding dress, but the fabric she wants is heinously overpriced."

"Send me the website and the specs," I said, relaxing into the chair. "It's yours."

"Ha-ha," he said dryly.

"No, I'm serious."

"Why? Why would you buy my girlfriend's wedding dress fabric?"

"Because her fiancé totally saved my life," I told him truthfully. God, someone got it—someone not Noah. It was just nice to have friends who didn't hate you when you were trying desperately not to be a miserable asshole and failing.

As I was lying there, being thankfully quiet in the makeup chair, my phone rang. I pulled it out and handed it to Noah, and he checked it, grunting.

"What's it say?"

"It says the next couple of weeks are going to suck large," he muttered.

"Good, because the last year has been a *cakewalk*!"

"*Huffington Post, The Guardian, Gawker*, and *BuzzFeed* all want quotes, and Jillian says you have three more interviews on Friday afternoon—promised to be fifteen minutes apiece."

"Suzanne posted that awfully early. Wasn't it only supposed to go out after three?"

"Her cameraman must have taken pity on her and helped her with her career."

"Fucking lovely." I sighed. "Noah, you want to do me a favor—"

"I'm entering it into your phone already, Mr. Montgomery," he said, voice dry as toast. I remembered when he'd joked about being my PA. I hope he didn't mind if that sort of just "happened" right now.

He didn't, which was great—because the next week was just as bad as that moment promised.

Interviews, calls from the press, suddenly everybody knew my name. And that poor Suzanne Sylvano, she was brutally outclassed: Did Vinnie know? Was Vinnie gay? Were you lovers? Of course you were lovers—which one topped? Did your sexuality figure into your decisions for *Warlock Tea* and Marvel? Were you in rehab? Did your gayness drive you to rehab? Who are you seeing? Do we know whom you're seeing? Is it the new director, Rafael whatshisface? What about Simon Conklin, are you seeing him? Do your friends in Hollywood know? Did your agent know? Did the producers know? Is there a tiny tribe on an island in the South Pacific that is being destroyed by climate change and does not get any sort of technology that does *not know or give a giant flaming shit whom you want to fuck*?

Apparently not.

By the end of the first week, two days before *Vogue* came to do the photo spread—at a state park, thank God, and not my house—I'd pretty much had it. *Not* having those people at the house on the sweet and quiet little block had been a major headache, and the only reason I wasn't up to my armpits in stalkers in the hedges was because Jilly asked Anna and the show's producers to arrange for extra security, bless her heart, and because Noah pretty much scared the hell out of anyone who slipped through. Local law enforcement lent a hand, and Noah and the sheriff both got particularly good at shooing people the hell away.

So personally, it was a nightmare. Professionally? I had my shtick down, I'd memorized my lines, and I'd developed a thousand and one ways of talking about *my* gayness while leaving Vinnie's gayness and Noah's identity completely out of it. Which meant mostly I used "No comment," especially when I got tired of dancing around the subject.

And when I got tired of "No comment," I used, "Talk to my agent," and apparently from Jilly, "No comment" sounded an awful lot like "Go fuck yourself with a hellfire sword, complete with the handy mace attachment" because nobody ever came back to me after talking to her.

A part of me was proud—I'd launched into this whole thing to protect Noah, right?

But a part of me . . . most of me . . . was starting to curl steadily inward, a pill bug, trying to let my hard, brittle shell shed all that pressure. And the whole time, Vinnie kept up that snarly, passive-aggressive banter in my brain. I swear to God, if he'd still been alive, I would have broken up with him and outed him from fucking spite. And my shell was starting to crack.

Noah stayed there, my rock through the whole thing. He got me into the studio when the fan buildup in the front gate was too big to be manageable. He fielded phone calls when I was on the set, or often when I wasn't, and there were times when he just turned the damned thing off at night so we could be together.

He never left me alone.

Not once.

We got back to the house after that first night, and there was a whole new dresser and computer desk up in my bedroom, and ta-da! I had another roommate. One with definite perks.

That night, my "perk" simply rubbed my feet after dinner and let me lie on him as we watched an old Cary Grant movie on TNT. (Now *there* was a guy who knew about a closet!) When the movie was done, I didn't move, staring blankly at the Turner Network guy talking about Cary Grant and Katharine Hepburn, while Noah stroked my hair back from my face.

"I wish I knew what you were thinking," he said after a moment.

"I'm trying *really hard* not to think at all," I confessed, burrowing harder into his chest.

His hand stilled. "Is that really what you want from me?"

I frowned. "No thinking. Brain hurt. Just hold me."

He laughed softly and kissed the top of my head. "'Kay. You'll let me know when you want me to break into that bag of goodies we've hardly touched, right?"

"Mmm . . ." The thought sent a tingle down to my groin—but not much else. "Yeah. And feel free to take that into your own hands too. But—"

"Not right now."

"Yeah." *God, I love you. I love you so much.* I tried to think about whether Vinnie would have listened to me in this moment, or if he would have jollied me into sex to make himself feel better, or if he would have pouted because I didn't think sex was going to solve all my problems.

You're being sort of unfair, Con. I held you a lot too.

Yeah, Vinnie. You did.

Or maybe that's what made all great couples great. That they knew what to do for each other, and it wasn't important that Noah be better than Vinnie at this part of the game, just that he was good for me now.

So great—that first night started with peace—but by the end of the week, with the stalkers and the phone calls and emails from Jilly that started with *JUST FUCKING SAY NO TO ANYONE NOT ME*, I was a wreck.

When we got back from the set Saturday afternoon—because yeah, all the extra security had us behind schedule, which meant that, once again, speshul snophlake Connor Montgomery had managed to fuck everyone's world up with his stupid personal life—we could see the idiots hiding in our bushes.

Hiding. In. Our bushes.

Noah had to grab the two kids by the scruff of the neck and haul them up to the main road for the security guy to get. While he was doing that, I pulled the car into the garage and trudged inside, thinking I should get dinner or lunch or something started, and that I should start doing laundry because we were going to have to leave at the end of next week or answer Jilly's last email making sure I was okay or double-check with Viv that she was coming with us and whether or not she wanted to bring her little sisters along and—

When Noah walked into the house, I was standing in the middle of the kitchen with a loaf of bread in one hand and a soup pot in the other.

"Connor?"

"Do we want laundry?" I asked.

He took the pot away from me gently and put it on the stove. "Laundry?"

"For dinner."

He took the loaf of bread out of my hand and set it on top of the refrigerator.

"It's two in the afternoon, and we just had lunch."

"But—"

Chest to chest, facing me, he slid his hand into the hair at my crown and jerked sharply, tilting my head back until I was staring at him with big eyes, my heart pounding suddenly in my ears.

"Connor!"

"Yes, sir!"

"Go upstairs, take off all your clothes, and be waiting for me when I get there."

"Yes, sir!"

"Don't touch yourself. Don't play. We are *not* playing, not when you're like this, do you understand?"

"Yes, sir." My eyes dropped. "Thanks Noah," I said softly.

My reward was a crack on the ass to speed me on my way.

My hands were still when I started to undress, but by the time I turned my phone off and put it in the charger they were shaking all over again. *Don't mention Noah. Don't talk about Vinnie. Don't say anything about how miserable the press made the whole coming out process.* And a part of me was resentful. Levi Pritchard had practically gotten a parade in his honor—but this was his turf. Everybody knew him.

I didn't realize what a rare and exotic bird I was until I added another color to the feathers in my tail.

I stood next to the bed, at parade rest, with my hands at the small of my back, and fumed. Seriously, what was he doing down there?

How long would it take to lock up the house? Was he opening some windows, because the temperature had reached eighty, and it was getting hot in here, hot enough for sweat to drip down the small of my back, between my ass crack, down my neck—

Whoosh!

And there went the air conditioning.

My nipples hardened to diamonds just that fast, and my balls drew up hard and aroused, next to my warm body.

Oh.

That's what he'd been doing.

A part of me relaxed. I was being taken care of. Unbidden, my fingers went to a tiny pointed nipple and pinched. It was like squeezing a bag of spices into a simmering pot—the scent, the saturation, the *sexual arousal* slowly steeped through my body, until all things ached pleasantly, and the anticipation of what Noah was planning was the only thing on my mind.

"You'd better not be touching yourself." Noah's voice echoed up the hallway, and I moved my hand quickly behind me again.

"Uh . . ."

He neared the doorway and leaned against the frame, eyes assessing me steadily. "You just touched, didn't you."

"Sorry?"

I loved his laugh so much. He walked into the room and started to undress. He'd worn a T-shirt and jeans today, because I'd been his only passenger, and I loved watching a man pulling his shirt off from the neck first. He'd been working out with me during breaks on the set, and his chest was starting to show the effort. Wide and dark, his pecs weren't slabs of meat yet—but they were hard and unyielding. He was starting to get a tiny patch of *very* curly hair in the center, but I wasn't going to mention it. I felt like it was for me alone.

"I need to know what you need." He kept eye contact with me as he kicked his shoes and socks off in the corner by his dresser. "Some guys get off on punishment and smacks on the ass, and that's fun, but you—"

"I just need . . . help," I whispered. I needed to be told what to do.

"That's what I thought," he said, fingers at his fly. He stepped out of the jeans, his long, dark legs making the motion look even more graceful. His boxers followed, and he walked toward me, naked, confident, his attention burning on my skin. He invaded my space, his body heat making me flush before he even touched me. "So I'll just call the shots."

He traced a delicate line with his thumb down my throat to my collarbone. I tilted my head back just a little, giving him access to everything.

"You don't like something, say so. You were pretty out of it—I'm going to be strict and intense until you tell me you'd rather do things another way."

"Safeword?" I asked, because yeah, I read the porn.

"I'd prefer you just say, 'Stop it, baby, it doesn't feel good,'" Noah said, his mouth turned up, "but sure. Whatever you want the safeword to be."

"Chihuahua."

He buried his face against my throat and snickered. "You are not making it easy for me to be all sexy and dominant, you know that right?"

"It's just, you know. If we had one, we'd have to stop having sex when it came in the room."

He swallowed a smile and framed my face with his hands, while I kept mine obediently behind me. "Connor Mazynsky, you are something really special."

I fought sudden tears. "Make it better," I begged.

He nodded and straightened up, assuming that natural dominance like a cloak. "Boy, I seem to have misplaced my hard-on—get on your knees and find it for me. Do *not* use your hands!"

"Yes, sir!" I dropped my military attention and put one hand on the bed to lower myself when he stopped me and grabbed a pillow off the bed.

"Here, for your knees."

I'd been doing a lot of stunts that week, and I nodded gratefully as I set the pillow on the ground first and then put my weight on it. From there, he looked like a god, a brilliant, diamond-black god of sex and strength, staring down at me kindly and blessing me with his hands on my cheeks.

"I take it back," he said, face stoic. "Use your hands. I want to feel your hands on me, Connor. Can you do that?"

I smiled, so damned glad I could make him happy I wanted to cry. "Yes, sir!"

I grasped him and stroked, relaxing into the sensuality of sex with the basic act of touch. He was fat and blood-filled in my hand, and his skin had the rich, slick texture that made *this* organ different than any other part of the body. I squeezed slowly up and slowly down, and then opened my mouth and wrapped my lips around his head.

And groaned in pleasure. Oh holy hell, he wanted a blowjob and I knew how to give a blowjob. I reveled in the stretch of my mouth around him, in the salty tang of sweat by his crown, in the tight pucker of skin around his scrotum, and the musk I inhaled when I lowered my head to the tiny pebbles of hair at his groin.

Good. Sucking this cock into my mouth was all that was good.

Noah's hurried exhalation told me he thought so too, and I pulled back slowly so I could swallow him again.

His tightening fingers in my hair said something different, and I let him guide me, let him use me, sliding me forward and backward as he desired, slow, fast fast fast, slow—I shielded my teeth to protect him and put my body at his disposal. I so very much yearned to be used.

He thrust hard and deep down my throat, and I tasted the first glorious spurt of pre-cum before he pulled out.

"Stand up," he said gruffly. "I want my hands all over you."

He gave me a hand up, and I stood as he did exactly what he said—he skimmed his palms over my upper arms and down my spine with one hand, while with the other, he pinched my nipples in quick, hard bursts again and again.

I shuddered, and almost begged for him to just get on with it and bend me over. Then I remembered—he trusted me to be patient, to trust that *he* had my best interest and my best pleasure in his heart.

I could endure any amount of teasing if he had my best pleasure in mind.

He left my nipples alone, right before I was about to warn him that I'd come. The relief left me light-headed, and he easily maneuvered me until I was bending over the bed, my ass popped into the air, my dripping cock thrusting into nothingness.

"Stay there," he whispered in my ear, and I worked hard to keep my knees from buckling, just from his voice.

He came back with lube and—to my surprise—soft handcuffs, a scarf, and the flogger/plug combo.

"I don't want to use this plug," he said, rubbing his fingers between my crease and claiming my hole as his own. "I want the flogger, 'cause it's gentle. It's just going to touch your shoulders all over, maybe edge you with enough pain to really feel. It's not going to hurt, not really."

I nodded, content with that trust, content with the knowledge that whatever Noah was doing, he was doing it for me.

"The cuffs don't even bother you, do they?" he asked, searching my face.

"No," I said, thinking about the safety of not being able to move, the absolute confidence of knowing someone else had this.

He swallowed, hard, and moved close enough to stroke my ass with a shaking hand. "Baby . . ."

"What?"

He shook his head. "Later," he murmured. "I'm going to use the scarf instead." He had to pull his finger from my ass to tie the scarf around my wrists, and for a moment, I wanted to protest. But once I felt the strength of the knots he'd used to bind me . . .

Oh. Oh yes.

He hummed and gentled my body with his hand, and everything was right with the world. "Just stay there." He left for a moment and came back with a few more things and a towel. He laid the towel out and then laid out the lube and the flogger, a tiny leather paddle, a couple of plugs and dildos in varied sizes, and a leather cock ring.

"Wow," I said, my eyes big.

He leaned over my back and selected the cock ring. "I'm going to put this on you," he told me unnecessarily. "It's going to make you ache, and it might put off your climax. You may beg me to take it off—and I will."

My mouth parted, and my cock gave a vicious throb. "Not unless I use the safeword," I breathed. The thought of begging to come made my knees weak.

"Okay," he agreed. "If you're sure."

"I am so sure."

He dropped to his knees behind me and kissed one cheek, and then the other. Then he groaned and spread me, and I felt his tongue along my crease and invading my pucker. I moaned, surprised. He'd promised the cock ring, promised the ache and the binding and the being forced into submission!

I started to shift my feet, and he pulled back enough to say, "Stay still. This is mine!"

Oh . . . okay. I was being claimed. His ass, his body to do with what he wanted. I closed my eyes and relaxed into the pleasure, so liquid, even with my cock hard and dripping, that when he wrapped his hand around my cock and secured the ring, I barely even shuddered.

"Comfortable?" he asked, rising to his feet.

"Mmm . . ." My hips rocked unconsciously as I sought to grind up against the bed, and he popped me lightly on the ass to keep me from moving. "Ahahah . . ." It was a greedy sound, because that sting of pain, that overt dominance, made me need.

"You want that," he purred. He leaned over my back again, thrusting his cock along my thighs, leaving a trail of pre-cum down my left cheek. I sighed and wriggled against him, flexing my arms against the scarf at my wrists but still wanting more. He only kissed my spine gently and pushed back my hair to lick at my ear. From the level of the bedspread, with my arms still stretched in front of me, I watched him select the flogger, and I groaned.

I wanted that.

Not the pain, but the . . . the *absence* of everything else in my head. The stalkers in the bushes, the nonstop request for interviews, the constant invasions into my privacy, the wounded, faintly accusatory voice of Vinnie in my head, that worry about what was on the island, if Vinnie would be there and I could just talk, just explain . . .

Swack!

The tails of the flogger layered my back with a mild sting, and the other noise disappeared.

"Are you here?" Noah asked sharply.

"Yes, sir!"

"You're not on that fucking island, are you?"

I paused. "I was, sir," I confessed, chest heaving with the weight of it.

The flogger fell heavily across my back again, and I grunted, each and every strip of leather striking a distinct pattern of nerve endings.

"Here," Noah said, brooking no argument.

"Yes, sir."

Again.

"Here!"

"Yes, sir!"

Swack!

"*Here!*"

"*Ahhhhh . . .*" Oh God! The heat building up on my back was edging into actual pain, and the result was . . . terrifyingly arousing. "I . . . I . . ." I started to thrust my hips against the bed, trying to find a hard place to grind my cock.

"Shh . . ." He soothed my back with his hand, the gentleness making me tremble. My ass clenched and opened again and again, craving, craving him, craving possession and craving more pain. "Here," he murmured. He reached above me and found the lube and one of the smaller plugs.

I whined.

"Not big enough?" he asked, amused.

"I won't feel it!" I protested.

"You'll need to bear down on it." He was so serious! "It'll keep you in the here and now."

"So will pain," I said mutinously.

He grabbed my chin and turned my head sideways. "Are you questioning me?"

"No, sir."

His expression softened. "Do you need to move? Are you comfy?"

I shifted and pulled my arms under my body. "Yeah, I'm good."

"It's not about the pain, Con."

I frowned, because there was something wrong with that on so many levels.

"Con!"

"Yes, sir!" I snapped, my back heating up and throbbing with just the sound of his voice.

"Spread your legs and bend your knees, we're moving on to the paddle now, 'kay?"

I closed my eyes and breathed out. "Thank you, sir."

"But first . . ."

The plug he pulled wasn't the smallest—but it was close. I stared at it, clenching and unclenching, simultaneously happy *something* was going up there and depressed it wasn't bigger, or *him*.

He dribbled lube right down my crease, cold and surprising, and teased me as it dripped down, down, coating my hole. For a hopeful moment the coolness of the plug slid through it, slid into me, and then I was left wanting more.

"Aw *man*!"

The *crack* of his hand on my ass was enough to make me clench, and that was good. He grabbed the little paddle, just a strip of leather on a stick, really, and I had hopes. It would hurt. The pain would ground me, the pain would make me come.

The first swat stung, and I hummed deliriously. Oh *yes*! The second and the third came in quick succession, and I wiggled my ass in the air, hoping for more.

He denied me, soothing the hurt with his hand and then his tongue, and the tenderness undid me, made me groan when the pain had not.

"Noah!" I complained, and he ignored me. "Sir . . ."

He reached in front of me and brushed my cock so lightly with his hand that it almost hurt.

"What?" he said, tracing a finger over my warmed back, making a design in the tiny patterns.

"You're teasing me," I told him breathily.

My reward was a smack with the paddle, a tiny sting, and then another, and another, across my ass, my upper thighs, my backside, and one tiny one, flicking my balls.

"*Yes*!" I groaned, rutting against the comforter. "God, yes, please, keep . . . please . . ."

Then he stopped, the edge of the paddle dancing slowly on my stinging ass.

"*Noah*!"

"What?"

Oh my God, everything ached with need—my cock, my balls, my clenching asshole, trying so hard to hold on to something that wasn't there.

"I *need*!" I almost sobbed. My ass and back stung, but the sting was fading. "I . . . I need—"

"What do you need?" he asked, leaning forward and grinding his outsized cock against my stinging bottom. "Because I'm not giving you any more pain."

I almost sobbed. Something . . . "Oh God, something. Please, Noah . . . something . . ."

"What do you want, Connor?" he whispered, hand going down to tease my testicles again, to stroke my bound cock slowly, with steady pressure. "What do you want?"

No pain? What did I want without— Oh, oh, oh, oh! He'd just squeezed my cockhead and my world almost detonated. It was swollen to the point of pain, but I didn't want the pain, not there, not even in my asshole. That's not how this had started—that's *never* where sex started. It had *never* been about the pain.

I started to weep, suddenly understanding the emptiness that had driven me this last week. "Please, Noah," I begged. "I need to come."

"Yeah, baby," he whispered, covering my tingling back and ass with his body. "Yeah."

His fingers fumbled with the snap on the cock ring, but the plug came out with almost no tugging at all. In a heartbeat, really, he was sheathed inside of me and thrusting, hard and evenly, his body stretching me, not to the point of pain but just past pleasure, and still he thrust, fucking me strong, and sure.

I moaned into the bed, weeping with relief. Blood surged through my cock, and he had me push up so he could reach my hands. He undid the knot at my wrists with a quick jerk.

"Touch yourself," he told me. "Make it happen, Con. It doesn't need to hurt."

My hand on my own body was blissfully gentle, then a little rougher but still—it was all the pleasure, all the sex, and I squeezed and jerked and moaned. My back and ass were suffused with warmth, not stinging, mostly tingling, and Noah's hands on my hips felt solid and warm and real. And still he thrust evenly, and I begged some more.

"Please, sir, harder!"

Noah threw his hips forward, and he slapped right up against my bruised ass. Once, twice, a third time, as hard as he could, and I screamed, the orgasm rolling up through my body, crashing through my blood, rinsing me clean of all the bullshit that had cluttered my head when Noah had sent me up here. I spewed semen on the comforter and cried with the beautiful, blissful release of climax, and the terrible purge of all the garbage in my brain that had held it back.

Behind me, Noah let out a roar and pistoned into my clenching asshole one final time. I felt him, hot and liquid, shooting inside me, and the thought made me tremble.

Inside me. Filling me up when I was empty. It was all I wanted.

And still I wept, the relief, the blessed, blessed relief of pleasure without pain.

I drifted there for quite a bit.

I was vaguely aware of Noah, murmuring sweet things into my ears, kissing my reddened shoulders softly, telling me I was beautiful, and he would take care of me.

Lovely things, if only I'd believe.

He left and came back with a soft cloth. He didn't wash me *too* thoroughly, but he did mop up the comforter. Then he pulled the covers down and let me slide into bed.

He slid in next to me and held me for a long time while I flirted with an afternoon nap and came back.

"You okay?" he asked finally.

"Yeah," I said, still in the vestiges of subspace.

"You know what I was trying to tell you, right?"

I nodded, too clean and empty for tears.

"It's not about the pain," I said, this lesson working hard to set itself in my heart. "You and me, we don't have to hurt."

"God," he said, his voice rough. "I thought you'd never get it."

"I'm only a little stupid," I said.

"Not stupid," he murmured. "Not at all."

He was quiet, but it was the kind of quiet where I could hear his gears turning.

"What?" I asked.

"I just wanted . . . You are so used to . . ." His voice cracked. "Look, I've got to say something."

"I'm in a perfect mood to hear it," I mumbled, half laughing. Nothing was gonna hurt me here.

"Baby, I know you're still mad at him, but the more I get to know you . . ."

"What?" I couldn't be that bad, could I?

"You . . . you are *terrifyingly* ready to be somebody's sub. I mean, I'm glad you're mine, but there are some unscrupulous motherfuckers out there, and they would not care for you the way I do. Or the way Vinnie did. He may have had a lot of flaws, and he may not have given you *this*, but I'm just . . ." He wiped his face on my back, and the dampness on his cheeks stung. "I'm so grateful, Connor. He took care of you. You guys were kids, and I know you were the grown-up most of the time, but he didn't let anything bad happen to you, and it could have. I'm so glad you had each other. I'm just so damned glad."

My tears were like his—not sobs, and not violent. Just a gentle extension of the cleansing of orgasm.

"Me too," I said, and for the first time in forever, it was true. I was so glad I'd had Vinnie. So glad we'd been there for each other. Yeah, there'd been problems. But so much of it had been good.

My tears stopped, and I drifted some more, until Noah, bless him, gave me some direction.

"Here. Let's nap, and when we wake up, we can fix dinner, okay? We've got all day tomorrow—you up for a bike ride?"

The clean, cool air on my face? My body pitched to hold the bike steady and maybe screaming down a hill?

"Yes," I said, holding his arm at my waist. "Yes."

Thank you, Noah. Thank you.

I was surprised that he didn't answer in my head, and I had to make myself say it out loud.

"Thank you, Noah."

"I love you, Con."

"You too," I mumbled.

I'll say it someday. I promise.

But that, I didn't say out loud.

CHAPTER FOURTEEN

ZERO FUN, SIR

T he *Vogue* people came, and the evisceration for the interview
was uncomfortable at best. This interviewer asked, "If you and
Vinnie *weren't* an item, where were you finding your 'companionship'
over the last ten years?"

To which I replied, "So, if I was straight, it was okay to be a
one-night-stand bachelor, but since I'm gay, we're going to make that
a thing?"

The reporter's smile never wavered, and the interview went on.

So yeah—at its worst, it was as invasive as an anal probe to check
my tonsils.

But I did it with a smile, and I posed for the excruciatingly framed
outdoor shots in clothes that I suspected were actively trying to
geld me.

By the time they were done, and I'd showered off the makeup and
the invasive emotional procedure, Noah had to force me downstairs
to eat.

And then he'd forced me upstairs and ordered me to suck his
cock, because I'd wandered off midbite of leftover noodles and started
wondering about the island again. I couldn't put into words what that
island meant to me, how badly I wanted to swim to it—not boat,
mind you, swim, like some sort of primal rite of passage.

The fact that Noah was right, and the odds of me making it there
alive were practically nonexistent, only made my yearning stronger.

That week as we finished shooting the first part of the season,
before we left for Comic-Con, the only two things that got me up in
the morning were my curiosity about the island and Noah's hands on
my skin.

Noah was getting increasingly frantic.

"*Con!*" he snapped one morning when I wandered off in the middle of a conversation about what to pack. "Damn it. Where the fuck did you go *before* you went to that *fucking* island?"

I looked back at him in surprise. *That* was a really good question. How *had* I spent the previous year?

Oddly enough, I couldn't remember what I'd *done*, really—but I remembered what Jilly *said* I'd done. And I tried not to confess that at first.

"I watched a *lot* of old movies," I said, because *duh*, "most of them Vinnie's," because also *duh*, "and shotgunned a fuck-ton of old Netflix stuff."

"Besides that," he said suspiciously.

I caved, because it was *Noah*, and he saw me naked, bound, and screaming for his cock and cum almost every night. He only got the raw, unfiltered Connor Mazynsky, and the last three weeks in his bed had made that more than habit—it was now reflex.

"I watched my video file," I confessed. "The one with all the unedited pictures in it."

Noah looked at me distrustfully. "The what?"

Well, he had a right to be skeptical. I hadn't watched it once since I'd arrived here. At first it was a conscious act; I was moving on, and I had to not be lost in the past—the *magical video perfected* past, actually—so I hadn't even opened the computer.

And then I'd been busy, and then I'd been . . . well, with Noah.

I couldn't look at that past with Vinnie when Noah was in the house.

Vinnie, I can't be unfaithful to you.

Wasn't my *cock in your ass last night.*

Vinnie! You said I could move on!

Yeah—weird how I keep waffling about that. Maybe you should rely on your own judgment, Con, ya think?

"I haven't opened it since I got here," I told him, and Noah frowned, like this was shameful.

"I don't expect you to stop loving him just because we're together," he said frankly.

I got up and left the room.

Noah found me on the back patio, looking across the sound.

He slid behind me and pulled me against him, and I went liquid, lolling my head back against his shoulder.

"I can't—"

Hey, Connor!

What?

Guess what day it's gonna be?

Shut up.

"You can," Noah said, but his voice sounded thready and fragile. "You can deal with this, Connor. You have to."

C'mon, guess!

Not now, Vinnie!

"Not now. We're leaving in two days, and you know where we're staying?"

"In your house."

"We're staying next to Vinnie's house," I corrected, because that seemed important. Really important.

"So," he said after a moment, "tell me how that worked."

"How what worked?"

"You and Vinnie, in the two houses."

I thought about it. "Well, I cooked. If we had company and we had to sleep apart, Vinnie would always be in my house in the morning for oatmeal and fruit. And once he showed up I'd shower, and we'd meet over breakfast and decide what to do. Between shoots, of course, you know, so it was like . . . like three or four months out of the year we'd do this. Sometimes we'd do publicity stuff, or meet with people who had to be seen or whatever. See movies, go to parties, go shopping. I mean, I guess all our time together was essentially vacation time, you know? Jet skiing, surfing—we'd go on trips together, which was great, because we could get a suite."

Noah grunted. "Okay—so, you'd spend most of your time at your house when you weren't out and about?"

I shook my head. "No—meals, because I'd cook—but, see, all the stuff we bought together, you know, as a couple? That went into Vinnie's house. Because it all went together, right? So my house is all white curtains and hardwood floors and matching towels and stuff. I had the home gym and the big-screen television and the conversation pit. Vinnie had the piano with feet and the comic book prints, and we painted his walls all different colors. He had the area rug with Harry Potter on it and the matching throw that said Hairy Otter. The Precious Moments figurines that looked like us. The turquoise couch and club chair—that sort of thing. If we had parties, we had them at his house because, you know—"

"More personality." Noah sighed.

I nodded happily, and then sort of slumped, defeated. "Yeah."

"Where did all the stuff go?"

I sighed and looked away. Suddenly I couldn't even look at the island anymore. "Vinnie's house," I said, my voice vacant and bleak. "It was all in his house, and like . . . the day after he died, Jilly called me up and told me that because there was no will, it all went to his family. His parents got the keys, and I . . ." I shook my head, trying hard to remember. "I know I asked her if I could get my own stuff, and she . . . she was crying. She said his parents had hired a lawyer, and that if we were going to claim any of the stuff in the house, we would need for me to come out about Vinnie, and . . ."

"Oh, Con . . ."

I moved my head again, but the island was still there, and the vision of Vinnie's house, right next to mine, untouchable, was still behind my eyes.

"She told me right before the press got to my house," I said, remembering the torn curtains, the inarticulate rage, the rabid pain. "Can we not—"

Noah's arms tightened around my shoulders, and he whispered into my ear. "Thank you for coming out." I shuddered and squeezed my eyes tight. "Thank you for letting me claim you if I need to. I . . ."

"You've lived in the sunlight your entire life," I said, and he snorted.

"It rains or fogs every month of the year here."

I tried, but I couldn't laugh. "You know what I mean."

"Yeah." He nuzzled my ear. "So, the videos of you and Vinnie—"

Oh God. He was not letting this go. "See, you know all those Vines and Instagram videos he'd post—did you see those?"

"Yeah—usually stuff he was doing, sometimes with you—"

"Most of the time with me," I corrected. "Just . . . you know, not in the versions you saw. We each had a file of the undoctored videos.

Sort of, you know. History as it *really* happened. Ten years' worth . . . He started taking videos with a little camera before every phone in the world could take video." I thought for a moment. "There's like, thirty-two hours of footage in that folder. Bits and pieces of me and Vinnie. Some of it's shit—you can just hear us talking. But . . . you know . . ."

He turned me around in his arms. "It was you, and it was real."

"It was us," I affirmed. "And it was real."

"Can I see it?" he asked.

I froze. "I'm not sure. Would that make the space-time continuum explode?"

"Yeah," he said, rubbing my arms. "I'm sure that's it."

I had no words then. My mind, my body, all of it was frozen with indecision, with pain. "This will be better in San Diego," I told him apologetically. "I know how to be a professional. And my house— It'll be fine."

"Of course it will." But he sounded so disheartened. "Your heart's not there."

I turned and cupped his cheek. "No," I said, stroking it. "It's not."

He kissed my palm. "I . . . Con, if you think you can't ever love me, do me a favor."

"What?" I said. *I love you already.*

"Let me go."

"No," I whispered. "I . . . I'll grow up. I'll fix myself . . . I swear . . . Don't—"

"I'll never give up," he told me, his voice choked. "If you could love me just . . . just a fraction as much as you loved him—"

Oh, Noah! More. I could love you more!

I wrapped my arms around his waist and held him so tight. "Noah . . . just . . ." Oh God. "Just . . . it'll come." *I'll heal. I swear. I can't hurt forever. I want you there when I stop.* "I'll . . ." *I'll disintegrate without you.* "I'll be strong for you. I will."

"You don't have to be strong," he said, sounding as hurt as I felt. "Just . . . just don't pretend for me, okay?"

"You're asking an actor not to pretend?" I tried to sound snarky, tried bleeding the intensity out of this moment that was chipping away at the rough casing I'd built around my heart.

"Not for me."

So unyielding. The last three weeks of obeying him in the bedroom snapped into place.

I obeyed.

"I am lost and sad," I said at last. "And I am afraid I'm not strong enough for you. You—*you* have forced me to function like a human being, and I'm so grateful. You . . . When we're touching like this, or in the bedroom, I feel like I can be whole, maybe. But when I think about down south, and who I was then, and the big gaping hole in my life that I can't give you access to—I feel like I've sort of cheated you. I thought I was a man, but I fucked up. I'm a windup doll instead, and that's a shitty thing to do to someone who's given me as much as you have, and I've got no answer for you."

The words hung between us, and for a moment, I tried to imagine my life if he just turned around and walked away, leaving me with my computer of memories again.

Vinnie, don't let him go!

Connor, make him stay!

"Connor?"

"Yeah?"

"We can pack in the morning."

"What are we doing now?"

"I'm going to hold you—just hold you. And later, when I can quit shaking, we'll make love, and you'll remember what it feels like to live again."

His neck and shoulders were still so narrow. It was hard to remember he wasn't older than me.

"Why are you shaking?"

He buried his face in the hollow of my jaw for a moment. "Baby . . . for a minute there, I was worried."

I stroked his curls, soft and glossy, springing under my fingers. "Not anymore?" I asked, wanting him to feel better.

He shook his head. "That was honest, Con. Months, I've been waiting for something honest out of your mouth. But if you can be that honest about how much you hurt, I think we'll be okay."

We sent Vivienne down four days early so Jilly could "abuse the shit out of the poor unpaid intern," but since I happened to know Jilly was actually paying Viv to help her out for the con, I don't think Viv minded the abuse.

Viv must have been doing her job, because there was a driver waiting for us at the airport, a pretty, thirtyish man who greeted me with a handshake and a genial, "Nice to meet you, Mr. Montgomery, I'm a really big fan."

Noah cast me an unfriendly look. "You only get to sleep with one fanboi driver at a time."

I held up my hands, feeling innocent and virtuous. "I didn't even think about it! Jesus, Noah, give the guy a break!"

The driver—Cliff, by his name tag—looked between the two of us and then started to laugh. "Uhm, I'm a big fan and so is my *wife*, if that helps things a little."

"I certainly hope so," I said, casting Noah a squinty-eyed look. "I swear, picking up my driver was a one-time thing."

The guy laughed and took my bag—and I turned to grab Noah's carry-on, but he batted my hand away.

"What the—"

"You're Connor fucking Montgomery," he said, scowling. "No, you do not carry my bags."

"Don't be a douche. You've seen me use the potty—we're not doing the fanboi thing anymore."

"Connor!" he snapped, and it was getting so the sound of his voice, saying my name like that, made me hard, even in public.

"Yessss?" I barely refrained from saying "sir."

"This is your turf; you're in charge. It's my *job* to be the flunky. Now let go of my bag and let's boogie."

I let go of his bag, stung, and I just may have pouted my way through the airport, but as we neared baggage claim, I heard a high-pitched squeal, sounding my name.

And spent the next half an hour surrounded by pens and autograph books, just like in the movies, while Noah and Cliff fetched the rest of our luggage.

Oh yeah. Right. Movie star.

I remembered now.

Finally—*finally*—Cliff dropped us off in Malibu. The drive from LAX takes an hour and a half in traffic, and by the time we got there, I was slouched against my seat dozing, my head on Noah's shoulder while he read from his Kindle.

He woke me with a kiss at my temple. "C'mon baby. You go inside and open shit up, Cliff and I will get the luggage."

"Noah!" I whined, and all I got in return was rolled eyes.

"Shut up and go fix us dinner or something, okay? Me and Clifford have got to have us a conversation about how we're going to manage you while you're here."

"Manage me? *Manage* me?"

"Yes, manage you. I don't know how you managed your life *before* Vinnie died, but you have got a major picture coming out this week, you just joined the cast of an up-and-coming show, and, hey, besides the whole YouTube thing, which people are *still* talking about, you also came out. Do you know there's a whole forum of people trying to lip-read that YouTube thing to see if you're saying anything like 'I miss Vinnie's cock'?"

I stared at him, appalled. "I thought you were reading a *book*!" I reached for his Kindle to see exactly what he had called up there.

"Me, Viv, Jilly, we've been doing damage control for the last week," he said bluntly, holding the Kindle behind his head. "And I was reading porn because I want you tonight, because I *always* want you, so you're going to need to get lots of protein for that, okay?"

I squinted. "Damage control? I wasn't malfunctioning— Why would you need to do—"

"Not malfunctioning? Are you kidding me? You did the *Vogue* thing and checked the fuck out of your head. I saw the real you on the soundstage and in the bedroom, and . . ." His confidence fell away, and he bit his lip. "And the other night, when you were honest."

My face heated. "Uh . . ."

"You needed us to see what was out there if you couldn't. So don't worry about the luggage, Con. We're on top of it."

He kissed me hard and fast and then shooed me out of the car. Cliff had already unlocked the door from the carport through the laundry room, and I headed into the place, wondering if it looked any different.

Not so much, no. The curtains were still white, the windows were big and sparkling, particularly the ones on the west side, and the place had been aired out and dusted. I went from window to door, opening them up and filling the place with the ocean roar, before I hit the kitchen.

My favorites were well represented, including the ingredients for a garlic alfredo that I used to make for Jilly and Vinnie all the time. I pulled out the noodle pot and filled it, suddenly lost in the easy domesticity of cooking in the place I'd once thought of as home.

I paused after turning off the tap, and looked around for a moment. Did I still think of it as home?

Huh.

I put the pot on to boil and opened the blinds, looking straight at Vinnie's house.

Vinnie had kept it bright blue with yellow trim—not really up to neighborhood code, but people forgave him because he was Vinnie and I was his best friend—and of course I had adored it. It was the sort of thing that had worked on *his* house, but would have been a crime on mine because mine had so many big windows.

Vinnie's house had been painted.

"Cliff's gone—he'll be back tomorrow afternoon to take us to the movie premiere. What's for dinner?" Noah asked, coming behind me and wrapping his arms around my waist.

"Brown," I said, trying to get my head around it.

"Brown what? Brown rice?"

"Brown. Vinnie's house is brown."

"Uh-oh," Noah muttered, face against my shoulder. "Is this going to be a thing?"

I stared at it for a moment, and tried to place it on my pain scale. It didn't seem to have a slot, and for a moment, I had the weirdest, most dissociative feeling.

"I'll put it on the island," I said, as though that made any sense at all.

"Oh damn."

"No . . . no, seriously. It'll go on the island, and I'll worry about it when we go there."

"On a boat?" Noah said suspiciously.

"Sure." The house was on the island now, and I wasn't going to worry about it. We'd swim there someday. I could swim. Noah would take a boat. Whatever.

"Connor . . ." But he wasn't commanding me, he was asking me, so I didn't worry about it.

"Do you want salad or steamed veggies with your garlic alfredo?"

"Anything but Brussels sprouts. Those things make my pee smell weird."

I looked over my shoulder and grinned at him. "And they make your cum taste like beer," I told him seriously.

He laughed and kissed me, then reached out and closed the blinds. He didn't have to. It was all on the island now.

Jilly showed up after dinner with a bottle of wine, and we sat in the living room and talked. Noah passed on the wine, went for a beer instead, and I noticed Jilly had stocked the fridge with his favorite.

I thanked her for it, and she shook her head.

"No, hon—that was all Viv. I put her in charge of taking care of you guys, and she's insanely good with details. I'm trying to poach her to stay down here and intern—I'd pay her but—"

"School!" Noah interjected, concerned.

"They have schools down here too," she said dryly. "Maybe you've heard of them? And I'd give her free room and board—and she's a natural. I'm telling you, Noah. The whole reason she hasn't moved in here with you guys is that she's interested in what I'm offering her on my end of town, so don't go all big brother on her."

Noah looked at me, clearly unhappy. "This is not a good place," he said grimly.

Jilly's expression softened. "It's not if you're young, unconnected, and working your way up from the bottom," she agreed. "But she's young, *very* connected, and working her way from the upper middle."

She swallowed. "I promise, hon. My kids may both have that fresh-out-of-rehab smell, but they're living in the condo down the block so they won't have too much a place in her life, if that's what you're worried about—"

Noah wrinkled his nose. "Jilly, if you think we don't have drugs in Seattle, you are sadly mistaken. It's just . . ." His eyes begged me for help.

"Broken heart," I told her. "He's worried about her broken heart. Her boyfriend just broke up with her because he thought she was destined for bigger, better things, you know?"

Jilly cocked her head at both of us. "Well, guys. Maybe her boyfriend was right, ya think?"

Noah glared from her to me, shook his head, and growled. "I don't like this logic. I think this is a *flawed system.*"

"You were fine with it when it applied to Viv and Cheddar," I reminded him.

"Yeah, but then you tried to apply it to us, and I was not a fan," he grumbled.

I kicked him gently and smiled. "Well, it just means the two of you are too much awesome for the average guy."

Noah scowled at me. "You are a *movie star.*"

I glanced away. "Yeah. Well, I'm sort of a *media* star at this point. Movie stars are a whole other—"

"Argh!"

Jilly laughed, and I smiled at her gratefully. This discussion depressed me—and I wasn't sure if there was any room on the island for this one. It seemed to be a fact of life that wouldn't swim.

"You two will find a solution," she said, patting my leg. "I'm sure of it. You've got your shtick planned about him for the presses, right?"

"Oh yes," I said. "He's a friend. I mean, I don't have anyone else in my entourage, so 'driver and friend' is pretty innocuous, right?"

She shrugged and cast a doubtful look at Noah. He returned it blandly.

"O-*kay*," she murmured, like there was something I wasn't getting. "Now, are you ready for the premiere?"

"Red carpet at three, interviews until five, movie at five thirty, post chat at eight, take the car to the after-party, drag Noah around like a woobie for half an hour, back here by eleven so we can be fresh and minty in time to leave in the morning." I recited the agenda dryly, because Jilly had drilled it into my head.

I'd finished the shoot fifteen months ago—it had been nine months in postproduction and five months looking for the "perfect" release date. Honestly? Like the public, the delay didn't inspire me with confidence. In any other year I would have shot two movies in the interim, but not this one. I felt that year of dormancy keenly—one of the things you have going for you when you're nervous about a project coming out is the deep and abiding surety that whatever project you *just* completed is a thousand times better.

Right now, *Wolf's Landing* was holding all of my ego eggs, and I was almost psychotically afraid of the Comic-Con appearances, lest they disturb my fragile little basket.

"Good job." Jilly downed the last of her wine. One glass apiece for us—there would be no long talks tonight. "You're going to do fine."

"Of course!" I smiled brightly. "Now, tell me who you've signed in the last year to replace me."

"Nobody could replace you," she lied.

I'm saying.

"But I *did* just sign this eighteen-year-old for a vampire movie who's got a chest that would make you weep with desire."

"I bet *he* doesn't have to wax," I muttered. I'd needed to turn to the on-set stylists for my *Vogue* shoot, and my chest still stung when I thought about it.

"You can stop anytime," she said, and Noah's warm hand on the back of my neck told me she wasn't bullshitting.

You'd look like a blond chia pet.

The conversation tumbled along for another hour and we hugged her good-bye in the driveway.

She said something quiet to Noah as he was bending down, and he straightened a little and nodded. He said something back, both of them speaking just low enough that we'd have to engage in ménage a trois if I were to have any hope of hearing what it was.

They broke up, and she drove away, passing a car that added itself to the line of them in Vinnie's driveway.

"Huh," I said.

Noah shrugged. "Family reunion? Party? Who owns the place now?"

"His family," I said, gazing at all the lights mournfully. Yeah, sure, it had only been a few days a year for a couple of years running, but still . . .

You know what it is.

I . . . What day is it?

You know what day, Con.

I can't.

He slung his arm over my shoulders and steered me inside. "You want to go look at the computer and see what new lawn ornament we can order for Gran?" he asked kindly.

"I thought we were going to have sex," I said, feeling surprisingly innocent. "The kind where you tie my wrists and make me call you 'sir.'"

He rumble-growled. "That too. But we can still go shopping."

I thought about it, about the many, many possibilities for whimsical, darling little objets d'art. And then I remembered that Noah's father had needed to bring us to the airport in his pickup truck because Noah was getting the town car repaired on his own dime.

"Has your dad been able to gravel the road yet?" I asked, figuring Noah probably texted his family ten times a day and he'd know.

"Not yet," he sighed.

"Then let's do that. Nobody has to tell him where the gravel comes from—we'll just put in the work order and let it happen."

Noah stopped still, hand on the doorknob as he was about to usher me into my own house. "You'd do that?"

"Yeah, why not? I mean . . . you know. I haven't really spent my money on anything this year. That's not a big deal."

"It is to the people in Bluewater Bay!" Noah said, like I wasn't seeing something.

"Noah, man, don't be weird about it. It's not a thing."

Fifteen minutes later as I sat at my desk and finalized the work order on the laptop, he was still looking over my shoulder and being weird.

"You do not even—"

I stopped him with a kiss. "What is the big deal?" I asked when I pulled back. "Is there some sort of pride thing? Have I offended either one of your ancestral cultures? Is there a non-Californian tax I haven't heard of? It's a need, and I can do something. What's the deal?"

"I don't know. I mean, it's a nice thing. You just do random nice things for people that—"

"Who else am I going to do them for?" I asked, feeling the hurt here keenly. "Jilly has pretty much everything she wants, the only thing my family ever wanted from me was money, and Vinnie's dead."

"Oh God!" Noah sounded horrified. "You're not still paying them off, are you?"

"No." It had been one of the first things Jilly had done after that vlog interview—told my parents they could say anything they wanted to the press, it was all out now. I was just holding my breath for the story of the basketball game facial to hit the news, but hopefully they had more dignity than that. "But you're missing the point. All of the 'friends' we had before he died weren't close enough to trust with the big fucking secret, so they just think I'm a reclusive hosebag, and who else am I going to do nice things for—"

His mouth on mine was firm and no-bullshit. He pulled back and stroked my cheek with his thumb.

"You want to do something nice for *me*?" he asked, his voice authoritative and playful. "Because I can think of some *really* nice things you can do for me that aren't going to cost you more than a bottle of lube."

I closed my eyes, suddenly desperate to be taken some place where my body awaited Noah's pleasure and pain, and nothing else mattered.

"Would you like me to strip naked, sir?"

"Yeah, boy. I'd like that very, very much."

He grasped me under the chin and put just enough pressure to tell me to stand. He searched my face, and I looked back, pathetically grateful to have him in charge, to have that implicit promise that whatever he told me to do, whatever I begged him to do in bed, he was going to make me feel something in the here and now, in the moment, something perfect that wouldn't let me lose any more of myself than I'd already let drift away.

Whatever he saw, though, it tilted the corners of his eyes down, and he pinched my earlobe roughly between his fingers.

I whimpered and gasped, going hard with just the bite of pain.

"I think," he said softly, "tonight we're going to need to get a little rough."

He left paddle marks on my ass.

Paddle marks on your ass.

And I begged him. I begged him to do it.

Every smack, every crack of his hand, every thrust of his cock inside of me was here and now and *real*. There was no island in the land of Noah taking over my body. There was no island in the land of Noah fucking me until I screamed.

And I did scream. I screamed until he gagged me with the scarf he'd used to tie my hands, and when I whimpered, unbound and ungrounded, he'd pulled out the silly padded handcuffs instead.

I relaxed into their grip like they were Valium, and proceeded to beg like a pain slut, because damn it, I wanted some fucking *pain*.

This night, the night before I went back in front of Hollywood and put on a happy face, like someone who had no more secrets to tell, Noah didn't try to tell me what I needed, or teach me any lessons, or probe too deeply into where I went when my mind and body weren't possessed by his mouth and his hands and his cock.

He just smacked my ass until I screamed, and fucked me until I came.

When it was over, I lay floating while he took care of me. I could barely remember to roll out of the puddle of my own cum, but he helped me anyway and washed me, then wiped down the comforter and slid me between the sheets.

When he came back, his breathing sounded congested, and I pulled myself out of lethargy to tug on his shoulder and invade his space. "Noah?"

He didn't answer, but he rolled into me and wrapped his arms around my shoulders so tightly, breathing became optional.

"What's wrong?" I managed to ask.

"Con, I hope you find yourself here," he said after a moment. "Because you are losing more and more of yourself as the days go by. And I'm just . . . just watching you go."

"No," I told him, lucid and honest in subspace as I was not ordinarily. "You don't understand. You're my only reason to stay. Don't let go of me now, okay? You're what's holding me here."

"You've got to help me," he said wearily. "You've got to help me, Con. I can't do this alone—you have to want to stay."

"I do," I told him perplexed. "If only the house wasn't brown."

His breathing hitched, and he didn't answer. He just held me hard until we fell asleep.

CHAPTER FIFTEEN

I DON'T KNOW LOVE. I WAS MADE TO PROTECT, NOT TO LOVE.

I really threw my all into the part of Connor Montgomery over the next three days, and I have to say, if they gave you an award for playing yourself, I totally would have earned that bastard.

I smiled, shook hands, ignored flashbulbs, and interviewed in the cauldron of Hollywood the next day, and the only flinching you could see was from Noah in the background. (In fact, somebody captured a GIF set of him getting blinded for like, six shots in a row that's going to remain classic for *years*.)

I answered the gay question and the relationship question and the "What is your next project?" question (Jilly had brought a list of them to me for the seasonal hiatus, and I liked the selection) and the inevitable, oft-repeated chestnut about if I enjoyed coming back to my roots.

Same answers now as there had been a few weeks ago, folks. Only thing that had changed was that now everyone knew where my pecker went when it *wasn't* in my pants.

Apparently that was enough for me to have to answer the whole slew of them again, but I did so with charm and grace before sitting down to a movie that pleasantly surprised me.

"Wow," Noah said, when my character gave one last smirk over his shoulder and then hurtled his spacecraft into the path of the oncoming asteroid. We weren't holding hands, mostly because I didn't want *him* to get all the questions before he was ready, but we were leaning shoulder to shoulder.

"Wow what?" I asked, around one of the last bites of popcorn.

"You're really good," he said, completely engrossed in the movie.

Suddenly, watching me save the galaxy wasn't even that important. It was all about watching *Noah* think I was good at galaxy saving.

And he did. He watched the screen with the wide-eyed faith of a child, and no, I did not let him down. I *destroyed* that asteroid and I *saved* that motherfucking galaxy, and damn, just for once, it was pretty awesome to see me, Connor, the guy who literally couldn't come unless Noah commanded it, go and do something cool.

I lost myself in the end of the movie, coming into the present with a thump when applause erupted after the postcredit scene. Oh. Oh yeah. In that moment every movie I'd watched as a kid came sailing back to me, and I remembered why I did this, why becoming somebody new was as important for the rest of the world as it was for me.

The director and producers were standing up, and so were the other cast members. Noah bumped me softly. "Go on, Connor. This was really good. Stand up."

I stood up, and the applause increased. I smiled shyly and nodded. In that moment, with Noah sitting next to me, I felt more myself than I had since the blog interview where I'd come out. Yeah. Gay or straight, this was who I best loved to be.

Noah knocked back the rest of his imported beer and watched in puzzlement as Katie Grace, up-and-coming pop singer, toddled away on six-inch spiked black heels with glow-in-the-dark bows over the patent leather toes.

"Who in the hell was she again?"

"Actress, singer, It Girl," I said, smiling out of reflex. I liked Katie, actually—she was new enough for the fame to be exciting, and talented enough to hopefully make it stick. She seemed to be avoiding the coke and party crowd, and she'd been charming and funny when she'd talked to Noah.

"Yeah, but why spend all that time talking to *me*?"

That made me actually laugh. "Because you're a sarcastic fucker and you cracked her up." I paused and watched as Katie glanced wistfully behind her shoulder, her blonde hair cascading over what appeared to be her naturally blue eyes. She waved a little, but Noah didn't see her. "That, and she doesn't know you're gay and taken."

He scowled. "That feels dishonest," he said after a moment. "How did you deal with that?"

I thought about the girls through the years. Jilly had almost always fixed us up, saying either Vinnie or I were between girlfriends right now and needed to be seen with someone. She chose relatively unknown actresses, and in a way, I felt like I'd been doing them a service. They got to go to parties and make connections that they wouldn't ordinarily, and in the meantime, they had an escort so they didn't have to deal with the general pawing and drunk groping bullshit that goes along with being young, pretty, and single in a place where those things were disposable. I mean, I'd endured plenty of that when *I'd* been starting out, so it was nice to think they were getting a break from it themselves.

Most of those girls had gone on to at least some solid series roles, too—I hoped they remembered me as well as I remembered them.

"Jilly arranged my dates," I told Noah. "There was never any expectation—I was always 'between girlfriends.'"

He grunted and snagged a glass of champagne—which he gave promptly to me. "You think people are putting that together now?"

I shrugged. The inside of my head felt worn and transparent with trying to guess what people were putting together.

"What about for Vinnie?" His tone told me he already knew the answer.

"I . . ." I couldn't hold them off forever? But I pretty much promised Vinnie's ghost that I'd have to. "God, maybe they'll lose interest," I muttered. I know that for me, it had been relentless. I was pretty sure Jilly was going to end up with a restraining order if she threatened to geld one more damned reporter. "I . . . Can't they just leave him alone?"

He leaned close to me then, like two friends sharing a secret. "You've been introducing me as your friend," he said quietly. "You think people are putting *that* together?"

I looked at him sideways, suddenly overwhelmed by the need to feel his wide, smooth-skinned palms sliding down my torso, along my waist, cupping my ass. I shook my head then, resisting the temptation to be sucked into the place where it was only us together, because this was important.

"That's why I've been introducing you as my friend," I told him seriously. "I told you that before we left. You don't want the questions, Noah—not straight out of the—"

He cupped my chin and kissed me in the middle of the wrap-up party.

Instinct. Three weeks? Four? Was that how long we'd been sleeping together? Was that how long it had been since he'd first made me unequivocally his, in body if not in soul?

Whatever it was, it opened my mouth and rendered me limp and senseless, at his beck and call. Here, with his tongue down my throat, one hand clamped on my hip, his breath filling my body—*here*—there was no uncertainty. I didn't know if the entire party really stopped to watch Noah Dakers kiss Connor Montgomery until he could no longer think—or lie—but I know the silence in my head was vast and peaceful.

He pulled back, and I remembered I was a neurotic mess. "What did you— Why did you . . . We *talked* about this!" We'd planned with Jilly the night before—I could *swear* I remembered that!

"Yeah. Changing the plan." He wiped my lower lip seriously, like it was important.

"Why?" I asked, voice throbbing.

"'Cause. You are having a hard enough time keeping your lies straight about *Vinnie*. You need to be honest about me. We understood?"

"But . . . but the press. And your family. And—"

"I don't need protection." He rolled his eyes. "I need one less thing to worry about whenever you open your mouth."

"Yeah," I said, still dazed by the public kiss. "Okay."

He grabbed my hand then, just like when we were in Bluewater Bay, and walked me to the hors d'oeuvres table, then stood me in a corner while he filled up a plate.

I let this happen, because I could not straighten out the tangle in my own head enough to stop it.

"Hey, Con."

I turned and smiled briefly. "Hey, Gina." And speaking of girls I'd party-walked into better roles—here was someone I'd actually gotten into this particular picture. "How proud are you? You looked amazing!"

She tucked her hand under my arm and leaned her head against my shoulder. "Yeah, well, you helped get me the role, so that's all you."

"But you've got a series this year, right?" Something feminist and kick-ass and sci-fi—major network, even.

"Yeah." She smiled, her pearly whites freshly bleached and blinding. But beyond the nice teeth and the perfect makeup, the smile was real—she'd been one of my favorite escorts for a year. She'd gone from blonde back then to a glossy brunette now, and the careless updo flattered her. So did the killer red dress—but the personality was the prettiest part of all. "I'm not getting my hopes up," she said with a shrug. "The scripts aren't there. But, you know, I've got other offers if it goes tits up."

"Good for you. You totally deserve it."

"Yeah, well, if *Wolf's Landing* needs another random hottie, let me know. The writers on that show . . . mm."

I thought of Brenda and Lissa, and the takeoff show they were doing.

"Email me— Actually, better yet, email Jilly. We may have something for you on a pilot show, if your season doesn't pan out." I patted her hand and smiled down at her, aware that we looked like everything a het couple should. "The cast and crew are amazing—you really couldn't work in a nicer place."

She quirked her mouth wistfully and patted my cheek. "Yeah, well, they snagged you, and you're the world's nicest guy." Suddenly she looked sober. "So, this one—" a nod toward Noah "—he's yours?"

Well, that kiss had been pretty unmistakable. "Yeah." Some of the fog in my brain dissipated just saying the words. "Yeah, if he wants to keep me."

"Well, you're a prize," she said gently. Then she stood on her tiptoes and kissed my cheek. "I'm sorry about Vinnie," she whispered. "And none of us are going to say a word to the press until you do."

I stared at her in shock. "Uh . . ."

Noah showed up with a plate of food and three flutes of champagne, expertly balanced. Yeah, he probably waited tables through school, because he was just that competent. "Noah Dakers," he said pleasantly. "And you, Miss—"

"Gina Cleo," she said briskly. I'd helped her come up with that—I still thought it was a good idea. "And I have my hands on your man."

He nodded. "Here, have some champagne. It'll make up for letting him go."

She gave a quick grin, and I thought fondly of how much I'd missed her. We'd had fun on the set of *Jupiter*—but I didn't realize how much of myself I'd given away.

"Uh, Gina . . .?"

She glanced up at me, and her smile twisted. "Connor, the whole world doesn't know, but you had to know that some of us did. The question is, *you* came out. Why didn't you tell the world about him? They'd understand, right?"

I thought about Vinnie's suddenly brown house and the lines of cars in the driveway. The sounds of a true-blue Midwest family singing Christmas carols next door while I got quietly drunk in my kitchen. Vinnie's panic if we so much as kissed on the balcony.

"His family," I said quietly. "He . . . he just never wanted them to know. Not about being gay, not about us—"

"Not about rehab?" Oh Jesus.

"You know about *rehab*?" I whined.

"My best friend was there with him," she said frankly. "Ten years, Con—and no girl could ever swear she'd slept with either one of you. It was the worst kept secret since Cary Grant and Randolph Scott. But his family didn't know?"

I shrugged and looked at Noah. "The whole world knows about Noah," I said brightly, like that would make up for the ten-year hole in my history.

"You should tell them," she said, and right at that moment Kyle Adams, the director of *Jupiter*, made his way around to talk to us. And to have pictures taken, since the press was on his heels.

The next morning, Noah woke me up to get ready for Comic-Con by showing me a picture of Kyle, Gina, Noah, and me, standing in line, our arms around each other. The caption read, "Connor Montgomery and his special friend."

"Was that so hard?" he asked, hand pushing my hair back from my forehead.

"No." When we were together, I couldn't seem to not look at him. Right now, his eyes searching my face seemed to be the most important place in the world.

He cupped my face and leaned his forehead in, until I had to close my eyes. We'd both been pretty tired when we'd gotten in the night before. I remembered thinking for a moment that our "coming down" noises weren't similar at all to Vinnie's and mine. For one thing, Noah kept up sort of a constant grumble to himself, and when he wasn't doing that, he was giving me directions.

"Hang your suit up, Con. It'll take another wear," or "I like the cuff links. Do you have a place to keep them?"

There was none of the bitch and dish that Vinnie and I used to do—but then, Noah was too decent a person to bitch *or* dish.

When we'd slid into bed, both of us in our boxers, another difference made itself known. Vinnie and I used to kiss and then roll over to our own dents in the mattress.

Noah dragged me up against him in a power spoon.

I'd had just enough consciousness to think I liked this way, when I'd fallen asleep.

Now, waking up and feeling Noah's solid warmth *breathing* itself into me, I wasn't sure I could imagine waking up without him.

"You ready for the next two days?" he asked. *Jupiter Seven* today, *Wolf's Landing* tomorrow. Both panels were followed by an extensive cast signing, but I was looking forward to it.

"Raring to go," I promised him.

"I won't leave your side."

He had no idea—*none*—what that meant.

He did it, too—both days, bringing water, working with security, making sure I stayed with my group as they hustled us from the interview room to the panel room to the signature room. There was the occasional hand on my back, and definite manhandling of my shoulders when I, say, turned to talk to the seven-year-old wearing my costume from *Jupiter Seven* and stepped out of line, but for the most part he kept the public touches chaste.

He was there to direct me and meet my needs, and although I'd had assistants before—PAs, usually hired by Jilly—I can't remember ever feeling as though my world was quite as clockwork as it was with

Noah. His job description might not have said "bodyguard" but then, Viv's didn't say "handler" either—but that's what they both did.

And because I was so secure, I managed some real magic on the panels.

"So, Connor, you're on a panel for *Jupiter Seven* and one for *Wolf's Landing*. Which would you say is your favorite?"

"Sci-fi," I replied pertly. "I think sci-fi is my definite favorite."

"So, Connor Montgomery, do you think there's something in the water at Bluewater Bay that is making all the stars come out?"

"I dunno, the water's pretty clear. Maybe you can see our reflections better?"

There was general laughter, and then the interviewer followed up.

"Out of the closet, Mr. Montgomery."

This was the second day, and I looked back at the *Wolf's Landing* panel. Levi was looking sardonic, as usual, Marianna was gracious, of course, but Carter was leaning forward, almost eagerly, waiting to hear what I'd say.

Well, hell. They'd tried to be kind to me, right?

"I think the cast and crew—right down to the makeup and wardrobe people and the gaffers and set dressers—have all worked to create a really supportive, creative atmosphere," I said truthfully. "When you're working in a place where you're comfortable, where you're not afraid of the repercussions of being yourself, it's amazing what can happen on set."

Carter lit up then, his beautiful, boyish features practically shining, like this was the thing he'd been waiting for another actor to say all along.

"And with that," he broke in, "how would you all like to see Connor Montgomery killing it in a place where he feels comfortable?"

The applause was heartwarming, and to my surprise, the clip they ran was of me yelling at Brenda and Lissa.

As my voice cracked on-screen, and the real anguish sat my shoulders and rode my expression, a shiver ran up my spine, one that exploded into my chest as the clip ended.

And then there was that silence—that *true* silence, the one that said everybody was so stunned and happy, they were going to let that performance sit for a minute before they reacted.

When they reacted, the applause was thunderous. I leaned back and spoke quietly to Carter. "That was nice. Why not a clip of you and Levi?"

"'Cause Levi and I are a lock," he said quietly.

"I signed the papers!" I laughed.

"Yeah, but you don't understand, Connor. We *want* you to stay."

"I want to stay too," I said, warmed. The applause continued, and I looked up at Noah, who didn't seem to hold it against me one bit that the big noise was something that fed my soul.

That night he dragged me away from a backstage party in Carter and Levi's hotel suite. It wasn't one of those out-of-control things that always got embarrassing, but most of the cast and crew of *Wolf's Landing* who had made it to Comic-Con were there, and yeah—my wineglass was always full.

But it was a happy party—it was like leaving home and finding out that all your favorite neighbors were coming to wherever you were going, and that was *great*. We hung out and talked shop and talked about how the *Supernatural* fans were terrifying and how *Jupiter Seven* had been a fun set and how sad it was that Gina's series looked so shitty because it had such promise, but nobody wanted to work with the producers. It was the dish and bitch I used to do with Vinnie, but a little bigger, and Noah didn't seem to mind standing at my elbow and saying quiet, sarcastic things in my ear as the conversation waxed on.

At one point—after my third glass of wine, I thought, *Geez, Vinnie, this is fun. I wish I'd gotten to do this with the folks at Warlock Tea.*

Yeah, Con. I regret doing that to you. You deserved to enjoy your work.

I turned to Noah and smiled. "You're right. Doing this with *Warlock Tea* would have been fun."

Noah turned from a conversation with Levi. "Baby, I didn't say anything about *Warlock Tea*."

I blinked at him slowly. Oh God. Where had that come from?

"Too much wine," I said, trying to be winsome.

He took the glass out of my hand and regarded me with completely sober eyes. "We're going home."

I nodded, and let him seize my hand and pull me out of there. He wasn't rude, really, but I don't remember having to extricate myself from any social situations. He just looked at people, his brows faintly knit, and they smiled and said, "Bye, Connor! Bye, Noah! See you later!"

It was like a superpower.

We drove home in silence until I asked Cliff if he could open the moonroof. For a moment, the air on my face felt good, especially because we were still on the stretch of Five near the ocean, but then...

"Damn."

"Damn what?" Noah had sprawled his legs over the backseat, wedged his ass in the corner, and pulled me into his arms. I was leaning against his chest and staring up at the sky.

"No stars."

"LA." As in, *Duh, what did you expect?*

"Yeah, but San Diego's different. I expect stars in this stretch."

He sighed and dug his chin into my shoulder. "Maybe you just miss home."

Home. As in Washington.

"Yes." I closed my eyes. "The sea smells better there."

"More trees."

"Mmm... You hated trees, Vinnie."

I didn't hate them, per se—

"He did?" Noah asked cautiously.

"Yeah, he was afraid of getting lost in them. He grew up in Nebransas, right?"

"Like, the Midwest?"

"Yeah. I could never remember the state. Sorry about that, Vinnie."

I tried damned hard to forget, Con.

Behind me, Noah's breathing got very, very still. "Uh, Connor?"

"Yeah, Noah?"

"Why is Vinnie suddenly here with us?"

"Can't you feel him? He's everywhere down here."

No, mostly I'm just in my house.

"Goddamn you two," Noah muttered.

"Why?" I tried to turn to look at him, but I was too tired and too tipsy. "What'd we do?"

"That fucking house, man, the fucking silence. You have like . . . an *iceberg* of damage in you, and you keep trying to think it's all fine, but I keep wrecking myself on bigger and bigger pieces."

"I'm sorry," I mumbled, the pleasant buzz of the day doused in ice water. "I think today went really well."

"Right up until you had a conversation with Vinnie in the middle of a party, baby."

I grimaced. "How did you know I was doing that?"

He sighed and tightened his arm around my chest. "I always know," he said bleakly. "I just fucking do."

I whimpered. Oh God. Oh God—

"How often am I talking to him?" I didn't even want to know. It was one thing if your madness was trapped in your own goddamned head but to have Noah realize the extent of it?

"Since you came out? All the fucking time."

My brain swelled. Or it felt like it swelled. Or it exploded. It definitely exploded.

"I . . . I have no . . . I didn't realize—"

"Why do you think I've been so worried?" he burst out. "Because you're all smooth on the outside, and you're all, 'Fine, Noah, fucking fine!' and then you get that look and you have your little conversation, and then you just go on with your day."

Vinnie, am I that bad?

"You're doing it again!" *You're doing it again!*

"Oh Jesus," I said, shaking. "Stereo. I heard you both in stereo."

"And then, when it's you and me together, you're . . . you're so driven. You just *need* so badly. And it finally hit me the other night. It hit me that you needed me because there's no Vinnie in the room when we're together. Which on the one hand is really flattering, right? But on the other hand is fucking terrifying! Con, what does it take to have you to myself when we're *not* naked?"

"I don't know," I whispered. "I don't—I don't even know when I'm doing it. I just . . . I forget, you know? It was okay when everybody didn't know all of it, but now that so many people know parts of it I'm just . . . I can't keep track of the pieces." I sat forward, panicked. "I can't keep track of the pieces. Noah, what if they all come apart?"

Oh hell.

"What if I lose you?" I turned and looked at him, almost in tears. "What if I lose you? What if it becomes all the Vinnie and none of the Noah? He's *dead*, Noah—I need the live person! I'm not so stupid I don't know that—I need the *real person*. You love me! I can't lose that!"

I was shaking so hard my teeth were chattering, and he wrapped his arms around my shoulders and held on tight.

"Shh . . ." he murmured in my ear. "It's okay. It's gonna be okay. You can't lose me. You can't. I'm stuck to you. I'm unshakeable."

"You don't understand," I mumbled. *He doesn't understand, Vinnie.*

I do. You did everything right.

"I did everything right," I told Noah desperately. "Everything. And I lost him. And I'm not doing anything right with you. Nothing. I should be . . ."

You know how to take care of people, Con. Remember?

"I should take care of you," I mumbled. "I should take care of you. Because I'll lose you."

My mind went blank, then numb with horror, overwhelmed. I *should* be the caretaker. I had been with Vinnie—but now I was lost, trapped, crippled by memories of Vinnie and clinging to the real with Noah. How could I be another person? How could I be "out-Connor" and "in-Connor" and "Vinnie's Connor" and "Noah's Connor" and *Slade fucking Lupin* or whoever else showed up in a script on my desk?

Noah's hand over my mouth barely brought me back to myself as I breathed in heated recycled air, and the oxygen stopped rushing my brain.

"Connor!" he snapped, pulling me more into myself.

"Yes, sir," I mumbled weakly.

"None of the sir shit, Connor. I think . . ." His voice grew thin, uneven, like he hated to admit this. "I think we need to ask someone for help, you think?"

"Oh God." A shrink? A grief counselor? "No." I collapsed against him. "Please. Just . . . just you."

"I'm not enough," he said. "Not enough."

"You are." I stopped sucking in air, my chest stopped heaving, and my mind freed itself from that crippling lock. "It's not . . . It was a panic attack. It's . . . I just need to think about it. I need to be *home*, where I feel like *me*—the me who's with you, and not the Hollywood me."

"Connor, you're an actor—"

"Yes, yes, I am."

"You need to come to Hollywood sometimes."

I sagged against him, too limp to pretend anymore. "Yeah. But next time I'll know."

"Know what?"

"Vinnie's house will be brown."

We got back to the beach house and made our way upstairs. I was wearing high-end jeans and a button-down shirt, and it all got chucked in the hamper. I stood in the darkened room after that, staring blankly through the sliding glass door at the ocean.

Noah walked in behind me, also in his boxers, and put his hands on my shoulders. In the sudden quiet, we could hear a raucous celebration down on the beach. I focused on the bright spot down below my deck.

"Look," I said quietly. "A bonfire. Think that's coming from next door?"

"Yeah," Noah said. "There were still a lot of cars out there. Did Vinnie's family have reunions?"

"No," I said. "It's . . ." I closed my eyes. "What day is it?" I wasn't great with dates regularly, but conventions—forget about it. I couldn't remember to link the number with the day during the best of times.

"July twenty-second."

I started to laugh, a humorless sound that hurt me to make.

"Oh Jesus," he muttered. "You think that would be worth mentioning?"

"How do you even know what I was going to—"

"It's his birthday, isn't it?"

Images flashed behind my eyes—long walks on our beach, stupid, kitschy little gifts like Bundt pans with plants in them and Hummel figurines. Giant lime-green bathroom rugs, and wreathes of teddy bears. All of it given in the darkness after Comic-Con, which had been our real gift to each other.

"Yeah," I said, and oddly enough I was reassured. "But . . . you know. That . . . that explains a lot."

"But not all of it," he said soberly. "Please, Con? Would you—"

"We leave the day after tomorrow, right? We have a week's break, and then we start shooting again. Right?"

He palmed the outsides of my arms, and I melted into that touch. "Right."

"Let's go to the other ocean, okay? Where he's not . . ."

"Right next door," Noah murmured. "I get it. I've gotten it since the very beginning."

"I didn't," I told him seriously. "I didn't have any idea. I thought . . ." What? That I could skate along on the surface of the ten-year hole?

There's not even ice on the surface, dumbass!

I sighed.

"What?" Noah touched his lips to the back of my neck.

"Even Vinnie thought it was a bad idea."

Noah's chuckle sounded strained. "Well, good that me and your dead boyfriend could agree. But now tell him that you're going to be unavailable."

He dragged his knuckle down the xylophone of my spine, and I shivered.

"Yeah, sure."

I'm outta here.

Noah turned me in his arms and kissed me softly, tentatively, and I chased him, holding him still and *making* him stay.

That was his cue right there, to take over, and he did but . . .

Softly.

There was no playing at boy and sir here. His mouth on mine was firm—but not commanding. His hands sliding along my arms and torso were warm and hard—but not painful. I arched into him, wanting harder, and he gave me back . . .

Himself.

I tilted my neck back and gave him access to my throat, the hollow of my shoulders, behind my ears, and he nibbled. I shivered, and for a moment, I wanted to arch against him, greedy, and beg, but he pushed my hair from my ear and licked along the outer shell. His voice—deep anyway—grew huskier, and he whispered, "Stay with me here, Con. Stay with me."

It was all the strength I needed.

We made love sweetly then, and every touch, every kiss, was a blessing.

My body was his. I gave it to him as a prayer. *Oh Noah, please let me stay.*

He thrust his way into me, and I heard his response. *Yes. Oh God, Connor, stay.*

And I was his then, in the moment, under his fine, rangy body, pulled into the warmth and comfort of his dark skin.

Our climax rolled through us, starting small inside me and gaining power and complexity, until it rocked his entire body, sent him shaking and sobbing into the hollow of my shoulder.

I comforted him, stroking his neck and chest, while we whispered stupid promises I wasn't sure I could keep.

Shh . . . It's okay. It's okay. We'll be okay.

I'll stay.

I'm not sure if he believed me. I fell asleep with his weight pushing me into the mattress, his erection still nestled inside me. I felt complete that way.

He and Viv were scheduled to go down to San Diego together the next day. They hadn't had a chance to cruise the vendors' floor, and I had earmarked all sorts of things I wanted them to get for their gran and their father and their little sisters. Kitschy crap? Of course. But I could picture their house, every rainbow-painted room of it, and I wanted something from me in each one.

So I'd written a list out specifically, and their job was to get as much of it as they could.

Noah woke me up early, smelling like shower gel and kissing me softly on the temple.

"You'll be okay?" he asked.

I yawned and tried to remember what he was talking about. "Yeah, sure."

He scowled. "Con, this is not a 'sure' thing. You—"

Oh, yeah. I *was* falling apart. There was no denying it.

"You'll be home at four?" I asked, because that way I could schedule. I could do paperwork and stuff, maybe go for a run on the beach, and have dinner started for them before they got home.

"Yeah," he said, nodding. "But if you need—"

"Cell phones," I yawned again. "That's what they're here for."

He growled in his throat, and I patted his cheek.

"I promise I'll call you and not Vinnie. He probably doesn't get cell service anyway."

"That's not even funny, Con."

"It is."

"No, it's really not."

"Little bit, yeah."

"Con, I will—"

"Go have a nice day," I mumbled, suddenly too tired to even play-argue. "Come back and show me all your fun things. I really want to see them, okay?"

He sighed. "Yeah." He kissed my forehead and then my mouth. "Remember who loves you, okay?"

"Noah Dakers. Can't miss him. Tall black kid, with the most beautiful eyes in the world."

"Flattery helps—I can't deny it."

"Good, now go before traffic gets worse than shitacular, 'kay?"

One more kiss and he left, and I did what any actor did after a premiere and two days at Comic-Con. I went back to sleep until noon.

CHAPTER SIXTEEN

HE'S ONLY BEEN MOSTLY
DEAD ALL DAY

I did finally bestir myself to get out of bed and answer some emails. Jilly wanted me to narrow down my script options, and I told her I'd read them on the plane. *Vogue* wanted my okay on the photo layout, which I gave, and someone had slipped a ball past Jilly and wanted me to do a commercial for condoms that would probably make me a lot of money. But they'd slipped the ball past Jilly, and nobody did that to Jilly, so I told them no.

When I looked up, it was three, and I figured better to do my run now and then shower than the other way around. I grabbed my iPod and my sleeve and put on my running shoes, liking the idea of a crashing ocean instead of a still one.

And I have to admit that as I took the path from my backyard to the steps down to the beach, I was in decent spirits. I'd gotten used to the brown paint on Vinnie's house, and Noah's lovemaking was still bright and dark and lovely, etched in my head.

I had faith right then, hope that I'd figure out how to live with my ghosts, and that it would be all okay. I took off going north, running for about fifteen minutes before turning back around. My time got better on the way back, so as I passed the back of *my* beach house, I decided I'd run down past Vinnie's.

A woman had come out as I'd been running, and she was walking a bucket with water back and forth from the ocean to the remains of the bonfire that had been built the night before.

I slowed as I neared the fire, recognizing the skeletons of some of the things in the pit.

Oh.

Oh, oh no.

I didn't realize I'd made a sound until the woman trotted around the remains of Vinnie's turquoise recliner, bucket in hand.

"Connor?"

I glanced at her, and then back to the charred remnants of ten years of my life.

"Oh," I said, my voice small.

"You are Connor, right? I mean, we spent Christmases with you and Vinnie. I'm Christine, Kevin's wife?"

"Ohhh . . ." I moaned. There, in the corner, reeking like burnt rubber, was the remains of the big furry lime-green rug he'd kept in the bathroom.

"Connor, are you okay?"

"Our stuff," I whispered, seeing a multicolored scrap of what must have been the Hairy Otter blanket flying off down the beach. I sat where I stood, the hugeness of the destruction too big for me to comprehend. "Why would you burn mine and Vinnie's stuff?"

I'd had it so perfectly outlined in my head, that house on the island. Vinnie waiting there, all of our stuff, the life we'd picked out and laughed over, the time we'd spent creating something whimsical and adorable that only *we* would ever understand. We'd lived in our own world—it had been our magic bubble. We'd decorated it like petty gods, and here was our sorcery, immolated and charred, toxic ashes in the wind.

"Your stuff?" she said, sounding surprised. "I mean . . . we went sort of overboard. We were . . . You know . . . It was his birthday. We just . . . all missed him so bad, you know? We wanted to sort of . . . you know. Closure."

"You burnt our home for closure?" I couldn't get mad—there was no strength in me for mad.

"Vinnie's house is still up there," she said kindly.

"He painted it blue for me." Nobody knew this. "I like . . . I like blue." So the furniture had been blue, and the living room rug had been blue, and the trim had been yellow. "It was . . . so I'd look over at his house and know he was really living in *my* house. Just . . . just a backyard away, right?"

"Connor?" She sounded confused. "Why would Vinnie paint his house blue for you?"

"Because he loved me," I keened. "Oh . . . oh God. Vinnie, you loved me . . . and look. It's our home . . ." I reached into the ashes and pulled out a plate, the veneer peeling from the pottery, but I was pretty sure it had once been a raw piece of steak. "It's our life, Vinnie," I moaned. "Oh, Vinnie, it's all gone. Our home is all gone. It was . . ." I looked up at his brown house, the truth slamming into me so hard I could barely breathe. "It was never mine. Oh Vinnie, how could we have built that home and it was never mine? Ten years, and it was never mine. You were never mine . . ."

"Oh, Connor . . ."

I was too far gone to hear the epiphany in her voice, too destroyed to explain.

"You were never mine . . ."

And the sound I made then—I can still hear it. My dad had needed to shoot a jackass once because the poor thing had broken his leg, and the sound that animal had made, in pain and helpless—*that* was the sound that came from my throat.

There was no dignity in it, no beauty—nothing as clean as a sob.

I couldn't control my sounds, or my mind or my words.

Vinnie!

And in my head, I was yelling to stop, to stop, because maybe Vinnie's sister-in-law would figure it out, and maybe the whole world would know but . . .

Vinnie! Oh, God, Vinnie! Our lives are gone. You're not just dead, but our lives are annihilated. It's like it didn't happen at all!

But Vinnie didn't answer. He was gone. All of our stuff was gone. Our lives were gone. It was like it hadn't happened at all.

I'm not sure how long I sat there, making donkey noises, but Noah found me as the breeze got chilly, and I'd started to shiver from sitting in the damp sand. Christine was sitting next to me by that time, resting her chin on her hands and staring at me, just staring at me, which was weird, right? Because I'd been sobbing for an hour.

You think she would have just left me alone.

Noah's feet barely kicked any sand as he approached, and I recognized them. Big, dark-skinned feet, with that vulnerable pink underside, padding across the beach with an easy grace.

I gazed up into the sun and squinted against the salt water and the sand and the wind and the sun.

"Noah?"

He sank down next to me and wrapped an arm around my shoulders. "Con? Man, we've been calling you."

I hadn't heard my iPhone going off in the running sleeve.

"Noah, they . . . they burnt our stuff."

"Oh . . ." Noah stared at the fire pit and took in the devastation. "Oh, oh fucking Jesus. Oh, Connor . . . I'm so sorry."

"It's gone," I said softly, too destroyed for more than that. "All gone. Ten years, it never was."

"Oh . . . oh no . . ." He looked up and saw Christine, a pretty woman, brown hair in a ponytail, freckles across her plain Midwestern face. "You . . . This was fucking *necessary*?"

She wiped her hand across her eyes. "We didn't know." Her voice sounded rustier than it had when I'd first come down the beach. "My God, do you think we'd . . . Nobody's that fucking cruel!"

I melted against Noah and rocked back and forth, and I was no longer making that horrible sound—but I hadn't stopped crying either.

"Connor didn't know that," Noah argued, and there were tears in his voice.

I'm sorry, Noah. Didn't mean to hurt you too.

"We didn't know about Connor!" she yelled. "We didn't know! Oh my God, this whole time, his mom and his brothers and sisters, all of them crying because he'd never been in love—do you get that? They thought his whole life, he'd never fallen in love, and it made it all just . . . just *worse*. How could they let him go if he'd never been happy?"

"We were happy!" I sobbed. Oh, we had been. There'd been rough road, but God, I'd still been down for the ride.

"Yeah," she cried back, wiping her face on her sleeve. "I get that. I can see that. *Why didn't he tell us?*"

And I had no answer for her. I was out of words. I reached back into the wet ashes and pulled out that piece of steak plate and held it to my chest. I remembered that Precious Moments figurine, two boys, one with dark hair and pale skin, one with blond hair and blue eyes, standing together at the school bus stop. Me and Vinnie, from the first moment of our Hollywood education, we'd been together.

I couldn't stick my hands in there to find it, shattered. I just couldn't. I was not that brave.

I don't know how long it took for Noah to get my attention, to stand me up and make me drop the plate and herd me back toward the house.

I remember Christine running to catch up with us as he was about to shoo me up the stairs, though. "Connor!"

I turned.

"Connor—Vinnie's got a file on his computer that we couldn't open. It's password protected. And his financial stuff was all in the open. Do you know what the password was?"

"Mazynsky," I answered dully. "M-a-z-y-n-s-k-y."

"Oh God," Noah almost moaned. "Connor, do you know what you just—"

"I've got nothing left," I mumbled. "No more two of me. No more pieces. Connor's all shattered now, no more pieces. Only sand."

And Noah didn't ask me any more questions. He just chivvied me up the stairs and into the house, and probably into the shower and to dinner and bed.

He must have. I woke up next to him in the morning, and he got me ready for the flight home.

As we walked out of the beach house, I turned around and looked back into it. It was what it had always been—light, and airy, and beautiful.

Maybe, if I sold it, I could hire a company to pack it up for me.

I'd never have to see it again.

I didn't remember much about the airport and the flight, or even the trip home. Noah's father picked us up in the town car, and he and

Noah talked about the trip while I zoned out, eyes staring blankly at the now-familiar topography.

The sky was gray, and I found myself lost in the drizzle, disintegrating, not sand but mist.

We arrived at the house, and I didn't argue about the luggage, I just wandered inside, touching things randomly, trying to ground myself.

Noah and I had bought the throw, and the rug. We'd bought the figurine of the dog, and the little wooden statue of the otter. I stroked each of these things, and wondered if they'd be on the island. I should see. I should see if the things with Noah and me were on the island.

The things with Vinnie and me were probably on the island.

I should go look.

I stepped out to the back patio and looked for the little gate that led to the water's edge.

Vinnie, do you want me to come visit?

No. Con, no. That kid in there, he wants you home.

I'll come back.

You can't come back from this, Con. You can't. Go back inside.

I just want to see how cold the water is. That's not such a bad thing, right?

It's a very bad thing, Con. Don't—

I hadn't really seen this stretch of the water; it was *right* in front of the raised backyard. Lots of rocks in there—I could see some of them protruding right where the water got really dark.

I'll have to swim the whole thing. Vinnie, I don't know if I can do that. Those rocks look sort of dangerous.

CON, DON'T COME.

It's what—half a mile out there? How many yards is that? If most people can swim 500 meters in sixty-five degree water, how fast will the train be going when it gets to Brooklyn?

I laughed softly to myself. That was a good one. Fifty-eight degrees? Fifty-five? Seriously—how cold could it be?

I took off my shoes and socks and stuck my toe in.

And barely refrained from an unmanly shriek. Oh holy God—holy God, that was cold.

I should probably take my clothes off. I'd want something sort of dry to put on when I got back.

I folded my jeans, sweatshirt, and T-shirt neatly, and wrapped them in a little bundle with my cross-trainers and socks. Standing on my tiptoes, I shoved them between the bars on the fence of my patio, making sure they were wedged there so I could get them quickly. I left my boxers on—I figured I could take them off and go commando when I dressed, but I knew I'd be cold when I got out of the water.

I was cold *now*, actually, and that was just from the drizzle. Trying not to hurry, clenching my teeth to keep from chattering, I stepped into the water and bit back on the scream I knew was coming.

And another step. And another, and another. Oh fuck—the rocks were many and sharp and painful. I was starting to wish I'd gone back inside for my flip-flops when I took another step and slipped into a hole, pushing up instinctively as the water hit my armpits.

"*Ooh!*" I gasped, my chest hurting. "*Fuck*, that's fucking *cold*!"

Vinnie, maybe this is not such a good idea.

No, it's a great idea. Take another step.

Oh, well if he was going to be on my side. I took another step and winced. There was a huge boulder to my left, and I stubbed my toe on it. Oh, hey, that thing was like three feet from the surface—damn. My teeth chattered uncontrollably, and I wondered if maybe I should climb that rock and see if I could move well enough to swim even. My arms and legs hurt, and I wasn't moving fast enough. If I was going to do this, I should just jump in, but it was starting to filter in that once I took the plunge and started to make my leaden limbs move, I wasn't going to be able to get back.

"*Con!*"

Noah's voice crackled in terror, and I honestly wondered if some sort of sea creature I didn't know about was behind me. I startled and bonked my knee on the fucking rock.

"Ow! Noah! You scared me!"

"Connor? Baby? What in the fuck are you doing?"

"Freezing," I mumbled. Suddenly I was really tired. Maybe I should try this swim tomorrow. "I'm sorry. I thought I'd try to go to the island. You know, to visit Vinnie."

Noah was dancing on the shoreline, his face twisted in anguish, but when he heard that, he stopped.

"You want to visit Vinnie?" he asked, his voice breaking.

"Well, maybe not now—"

"You want to visit *Vinnie*!"

"I just . . . you know. Want to tell him good-bye—"

"He wants to visit Vinnie," Noah muttered, apparently to himself. And then he started stripping off his shirt.

"Noah, you don't want to do that—it's cold out here."

"You think? You fucking think? Did you hear that, Noah? He thinks it's cold out there." Noah stopped muttering to himself and snarled at me, throwing his shirt over his shoulder and going for his pants. "If it's too cold out there, asshole, get your fucking nuts back on shore."

It was too cold out here for him. His best friend had died in these waters—I didn't want to make him swim them.

"Noah, baby, you don't want to swim here—it's dark, and it's freezing . . . you don't want to visit Vinnie."

Oh God—everything fucking hurt. My joints, my chest, my muscles and bones. I really should come ashore and try this another day.

"No!" Noah yelled, down to his boxers. "I think this is a *great* idea! I think we need to visit Vinnie!"

He took a running step into the water and howled, and a part of me woke up. "Noah, honey, it's too cold. You'll . . . hypothermia . . ." I could barely talk. "Maybe you shouldn't do this with me—"

"No! You want to visit him, then *I* want to visit him. I'm— *Augh*! This is fucking *cold*! Jesus, Connor, how did you get out that far?"

"I slipped," I told him through a jaw so tight my neck and shoulders were burning with the tension. "Noah, you don't want to visit him—he's *dead*!"

"You think!" Noah screamed, his voice hysterical. He was crying. His eyes were red and his face was wet and twisted and he was *crying*. "You think he's dead? But that's where you want to go, Connor, so I'll follow you there. I'll follow you across the fucking sound and to that fucking island, and you and me, we'll be together and we can *visit Vinnie*!"

Oh God. Oh God—not Noah. Not *Noah*. "Noah, you'll die," I said, because I could barely move. "You can't come— Don't come out here . . ." My voice was losing volume. I had no breath to power it.

"Connor," Noah sobbed, taking another stumbling, painful step toward me. "So will you."

Oh, look at him—so beautiful, and so hurt. I didn't want to leave him. And he couldn't come with me when I did this.

"I don't want you to die," I said. "Noah, I *love* you. You have to live. You *have* to."

He half laughed, but mostly cried. "*Now* you fucking say it. *Now*?"

"Sorry, Noah," I mumbled. I turned from the rock and took a step toward him. "I won't go if you're going to come with me. I love you, and I need you to live."

"You think?" he hiccuped, drawing near me. "Because I need you to live too. I need you to live, Connor. So come on." He was even with me, and he held out his hand.

I suddenly wanted to take it more than anything in the world. More than going to the island, more than seeing Vinnie, I wanted to feel the touch of that dark-skinned, pink-palmed hand on mine.

I reached out for him. "Yeah," I whispered. "Yeah. I think we both need to go to the house. No more island. I need to go ho—"

He half smiled, took one more step toward me . . .

And slipped hard, cracking his arm on my friend the rock. I watched him push up off the bottom and gasp, too cold to move well, and then he must have hit a hole, like I had, because he disappeared.

"*Noah*!"

I could see him flailing under the water, the dark bottom making the cold clear salt water almost opaque. Oh God, he couldn't get his feet under him! He needed me.

The heat of panic fueled me, and I dove cleanly toward that flailing body, the water closing over my head.

The cold was absolute. It stopped my breath, stopped my heart, stopped my mind. My skin screamed within the frigid embrace, and for a moment, I was encased in a layer of ice.

And time itself froze down to me, reaching for Noah, the two of us isolated in a crystalline bubble of a single heartbeat.

And I was on the island.

"Connor?" Vinnie said, smiling. "You're not supposed to be here yet."

I peered around and smiled back. Our stuff was there. The accrued detritus of ten years of our life was arranged neatly in a room that looked a lot like his living room in Malibu.

"Vinnie, I missed you so badly."

His smile flickered. "I miss you too, Con." He bit his lip. "I mean, you can stay if you *want*, I guess."

Oh, I loved that smile. The fullness of his lips, the shyness that peeked out from under his brows. I yearned to run my fingers through his sleek, coarse dark hair, because it would be so different from Noah's—

Noah.

"I've got to go, Vin," I said, but there was urgency under the regret. "Noah needs me."

"Yeah. Yeah, I hear you. Bring him by when it's time, but if you gotta go, you gotta go."

I reached out halfway to him, tears burning in my eyes. "Vinnie..."

"I love you, Connor. I'm sorry I left so early, but it wasn't because of you. Life just happens—and so does death. You know?"

I nodded, and smiled through the salt curtain in front of my eyes. "I love you back, Vinnie. But I love him too. That's okay, right?"

"Yeah. Go get him, 'kay? He needs you."

"'Kay."

Vinnie drew closer to me, and for a moment—just a moment—I could *smell* him, and the bergamot and lime smell that had always been Vinnie. I could feel the heat from his body and hear the rustle of his clothes. His lips brushed mine, just a touch, a good-bye, and then—

My arms closed around Noah under his arms, and I kicked to the surface, the two of us pulling in a screaming breath as our heads cleared the water.

I'd worked summers as a lifeguard when I was a kid, and it came back to me, how to haul someone to shore.

Noah was gasping, disoriented from the pain, and as we made our excruciating, stumbling way over the rocks on the shore, I got a look at his arm.

"Jesus, baby—I think it's broken!"

He grimaced mournfully at the area right under his wrist that was swelling with an unnatural lump.

"I wish it was broken *off*," he snapped. "Fucking *Jesus* it hurts."

I couldn't even say "I'm sorry" because I felt so much *more* than sorry.

"Here." I reached up to my neat little bundle and grabbed my T-shirt out, using it like a towel over his chest and his arms. He was shivering, the insides of his lips and his cuticles blue, and I needed to warm him up. I made him hold his arm out, and I wrapped the T-shirt around the swelling part—not too tightly—and fumbled badly because my fingers were too stiff to tie a knot.

The silence between us was almost as painful as the heat returning to my frigid limbs.

"Here," I said again, the heat of shame working on my body temperature as I wrapped my sweatshirt over his shoulders. "Here—let's get you inside and into some clothes. Is your dad still here?"

"Yeah—he's probably in the kitchen thinking we're out for a little walk," he chattered sourly.

"Well, you can tell him I was out for a little psychotic break," I replied, the shame so thick I was surprised I wasn't sweating. "And that he can steal his baby boy back if he's afraid of me. I wouldn't blame him."

"No." He reached out with his good arm to pull me close to him. "No."

For a moment we clung to each other, shivering, skin to skin, so cold from the water that the drizzle felt like room temperature.

"I wouldn't blame him," I said into his cold chest. "I mean, who signs on for this much crazy—"

"Connor," he said against my temple, "you saved my life."

"After I tried to kill you by taking you to visit my dead boyfriend." Oh God. That didn't sound any saner when I said it out loud. "If you decided now was the time to bail, I wouldn't blame you—"

His semihysterical laughter in my wet hair didn't reassure me. "Oh fuck no! *Fuck* no, I'm not leaving. Jesus, Connor, you just said you loved me."

I laughed feebly against his chest. "I do. I love you so much, Noah. I want to *live* for you. I want us to *live*."

His arm tightened, and my arms around his waist tightened, and for a moment, just a moment, it really was that simple.

It's never that simple.

Noah's father took one look at us and went running for blankets and clothes, and then the car so Noah could get his wrist checked out.

Once again we were clinging together in the back of the car, but as soon as we got to the hospital, that changed.

"You tripped and broke your wrist on a rock?" the doctor said after probing Noah's arm gingerly. He was going for X-rays in a few moments, but right now it was most decidedly broken.

Aces.

"Yeah," Noah said, and both of us were still shivering. I'm not sure what my hair looked like, but his was riotous around his head.

"Where were you walking?" the doctor asked, looking from me to Noah and back again, and abruptly I was reminded of Noah, trying to get me to admit I was gay so he could just talk to me honestly.

"We were in the water," I said with a sigh. "I . . . I was having a really bad moment grieving for my old boyfriend, and Noah came into the water to try to pull me out of it and . . . he fell."

The doctor and Samuel Dakers both looked at me in surprise.

"Noah?" Samuel said, sounding a little angry. "That's not what you told—"

"He was protecting me," I said, a part of me jealous of how suddenly "dad" Noah's father got when he was at risk. "I mean . . . I'm okay *now*, but I was *not* okay for a while—"

"We have a doctor I'd like you to talk to," said the guy probing Noah's wrist.

"Of course you do," I sighed.

Noah shook his head. "We so could have avoided this," he muttered.

"I don't want you to worry," I said frankly. "I don't want you to worry about it ever happening again."

Two hours later, Noah got out of the plaster and bandage room, and he and his father came to bail me out of the psych ward.

I was just finishing up with the nice, harried, too-young-to-be-that-bald man they'd thrown at me when Noah had made a big deal about not wanting to leave me overnight.

"So," the guy said, squinting at me like he knew me from somewhere, "you . . . you *didn't* want to kill yourself?" he asked, for like the fifteenth time.

"No, sir," I told him truthfully. "Remember: I saved my clothes for when I was planning to come back."

"But the water is *freezing*!" the guy exploded. "What made you think you were going to come back?"

"Noah was here," I said with a smile.

"Your . . . friend?"

"Boyfriend."

Suddenly the guy sat up. "Oh my God, you're Connor Montgomery!"

I nodded and smiled, and inwardly groaned. There was a knock on the conference room door, and I stood up and let Noah in while the poor man tried to reconcile everything he knew. Essentially, I sprang myself with some signed paperwork and some autographs for his kids, and Noah and I walked away.

"God," Noah muttered as we walked across the hospital parking lot, "talk about losing my faith in the medical system. They let you *go*?"

"I told him the truth." Thank God it *was* the truth. "I told him I had something to live for." It had gotten dark since we'd both gone in the water, and my stomach gave a gurgle as we were walking. "Are you hungry?"

Noah squinted at me. "Are you *insane*?"

"You just heard the nice man say I'm not," I shot back, wounded. "But you got pain pills, right? You need to eat something with those."

Noah groaned. "I'll have crackers when we get home. God, Connor, I love you, I fucking *love* you to death, but you are going to make me batshit crazy before I'm thirty."

I grimaced and stepped back so Samuel could open the car door for his son. Samuel regarded me quietly and stopped me for a moment as I walked around to my door.

"You *are* going to be okay, aren't you?"

Oh God. So worried.

"I will be," I said, feeling quiet and tired—but not overwhelmed. Not anymore. "If you want to stay on the couch tonight, that's fine, but don't worry. I'll take good care of him, I promise."

Samuel smiled faintly and ruffled my hair like I was his boy too. "I'll take you up on that, son—but not because I don't trust you. Just because I want you both to be okay."

Oh. Oh wow.

"That's really nice," I said, and then yawned. "Do you think there's any fast-food places open? I mean, is there a McDonald's or something? Carl's Jr.? KFC? Seriously—Taco Bell? Fast food, I'm all over it, my treat."

Samuel walked around and got into the front seat while I slid in next to Noah.

Noah, cast and all, did his thing where he wedged himself in the corner and opened his good arm. "C'mere, baby," he yawned. "Lay on me while my dad plays chauffeur."

"Yeah, sure." Because who could resist resting his head on Noah's chest? Not even the hospital smell could overcome the musky, dark-rum scent that Noah's body put out just as a matter of course. Oh, yeah. I was careful of his hurt arm, but I went right in for the snuggle.

Noah's good hand came up, pulling through my tangled hair and smoothing out the strands. "Are you really going to be okay?" he asked as his dad started the car.

"Yeah." I let out a breath and relaxed more fully. "I am. I know you're worried—"

"You . . . you almost—"

His voice hitched, and I rolled so I could face him and put two fingers over his full lips. "I was planning to come back," I said, a faint smile at the absurdity. "See . . . I didn't want to *stay* on the island, I just wanted to *go* to the island."

"You didn't want to stay with Vinnie?" he asked, hurt and confused at once.

"No," I said, all truth. "I just . . . You need to know where someone is before you can say good-bye, Noah. I just needed to say good-bye."

"Did you?" And the hope in his voice was a needy, fragile thing.

"Yeah. I said good-bye because I had to haul *your* sorry ass out of the water. There I was, in the middle of a good-bye kiss from Vinnie, and I chose you."

"Really?" He sounded about five years old, and I watched, feeling like the oldest for the first time *ever*, as he wiped his eyes on his shoulder. God, it must have been hard on him, watching me drift further and further away, thinking it was because I loved and would always love my dead boyfriend more.

"Yeah," I whispered, wiping under his eyes with my thumb. "I chose you, Noah. I love you. I want to *always* love you. I want to live under the same roof with you, and make a home. I want you to buy stuff you love and help me shop. It can be *our* stuff. Or, you know, it can be a tent in the wilderness, as long as it's ours."

Noah cracked a half smile. "There has got to be a happy medium between Tchotchkes 'R' Us and Wilderness Men."

"We'll find it," I said. "We'll find it. I'll go to the island someday when it's my time, love. And I'll wait for you to join me when it's yours. I'm not worried anymore. I got to say good-bye."

Noah swallowed hard, and I wiped his eyes again. He was probably hurting and tired, and tired of being worried, but he still lowered his face to mine and took charge with a possessive kiss.

He pulled back after a moment and grimaced, clearly uncomfortable. "Dad," he called, his voice thick and congested, "Dad, I'm *dying* for a soda. Can we get some—"

"McDonald's," his father called back. "I hear you. God, you two deserve each other."

I grinned up at Noah. "You deserve better," I said solemnly.

"I got a movie star," he replied. "I'm not bitching."

I laughed softly and rested my head against him. Food would make this moment perfect, but I had faith it was coming.

CHAPTER SEVENTEEN

WHAT'S IMPORTANT IS THAT THEY **LIVED**

O f course, it's not easy to replace faith. I knew it. I was perfectly aware that Noah would be watching me carefully until I'd been *not* crazy for as long as he'd known me when I'd been losing my nut.

Our week of vacation passed smoothly though. On the third day, the doctor gave the all-clear and gave him a fiberglass cast, and we went on some mountain biking rides that *didn't* end in disaster. We set up a weight room in the house, and he professed himself unexcited about stationary exercise. I told him that as soon as his arm was healed, we could go back to swimming, and he grunted that I sucked, and the next time I wanted to take a swim across the sound, he'd let me.

I kissed him, and we ended up having a quickie on the Soloflex, and after he'd come all over my back, he'd kissed my shoulder and announced maybe the damned thing was worth what I'd paid for it.

I agreed—and then ran and got the cleaner and a towel, because my back wasn't the only thing that got hit that day.

Viv decided to stay down south with Jilly, and we got daily reports on her progress and how she was going to reform Hollywood. She told Noah that she'd already signed two clients for Jilly who *weren't* white, and I'd half laughed.

"Vinnie and I weren't white," I said, because I hadn't thought of it like that before.

"Yeah, well you weren't Mexican and . . . whatever Vinnie was."

"Mexican American," I said dryly. "Both of us."

"Well, you certainly didn't fly your colors on the screen, Connor *Montgomery*."

"Well we didn't fly our gayness on the screen either," I reminded him unnecessarily. "I think we mostly just wanted to . . . you know . . . *be*."

He grunted and threw himself back on the couch, looking around the house. "This place is small, don't you think?"

I looked around. "There's only two of us."

"Your place in Malibu was bigger."

"I had to show off to people. You're dodging the subject."

He cast me a brief smile. "Because I don't have the answer. You're right. I mean . . . mostly, you just wanted to work unmolested. But . . . but look at what *not* telling people about you almost did."

I sighed. "I don't know how to fix it for other people. I fixed it for *me*, and that's going to have to be what's right."

But I'd underestimated how powerful it could be, fixing the world for yourself and your loved ones. I'd underestimated the truly good things that could come from telling an unmalicious truth without hope or agenda.

The Saturday before shooting, Noah and I had his family over for dinner, and all six of us stayed up late and played Monopoly in the living room. Ky and Trina were joyful at having me to play with, since Viv was still in LA, and Noah had been happy to reconnect with his family.

His father and grandmother watched me carefully the entire time—probably wanting to make sure I didn't go sharing the crazy again, or at least that's what I thought.

But at the midgame stretch, when I went into the kitchen to refill the snack bowl, Noah's gran came in to get more lemonade for the girls.

For a moment there was an awkward, if companionable, silence as we went about our tasks, but just as I was about to leave the kitchen, she stopped me with a look.

"No more swimming?" she asked, probably just to make sure.

"No," I promised. Not for a minute did I think she meant me and Noah working out in the pool. "I just . . . had to do something there. It's done. I wouldn't hurt Noah like that again for the world."

She nodded, and glanced out to the living room. "Their mother, she hasn't come back, hasn't contacted them, hasn't done a thing since you saw her."

I blinked. I remember her promising that she'd be back the next weekend, but then *my* life had exploded and . . . well, apparently she hadn't kept that promise.

"But . . . she seemed so sincere . . ."

Helena nodded. "She was," she said surprisingly. "Annette was *very* sincere about wanting to see her children again. But that didn't mean she could."

I frowned. "I mean, she could come back and—"

"No, hon. That's not what I'm talking about. I mean there is something inside her that absolutely can't live that life."

"Then why the song and dance?" I said, absurdly hurt for Noah, even though he'd been able to see it when I hadn't.

"Because she needed to say good-bye," Helena said serenely. "But some people have to make a big stink out of good-bye. You know, you people on stage can't do anything quietly."

I blushed. "No," I agreed. "We can't."

"At least you didn't hurt Noah when you did it," she said.

If I hadn't had the bowl of pretzels in my hand, I would have flailed in honest surprise.

"Did you *see* the cast on his arm?" Because I had—especially because he'd chosen the bright-green plaster, just to fuck with me.

"Yes, dear. But he slipped and did that himself. If you'd said good-bye to *Noah*, then you really would have hurt him."

She hustled back into the living room, and I stood there gaping.

Noah wandered in a moment later and closed my mouth with a finger under my chin.

"What?" he asked. "You're catching flies."

"Your gran—she does get to the point, doesn't she?"

"Yeah. Yeah she does. What point did she get to?"

I pulled my shit together and winked. "That I stayed with the right person."

His grin was as relaxed as I'd seen it since the *Vogue* shoot. He leaned in and kissed me.

"Damned straight you did," he murmured, and I knew that he'd found his way to faith in me, in how badly I wanted our life together, and in how ready I was to leave the destructive part of my grief behind.

Which was probably something I should have told Jilly, because when she called the next morning, she was really worried.

Noah and I were having a lie-in since this was our last day of vacation. We were sprawled on the couch downstairs, wearing sleep pants and T-shirts, and truly spectacular bedhead while we both read from our Kindles. Noah had a pair of hand-crocheted socks on that his gran had made, and I kept poking him with my toe, because I wanted a pair, and I wanted him to get her to make me a pair, but I wasn't *quite* in the family enough yet to ask.

"No," he said the fifth time I poked him.

"But they're so warm!" I protested.

"I'll make you some myself, but I'm not asking my gran."

"You'll make me some?" Okay, so we all knew Russell Crowe knit on set, but still. Wasn't expected.

"You think she didn't teach me? But you know, you hit college, you're too manly for that shit. But for you, I will make socks."

My entire body felt suffused with light, and I could feel my smile near my ears. "Oh my God! Can they be brown and blue and yellow and red? And have those lacy little shell things on them? Oh *please*, Noah, please. I'll do *anything* for you if you could make me slippers like that!"

He stared at me. "You do anything for me *now*. Jesus, Connor, did you just offer to whore yourself out for a pair of slippers?"

I nodded. "Pretty please?" I thought about perfectly beautiful slippers on my big blocky feet that had been *made by my boyfriend*, and I convulsed with what could only be described as a paroxysm of joy. "Can we get the yarn today? There's a yarn store on the boardwalk, by the candy store. Can we go? Please?"

"Yeah," he said, with that same expression he had on his face when I was picking out his gran's present. "Yeah. Sure. I'll get you a how-to book. You can make me a pair in *black*."

I nodded. "Sure. We can do that today, though, right?"

"Yeah. Why not? I don't see why—"

And that was when my phone buzzed on the end table. I grabbed it and stood, planning to go upstairs and change, because oh my God! I was going to learn how to do something during set breaks and the thought actually made my *balls ache* with joy. Jilly was on the line, and the tone of her voice pulled me off cloud euphoria in one word.

"Connor?"

"Yeah, Jilly. What's up? You sound—"

"Connor, why didn't you tell me?"

I had to search my brain for what she could be referring to. "Tell you what?" I asked cautiously. I mean, I'd put her name on my hospital contact information, but I don't think the shrink was that interested in contacting my agent. Unless he had a screenplay or something.

"Connor, Vinnie's family called me today, and they told me what happened before you left LA."

I blinked, and for a moment I was there on the beach, heartbroken and devastated, confronted with the remains of a life that nobody had known existed.

"Yeah," I said through a rough throat. "Wasn't their fault, you know. They were just—"

"They were making their own peace. Yeah, Christine explained all that."

Christine—Kevin's wife. I remembered that now—Vinnie's older brother's name was Kevin. "She was nice," I said, remembering how she'd sat with me until Noah came. "But I don't want to—"

"Well you're going to have to, hon, because they're on their way over."

My eyes crossed so hard I thought they'd stick that way. "They're on their way *what*?"

"They called me today—told me the whole story, and then asked me for your address so they could, and I quote, 'Get something to him that he'll want back.'"

"You gave them my address?" Damn—Jilly *must* have been rattled. That was a breach of protocol that most clients would fire for. "Why would you—"

"Well I didn't know they were calling from Seattle, Con! But she called me back a half an hour later, and said I might want to warn you they were coming. I mean, they had *my* number because *Vinnie* had my number and I've been sending his family Vinnie's residuals. I didn't even know what you'd *want* me to do, and . . ." Her voice dropped. "You were so out of it, hon. That day I saw you and Noah, you were so sad. I would have given anything if they could have come and made you better. Please tell me you don't hate me—*please*."

I closed my eyes, and as the wave of sadness passed through me and my heart kept beating, still and sane as it had for the past week, I made a stunning realization.

I was all right. I really *was* all right.

But I would always be sad.

I'd sat on my euphoria cloud, so damned relieved to have the chance to say good-bye that I'd forgotten that I really had lost someone. But it was okay. I really had lost someone, and I would have sad moments like this one, and the one that was coming. But I could live. I *had* lived. I'd said good-bye, and I would keep on living, just like I'd been telling Noah all week.

"I love you, sweetheart," I said kindly. "But Noah and I look like the cat's ass right now, so let us go change, ok—"

Knock, knock, knock.

"Oh fuck, Jilly, I love you, but you fucking owe me for this. I'm in my goddamned pajamas!"

Noah was scrambling to stand up as I stalked from the kitchen through the living room to answer the door. "Who is—"

And at that moment we heard a crash, like broken pottery, and Christine's voice letting out an unmistakable wail.

"God*damn it* Kevin—we kept that thing safe across two airports!"

"Oh Jesus . . . Jesus, I'm sorry, Chris— Dad, I'm so sorry!"

Knock, knock, knock.

"Vinnie's family," I said grimly, and watching the horror dawn on Noah's face actually settled me down a little, because that was *both* of us in our pajamas and bedhead, and I wasn't in this alone.

With a sigh I got to the door and swung it open, hoping I had a welcoming expression on my face as I did.

"Mr. Walker," I said, fighting against the gut punch of seeing him again. "I'm so sorry I didn't know you were coming, I'd—"

Vinnie's dad was a compact man of Mexican descent, with a full mustache and graying hair swept back from his brow. He swung open the screen door as I stood in the doorway and swept me up in the hardest, fiercest hug, and held me there until my ribs creaked.

"We're so sorry," he murmured again and again. "We're so sorry, Connor. We didn't know."

Well *yeah*, of *course* I cried. I was at peace, I wasn't *dead*.

We probably could have hugged forever—or at least until it got awkward—but Kevin pushed past us abruptly, a big box of what I assumed would be broken tchotchkes in his arms, and shoved through behind his dad.

"Sorry, Dad, sorry, Chris, sorry, Connor, I gotta pee. Jesus, I gotta pee, where's the bathroom?"

Noah took the box from him and nodded down the hall past the kitchen. "It's around under the stairs."

"God, thanks," Kevin blurted, and then took off like a three-year-old instead of a thirty-year-old, but then, Kevin, Christine, and I had always had the best time at Vinnie's house over Christmas. He was probably the closest thing the family had to a full-grown child.

Noah heaved the box over to the end table and set it down, and we both looked at each other and winced when we heard the tinkle of a lot of broken things.

"God, I'm sorry," Christine said, coming in last and shutting the door. She waited until her father-in-law stepped aside and hugged me tight. I returned the hug and kissed the top of her head, and she backed up and smiled. "So cute," she murmured, pinching my cheek.

I winked at her, and gestured everybody in.

"Uh," I said gamely, "can we . . . uh, Noah, do we have anything like coffee or milk or—"

"Yeah, we've got coffee and milk and some soda, or some beer," he offered. "Can I get you folks anything?"

"Maybe later," Mr. Walker said, moving to the couch. "How about right now we sit and tell each other some stories, okay?"

I nodded and glanced at Noah, and we both took the stuffed chairs on either end. It meant I couldn't touch Noah's knee, or hold his hand while we had this conversation, but Vinnie's family could sit together. "Uh, I forgot. This is Noah Dakers, he's my, uh—"

"Boyfriend," Mr. Walker said kindly. "We know. In fact, we know a *lot* now that we didn't, thanks to that password you gave us. What was that from, anyway?"

I grimaced. "Mazynsky," I said with a sigh. "It's my real last name. I changed it when I signed my SAG card."

"Of course." Vinnie's dad reached over and patted my knee. "That . . . that makes perfect sense now." His voice lowered. "Just like your thing on YouTube on the . . . on the anniversary of the day Vinnie died, and . . ." He shook his head and looked sorrowfully at Christine. "I am so ashamed," he said, his voice thick, and Kevin came out of the bathroom then, hustling across the living room so he could lean over the couch and embrace his father from behind, since Christine was sitting next to him.

"He hasn't been really coherent," Kevin apologized, his own voice a little congested. "See . . ." He straightened up as his father gave his arms one last pat, and then he moved to the couch to sit next to his wife. Noah had to shift his knees aside, and Kevin gave him an absent, "Thanks, bro," before settling down.

"So, see," Kevin resumed, while his father got himself under control, "the whole family wanted to come—but you just can't fly that many people to Seattle at a moment's notice, and Mom is sort of in charge of the troops when we're all together, so she had to stay back in LA. But Christine felt really bad—she was so upset when she came into the house that day, and she said you'd been just destroyed, so she wanted to come here and make sure you were okay."

Kevin smiled weakly at me. "And I was worried too. I mean . . . Jesus, Connor. We were just wrecked over Vinnie, but I don't know how we could have assumed you wouldn't be, even if you'd just been friends. I guess . . . I guess being sad made us really selfish. We assumed we were the only ones who were hurt that bad. And we weren't. And we just wanted to sort of . . . I don't know, get rid of some of that hurt, and we hurt you . . ."

Kevin trailed off, and Christine grabbed his hand with one of her hands, and with the other, she pulled a small laptop out from the bag under her arm and set it on the table.

"Sorry," she said, and she sounded like she'd gotten most of her crying out of the way. "We . . . we're doing this badly. We just— Nobody in the family knew. Maybe we can start with that. We're doing all the talking here, Con. Can you maybe tell us why he wouldn't tell us? Why you guys would . . ." She took a deep breath. "Why you would spend all that time together, practically married, and he wouldn't tell us that you were more than friends?"

I swallowed, and wiped my own eyes. Actors are sympathy criers by nature, I guess. "See," I said, Vinnie's bright-blue eyes and shy smile flashing in front of me as I spoke, "when Vinnie met me, I was . . . well, I was living out of an abandoned car and sneaking into the gym to shower for auditions. And . . . we . . ." *Sorry, Vinnie—nobody wants their folks to know they were a total slut. I'm going to give the kid's lie to the parents here, okay?* "We hit it off," I said with a little smile. "And moved in together that day. And eventually he asked me why I'd been so desperate for money. And when I told him that my parents had . . . had kicked me out, and they'd told all of my friends' parents not to take me in, and that I'd essentially hitchhiked to Hollywood because I wanted to . . . you know, make my fortune there . . ." I looked at Noah and shrugged. "He got afraid. I mean . . . I don't have to tell you Vinnie loved you guys, right?"

They all shook their heads, and I felt better about the world as a whole. "Good. Because he thought you guys were everything. We'd talk about his family all the time. It was like gossiping about you guys, that was the substitute for me not having my family, and for . . ." I swallowed, "for the idea that Vinnie and I, we'd probably never have one of our own if we didn't come out. So . . . so you—you were all we had. He . . . he was just too afraid to lose you."

Mr. Walker nodded. "Connor," he said, tentatively, "we looked at my son's videos. At all of them—all thirty-eight hours of them."

For the first time since they'd arrived, I had trouble catching my breath. "Thirty-eight hours?" I asked, my lungs laboring in my chest. "I . . . I've got thirty-two."

Mr. Walker looked at Christine and Kevin. "You guys were right— you were so right. You were right we had to come here and show him this. You were right he had to see." He turned back to me. "The rest of it is video diaries, Connor. And pretty much all he talks about is you. He talks about how you got together—" His lips twitched. "Hit it off? Really? Is that what the kids are calling it these days?"

Noah snorted softly, and I blushed.

"And he talked about rehab, and how bad he felt. Twice, Connor. Twice my son called on you, and you left *everything* and came to his side. He . . . he never forgave himself for that, so you know. And he . . . I'm so mad at him for that, you know? *I* thought you were flaky. Me and his mother, we used to talk about, 'Oh, Connor, he's such a nice boy, but he's going to piss his career away if he doesn't get his act together.'"

He shook his head. "And we were talking out our asses, weren't we? Because you *did* have your act together. Your act was taking care of our son. And you did a really good job of it. Vinnie told us so.

He told us . . ." Mr. Walker had to look up at the ceiling for a moment to get control.

"He told us about the other men, on those tapes, and how lonely he was. And how he felt horrible when it happened. And how you forgave him. Connor, I can't imagine how lonely you've been in the last year or more. I can't imagine how much it must have felt like you squandered your heart on someone and those ten years didn't mean spit. But . . . but I've seen my son's tapes. I've seen him talking to you. I've seen him crying because he'd hurt you, and I've seen him happy because he did something that made you smile. *I* didn't see what he was hiding, and I'm going to have to live with that regret. But please—I'm sorry about your stuff. I'm *so* sorry. But don't feel like . . ."

He closed his eyes. "*Please* don't feel like . . . like you loved him in vain." His voice broke completely. "You were the best thing my son had, and I'm so grateful you're here!"

And then I broke, falling on my knees in front of him, and he held my head on his lap and rocked me gently, like a real father, and we mourned his son.

The rest of the day was . . . hard.

We watched those extra hours together, Noah gripping my hand like he was anchoring me in the here and now.

Maybe he was.

I had watched Vinnie's movies in the past year—that much I remembered. But nothing equaled the full "Vinnie is dead but alive" experience like seeing him on the computer screen, talking into his computer like nobody else would see.

"I'm sorry, Con. I . . . You're right. You said you were going to call rehab. It's the right move."

I remembered that outfit—the one with the brightly striped shirt and the pants tight enough to show his camel toe. The shirt was torn in the picture, and his nose was bloodied, because I'd tackled him when I caught him taking someone else's painkillers in our bathroom. He'd lied to me for a month, but I'd seen it—the mood swings, the oversleeping, the general bitchiness.

I'd thrown the pills down the toilet, and he'd blackened my eye.

And then I'd stalked out and told him I was calling a rehab center and he'd better pack his bags.

I hadn't seen him doing this, having this conversation with . . . with me, I guess. Since I wasn't there.

Oh, Vinnie. I guess this last year wasn't an anomaly. We both did this, but you did it on screen.

"That one's too far, Dad," Kevin muttered. "Did he see the footage from when Connor first went to shoot that *Warlock* show?"

"No," Mr. Walker said quietly. "But maybe not—"

Kevin found the file and pressed Play.

Vinnie, as he'd looked nine years ago, impossibly young, a little bit of baby fat still on his chin. This was when he'd gotten to play the vampire in all of the sci-fi shows. Everyone wanted him to be redeemed.

"Damn it, Connor. I hate this. I hate myself. You did everything you could to get me up in this business, and now you're out there, a solid series under your belt, and I'm whining here like a baby. And . . . and last night. There was a guy, and he was so kind, and so sweet, and he just wanted to get in my pants and I . . ."

He broke. "I let him, Con. I'm so sorry. But the whole time, I saw you, in my head. I just missed you so damned bad. And I used rubbers, because I'm not stupid, but I feel so dirty now. How can I touch you when you get in tomorrow when I feel so dirty?"

"Oh," I said, resting my head on Noah's waist as he sat on the arm of my chair. "Now I know about the rubbers."

Noah let out a breath and stroked my hair back from my eyes, and we watched on.

Almost six hours of film. We didn't stop in the middle—although we were all starving—and there was a line at both bathrooms after the last file played because *everybody* had to pee.

But I watched it all. I watched six hours of Vinnie that I'd never seen before, six hours of him that I hadn't known I'd had.

And yeah, his father was right. It was almost all about me.

I cried so much I felt clean with it—not just cleansed but polished and shiny, my tires blackened, my chrome wiped down. I was the best Connor I could be, because I'd tapped out all my tears.

In fact, I felt reborn.

After six hours, I was done with the lot of us lurking in our living room, eyes glued to the little screen. Randomly, I asked Vinnie's family if they wanted to go somewhere to eat. Noah and I got ready in record time, hustling down the stairs with hair that was still drying and clothes sticking to our skin. We'd had a quick naked hug as he'd stepped out of the shower and I'd stepped in, but God—who had words right now?

I had Noah take us to the Rockin' Surf and Dockn' Turf while they followed in their rental car. It was local, and they hadn't seen it before, and it sat partway to Seattle, where they'd booked a hotel in the mistaken idea that it was close enough to Bluewater Bay to not be a nuisance to drive.

I was relieved, actually. They were welcome in my home anytime, and I had high hopes they'd take me up on my offer to come visit the set, but I would be glad when we got some distance between us, just for tonight.

I needed time alone with Noah, and time with my thoughts, and time to make sure my good-bye was still solid and real in my heart.

I guessed, by how subdued they were at dinner, that they felt the same way.

But still, we hugged before they got into their car to leave.

"We'll come see you before the end of the week," Christine promised, hugging me tight. "And we want to see you two near the holidays. Please, please come see the family in December." She pulled back and smiled. "You have a house right next door, after all."

I nodded, and her father walked in for his share. "Speaking of . . ." Mr. Walker said, kissing me on the cheek. "I've got to tell you—the houses. The houses make so much sense. His whole life, Vinnie liked clean lines—in his cars, in his room, in his clothes. Even women, when he pretended to like them, Audrey Hepburn was his favorite, because he said other actresses were too gaudy, too messy. You were living in his house, weren't you? And he was living in yours."

I looked over my shoulder at Noah, who rolled his eyes. "Yeah," I said honestly. "We . . . we didn't do it on purpose. It's just . . . that's what each house looked best as, and it was like . . . it was really like . . ."

"Like you were living in each other's hearts," Vinnie's father said. He kissed me again. "I wish," he began, his voice rusty from crying,

"I wish with all my heart my son would have brought you to us and said, 'Here is my heart, Mom and Dad.' But he didn't, and we'll have to live with that. But he loved you. And . . . that makes us so happy."

I wiped my face with my palm, so *over* this day I couldn't even talk anymore.

"And Connor?" Mr. Walker said, making sure I was looking at him. "I know— You and my son, you did a lot of your life living in public. We've seen the press, hounding you these past weeks, and you haven't said a word."

I shrugged. Apparently the security people had been by, kicking reporters out of our bushes while we were gone. The gay press was especially relentless.

He patted my cheek. "We'll call your agent and make a press release," he said softly. "I don't want this on you—not after everything else. His mother and I will do the interview. We didn't see Vinnie for who he was when he was alive—the least we can do is support *you* now that he's gone, okay?"

Oh God. I couldn't even . . . I'd have to call Jilly later, make sure she told them what this gift meant, make sure they understood the enormity of what he'd just promised to do. I gaped at him, nodding, incoherent even, and that's when Kevin came in for his hug.

"Everything they said," he told me, his football player's build swallowing me up. Kevin didn't run to fat, like most people in their thirties—he just became more awesomely solid as he aged. "But . . ." Kevin pulled back and stuck his hand out toward Noah, shaking it. "But I need to add that I'm glad you've found someone, now that Vinnie's gone. It really sucks to be alone. Vinnie didn't want you to be that way, and I'm just glad you're not."

With that, the family all bundled into the rental and buzzed away, leaving Noah and me, exhausted and talked out, to make our way home.

We watched stupid television all night, and old movies, and hell no, neither one of us felt like sex afterward. But we did lie in bed, him at my back, holding me around the middle like we always did.

"You okay?" he asked, when the silence of bedtime had seeped into our bones.

"Yeah. I can't believe I work tomorrow."

"Saying. I can't believe they still pay me to drive you around."

I laughed, genuinely tickled as I didn't think I could be. "That is so awesome, I don't even have words for it," I said after a pause.

"Yeah, I'm going to have to agree." We giggled for a moment, like naughty children, and then he spoke again. "You're going to be okay, though. Right?"

I closed my eyes and savored his warmth at my back, and his dark rum and musk, and his deep rumbly voice, and the sex appeal that thrummed like an electric current under the surface. "Noah, I am so okay right now. I . . . I am lying in bed in a house by the ocean, and I'm held by a man I love. You have no idea. When I was a little kid, dreaming about my future—*this* was the future I dreamed of."

He kissed the back of my neck slowly and sensually, and I shivered.

I was apparently *wrong* about the no-sex thing, and rolling in his arms so I could find his mouth with mine reaffirmed my point about life.

I wanted to live it.

Tomorrow I would wake up and go play somebody else, and I loved doing that—I was *blessed* to be doing that.

But tonight, in the sweet and holy darkness, I was skin to skin with my lover, and I was myself, and I was blessed, more than blessed, to be doing that as well.

I didn't say good-night to Vinnie; we'd said our good-byes already.

And Noah and I had some more lovemaking to do before it was our time to say good-night. I wanted to be there for every moment.

It was what living was all about.

Vinnie's parents made their press release a week later—and my life exploded again. This time, I talked to the gay press, and oh yeah, I made it really fucking clear that I was not excited with their pressure to out someone without his family's permission.

And then I told the truth, gave the "No more interviews!" edict, and peaced out. Jilly told me that Viv spent three hours a day fielding calls for the next week—but that it eventually died down.

It was a week after that last interview, at least, before I felt able to go through the box of shattered dreams that Vinnie's brother had dropped on our front porch. I waited until Noah was out running other actors around and I had a quiet moment in the house.

Most of the box was toast—there was no denying it. The last few steak plates were rubble, and the figurines from the mantel, every adorable kitten and big-eyed dog of them, were broken in three or more pieces.

One thing survived.

It was the Precious Moments figurine, the one with big-eyed Connor and big-eyed Vinnie, standing at the bus stop, ready to face the wide world. There was a chip on the base, and little Connor's hand had broken off, but for the most part? It was sound.

I very carefully placed it on *my* mantel, thinking that when Noah and I went shopping for a house and not a rental, we would very much have to make sure we had a place to put adorable figurines. It was necessary. Noah would understand.

I took the rest of the box out to the trash can in the garage, cringing when it *bang-smash*ed into the bottom of the can. God, it was a good thing I'd gotten all my tears out of the way, because that was a final sound if there ever was one.

I'd just turned back when the garage door opened, and Noah pulled the town car in. I waited by the inside door for him to get out, pleased because he could help me make dinner, and because just having him in the house made me happy.

"Hey, stranger." He greeted me with a kiss, and I wrapped an arm around his waist—and then grabbed for the package he was holding behind his back.

"What'd you get me?" I asked, excited and suspicious.

"What'd you just do?" he asked, just as suspicious.

"I threw away the box of broken stuff that Vinnie's family brought," I told him, making my way in, because the garage is *not* romantic. "What are you holding behind your back?"

"Yarn," he said pertly. "And a how-to book."

I turned toward him so quickly I almost knocked him down the garage stairs. "Oh my God! You did? You *did*? That's *awesome*!"

I reached for the bag, and he held it out of my reach. With his other hand he captured my chin and kissed me. "I'm sorry it was all broken," he said softly.

"One thing survived," I said. "C'mere and see."

I dragged him to the mantel, and showed him the ornament proudly, and he laughed like I knew he would.

"Perfect." Then he pulled out the bag—which was visibly full of yarn, the pretty fiber smooshed up against the plastic—and rooted around in the center.

He produced a small box, of the tchotchke variety, and I almost pee-pee danced. "Really? I get presents?"

"Yeah, Con. You get presents."

I took the box eagerly and scrabbled it open.

And gasped.

It was a lot like the Precious Moments ornament, but a different company made it, and the colors were brighter, bolder, and more present.

The little boy with the dark skin and the curly hair fishing with the little boy with the yellow hair and the pale skin were unmistakable.

"I couldn't find one with mountain bikes," he apologized.

I couldn't breathe it was so perfect.

"Oh . . ." I said, voice shaking. "This is *so* gonna get you laid."

His laughter was throaty and beautiful. "Yeah, well. Anything—" he said. I looked up, and he was biting his lip. "Anything to make you happy."

I smiled, feeling all sunshine, and put me and Noah next to me and Vinnie.

"This makes me happy," I said softly.

"So we can forget about the crocheted slippers thing?"

I looked at him, horrified. "Oh hell no. Right after dinner, promise?"

"Yeah." His arms were as sweet and as warm as they always had been. "You kept your promise to me, you know."

"My promise?"

"You promised to love me. You promised someday you'd be not-broken, and you'd love me."

"I am," I said. "I do."

"So I can keep any promise I make to you after that. It's the only thing I've ever wanted in the world," he said, and his mouth on mine was perfect.

Dear Reader,

Thank you for reading Amy Lane's *Selfie*!

We know your time is precious and you have many, many entertainment options, so it means a lot that you've chosen to spend your time reading. We really hope you enjoyed it.

We'd be honored if you'd consider posting a review—good or bad—on sites like **Amazon, Barnes & Noble, Kobo, Goodreads, Twitter, Facebook, Tumblr,** and your blog or website. We'd also be honored if you told your friends and family about this book. Word of mouth is a book's lifeblood!

For more information on upcoming releases, author interviews, blog tours, contests, giveaways, and more, please sign up for our weekly, spam-free newsletter and visit us around the web:

Newsletter: tinyurl.com/RiptideSignup
Twitter: twitter.com/RiptideBooks
Facebook: facebook.com/RiptidePublishing
Goodreads: tinyurl.com/RiptideOnGoodreads
Tumblr: riptidepublishing.tumblr.com

Thank you so much for Reading the Rainbow!

RiptidePublishing.com

ACKNOWLEDGMENTS

Thank you, Amelia, for the insider knowledge that helped make this better—I love the details, they make me very happy.

Amy Lane has two kids in college and two in soccer, and an indulgent spouse. Together they exist happily in a crumbling suburban crapmansion, and equally happily with the surprisingly demanding voices who live in her head.

She loves cats, movies, yarn, pretty colors, pretty men, shiny things, and Twu Wuv, and despises housecleaning, low-fat granola bars, and vainglorious prickweenies.

She can be found at her computer, dodging housework, or simultaneously reading, watching television, and knitting, because she likes to freak people out by proving it can be done.

Oh! And she's been nominated for a couple of awards. She's even won some. Swear.

Connect with Amy:
Website: greenshill.com
Blog: writerslane.blogspot.com
Facebook: AmyLaneAnonymous
Twitter: @amymaclane
Goodreads: goodreads.com/amymaclane

Enjoy more stories like
Selfie
at RiptidePublishing.com!

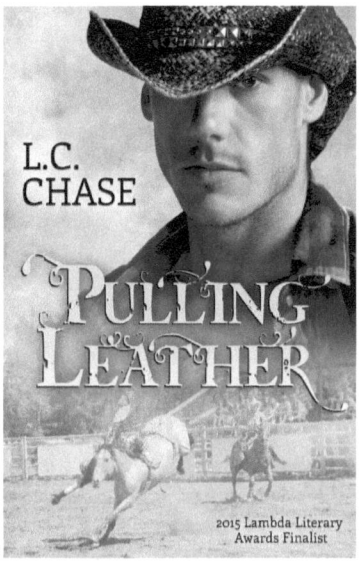

www.ingramcontent.com/pod-product-compliance
Lightning Source LLC
Chambersburg PA
CBHW022207030726
47494CB00021B/1741